Rainbow

Praise for Eileen Ramsay's novels

'From moments caught on canvas, a tragic relationship unfolds. And embroiled in this unfolding, two lives become entwined. *Someday, Somewhere* is a wonderful double-layered love-story, beautifully structured and a plain old-fashioned good read.' Isla Dewar

'Utterly captivating romance . . . The beautiful Scottish setting only adds to this poignant and poetic journey through the generations. This book is as unique as it is exquisite.' *Daily Record*

'Ramsay caps the success of her first book with another cracking good read.' *Livewire*

'A seriously good read!' *Woman*

'As is appropriate in the love story of a singer and an artist, the prose sings and is full of vibrant colour.' *Historical Novels Review*

'Ramsay's prose is vivid and flowing and the pages just fly by.' *Choice*

EILEEN RAMSAY

Rainbow's End

HODDER

Copyright © 2006 by Eileen Ramsay

First published in Great Britain in 2006 by Hodder and Stoughton
A division of Hodder Headline

The right of Eileen Ramsay to be identified as the Author of the
Work has been asserted by her in accordance with the
Copyright, Designs and Patents Act 1988.

A Hodder paperback

1

A CIP catalogue record for this title is available from the British Library

ISBN 0 340 83906 6
ISBN 978 0 340 83906 5

Typeset in Plantin Light by Hewer Text UK Ltd, Edinburgh
Printed and bound by Mackays of Chatham Ltd, Chatham, Kent

Hodder Headline's policy is to use papers that are natural,
renewable and recyclable products and made from wood grown in
sustainable forests. The logging and manufacturing processes are expected
to conform to the environmental regulations of the country of origin.

Hodder and Stoughton Ltd
A division of Hodder Headline
338 Euston Road
London NW1 3BH

For Alistair and Philippa, with love

ACKNOWLEDGEMENTS

Thanks to Morag Lyall who is a fantastic copy-editor and to my meticulous editor, Carolyn Caughey.

Thanks to my friend Lalita Carlton-Jones for help with the geography and history of the Barbican.

I have read too many books about orchestras including the fabulous LSO to mention them all – but thank you.

The American baritone, Michael Chioldi, was extremely helpful.

For help with clothes, thanks to Charlie Taylor of Dundee and her talented and very 'with-it' stylists, the wonderfully helpful Elaine Keir of Warehouse in Dundee, Penny Jordan and my daughter-in-law, Pippa.

I am deeply indebted to all the conductors I have studied over the years but especially to the inspirational Daniel Barenboim. I relied heavily on his lectures, interviews and generous autobiography, *A Life in Music*. The diamond story is true and so thank you, Sari Portley, for allowing me to use it.

Thank you to Tansy Hawksley for all her help with computing and Monika Bowler for help with the German Language.

And, as always, I would be unable to 'face the music' without the help and encouragement of my agent, Teresa Chris.

Eileen Ramsay

I

Juliet hurried up the steps from the Métro and blinked for a moment in the bright spring sunshine. April in Paris – was it as beautiful as the song said? Deliberately, savouring the moment and aware of her rising excitement, she stood looking across the Place de L'Opéra towards the Boulevard des Capucines but she could wait no longer. She turned, and there it was before her in all its magnificence, dominating effortlessly everything around it, the Garnier opera house.

The sun lit up the extravagant gilded façade of arches, winged horses, friezes and columns that held up the verdigris dome, and it shone alike on the solitary red, white and blue flag flapping listlessly on a tall slim pole just across the street on the left of the building, and on the traffic – cars, buses, motorcycles, and bicycles – that seemed to Juliet's astonished eyes to hurl themselves with no apparent plan, but a great deal of noise and occasionally eye-watering fumes, around the great island on which the enormous building had been erected. She wanted to pinch herself to verify that she, Juliet Crawford, graduate of the Royal Scottish Academy of Music, was actually standing there, and that, once she had ventured out into that rather unnerving sea of traffic and had then found a path through the hordes of people of all ages who were sitting on the steps talking, laughing or just looking at the living painting that was Paris, in a few minutes she would be inside. She wanted merely to soak in her first sights of this hallowed building – was there a music lover in the world who did not know of its wonders? – but there was not time. The first meeting was at eleven; she had only a few minutes to find the correct entrance.

Juliet waited, watched and strode out; one sustained note on a car horn, one motorcyclist who stopped centimetres from her best thigh-length boots and then revved annoyingly while he waited for her to cross. Clutching her music case with familiar ease, she picked her way through a good-natured group of French students. It could not be her clothes – for she wore the knee-length frilly gypsy skirt, the tiny T-shirt and the short leather jacket so beloved of many young women internationally – that made her instantly recognisable as British. It must have been the large well-shaped blue-green eyes and the shoulder-length mane of reddish brown hair that immediately proclaimed her nationality, since the ones who spoke to her, inviting her caressingly to sit with them in the sun, spoke in English.

She smiled, said no thank you, *Non, merci*, very politely in her best French – conjured up from hideous memories of St Ninian's School for Girls – and walked on past the tall iron lamp standards holding aloft not only a circle of white globes but a lyre, symbol of Apollo, god of music, hurried on past colossal marbles of naked ladies, through the first unguarded wrought-iron gate. A guard stopped her at the second entrance. Juliet smiled, crossed her fingers in the forlorn hope that he spoke English, and said clearly, 'Good morning. My name is Juliet Crawford and I am one of the competitors in the Prix d'Argent conducting competition.'

He looked at her uncomprehendingly, said something she did not understand, and moved as if to close the gate. Over his head Juliet caught her first heart-stopping glimpse of the foyer which, even in the dim interior lighting, was dominated by a staircase, the Grand Escalier. It was everything and more that the guidebooks said and she looked forward to seeing it properly, to being part of it, to standing quietly listening as music poured out from the auditorium, to running up and down its magnificence with loving familiarity, recognising and perhaps pointing out the chandeliers which would light the steps of beautifully gowned women while it caused their gems to sparkle as they progressed upwards to the world-renowned Grand Foyer. Desperately she parroted her carefully worked out and learned French sentence of explanation. He was singularly unimpressed and told her slowly and painstakingly that she was not allowed to enter here but must go outside and round the building to the library door. His whole demeanour told her exactly what he thought of foreign students who had not had the good sense to learn French.

Some day, she told herself as she hurried round the monumental building, some day I will be welcomed – as a conductor – through that door.

Three hectic days later Juliet was standing off stage with the nine other semi-finalists, eight men and one woman, waiting for the judges to finish their deliberations and announce the names of the three finalists. The long corridor was dim even though the lamps that were attached to the walls at intervals were lit and cast the shadows of the contestants on to the cold marble mosaics beneath their feet. They had been warned to keep quiet and as still as possible but every now and again someone moved and his shoes beat a little tattoo, and drew an agitated '*chut*' from Madame de Champs who stood, like Matron at a preparatory school, waiting for permission to enter. Juliet was physically exhausted. The preliminary stages in this most prestigious competition had been arduous, the strain of trying to conduct unknown musicians in an unfamiliar hall unrelenting. But the stakes were high. The finalists would see their names, their plaudits, fly around the world, and the winner would immediately become assistant conductor of one of France's most famous orchestras for an entire year. Not only that, he, or she, would take home a cheque for twenty thousand euros – a great start to what could become an international career.

Juliet swallowed and tried to disengage herself from the air of tension and the drama unfolding in the magnificent red and gold auditorium by looking down the line of her seemingly patient fellow competitors. She almost smiled. Each and every one wore black trousers and a white shirt, some tucked in, some not, almost a uniform. Bryony Wells, the American entrant, still managed to stand out: she had tied her luxuriant black hair back with a scarlet ribbon – there was nothing in the rule book about acceptable ways to deal with long hair; perhaps the organisers had not yet come to

3

terms with the fact that every year more and more women were climbing the barricades of that most male bastion, conducting.

Juliet, much taller and very slim, was more interested in the result of the competition than in her appearance. First and foremost she was a musician. She took a deep breath as she felt the adrenalin, which had kept her buoyant throughout the long evening, draining away. Her stomach was churning, and the palms of her tightly clenched hands were wet. She prayed that what she was feeling was not evident on her face. She wanted no one to know just how much this competition meant to her. Silly, actually. They all knew; was it not vitally important to all of them? She had to win and this time she felt that she had a chance. Juliet had never believed in self-delusion but she knew that, for her, everything had gone well. The orchestra had responded and played exactly as she had dreamed they would. The performance had been as perfect as it could possibly be. It would be fine. She must try to relax.

She turned to Claude Morrisett, a French contestant who stood beside her nervously chewing his thumbnail. Claude was short and stocky and he had run his hand through his thick dark hair so often that it stood out wildly around his head. 'You were good, Claude.'

He tried to smile. 'This is the dreadful time, Juliet. Twice before I have reached the final. Is it, how you English say, the third time for luck?'

Could she say, I hope so, Claude. She wanted to reassure him but even more she wanted to win. She took refuge in the banal, 'May the best man win,' and he did laugh a little.

'Or woman? You, I think, are this time my rival.' He gestured to the end of the corridor. 'Just listen to them go on and on. This is, for us, so vital, but for them, just another evening.'

She smiled at him. 'If it helps, Claude, I think you're the one I have to beat.'

He looked at her seriously. '*D'accord*. Someone wins and the others lose. It is not easy. Look now at that one. She has . . . something . . . and some talent; but you . . .'

They looked along the line of young hopefuls towards the vibrant and attractive Bryony who was chatting casually with

4

her neighbours. How could she possibly be casual? Was it all an act and merely the way she coped with fear?

Juliet looked down at her clothes; Bryony might not be quite so elegant but she did exude sexuality. Was that a winning combination: undoubted talent, flashing dark eyes and sex appeal? I have talent, she thought. The performance was good. A door opened behind them and someone hurried out and along the corridor, high-heeled shoes announcing their departure, and once more there was a loud '*chut*', from Madame. Juliet sighed, trying to keep her thoughts positive. She felt as if they had been standing for hours but it could only have been ten or fifteen minutes, just long enough for the competition's sponsor to tell the invited audience about his company and how pleased it was to be securing the future of orchestras all over the world by financing this competition to find the best of the world's young conductors.

She tuned in for a moment but he was still talking about his company's future plans. Did he not care that ten young people from all over the world were standing in the dimly lit wings, each of them hoping, praying, to hear his or her name called, waiting to walk confidently across the stage to a burst of enthusiastic applause?

Think about the theatre, about the privilege of actually being here in this glorious building . . . It was impossible to think about anything but the results.

The voice had changed. '*Et maintenant*, and now it is time for us to congratulate our finalists,' and at last they were walking out on to the brightly lit stage, bare now, except for the five judges – four men in dinner jackets and a woman whose mother had never said, 'Look at yourself in the mirror before you leave the house, and take something off' – and the sponsor, the rather elderly, frail Vicomte de St-Nectaire. The judges, their job done, moved to the side, and the vicomte, in a strong voice that was at odds with his seeming fragility, began to talk again.

Juliet found it difficult to see anything until her eyes adjusted. She looked up and any feeling of insignificance she had felt outside was magnified by this spectacular auditorium, with its fluting gold

5

columns and superbly carved arches that together held up the sublime cupola on which the artist, Marc Chagall, had painted his homage to fourteen great composers. Juliet looked out over the auditorium but, even if she had been able to distinguish individual faces, there was no one there whom she would recognise. To-morrow, tomorrow for the final, her parents would come, her father fussing about having to find a replacement but deep down – surely – he would be pleased.

She crossed her fingers. I have to place, I have to. This is the most important moment of my life. I win here and a contract is in my hands; I lose and . . . to lose did not bear thinking about.

The atmosphere was electric; the tension felt by every one of the ten semi-finalists was almost palpable, and the hyper-imaginative among them could almost smell fear; it seemed as if even the audience held its collective breath. The vicomte bowed, everyone clapped. What had he been saying? Juliet had little idea but at that moment the chairman of the judging panel, Madame Geneviève Michau, stepped forward to announce the short list, the three finalists. For a moment there was silence as everyone both on the stage and in the stalls focused on her glittering figure. She spoke in French much too quickly for Juliet to understand but the names – she could understand the names.

'Bryony Wells.'

The contestants on either side kissed the American while Juliet tried to remain calm, clap dutifully and sincerely. Well done, Bryony. Mean it, Juliet. There are two more chances.

'Claude Morrisett.'

A huge cheer from the home crowd and Juliet turned to Claude, took his hand and shook it enthusiastically. 'Well done, Claude, well done.'

He hugged her and then kissed her, French fashion, three times. 'You next, Juliet. It has to be your name next.'

Was the interval even longer between the second announcement and the third? To Juliet's frayed nerves it seemed so. She found that she was holding her breath; there should not be the slightest sound that might prevent her hearing her name.

'Jaime Jimenez.'

Tears that she fought welled up in Juliet's eyes. It was impossible; it could not be correct. Disappointment lodged in her throat and threatened to choke her. She wanted to call out, 'Wait, there has been some terrible mistake.' But she could not do that. The thin skin of civilised behaviour that is all that lies between our untamed four-footed brothers and us kicked in and she held her tongue, literally. She bit down. It was unjust, wrong; there had to be a mistake. This was not ego, arrogance. She knew she had been the best. She was quite certain of it and yet she had not even been short-listed. But education, breeding, good manners, call it what you will, some code of behaviour was demanded and she could hear her voice congratulating, commiserating. There was a smile pasted across her face. The critics would write once again about her exemplary behaviour. Just as well that they could not see behind the mask.

Less than an hour ago this hall had echoed with the sounds of beautiful music, piping flutes, the exquisite drawn-out note from a masterfully played violin. Now it was full of laughter, happy, noisy, multilingual chattering voices. People were kissing, hugging, congratulating . . . sympathising.

Claude looked confused as they walked backstage, along the same marble corridor with its illuminated alcoves to a reception room – almost as opulent with its huge gold-framed mirrors and period furniture and exquisite, perfect wooden floor – where everyone mingled, winners and losers, judges and sponsors. 'I really thought you would beat me this time, Juliet. The orchestra seemed to respond to you more than to the rest of us.' He shrugged, raised shoulders, a small moue of distaste, embarrassed, honest enough to know that all was not well. 'Who knows what they look for, *mon amie*?'

She took pity on him. He was her friend and should be allowed to enjoy his time of triumph. 'Who knows, my friend? Claude, you won and I am pleased for you.' And that much was true, for Claude was decent, talented and hard-working. It was so much worse to lose to the arrogant, preening Jaime Jimenez.

As if thinking of him had conjured him up, the South American was before her. She could smell his hair oil before she saw him and managed to step back in time to avoid an over-exuberant and totally meaningless hug.

'Bad luck, Juliet. They say in your country third time lucky: not so in your case. Such ill fortune. Maybe you should face the facts.' He gripped her by the upper arms and looked solemnly into her face – a kind friend saying something unpalatable that had to be said – his over-white teeth grinning at her. 'Women can't conduct; they just don't have the charisma, the ability, the moral or the physical power to make the orchestra do what they want. You are tall but, beside me, see how slight.'

She struggled to control herself. She would not disgrace herself by rising to his bait and she would not dwell on the fact that he was interested enough in her progress to know how many competitions she had entered: this was indeed her third competition. Juliet felt threatened by the illusion of power that his strutting posture and height awarded him and stepped back a little further. 'Luck doesn't come into it, Jaime,' was what she chose to say.

'Now, now, *querida mia*, not the old chestnut about the odds being stacked. All women say when they lose, "Oh, it's a man thing; they try to keep us out." Ever think maybe you're not good enough?'

Juliet tried not to grit her teeth. 'Never occurred to me for a moment, Jaime. And, besides, Bryony is a woman.'

He smiled and it was a most unpleasant smile. 'La Wells has, what shall we say, a very powerful friend? But she won't win: even he isn't that mighty.' There was a note of doubt in that last piece of bravado. Whatever he wanted to believe it was well known that powerful friends helped at the start of a career.

Juliet would not listen to such nastiness, even though she did not particularly like Bryony Wells. She began to move away from him and then turned as another thought struck her. 'By the way, *querido mio*,' she added with heavy sarcasm, 'even without Bryony and her "powerful friend", Claude is light years ahead of either of you. I look forward to congratulating him when he wins tomorrow night.'

For a moment she felt better as she saw her blow hit home and then the adrenalin stopped flowing and the shock waves of soul-destroying disappointment threatened to swamp her. Oh, God, I have to get out of here so that I can cry. But there were others to talk to, other contestants, the judges, the sponsors. There was wine to be drunk and food to be eaten, although the wine tasted like vinegar and the artfully constructed hors d'oeuvres like cardboard. She looked for Bryony Wells, the only other woman in the competition.

Remember your manners, Juliet. Grin and bear it. Trot out all the old clichés which are sometimes the only things to say that help. She shrugged, looked around for Bryony again but could not see the American anywhere.

'Miss Crawford?' It was the most senior of the judging panel, the distinguished Czech conductor, Alexander Stoltze.

She looked up into sympathetic, understanding and very friendly eyes. And her heart skipped a beat. 'Maestro.'

'If it helps, Miss Crawford, I really felt that you should be in the short list. You were a revelation to me.'

Her depression lifted. Alexander Stoltze, the great Alexander Stoltze, had admired her conducting. 'How kind, Maestro. Coming from you, I can't tell you . . .'

'Then don't try. Your turn will come. When things go wrong, and they do and will in this claustrophobic world of ours, remind yourself that Stoltze thinks you remind him of Haken.'

She could scarcely speak, thrilled and yet humbled by the magnitude of the compliment. Karel Haken, another Czech, was the protégé of Alexander Stoltze. He had won this self-same competition at the unheard-of age of nineteen and now, eleven years later, was sought after by orchestras around the world. Juliet herself had followed the career of the young maestro, collected his recordings, read news items about him and reviews of his performances. To hear such praise was almost better than winning. She prayed she would not burst into emotional tears. 'Thank you, Maestro. I am honoured.'

He took her hand and raised it to his lips in an old-fashioned

Eastern European way as he looked straight into her eyes. 'We will meet again, Miss Crawford, and next time, maybe, the cards will not be stacked.' He squeezed her hand as he bowed, then walked off to join a colleague who was gesticulating wildly in another corner of the room and Juliet stood looking after him. Were he not so famous she might have been forgiven for thinking that he had been flirting with her.

Get a grip, Juliet. He knows he's attractive; he probably squeezes every hand he kisses. 'The cards stacked.' Was not that almost what the oily Jimenez had said? How odd. Coincidence?

She could bear no more. She needed to return to her hotel to ring her parents and her friends. Once more she would have to tell her parents that she had failed. She could not bear to talk to them while she was upset, for that would distress them more than the fact that she had not succeeded. Although neither was really musical they had tried to be supportive as she had studied and even now that she had finished postgraduate training and should reasonably have been expected to be earning money they were still sending small monthly cheques to keep her solvent.

She said her goodbyes, collected her coat, and slipped out. She would walk; the evening air would clear her head, and the beauty of April in Paris would soothe her wounded spirit. It did not. The skyline was as dramatic as it had been that morning when she had walked along, her heart full of hope, in love with Paris, in love with music and in love with life. She continued on down the Avenue de l'Opéra to the Palais Royal and the Louvre and carried on towards the river. The buildings on the banks of the Seine were just as magnificent, the trees along the wide boulevards were still springing into vibrant young life, the lights that illuminated historic buildings or played with ripples on the river were just as bright, but they failed to reach her, to cheer her.

Face it, Juliet, face it. Maybe it is time to quit, to say it's not going to work. It's high time you were supporting yourself instead of having to rely on an allowance from your parents.

She did earn some money by giving piano lessons or accompanying singers. Sometimes she played with her dearest friend, Hermione, who was a violinist and, like Juliet, going the rounds of the competitions circuit, but she was not earning a living wage. Her troubled thoughts accompanying her rapid footsteps, Juliet hurried along the pavements of a city built for love and did not even notice the appreciative glances she received. It was cool enough for her to wear her coat but she had not buttoned it and it blew behind her as she walked, revealing her slim body in her well-fitting trousers. For the final she had considered wearing an evening gown, but it would stay in its wrapping.

'It should be raining,' she said aloud and then hoped that the two young men leaning over the parapet on the bank did not understand English. Ashamed of her rather selfish outburst Juliet smiled an apology, '*J'aime Paris,*' and hurried on and, just as she reached her hotel, her mobile phone began to ring. She sat down on a bench, just outside in a courtyard full of sweetly scented potted plants, to answer it.

It was her agent, Aldo Navarini, who was exuberant and, as always, upbeat and supportive. 'I wish I could be with you. The results are already on the Net and the adjudicators' remarks are fab, Juliet; they can do you nothing but good. Reading them I find it hard to see why you weren't short-listed.'

She told him what Alexander Stoltze had said and he yelled 'Yippee!' so loudly into her ear that she felt she could have heard him without the telephone line.

'Fandabidozee. With Stoltze in your corner you're sorted, lassie. He is one powerful man. Pity he couldn't swing the rest of the panel though. You'd think if he was as influential as they say he is . . . Never mind that for the moment: we'll have lunch as soon as you get home and you can go over the whole thing with me and we'll try to see where you went wrong. There has to be something basic that we're missing.'

'Aldo, basically I think they don't want women. If the American wins all hell will break loose but Morrisett is good, almost as good as I thought I was.' She sobbed. She could sob with Aldo.

'You're sending me negative vibes, Juliet. Not allowed. We'll crack it. You're the best – even Stoltze said so – and with him in your corner there is only one way to go.'

She prayed he was right. A sponsor, even though she wanted to do it by herself, could make all the difference. Stoltze had watched her conduct, had heard the result she had achieved with the orchestra and had said that he liked what he saw and heard; but still she had not placed and he was the senior judge. How did it work? Next time. Next time she would win. For now she would go back to Edinburgh and she would work and improve and next time she would win.

She rang her parents, who wanted her to return home immediately and were displeased that she was going first to Edinburgh.

'We really need to talk sensibly about your future, Juliet,' said her father, using his calm, doctor-in-the-consulting-room voice. She could picture him, like her, tall and slim, his brown hair greying with age. 'Of course we're sorry that you're upset; we thought you would at least place. After all, at college you won everything. So what's different now?'

'I don't know, Dad.'

'That wasn't really a question, dear, but remember we're here for you. Now, if you have to go to the flat with your friends, fine, but then, as soon as possible, come home.'

'I have to plan a strategy with Aldo, Dad. He is one of the best agents in the business and I'm lucky to have him.'

'He hasn't done much for you so far.'

How often did she have to explain that every orchestra in the world already had a conductor, and that it could take years to achieve anything worthwhile?

'Dad, tell Mum that as soon as I've had my meeting with Aldo I'll come home and we'll talk.'

Once back in Edinburgh Juliet arranged to meet Aldo Navarini for lunch at one of his favourite restaurants, Bouzy Rouge, on Alva Street. The décor, wood tables, bright tiles, modern art on the walls, cheered Juliet as Paris, latterly, had failed to do. Before ordering a meal they sat with some fresh warm French bread and a glass of wine and poured over the adjudications, not only her own but the others. Aldo finished reading and leaned back in his chair and, as always, Juliet found herself praying that the frame would take the strain. Her agent was a big man in so many ways and she worried, not only that he would disgrace himself by breaking a restaurant chair but that his overburdened heart would cease to function. She had warned him several times but he laughed, talked about bones and genes.

'We're all big, Juliet. My grandmother – dear God, she was one formidable woman. Six feet in her stocking soles.' He tore off a piece of bread. 'What a smell, freshly baked bread; nothing like it.' He popped the bread in his mouth, straightened up and looked at her closely. 'For the life of me I can't figure out where you went wrong, lassie. Tell me again what you were wearing.'

'Brown trousers and a pink T-shirt for the initial heat and black trousers and a really beautiful white silk shirt for the semis; almost everyone else was wearing exactly the same – white shirts usually for the men.'

He frowned. 'You should have worn a dress or a skirt, short; you have great legs.'

Juliet threw her napkin down on the table in exasperation. 'I've told you a hundred times that I will not go that route. I have to succeed on merit. Besides, we were almost told to stick to trousers and shirts for the heats – androgyny or anonymity perhaps.'

Aldo smiled, his heavy-browed Italian face crinkling with amusement. 'Of course you'll be recognised – very soon – as a rising star but do you really have to look like one of the lads? You have to make your sex, your femininity, a selling point.'

Juliet's anger spilled over. 'What, great legs and – would you believe – she can read music too. You have got to be joking.' And then she took pity on him, for he worked so hard; and so far, since she had been spectacularly unsuccessful since graduation, he was earning nothing from her, and still he believed. 'Besides, Aldo, well-cut trousers are very sexy.'

He laughed, relieved that she was over the worst of her anger. 'Now we have to look at some of the other competitions. There are several, but which ones for you?' He took some papers from his bulging briefcase. 'How about the Grzegorz Fitelberg International Competition? You win if you can pronounce it. Sorry, rotten sense of humour.' He skimmed the page. 'No use. Every four years. You should have done it last year. Astrakhan Masterclass. Russia in October. Fancy it? We could find out more. I have the websites. Colin Metters' Masterclass in Leipzig first week in November: you could do them both: Russia and Germany always look good on the résumé.' He skimmed another page. 'Then you could try Chile or Argentina or even Australia or, closer to your home in Bonny Dundee, how about Orkney?'

The waiter returned with their order, saddle of venison with blueberry coulis for Aldo and a lighter selection, pan-fried chicken with foie gras and orange sauce for Juliet.

Although the smells wafting up to her were making Juliet's mouth water, she took the papers from Aldo and, while the wine waiter poured more wine, read. 'St Magnus Festival. Orkney Conducting Course. This isn't until June next year. I want competitions, Aldo, and auditions. Most of these are courses. And I need to earn some money. It's humiliating to have to depend on my parents. It's almost impossible to get a paying job when I have to drop out every few months.'

'I know and I have a few feelers out; let's see if we can get you an assistant's post somewhere, but, in the meantime, let's look at courses and competitions. And there's always teaching.'

She ignored that. She was meant to conduct, and although taking a masterclass in Poland or Chile or Australia could improve her skills, it all depended on who was leading the course. She had skimmed Aldo's lists and had heard of very few of the teachers. Not, she tried to be fair, that that necessarily meant anything. Even if they were not world-famous conducting names like Abbado, or Mutti, Ashkenazy or Barenboim, or any one of a dozen others, they could easily be highly gifted and successful teachers. She would look at the websites, gather information, and make decisions. In the meantime she would have to search for a job, just as soon as this delicious meal was over, and she would have to visit her parents.

On her way back to the flat she dropped in at an employment office and signed on as a client. Her confidence was so battered by the defeat in Paris that she was prepared to take almost any job that would earn her some money. Even in the Job Centre she was made to feel totally useless since it appeared that she had absolutely no marketable skills. She was a musician though, spoke reasonable German, and she could drive.

'This wee job might have been made for you,' said the manager. 'The Edinburgh International Festival needs people for all manner of jobs, picking up actors or artists of one kind or another from the airport, transporting the odd tuba, you name it, general dogsbody. I think you're a shoo-in.'

'Fine,' said Juliet. 'I'll apply.' She surreptitiously crossed her fingers and thought but did not say that she hoped some orchestra would rescue her long before then.

2

On the Friday after meeting her agent Juliet decided to visit her parents. Their home in the ancient east coast city of Dundee was on a tree-lined Edwardian terrace just a short bus journey from the railway station. Juliet loved the house and the location, partly because of the flowering cherry trees that line many of the streets of the city. In spring the dense clouds of pink blossom were quite beautiful and she gazed at them now from the bus, watching the slow fall of the flowers to the pavement. She had timed her arrival for early evening; her father would be on his way home from his surgery and her mother would be in the kitchen. She was looking forward to seeing them; she loved them. It was just that Dr Crawford had never really accepted his only child's career choice; he would have preferred that she study medicine and go into practice with him. Her relationship with her mother, however, was much easier. Mrs Crawford was rather surprised by the talents of her elegant and attractive daughter but she was very proud of her and was forever asking Juliet to play the piano for guests or visiting relatives. Juliet, who was, in fact, rather modest, found this 'showing off' an agony but would never, willingly, hurt her mother's feelings.

Now she revelled in the warmth of home-coming, in walking up the brick path to the dark green door with its lion-head knocker, in seeing the same tweed jackets hanging on the old hallstand, in smelling the potpourri in the blue Chinese bowl on top of the camphor wood box in the drawing room window; that box with its wonderful collection of heavily embroidered Chinese table linens had been one of the solid things that the infant Juliet had used to steady her in her early navigation attempts. She enjoyed exchanging hugs with her much shorter and more generously rounded mother, admiring her new, shorter hairstyle and turning round so that they could see how much her own brown hair had grown, and listening to cries of, 'But I would have picked you up,' from both parents.

'I'm so sorry to disappoint you both again,' she finally managed to say when they were all settled in the comfortable family sitting room. She looked across at her father, Dr Richard Crawford, at his tall, thin frame so like her own, at his rather austere face, which could crinkle into laughter lines, but rarely did. She sighed. How she had tried to be the perfect daughter: she had done everything he had ever asked her to do and had done it well – except that she had not studied medicine. 'I'm actively looking for jobs and have put my name down on all manner of lists. This is the year, Daddy. I will get a proper job this year. Actually I hope I've found one, unfortunately not until August but it's at the Festival.'

With a sinking heart she watched the smiles of joy on their faces. 'It's not a terrific job; I'll be driving people around, visiting musicians, singers, that sort of thing, meeting them at the airport and taking them to their hotels. It's a start,' she finished feebly.

Her father, who had been sitting sipping his one Scotch and soda of the day in his favourite chair near the rather grand tiled fireplace, almost jumped to his feet. 'Years of education and you do manage to get a job at the most prestigious festival in the entire world – driving people around. By this stage I thought you would be the one being driven.'

Juliet stood up to face him. 'Daddy, you know that it takes time to become established; we've gone over this before.'

'You didn't even place, Juliet. A whole extra year in Vienna, all the masterclasses you've taken and you didn't even place.' He waved his hand at her as she made a move as if to speak. 'And please don't say, "I was a semi-finalist, Daddy." Isn't it time you listened to reason? I know you're talented. Your teachers have been telling me that since you were five years old and I don't need this Alexander Stoltze to patronise you either, but what is obvious to me and should be to you too – unless of course there is more of your mother in you than I thought and you are able to blind yourself to the truth – is that no one wants a woman on the podium. Face it, Juliet, and save yourself and your mother and me some grief.'

She fixed on the word grief. When her father was in the middle of a tirade it was usually easier to catch just one of the many horses that went galloping past. 'I'm sorry that I cause you grief.'

Her mother patted the firm seat cushion on the comfortable pale blue sofa where she was sitting. 'Come and sit down, dear. That's not what Daddy meant.'

'Allow me to speak for myself, Lesley.'

Lesley Crawford smiled up at her husband. 'But why, dear? You've been speaking for me all our married life. Now, Juliet, I know how much this means to you but perhaps Daddy is right. It's not your ability: it's your sex. What is it they say, "Why fight City Hall?" Since you graduated you have taken part in three competitions, twice you have been short-listed but didn't win and this time, whatever Maestro Stoltze says, you failed even to place. Three people beat you into fourth place or twentieth; it doesn't matter which, does it? And don't say there was a female finalist. She didn't win, did she?'

'The Frenchman won.' Juliet ignored her mother's invitation and went over to stand beside the baby grand piano that was her mother's pride and joy. She looked out of the bay windows to the garden as, idly, she allowed the fingers of her right hand to play over the keys, experimenting with notes.

'What is that, Juliet? It's so annoying when you improvise something out of context.'

Juliet smiled at her father. 'It's annoying today because you're in a foul mood; usually you enjoy trying to place it.' She noticed the veins on his neck, always a warning sign. 'It's Beethoven, Daddy, the Fifth Symphony, third movement. I'm going to make it my shout of defiance; after all, that's what Beethoven himself wanted the symphony to be, an attack on complacency.'

He threw up his hands in exasperation as he turned to look down at his wife. 'Now she's second-guessing Beethoven.'

'That's what conductors do, Richard,' said Lesley and stood up. 'Let's go into the dining room. I've poached a salmon for supper. Cold salmon and salad, and some of my home-made salad cream. Then we'll have some strawberries, Spanish, but I did want something special. We can have them with ice cream. Won't that be lovely? For now, no more fighting, you two. We see you so seldom, Juliet, now that you've settled in Edinburgh. I did think while you were on the competitions circuit you might live at home.' The unspoken words, 'and it wouldn't cost anything', hung in the air.

There is no polite way to tell your parents that, no matter how deeply you love them, living with them is stifling, and so Juliet kept quiet. Discussing her living arrangements would undoubtedly bring a request that 'dear Hermione' visit and more astonishment that Heather and Gregor – both 'rather unsuitable, don't you think?' – were still sharing the large flat which was as close to the New Town of Edinburgh as the four of them could afford.

They made a tacit promise not to discuss Juliet's career for the rest of the weekend after her father made his final pronouncement, 'Give it till the end of the year and then choose a new career pattern,' and made concerted efforts to be as happy together as possible. Juliet went shopping with her mother on Saturday and played golf with her father on the Sunday. She was as interested in the finer points of the ancient game as he was in the subtleties of the symphony but they managed to keep smiling. She fended off requests that she stay one more night – 'Daddy can easily drop you off at the station on the way to the surgery' – with the excuse that Aldo often telephoned early on a Monday morning.

On Sunday evening she was on the train for Edinburgh and, as always, experienced pangs of both happiness and sadness as they were swept across the calm – for today – silver breadth of the River Tay. More than anything in the world she wanted to please her father, to be the daughter he wanted her to be, but she could not and that made her feel guilty. Never in her entire school life had she been at all interested in studying medicine; only music fired her and she knew that she could not change and, deep down, did not want to change. Could her father not accept that? She did not doubt that he loved her as she was sure that he knew that she loved him, but oh, how much easier it would be to have a father like Hermione's who thought that everything and anything his daughter did was perfectly splendid.

Her two best friends, Hermione and Gregor, were waiting at Waverley Station and Juliet laughed when she saw them. Hermione had dyed her spiky fair hair a royal purple and since Gregor's hair was a natural wild red, side by side they clashed horribly. They also looked odd together since Hermione was tiny and dainty while Gregor was very tall – at least two inches taller than Juliet – and ungainly; he had not yet, it seemed, grown into his bones. Obligingly she played the game that at least allowed her to avoid mentioning Hermione's clothes, which, to Juliet, resembled nothing more than a costume from a medieval film set. 'Tell me about the hair.'

'I'm making a statement. You should do the same, Juliet, make all those frumpy old conductors notice you.'

'They notice me; I'm taller than most of them. Mum's made you some raspberry jam.'

'Good, I adore your mother. My mother has no culinary skills.' Hermione's mother, the Honourable Chloé Elliott-Chevenix, had no need of housewifely talents since she ran, successfully, an international business and could afford to hire talented staff. 'You may share my raspberry jam, Gregor, if you promise not to eat out of the jar.'

Gregor, who was quietly walking along beside them, carrying Juliet's overnight bag, stopped in astonishment. 'But you do, all the time; and I use a clean spoon.'

'Good heavens, what is that woman wearing?' asked Hermione, probably to avoid answering Gregor. 'There should be a law against people who do not look at their back view before leaving the house, especially women members of parliament, don't you think?'

Juliet and Gregor merely looked at each other. They recognised this tactic. They managed to catch a bus almost immediately which took them down through the glorious New Town into Stockbridge and from there it was a few minutes' walk along quiet Sunday pavements to their building, a rather dull-looking grey stone tenement with a bright red door, courtesy of Hermione. Hermione pressed the bell and was able, a few seconds later, to push open the door. She had no need to explain that the fourth tenant of the flat was at home because they could easily hear a very lovely soprano voice singing scales.

'Mrs McDermott is out?' asked Juliet as she began climbing the wide, hospital-green, stone staircase to the second floor.

'No, she's in, as in our flat. Heather has an audition tomorrow and you know her, every minute counts. Ergo we have a guest for supper. Guess who?'

Juliet made a face, echoed by her friends. She did not have to guess. 'Mrs McDermott.' Still fraught with disappointment, she would have preferred not to have to entertain but it was vitally important to keep on the right side of their elderly neighbour since Gregor Morrison, a would-be composer, played the piano almost every minute of every day, Heather sang, usually scales, which, as she herself said, 'Only a mother could love,' and Hermione played the violin whenever she had time. Juliet, who also played the piano when she was studying a score, listened to recordings of great music at all hours. They tried to limit themselves to a normal working day and kept volume down, when they remembered, during evening hours and never, no matter the circumstances, made any noise at all after midnight, but occasionally mistakes happened and there had been several heated discussions with Mrs McDermott and their neighbour on the other side, Andy Morgan. They had realised that the only way to handle the situation was to invite Mrs McDermott to every late rehearsal. All four flatmates felt sorry for her. Her face, as Hermione said, was lived in and they wondered occasionally – when they were not too busy with their own worries – how she ever managed to stay in the flat since they were in a very high-rent area.

Mrs McDermott, dressed for an evening out, was a fashion disaster. Her hair was a brassy blonde and, since it was thinning, her pink scalp peeped out embarrassingly and poignantly from between the strands. Her eyebrows had been plucked into oblivion decades before and so she had drawn in two black arches that tended to make her look perpetually surprised. She was also a great believer in something called rouge – which she had used in her heyday and which she would have been better off forgetting – and liberal applications of musky perfume. The black eyebrows, the red cheekbones and the scarlet Cupid's bow that she painted over her rather thin lips made her resemble the mechanical doll, Olympia, in the opera by Offenbach, and perhaps that is why Heather chose to sing Olympia's song, the famous and difficult 'Les Oiseaux dans la Charmille,' usually known as 'the birds' song.'

'I know that aria,' said Mrs McDermott when it was finished, 'and how well you sang it, my dear. I heard the great Edita Gruberova sing it years ago. Oh, my dear, why you are not at Covent Garden I do not know.'

'Me neither,' said Heather. 'Come on into the kitchen and have some scrambled eggs, Mrs McD, and then Gregor will see you home, won't you, Gregor?'

Gregor, who had played for her, made a face but he agreed. What could he say when their guest was telling him enthusiastically that he too should be at Covent Garden?

Juliet and Hermione stayed behind in the living room with its eclectic mixture of bargain finds and good pieces supplied by Hermione's indulgent parents. After opening one of the tall windows to allow in fresh air to rid the room of stale perfume, they collapsed together on to what had once been a splendid red sofa. 'How was it?' asked Hermione as soon as they were settled, which meant as soon as they had thrown most of the colourful cushions that lined the sofa on to the floor.

'The usual. "Isn't it time you faced facts?" And maybe it is.'

Idly Hermione played with the leather laces of her little red leather waistcoat and smoothed them down over the flimsy material of her long dress. She began to laugh. 'Oh, my God, Juliet, I'm going to turn into a Mrs McDermott. We're wearing almost the same clothes. Shall I paint apples on my cheeks?'

'Don't be horrid. She's wearing what she wore when she was at her happiest, a Bohemian Rhapsody and it's come back in – unfortunately for poor Mrs McD – only for very young women. What does your mother say about the new look?'

'Really, darling.'

Juliet said nothing and Hermione said it again. 'Really, darling. It's the inflection, Juliet. That's what she always says, and then adds, "Why can't you be more like dear Juliet who always dresses like a lady?" In fact, "dear Juliet", you ought to go boho like me.'

'Aldo said something like that. He thinks my clothes should make a statement. My jeans are "token bloke" and I should wear short skirts because I have great legs – according to Aldo.'

'He's right about your legs. I think you should wear red on the podium. Just imagine it, a sweep of red satin, a very modest but beautifully cut white blouse; or perhaps cream and a red jacket.'

'Black, the jacket could be black. I don't want to blind the audience, or the orchestra for that matter.'

'Ghastly idea, the black jacket; you'd look like someone's idea of a Spanish equestrienne. Some wide boy would be sure to yell, "Where's your horse?" ' Hermione put her feet up on the very fine walnut coffee table. Idly she admired her little gold kid slippers. 'What do you think? Very in. Mummy says they remind her of ghastly over-dressed women in Florida.' She became aware that Juliet was not exactly enjoying the conversation. 'Never mind about my shoes,' she said. 'Were you serious about the black jacket?'

Angrily Juliet jumped up and began to pace around the beautifully proportioned, high-ceilinged room. 'Of course I wasn't serious. Clothes are the least of my worries. This is checkmate, Hermione. I have no idea what to do. Should I sign on at an unemployment office tomorrow morning? For hire. One unemployed but willing conductor.'

Hermione jumped up and joined her in the middle of the room. 'Double damn, Juliet. And I promised myself I wouldn't forget. Look, I even wrote it on my hand.'

She held up her hand so that Juliet could see the words she had written with a large felt-tip pen.

Margarita Rosa Grey.

'Mean anything? It was a phone call this afternoon from Aldo. Sorry, but he wants you to . . .'

She got no further, for Juliet had thrown her arms around her, kissed her exuberantly, and hurried from the room.

3

School auditorium, church or village hall, world-famous concert hall – it made no difference to Juliet. These few minutes before the start of the performance were always the best. The magic potion never failed: something wonderful was about to happen. How could it not? The expensively refurbished Usher Hall was a perfect setting with its fascinating plaster panels and gilded medallions which not only reflect the hall's Scottish character but also honour figures in the world of music: Robert Burns, the Scottish poet, and Wolfgang Amadeus Mozart, the great Austrian composer, and many others, can be found by the eagle eye. Myriads of lights illuminate equally both the expensively dressed patrons and the more casual. The roof, which for several years appeared to be held up by netting since it had, until recently, been marred by extensive cracks, was a subject of heated discussion among patrons.

'Dear Lord, it looks like a wedding cake.'

'Don't be ridiculous. It's quite magnificent.'

To Juliet it was simply the loveliest concert hall in the world, and not only was it lovely but its acoustics were far finer than anything Paris or London had to offer. Therefore the programme, a concert by the Royal Scottish National Orchestra, under the baton of its guest conductor, the world-famous Czech maestro, Alexander Stoltze, promised spellbinding pleasure for Juliet even before it began. Since the competition she had been spending her days studying scores, listening to recordings, looking for work, and wishing that something nicer than a plea from her parents that she visit them would happen, and it had. The postman had delivered a letter for which she had had to sign. Inside was a ticket for a seat in the conductor's box at the only concert that Alexander Stoltze would conduct in Scotland this year. The 'compliments slip' that accompanied it had told her that the ticket was a gift from Maestro Stoltze himself.

She had literally jumped for joy when she saw the signature. He had remembered her, and had taken the trouble to find out her address. Could it possibly be that one of the acknowledged great conductors was taking an interest in her career? Good omen upon good omen, since the ticket had come just a few weeks after she had found out that she had been accepted as one of the contestants in the Margarita Rosa Grey conducting competition. She was invited to visit him backstage after the concert and, at that time, she would thank him and tell him about the competition. Thank heaven that this time he was not one of the judges: there must be no hints of favouritism.

She opened the door of the box and slipped inside. Someone else was there already, sitting not up front in full view of the audience and the orchestra but in a corner towards the back of the box. That she would not be alone was to be expected; Alexander Stoltze was an international icon. Naturally there would be many people in Edinburgh whom he knew. She moved forward hesitantly, and immediately, much against her principles, found herself wishing that she had invested in a fearfully expensive but undeniably beautiful pink jacket she had seen – and tried on – in the lovely Princes Street store, Jenners. Hermione had almost wept because Juliet had refused to buy it. I should have listened, Juliet thought as she recognised the other guest of the maestro. Even from behind him she thought she recognised that beautifully shaped head, the slightly over-long straight black hair, the slender but quite broad shoulders. Instinctively she put her hand to her heart, which had begun to beat rapidly. Of all the people in the world that it could be. Her mouth went dry. She was about to meet her idol, the conductor whose career she had followed with profound admiration. Karel Haken.

He stood up when he heard her and looked slightly puzzled for a moment. Then he smiled and held out his hand.

'Miss Crawford, it is Miss Crawford, is it not? Good evening.'

Juliet shook the extended hand. 'Good evening, Maestro,' she said quietly and sat down where he pointed at the front of the box. She missed applauding the leader of the orchestra as he walked on to the stage because she was trying to school her beating heart. What did this mean? Not one but two influential conductors in the same evening and one of them this gifted young man who was admired and envied in equal measure by every student of conducting. And how did Haken recognise her? They had never met. He was taller than she had expected but not much taller than she was herself: his eyes – no, she could not really tell without gazing into them – were dark, but not brown, but then her questioning mind quietened while the hall shook with applause as the conductor appeared in the wings, threaded his way through the orchestra and stepped up to the podium. As always Alexander Stoltze seemed surprised by all the fuss. He stood waiting, baton raised, while the last frantic coughs disturbed the atmosphere. The orchestra looked at him expectantly and still the arm with its silver baton never wavered.

Silence, soft, breathless, hopeful. The arm moved and then there was nothing but sound, glorious sound. At the end of the first movement, Juliet found that she was sitting on the very edge of her seat and that she was holding her breath. She relaxed, deliberately settling herself into the surprisingly comfortable chair. She had forgotten where she was and certainly was no longer aware of the silent figure behind her. Until the interval she was attentive to nothing but the music and, of course, the maestro. How dynamic he was as he stood there like a charioteer in charge of not two but almost one hundred horses. Among them would be prima donnas who had to be handled carefully but with iron-strong hands. There would be shy, retiring, but gifted musicians who needed to be encouraged to give their best and Alexander would know each one, would have assessed strengths and weaknesses. To watch a great conductor pull from a world-class orchestra a sound that even they had only prayed that they could achieve was, to her, the most exciting experience.

Soon, soon – she crossed her fingers – she would be the one there on the stage of the Usher Hall.

'I'm glad you decided to breathe, Miss Crawford,' Karel Haken said as the orchestra left the stage. His voice was pleasant, low and musical, and with only a slight, but rather attractive, accent. 'Tell me, is the joy of the music more intense if you are holding your breath? Should I, too, attempt this?' He was laughing at her but the smile in his eyes took any sting away.

'No, I don't do it deliberately. It's just that I can never get over the excitement of hearing great music superbly played. I knew this would be good.'

'Because it is Maestro Stoltze or this orchestra or is it the composer?'

'All three, I suppose,' said Juliet as she tried to walk confidently with him through the rather austere whitewashed corridors towards the foyer. What was it about him that was affecting her? As they walked across the hall he was recognised, people drawing back to let him through, a few bowing their heads as if in acknowledgement of his fame or his prodigious talent, but he seemed unaware.

'I shall hesitate to ask you to watch me conduct, Miss Crawford. How could I concentrate wondering whether or not you were going to be able to breathe? I should hear you if you collapsed, you know, and what it might do to my poor orchestra. Champagne?' He had not waited for her to agree but was already ordering. He handed her a glass and smiled at her and she saw then that his eyes, in which the smile danced, were not brown but grey-blue, the colour of pebbles in a mountain stream. 'Delicious,' he said. 'I drink very little alcohol but when I do I enjoy champagne, and so do all beautiful women, do they not?'

Juliet laughed. 'I don't know if that's a compliment or a mere statement of fact.'

'Let us say that it is both. Now tell me, Miss Crawford, how is it that you are already so well known by the maestro?'

He was direct but she had been wondering the same herself. 'I don't think I am well known to him, Mr Haken. I met him at a competition in Paris. He was kind enough to encourage me in a moment, to me, of great distress. The ticket arrived out of the blue.' He looked puzzled and she explained. 'As a complete surprise, Maestro, something unexpected.'

He looked thoughtful. 'He is a very kind man, Miss Crawford, and very clever. Now, as it happens, I saw you conduct in Paris too. I was hiding in the mysterious Box Number Five. You know this box, the one they call the Phantom's Box, a wonderful place to be? Yet, no matter how much I wanted to meet you, it would never have occurred to me to send you a ticket to a concert. Unless, of course, you are travelling to Prague in the next few months, and then I would be delighted to send tickets. See how the maestro teaches me something new every day?'

He was flirting or was he merely being friendly? She decided to play it safe. 'You are perfectly safe, Maestro. I will be in Edinburgh for the next few months.'

They sipped their drinks and chatted easily about the concert and all the time Juliet was aware that they were under intense scrutiny. 'Do you like being looked at, Maestro?'

'I try not to think about it and besides, Miss Crawford, perhaps they are all looking at you.'

Juliet found herself blushing. He was flirting. Of course the concert-goers were looking at Haken, the phenomenon, the rising star, and, heady as adulation could be, he seemed to be determined not to allow it to affect him.

They finished their drinks and walked back to the box. 'Are you looking forward to the Mahler Fourth, Miss Crawford? I hope you will be able to breathe.'

'Oh, yes,' she said. 'Champagne is very relaxing.' It was also very stimulating, or was that the effect of his easy charm? She was surprised. Everything she had ever read, any photograph she had seen, had led her to believe that he was much too driven and focused to flirt but that was exactly what he had been doing. The iceman can melt, she thought, and settled down to listen to the music. For the first time ever the power of great music did not hold her completely. She could no longer see Maestro Haken and could almost believe that he was not there, that it had been a dream. I've been flirting with Karel Haken, the Karel Haken. Should I pinch myself? She forced herself down to earth. Get a grip, Juliet, and listen to the Mahler.

When it was over and all the bows had been taken they walked together down the steps to the foyer. The doors were open and they could see a perfect early summer evening. Had they wished they could almost have read their programmes by the soft blue light of the evening sky.

'How light it is in Scotland. Amazing. You are coming to see Maestro Stoltze.' It was not a question; he took her acquiescence for granted. He held her elbow as they walked down the crowded steps and turned right to get to the stage door. 'There will be a crowd waiting for his autograph but we can wait inside. You will have supper with us.' He looked at her face. 'He did tell you to come, yes?' He gestured with his right hand, his conductor's hand. 'We are in the hotel across the road; he will have ordered a supper.'

They were waved through the first set of doors by the security guard and then Karel opened the second wood and glass door and ushered Juliet in. They walked across the marble floors, Juliet's heels echoing but not loudly enough to drown the sounds of revelry coming from the conductor's room. There was a crowd, possibly not quite so large as the huge, highly polished mahogany Steinway that took up so much space made it appear, as it forced them all to congregate in one corner of the room, but, in the midst of it all, the famous conductor was laughing and talking in at least three languages; at the same time he was signing programmes and posing for photographs. He saw them and pushed his way through, his hands held out in a possibly theatrical welcome. 'Miss Crawford, you came, and Karel, my boy. Good, good. But you see here too many people. Go to the hotel and start without me.'

Karel spoke to him in a language that Juliet did not understand and which she rightly assumed was Czech. 'There are people from the consulate here, Miss Crawford; he will be twenty minutes or so.'

Juliet hesitated. 'But you should stay too, Maestro. I've had a lovely evening and I've thanked Maestro Stoltze. I am perfectly happy to go home.'

He held her elbow again and ushered her out of the hall. 'I saw them all earlier. Supper is arranged in the Exchange restaurant and he will find us easily when he comes. I know he wants to talk to you.'

She looked puzzled and he smiled. 'He would not have sent a ticket to a concert unless he wanted to speak to you. He is very influential, you know.'

Immediately she tensed and obviously he felt it. They stopped walking and stood quite still. 'It was the word influential, wasn't it? Everyone needs help in the beginning, Miss Crawford. There is no shame in that. Come, we can discuss this over some supper?'

She bent her head in assent and waited, conscious of his hand on her arm, until the lights changed and it was safe to cross the always frenetic Lothian Road. She tried to concentrate on what she would say, how she would explain herself. She had been pleased, an understandably human characteristic, when she had received the ticket. She was a conductor without a post and Stoltze was – Stoltze: a word here, a compliment there. They could do wonders. And Haken? Were he to recommend her or – could she even dream – hire her, how different the next few years might be. But always, always for a woman this age-old dichotomy: Is it my talent or my sex? I want to succeed as a woman in what has always been seen as a last stand of male dominance. Damn it, I'm good, not great yet as Haken is great but I'm prepared to work every second, to study, to sacrifice everything in order to achieve my potential – and I don't want to get there by being pushed up the ladder by two men, do I? She had argued long and hard with herself over this issue but Haken and countless other young musicians had been helped by older stars who felt that it was both a duty and a responsibility to share their abilities, to guide, to mentor. Would she feel better if a woman conductor offered help? There were, of course, so many talented women, Marin Alsop, Jane Glover, Sian

Edwards, to name but a few. Dash it. She wanted to do it on her own, to be judged only as a musician.

And that attitude, Juliet Crawford, she told herself, might well be labelled 'cutting off your nose to spite your face'.

She sighed but they had reached the stairs leading up to the revolving doors of the Sheraton Grand, which opened to admit them to the marble reception area. To the left of the magnificent corridor that stretched out before them were the Terrace and Grill restaurants but they walked past them, their shoes echoing on the tile floors. Karel gestured towards the door. 'This is Britain. Impossible to eat in a decent restaurant after ten o'clock.'

The word 'nonsense' hovered but Juliet was too political or too cowardly – perhaps they were one and the same – to say it.

Karel led her forward until the corridor opened out into the area known as the Exchange and since he said nothing else, perhaps awaiting a comment, she too waited until they were in the obviously popular bar before she spoke. 'How long will you be in Scotland, Maestro?' If he expected to be wooed by a despairing conductor he would be disappointed.

'Speaking of Scotland makes you sigh, Miss Crawford?'

'Not really. I was concerned about your comment about restaurant times.'

He laughed. 'That was nothing and here' – he gestured to the comfortable armchairs, the carefully arranged semi-private alcoves – 'the Exchange, is a pleasant place; you will see. I understand all the problems of long hours and working overtime. Besides, hospitality has really improved in Scotland. The maestro, as an example, says that the first time he was in Scotland he had no dinner at all; he lived on bananas.'

This time the 'nonsense' refused to be held back. 'Nonsense. He just didn't know where to look. There have always been really good Italian restaurants in Edinburgh, and fish and chip places stay open late. But you didn't tell me how long you plan to stay. I would be happy to compile a list of late-opening restaurants.'

His face was a study in concern. 'I'm sorry. I have offended you.'

'Not at all. I wouldn't want you, or any other visitor, to starve.'

'You are most kind. Unfortunately I am unable at this time to accept your offer. I have an extra engagement in Heidelberg and must go there tomorrow.'

She swooped on to this topic of conversation with relief. 'What a lovely town. Walking along the riverbank in the spring with all the flowers and then rounding a bend and looking across to see that amazing castle on the hill there is like being in a fairy tale. One autumn I was on a country road leading into the town. There were thousands of hazelnuts and walnuts just falling from the trees and I thought that it was a terrible waste. All that protein littering the pavements and thousands of people starving – in the world at large, I mean, not in Germany. Do they collect them? I never did find out.'

'I shall look for them next September and find out. You did not ask?'

She was relieved that he had not taken offence. 'At that time I didn't speak much German. I had a delightful encounter with an elderly lady who was tidying her garden and she talked at me for ages but I hadn't a clue what she was saying.'

He looked puzzled. 'But it was delightful?'

'Oh, yes, she knew I didn't completely understand but it was important to both of us to communicate.' She leaned back in the comfortable chair in a semi-private alcove near the bar where they could see and be seen but where their conversation could not possibly be overheard, and looked round. 'This is a lovely hotel.'

He ignored the hotel's appearance. Perhaps he saw so many that new ones no longer registered. 'Communication is so important for the conductor.'

She had no intention of discussing conducting, his or hers. If she spoke about his she feared she might be seen to be toadying; should she speak about hers, perhaps he would think she was angling. She could hear Hermione's voice in her inner ear: 'Networking, darling.' She could discuss communication with him and so she looked directly at him. 'Honest communication is important everywhere, don't you think?'

Just at that moment they heard an announcement calling Karel to the telephone. 'Excuse me for a moment. I did not turn on my mobile after the concert. Do order a drink; the waiter will take care of you. I do apologise.'

He hurried back along the mirrored corridor and Juliet, trying not to feel abandoned, waved away the hovering waiter. She could hardly start eating supper before her host arrived. She did not have to wait long, for only a few minutes later both conductors arrived in the room and, with many apologies, sat down.

'But why don't you have a drink, Miss Crawford?' asked Stoltze. To Juliet's surprise he turned to the hovering waiter. 'Did I not give orders that my guest was to be served immediately? Why does she sit with nothing?'

Haken said something Juliet could not understand at the same time as she tried to intervene. 'He did ask, Maestro. I preferred to wait.' She smiled at the waiter as she spoke but Maestro Stoltze merely waved his hands.

'We are ready now.'

The waiter opened and poured champagne and then set a mouth-watering array of trays on the table between them.

'I wanted it to be perfect for you, Miss Crawford,' began Maestro Stoltze when each of them was being served. 'It is Karel's fault; he should not have turned off his telephone, but enough, enough. This is a pleasant wine, no?'

Juliet sipped. The 'pleasant wine', she could see by its label, was a rare vintage. 'I would say rather, Maestro, that it is quite special.'

He laughed. 'Chosen especially in your honour, my dear. I have not forgotten your thrilling performance at the Paris competition, you know. Karel agrees with me – you seemed to us to be a clear winner.'

What exciting words: thrilling performance, clear winner, and, perhaps more importantly, 'Karel agrees with me.' Juliet tried to dampen down her rising excitement and remain practical, level-headed. 'But obviously the rest of the judging panel disagreed, Maestro,' she pointed out wryly. 'Participating was important, however, and I feel that I learned a great deal. In the meantime I have been accepted as a contestant in the Margarita Rosa Grey competition in November. All my eggs are in that basket.'

Karel offered her more champagne, which she declined, noting at the same time that he did not refill his own glass.

'You are eating like the sparrow, Miss Crawford,' said Maestro Stoltze, proffering a tray. 'Good, delicious. The Margarita Rosa is a most prestigious event and with a wonderful panel of internationally famous judges. I congratulate you, but, at the same time, may I suggest a few more competitions? I am reliably informed that there will be a fabulous competition in New York City next year; too early yet to give classified information but some of the finest conductors in the world are supporting it. What an opportunity. None of the great American orchestras has, as yet, a woman conductor; maybe you will be the first, and the prize will probably be in the region of fifty thousand to one hundred thousand dollars.' He turned to the younger conductor, slapping him on the shoulder in an avuncular way. 'Don't you think she should apply to enter, Karel, my boy?'

Karel Haken put down his empty glass and helped himself to some smoked salmon. 'Of course.' He winked deliberately at Juliet. 'Actually, if there is definitely such a competition next year I may well ask to be released from my contract in Prague so as to chase fifty thousand dollars myself. There were several international rounds a year or so ago, Miss Crawford. We could beg to be accepted for a European heat.' He smiled at her. 'What do you think?'

Juliet had been watching Alexander Stoltze while Karel was speaking and although Karel's wink, the tone of his voice and, in fact, his words, had told her that he was joking she was almost sure that there were underlying tensions in the room. What were the hidden agendas here? Stoltze had definitely been shocked or perhaps annoyed by Karel's light-hearted remarks. She decided to pretend that she took him seriously. 'I think it would be completely unfair if you were to enter, Maestro, and if you do I shall personally lead a protest.' She smiled at him as she spoke and was bemused by the answering smile in his dark eyes. She turned to Stoltze. 'It's so good of you to take an interest, Maestro. I will certainly alert my agent to the possibility of this competition.'

'You are most welcome, my dear. In fact I will have my secretary send you details of two or three other high-profile competitions. We don't want to think negatively about the November competition but it is always better to be prepared. And do remember that when they ask for a reference, you know Stoltze.' He half turned and held out his arm as if about to embrace Karel. 'And the brilliant Haken. My candle has burned as brightly as it is going to do, you know, but that of this pupil of mine has only just begun to light the world.' He laughed as if he were slightly embarrassed by his show of emotion and Juliet saw Karel look down as if he too were embarrassed. 'It will be a pleasure for us to help in any way.'

'You're too kind, Maestro. I'm most amazingly grateful.'

He waved away her thanks and offered her a plate of gravadlax but she declined. The waiter arrived at the same moment with the dessert menu and that seemed a perfect time to leave. Juliet stood up and immediately both men did too. 'No, please, you must be extremely tired and I have taken up enough of your valuable time. I am so grateful to both of you.'

'You have nothing to thank me for, Miss Crawford,' said Karel, 'and if I do not see you before I shall certainly make a point of being at the Barbican in November to wish you well. Allow me to see you home. It is very late.'

'It's a beautiful evening, Maestro, and I can get a taxi right at the front door. Really, I'd prefer that; you have both been too kind.'

They insisted on accompanying her, not only as far as the door, but also down the steps and across the plaza to the street. When she was in her taxi and the driver was attempting to interrupt the flow of traffic on Lothian Road she looked back. The conviviality that had marked the latter part of the evening was gone and it looked to her as if Alexander Stoltze was very angry indeed.

What on earth had happened to make him angry? Surely he had

not hoped that Karel would leap to his defence when he had said that he had gone as far as he could. Did his ego need constant massaging? She had been surprised too by his verbal attack on the waiter; he had seemed a man full of conviviality, both at the theatre and in Paris.

She lay back against her seat as the taxi raced down Lothian Road and on to Princes Street. Once again her heart was pounding, her mouth was dry and the palms of her clenched hands were moist. Her stomach was aflutter and she could not, in truth, say that it was the result of too much champagne. Those bubbles were long gone. Still, she would be hard pressed to give her interested flatmates a reliable review of the concert. To her consternation she realised that she had completely forgotten about it. Were the programme, signed by the conductor, not here in her lap, she would have had difficulty in telling them what had been played. Why? Stoltze's charismatic conducting or Haken of the laughing eyes?

Juliet sighed and stretched and then, ashamed of herself, straightened up in case the driver had seen her in his rear-view mirror. It was Haken. He had been at the same time exactly like his photographs and yet completely different, for the photographs did not show the smile that lurked at the corner of his mouth when he was sharing a joke and they did not do justice to his deep, dark eyes which seemed to have the power to stop all rational thought. Juliet hugged her elbow where he had held it and then touched her hot cheeks that both he and Maestro Stoltze had kissed as polite Europeans always do. Two spots seemed to burn and she assured herself that these were where Karel had kissed her, for Stoltze was taller and surely his kisses, which meant nothing, would have been closer to her eyes.

What's happening to me? I'm crazy. No. The salmon was dodgy. One has to be so careful with fish. I have the flu. That's it. I'm coming down with something.

For once all her flatmates were in and all were awake although, as usual, in various stages of undress. Juliet looked round at the loving, expectant faces. How wonderful to have such friends. 'Have you lot been waiting up for me?' she said casually.

Hermione, Heather and Gregor looked at one another in bemusement. 'Good heavens,' said Gregor. 'What conceit. Why should we be at all interested in a flatmate's night on the tiles with an elderly conductor?'

Juliet threw her jacket down on the sofa, deciding, as she did so, that she would certainly go to Jenners the next day in the hope that the pink one was still there. Stoltze had argued the values of being prepared. She would be ready for any eventuality. 'Not one conductor: there were two and neither is elderly. One is in his fifties, rather handsome, very debonair and sophisticated, and the other is . . .' but she found she could not describe Haken. 'He's quite ordinary,' she said and told them about the evening.

'Fab. Oh, Juliet, darling, with either one batting on your side you'd be fine but with both of them . . . The sky's the limit,' said Hermione. 'Now tell us about the food.'

'She won't have noticed,' said the perceptive Gregor. 'What's this about tension, Juliet?'

With three pairs of eyes gazing at her Juliet tried to remember the odd feelings of unease she had experienced. 'I can't put a finger on it, but when we went backstage Maestro Stoltze was smiling and chatting and then he saw us and, just for a second, his face changed. Silly, almost as if he didn't want to see us together. It was so fleeting that – perhaps I was imagining things. After all, he invited us or, at least, he invited me and he knew Haken was there, for Haken said they had spoken earlier. It was a bit childish actually. In the restaurant Karel pretended that he was going to enter a competition; it was so obviously a joke, but Stoltze tensed again, and there was something in the body language as I drove away.'

'Simple, darling. They both fancy you like mad and Stoltze is miffed that you seem to have hit it off with Haken.'

'Hermione, don't be foolish. Honestly it was a lovely evening and I'll be so pleased to have word of other competitions, and the promise of a reference. It's the way of the world, isn't it? We start out determined to go it alone but in any job a word in the right ear can work wonders.'

Heather Banner, a talented soprano and the newest addition to this quartet of friends, was already dressed for bed in a T-shirt that Gregor had been wearing just a few days before. She lounged back on the sofa. 'You're growing up, Juliet, joining the real world. Stoltze conducts a lot of opera. Can you put in a word for impoverished friends?'

Heather had been almost sure that, upon graduation, she would be offered a contract by an opera house with whom she had sung several times while at college. But sweeping cuts to the budget threatened to destroy the company and Heather, like her flatmates, was casting around for other posts. Gregor, of all of them, knew that his road would be hard and long and possibly unsuccessful. He was a fine pianist and managed to eke out a living accompanying choirs, and Heather and Hermione when they were auditioning or in recital, but his heart and his dreams were in composition. So far he had been spectacularly unsuccessful and to date his steadiest job was as scene-shifter and general dogsbody at the Festival Theatre. With that he managed to pay his share of the rent and his living expenses.

Hermione alone, on a generous allowance from indulgent and supportive parents, had no financial worries, and like Juliet and Heather she was doing the masterclass and competition circuit with varying degrees of success. Her instrument was the violin and she was so good that she had already been offered several positions. Fearing – wrongly – that her father's donations rather than her talent had got her the jobs, Hermione had declined everything.

The four had been together since their college days and their wholehearted support of one another was the envy of many other aspiring musicians. 'We chose one another extremely well,' was their own verdict on their friendship. 'A composer, a singer, a violinist and a conductor. What else do we need? All together now.'

'Contracts.'

Juliet took herself off to bed with Heather's last words ringing in her ears. The real world. It was an imperfect world where some-times, too often, talent was not nearly enough. Perhaps because she had been an only child and with no cousins of her own age she had grown more and more self-reliant as she grew up. She liked working things out for herself. Her mother moaned that her daughter's first words had been, 'I'll do it.' So it had always been. But the sense of achievement when problems had been sur-mounted without help was so fulfilling. In an ideal world, she felt, only talent should matter; she yearned for a meritocracy based on the old Venetian method. Sex should merely be a given and of no relevance. She did not want to be chosen because she was a woman, but even more she hated being rejected for the same reason. She had courted ridicule at school for advocating the abolishing of the old 'women and children first' rule.

'Why? It's nonsense,' she had railed in debates. 'There are women bigger, stronger, more capable than many men. Let's change this to "the frail first". Why should some poor skinny wimp of a man be left on a ship to drown when perfectly healthy ten-stone women are ferried away? And women float better too.'

She had been shouted down, by boys mostly, which, in itself, was a character trait she found interesting.

Now she found herself marshalling her equality arguments in light of the evening she had just spent. Just as well that she had decided to save all her energy for advancing her career. If she were at all interested in men as sexual partners she could easily have been drawn to Karel Haken and she assured herself, now that she was not near him, that she was not. Yes, he had a great deal of unconscious charm, a delightful voice, and his eyes were just the kind of eyes she admired, open and honest, the eyes of a man one could trust. As a conductor he was fantastically exciting, not that she had ever seen him in a live concert, but a measurable aura surrounded him. Even in repose he exuded energy; some might call it sexuality, but not Juliet. For the next ten years or so she had decided, very wisely, she thought, to focus on only one thing: she was going to be the first woman to be appointed to the Boston Philharmonic. She had turned down opportunities to appear with women-only ensembles. She wished them well, admired a great deal of what they were doing but to join them smacked of capitulation.

She intended to win and she would win without any help whatsoever from Karel Haken.

4

For once the flat was quite still. Juliet and Hermione were curled up on the sofa and the big armchair respectively and they were reading, Juliet, as usual, a score and Hermione, as was not usual, a novel, and not just any novel but the great Russian epic, *War and Peace*. Once or twice she sighed theatrically as if to get Juliet's attention and ostentatiously held the book so that the imposing title and the name of its even more imposing author could be read by anyone who happened to glance her way, but Juliet was deep in her score, marking lead-ins, echoes and questions and answers. What the flute was saying and which instrument was replying was of sublime interest to her at this point.

The shrilling of the telephone took them both from their self-imposed labours but neither was in a hurry to answer it. Eventually Juliet unwound herself and walked into the hall to pick up the receiver, knocking *War and Peace* on its face with a 'You'll never get through that,' as she passed.

She listened for a moment or two, said, 'I'll tell her. Bye,' and hung up.

'I do hate one-sided telephone conversations,' muttered Hermione.

'Overheard telephone conversations are always one-sided,' said Juliet loftily as she went back to her semi-recumbent position.

'I'm deadly when I'm roused.' Hermione, looking like a very angry chicken, feathers all ruffled, was glaring down at her.

'It was that smarmy bloke from BBC Scotland Heather's been seeing. He has an audition for her and her mobile is switched off. And no, I didn't ask about the audition; it's none of my business or yours and we can do nothing to help her until she comes home.'

'Let's hope it's soon then. And I will get through this,' she finished, as she buried her face in her book.

Juliet paid no attention and so Hermione threw her shoe and clipped the score. 'It's not good to be one-dimensional. I am broadening my mind.'

Juliet threw the shoe back without replying and Hermione gave up and returned to the march on Moscow.

Gregor, who spent some part of every day in the music library at the university, was next to come home. As usual he went straight to the kitchen. He did most of the cooking although the others helped with preparation and cleaning up. Ten minutes or so later he carried a tray of tea and biscuits into the living room; in his mouth was a large sandwich and there was another on the tray. 'Cup of tea, girls, and do either of you know where Heather is?'

They both sat up, Hermione waving her novel at him. 'Behold,' she said dramatically and Juliet looked at them both curiously. Was Hermione reading a classic in order to impress Gregor?

'She's had two calls today,' went on Hermione. 'One from that choir who want her to work with them and one, a few minutes ago, from the man she met at the Beeb.'

Gregor was pouring tea. 'I met him just now as I was crossing Queen Street. He's got a chance for her. Silly cow has her mobile switched off which means she's with some dreamboat she doesn't want to interrupt.' He looked at his watch. 'If I put the chilli on will one of you watch it if I run up to Shakespeare's to see if she's there?'

'Of course we'll watch it but she could be anywhere, Gregor,' Juliet pointed out. 'Eat your snack and rest.'

'Hate to think of her losing out on a chance to sing with a BBC orchestra.'

'For heaven's sake, Gregor, she's not a child; if she misses out because she turned off her phone, tough.'

It was so unlike Hermione to raise her voice except in fun that her two friends looked at her in some surprise. Juliet decided to ignore it but Gregor finished swallowing the large bite of sandwich he had taken and said in a low voice, 'We said we'd look out for one another.'

Juliet closed the score. 'What needs doing with the chilli?' she asked and gratefully Gregor got up and, teacup in hand, followed her into the kitchen.

'She won't get much money if she takes that choir job but the BBC will pay her a proper fee if she passes their audition,' said Gregor as he and Juliet began on the onions. 'I'm not sure of scheduling but it's to sing the soprano part in the *Messiah* for a Christmas broadcast. Great coverage for her; a fab opportunity. You'd be surprised at the number of people who listen to the radio.'

'Sorry I was grumpy.' Hermione had come in and was tying on an apron.

'Cooking a better option than Russian angst?' Juliet laughed.

'It's a fabulous book and I love Russian anything. Gregor, don't be cross. I just think you take too much out of yourself.'

He leaned down and kissed her cheek. 'Do the garlic,' he said and harmony was restored.

Heather phoned a few minutes later to check for messages. 'I forgot to turn my phone back on after the rehearsal. Fantastic,' she said when she was told about her phone calls. 'Look, don't wait dinner for me. I'll ring Peter and get the gen and then I'll telephone – what's his name again, the bloke who wants me to work with his choir?'

'Murray Thomson,' said Hermione, who had taken the original phone call.

'Great. Wish me luck. Maybe this is it.'

Heather contacted Peter Davis-Jones and arranged to meet him at a tapas bar on a street off the Royal Mile. It was a popular meeting place for every age group: an attractive staff served excellent food and drinks at a reasonable price and the venue itself was aesthetically pleasing with tables of light wood cleverly spaced so that one's conversations were private. While she waited there, oblivious of the admiring glances from Spanish waiters and male customers, she answered Murray Thomson's call. Murray had a pleasant enough voice and so it was no problem listening to him but he did like to talk and Heather had her eyes on the glass door while she listened and occasionally talked, hoping all the time that he would have finished telling her how wonderful he was and how lucky she was to have him choose her to be his choir mistress – a word he managed to inject with all manner of double-entendre – before Peter arrived.

'Murray, I'm really busy this evening. As it happens I'm seeing some people from the BBC, but if your group is rehearsing tomorrow I could pop in and we could chat. Great. I'll look forward to meeting you tomorrow. Bye.' The last uttered as Peter arrived, kissed her cheek, and slid into a seat across from her. He looked good, tall but not skeletal like Gregor, good shoulders, carefully contrived untidy hair and blazingly honest blue eyes. What more could a girl ask? A neat bum, Heather answered herself, but there was, she hoped, plenty of time to find that out.

'Don't ever turn your mobile off, you amazingly lovely creature,' he said, taking hold of her hand across the table. 'Covent Garden could be calling, Glyndebourne, the Met.'

She laughed. Heather knew she had a good voice and she knew she was pretty but she was not vain; vanity was not encouraged in the small Borders farmhouse where she had grown up. 'Flatterer.'

'God, you're so naïve, Heather. Things happen at the last minute. Emergencies do occur. Management don't waste time going through agents; they ring directly and the soprano who answers her phone first is likely to get the job. There are several after this job; two of them went to college with you and are prepared to scratch your eyes out if you get it.'

'Good.'

He smiled, knowing she did not take his last remark seriously. 'How about some sangria and a plate of tapas?'

There seemed to be so much to talk about and so they had some more sangria and more food.

'Singers shouldn't drink,' said Heather solemnly. 'It is very bad for the voice.'

'But you're not singing.' He really had such lovely eyes.

'True,' she managed. 'But I will need to sing tomorrow and, if my voice is off, I won't get the job; it's a brutal business. I think I'd better have some coffee.'

He stood up and pulled out her chair for her. 'Tell you what. Let's walk a little; it's such a lovely evening. I like walking in starlight, don't you?'

'Yes, if it's not too cold. Singers have to protect their throats.'

'How many throats do you have?' he murmured into her ear as he helped her on with her coat. 'May I please look for them?'

'I haven't had so much wine that I don't know you're trying to be naughty, Peter. I will walk a little if I get some coffee somewhere, a Starbucks on Princes Street, maybe.'

'There is a much better place in the Old Town.'

Juliet and Hermione waited up, Juliet still wedded to her latest score. Gregor came home from work and was surprised to see them in their pyjamas exactly where he had seen them several hours earlier. 'Don't you two have beds to go to?'

'Heather hasn't come home or called. We're just interested.'

'And you said I was being a nursemaid? You're daft, girls. Heather is probably sound asleep by now and if she's not, I'm bloody certain she's not thinking about you two waiting up for her. Goodnight.'

They looked at each other and Hermione made a face. 'He doesn't seem too disturbed, does he?'

'Why should he be disturbed?'

'All that super-protective stuff this afternoon.'

'He's a caring man, Hermione. He's like that with us all, except me, perhaps. He finds me a little of a control freak.'

'So do we all, darling,' said Hermione and took herself off to bed.

It was almost noon next day before Juliet spoke to Heather who had been in her own bed and sound asleep when Juliet had first walked past her open door on the way to the kitchen to make the early riser's coffee. She had closed the door, leaving Heather still in her day clothes face down and fast asleep on the bedcovers.

'Is there enough coffee there for me?' Hair tousled, mascara smeared, but now wearing rabbit slippers instead of her thigh-high leather boots, Heather slid into a chair opposite Juliet who was seated at the kitchen table, a tub of yoghurt, an apple and a pot of coffee beside her. A score was open against the coffee pot.

'You are the most annoying girl, Heather,' said Juliet as she reached for another mug. 'Even hungover you're lovely. What did you get up to last night?'

'How much do you want to know?' asked Heather as she absentmindedly began to eat Juliet's yoghurt.

'That had better not be the last apricot,' snapped Juliet. 'I'm only interested in your work opportunities,' she finished more calmly.

'Peter is dreamy, Juliet. He's just so different, so sophisticated, urbane.' Heather was waving her spoon in the air as if she were the conductor.

Juliet, who had heard exactly the same description of Paul, Joseph, Alfonso, Kurt and several others during the past three years, waited.

'I'm auditioning tomorrow for the BBC Symphony Orchestra. It's for Christmas broadcasting but is going to be recorded during the Festival; they've managed to talk some fabulous British bass into singing and he's only available late August. Oh, Juliet, can you imagine what this means? At last, a real job and to sing with real professionals, even though no one will hear it till December. I know I haven't got it yet and Peter can't fix it, not that I would want him to,' she added quickly, 'but I have a great feeling about it. And then this afternoon I'm going down to Leith to see a group of oldies who sing a bit but have always wanted to be in a real choir. They'll pay me about three hundred quid to coach them a little. It's not bad for one night a week for eight weeks.'

'Less than twenty pounds an hour and you have to teach the musically illiterate and do the solos? Not a bargain, Heather.'

'If I can teach them a few songs, some Christmas carols a bit later – some in harmony – that will be enough. They don't expect to be made ready for a performance in the Usher Hall. Besides, who knows who might be there, hear me sing?' She got up and walked across the room, more to avoid looking at Juliet than because she needed to move. 'Damn, I need some carbohydrates on my poor stomach; you can't believe how much wine I drank last night.'

'Nothing else?'

'You're not my mother, Juliet, but no, no matter how much I drink, I do stay in control. Can't afford to take risks with the voice.'

'Sorry. I suppose I thought that giving up my lunch for you gave me some rights. Only joking,' she added as she saw the look on Heather's expressive face.

Heather smiled weakly. 'I'm sorry too that I ate your lunch, not that I stayed out late. Can I make you some toast?'

Juliet declined the offer and picked up her score and took it off to the living room. There she sat down at the piano and began to play. As always, after a few minutes there was a sharp knock at the door and Heather ushered in Mrs McDermott who put her fingers to her lips theatrically and sat down quietly on the sofa, folding her gloved hands in her lap.

For some time Juliet played what she needed to play, and then, conscious of the old lady, she played some light waltzes. At that Mrs McDermott clapped.

'Oh, bravo, dear Juliet. I danced to that . . . a lifetime ago, in Vienna. I wasn't always an old woman, you know. Here is dear Hermione,' she said, starting up from her chair.

Hermione theatrically sank on to the sofa and covered her eyes with her hand. 'Hello, everyone,' she whispered.

'Bad lesson, my dear?' Mrs McDermott asked.

'No. Purple heads, Mrs McD. Purple heads.' She sat up. 'Remember I told you that Mrs Armstrong was *un peu* upset that I'd dyed my hair, not because I'd dyed it but because Rosemary loved it? Well, darlings, what am I to do? They've both gone purple. I couldn't concentrate on the excruciating noise Rosie was making for looking at heads; I could even see mine in the mirrors, two in the drawing room, would you believe. This is a hostess who enjoys seeing herself.' She lay back down. 'Everywhere I turned, purple heads – ad infinitum. We should write a children's programme: Patty and Polly, the Purple Heads.'

'Purple People, dear, better alliteration,' said Mrs McDermott calmly. 'I'll leave you to have a nice rest. Thank you for the waltzes, Juliet. I shall miss you when you go to London.'

'I haven't won, Mrs McDermott.'

'You will, dear, you will.'

5

In the months that followed Juliet explored every avenue that beckoned: she studied scores, practised at home with her flatmates as the orchestra, and with local orchestras when she found an opportunity, but spring slipped into summer and she had had no auditions.

The Edinburgh International Festival started with pomp and ceremony. International artists arrived and Juliet had the privilege of meeting one or two at the airport and transporting them through the historic streets to their hotels. One afternoon she sat in the car on a blocked Lothian Road with the elegantly curved bulk of the Usher Hall on her right; the world-famous conductor sitting behind her seemed oblivious of his surroundings and Juliet would have loved to engage him in conversation but dared not. He said nothing to her at all, not even 'thank you' when she deposited him safely at his hotel.

'High on talent, low on charm,' she said to herself as she reflected on being totally invisible.

But there were more high points than low points and one day when she was in the administration office she heard to her delight that Karel Haken was flying in at the last minute to replace an ailing conductor. She did not know whether to be pleased or unhappy that she was not asked to meet him at the airport, but as the box office opened on the morning of the concert she was there on the steps to buy one of the tickets that are held every day so that people, not on the mailing lists, or previously unable to apply for a ticket, have a chance to hear the greatest performers in the world. She got one, in the cheapest band, and almost danced to the offices with it. The rest of the day was a dream; grumpy conductors, bored basses, exhausted office staff, all were greeted with a smile of dazzling happiness. At last, at last she was actually going to see Karel Haken conduct.

'Wear the pink jacket.'

Hermione was standing behind Juliet who, clad only in bra and panties, was in front of the open door of her wardrobe, helplessly looking at her clothes.

'That's for best. This is just a concert, a seat in the gods' gods.'

'For heaven's sake, Juliet, you have worn it once since you bought it. Wear it; pink is lovely on you and then when you go backstage and he invites you for supper . . .'

Juliet tried not to listen. Her head was whirling and her stomach was a jangling mass of hysterical tiny winged creatures. She was going to see him, hear him actually at work. It was a learning experience, nothing more. He was a great conductor and she was going because she wanted to learn. No matter what Hermione said she could not join a queue at the stage door nor could she presume on slight acquaintance and ask to be admitted. But what if she just . . . if he just happened to . . .

Hermione's telephone began to ring and she hurried off to answer it. Juliet sat down on the edge of her bed. If she wore the pink jacket she would be wearing it because she hoped to meet Karel Haken and she certainly was not going to admit that she hoped to do just that. On the other hand surely a concert being given by a world-famous conductor and an even more fêted orchestra demanded that one wear one's best. It was only good manners, was it not? She selected a long brown suede skirt from the wardrobe, teamed it with flat shoes – easier to walk in on the many, many stone steps she would have to climb – and the pink jacket. The music deserved it.

Everything the critics had ever said about him was true. The music was outstanding; never before had she been so aware of the symphony's sheer beauty and splendour of sound. She was exulted and humbled. How did she dare to compete with his ability, to attempt to compare what seemed now to be such paltry efforts to his unique musical genius. Juliet was deflated and then she began to laugh, for every good concert sent her into these tailspins of mood. If the concert did not measure up to her ideals she hungered for the time when she would be on the podium to show that charlatan just how the music should sound. If, as tonight under Karel Haken, the orchestra was artistically thrilling she gloried in the overall effect and then descended into misery, fearing, knowing that she could never begin to achieve such heights. They were right, all the music teachers and well-meaning relatives who had told her that she should be content to be a good pianist, even a great pianist, but that conducting was for men and by trying to force her way into the gilded circle she was only storing up grief. She tried to shut out everything but the music, but memories intruded.

'Name me one woman who has successfully conducted X, Y or Z orchestra . . .' That was her father inserting the name of one or other of the world's greatest orchestras. How many times had he tried to persuade her to major in an instrument? 'Name the oldest orchestra in the world.'

'The Dresden Staatskapelle.'

'Give me the name of one woman who has successfully conducted it?'

And over and over she would say that just because there had never been a woman did not imply that there never would be one.

They had all been at the Caird Hall in Dundee to hear the BBC Scottish Symphony Orchestra. The conductor was the dynamic Israeli, Ilan Volkov, who was a mere three years older than Juliet. 'Look at it,' her father had hissed through gritted teeth as he prodded his programme with a well-manicured finger. 'He got his first post at the age of nineteen. Nineteen, Juliet. At that age you were only in your first year of college. Look what it says: "Volkov conducts with an authority that many conductors twice his age struggle to achieve." He's been principal conductor of the London Philharmonic Youth Orchestra. Well, I suppose that's nothing much, conducting children.'

Juliet looked at her mother while the harangue went on. He just did not understand. Since she was five years old she had been studying music, living and breathing music and he had paid for the lessons, attended every recital . . . No, he had not actually. Now that she thought about it, her father had missed several. Work, of course. He was a doctor. Doctors had to put family second many times. Golf. He had missed several concerts and recitals because he was playing golf, or watching golf. Doctors need relaxation. She did not mind that occasionally he had put watching golf ahead of watching her. Music is relaxing. She cleared her thoughts. She would not think disloyal thoughts. He was her father. He just did not really understand how much music meant to her.

He was still talking. 'You could do something like that, something simple to start, not this, "I want the Royal Scottish National Orchestra." Where are all the women conductors? We like music; we go to concerts. Never once have I seen a woman conductor; oh, sometimes women conduct wee amateur choirs but that's not real conducting. Women usually end up forming their own little orchestra or a music group. Is that what you want? The Dundee Orchestra of women who didn't quite make it.'

No, damn it, Juliet wanted to say. I want the London Philharmonic. I want Berlin, Birmingham, Cleveland, and I'm going to be good enough to do it, Daddy, with or without your support.

Don't think of that now, Juliet. Think of Maestro Haken and the Bruckner symphony. Relish it, enjoy it and then analyse it. What did he do to make it sound different from any other time you have ever heard it? Tomorrow, find time to see if he's recorded it, preferably with this wonderful orchestra. He won't have – he's only guesting with the Leipzig Gewandhaus.

She was not alone in enjoying the concert. The audience seemed to wish the orchestra, and the conductor, to stay there for ever, but after three bows, the maestro left the stage and did not return. The orchestra filed out and, reluctantly, the audience did too. Juliet, glad that she was not wearing heels, was almost swept along by a noisy crowd. She reached the door, stepped out on to the pavement, and stopped. If she walked straight across the pavement she would be on her way home; if she turned right she could go to the stage door. The debate went on in her head.

You've met him; you're a conductor too. Go in and congratulate him.

You're not really a conductor because you have no orchestra and anyway, he didn't send a ticket.

How could he? It was a last-minute substitution.

The artists' room will be full of Edinburgh glitterati and other musicians, famous ones. You are unknown. Go home, Juliet.

Juliet walked across the pavement but, at the last minute, passed the bus stop and started to walk. Her feet kept pace with her chaotic thoughts and in no time she was almost home. She could see lights on in the sitting room. That meant nothing except that someone, possibly Hermione, if the flat was empty, had left the lights on. When would she learn that not only was there not, for most people, an inexhaustible river of money but there was for the world an exhaustible supply of electricity?

Hermione was in the flat and Juliet apologised to her.

Hermione, who was sitting on the floor with a violin score, a glass of wine and a half-eaten plate of beans on toast before her, awarded her a cherubic smile over the top of her reading glasses. 'What for?'

'I saw the lights and assumed you were out.'

Hermione shrugged without rancour. 'Could well have been. The most divine toad asked me out but look, Juliet, the Mendelssohn.'

'I see. But why? And you have just dropped two beans on to it.'

'Some ghastly friend of Mummy, with an equally ghastly daughter, has asked me to play this at said GD's wedding in the spring,' explained Hermione, scooping up the beans before they left inexplicable marks on the score. 'Said nuptials to be in a fearfully upmarket country house hotel or a castle if they can find one.'

Correctly, Juliet translated ghastly as meaning middle-class non-deviator from the plans laid out by earliest ancestor and said, 'That sounds lovely. I take it you'll be paid, you'll be fed, and, who knows, someone "useful" might hear you.'

'And the watering, Juliet, let us not forget the watering. Now, darling, I had hoped to see you come in wearing an "I have just been kissed by angels" face. You didn't go backstage. Tell Auntie Hermione all.'

Juliet did while Hermione uncoiled herself from the cushions, fetched and filled another glass for Juliet and returned to her cushions.

'He is quite extraordinary, Hermione, amazingly gifted.' She closed her eyes the better to visualise him. 'He looks rather nondescript in photographs, and yet on the podium he's dynamic, so much energy and focus. I couldn't take my eyes off him.'

'Why didn't you go and remind him that you'd met?'

Juliet stood up. 'I am not a hysterical teenager. What on earth would he say if I pushed myself on him at this point?'

Hermione eyed her friend up and down quite frankly. 'Well, darling, if he's not gay, and who's to know, he'd probably be thanking God. Just think, Juliet, you could have introduced yourself, told him how much you appreciated his opinion of your playing at the Paris competition or how much you personally appreciate his flying in on such short notice.'

'As if my appreciation counts.'

Hermione ignored that as totally irrelevant. 'You really don't take advantage of situations, Juliet. It's perfectly normal behaviour. You buy a ticket for a concert; the conductor just happens to be someone you admire – professionally,' she added quickly as she read the storm warnings in Juliet's eyes. 'You go to the stage door. Maestro, remember me, Juliet Crawford. I just wanted to say how terribly exciting and sexy you are . . .' She ducked to avoid the cushion speeding its way towards her.

'I'm just not programmed to behave like that,' said Juliet and, wrapping her dignity around her, she went off to bed, firmly closing the door behind her.

Next day she spent the morning working in the Festival offices. She was free just after noon and, since it was a beautiful summer day, she decided to buy a sandwich and eat it in Princes Street Gardens. Roses were glorious in the many flowerbeds and, together with masses and masses of lavender, sent their heady perfume into the air. Juliet breathed in deeply as she walked beside them under the shadow of the castle until she found an empty bench. She sat down to enjoy the sun on the water in the restored fountain. The air was full of music, children calling to one another as they played on the grass, the continuous but, for once, low hum of traffic from the street, the folk group in the theatre and even the rattle of a train as it sped along between Haymarket and Waverley Stations, all contributing to an Edinburgh summer symphony. On another day, she was perfectly aware that she would have found the children a nuisance and the traffic annoying but today, for some unknown and uncared-about reason, she was at peace with her surroundings.

'Mood music,' she said aloud and, pondering on how mood affects one's appreciation of music, she got up and strolled towards the Mound or, rather, the art galleries that stood there. Juliet smiled; she was free as the air in the gardens. She could do something she rarely did. She climbed the great stone steps leading to the entrance and went into the gallery. And then she was lost in a joy of colour and form, accepting gratefully the beauty that was arranged before her and, before she knew it, it was four thirty and she heard an elderly lady say, 'I've missed tea.'

Juliet smiled at her and was rewarded with a frosty stare. Obviously one should stay in one's place even in such an acceptable venue as the National Gallery. Must ask Hermione if any of her elderly aunts are in the city. She was humming as she left the gallery and walked down the steps into the lower gallery.

There seemed to be two eating places. On the right of the doors was a rather elegant restaurant but on the left, a rather chic open-plan café. She queued for a few minutes at its counter and ordered some mineral water before she saw the four-inch-high slices of apple and walnut cake with thick, luscious, sour cream frosting. Irresistible. She found a table, sat down and attempted to look at a booklet she had bought which wanted to tell her about the exhibition she had seen but sour cream frosting and high art do not marry well and so she closed the booklet and gave herself up to the pleasure of taste.

'May I join you? Miss Crawford? It is Miss Crawford?'

A hesitant Karel Haken was standing beside the table and Juliet almost jumped to her feet. Instead she managed to finish the cake in her mouth and wave him into a chair. 'Maestro, what a pleasant surprise.'

He put his mug of coffee on the table and sat down. 'I have been in the galleries, so many lovely paintings. You have viewed them also?'

'Yes. I'm off today and . . .' Blinkety-blink: now he would be sure to ask what she had been doing.

'And you would take advantage of having some free time. I also. Last night I worked; this morning I recorded with the orchestra, and so now I can see paintings and perhaps the city without the guilt. Are you conducting at the moment?'

Her heart was pounding and she was sure that she could feel the blood rushing around her body. She prayed that none of her inner turmoil was evident to him. All night she had castigated herself for not having the courage to go backstage and had made up her mind to remember nothing but the joy of watching him conduct and now here he was, sitting at a table with her. 'No, Maestro,' she managed eventually. 'I am working in a very menial capacity at the Festival, driving important people, even instruments, around.'

He laughed and she thought immediately how much younger he looked when relaxed. 'My name is Karel.' He paused waiting for her to say it and, when she did not, he went on. 'I was once a waiter in a beer hall; I also washed dishes.'

She smiled. 'Did you enjoy being a waiter?'

'No. I learned to hate the smell of beer but it was good experience for a conductor. My arms, from carrying trays and lifting them above drunken heads, are very strong.'

Was he laughing at her? She realised that she did not mind. 'I was at your concert last night, Karel. It was wonderful.'

He leaned across the table towards her. 'You were there and you did not come? How I would have enjoyed to see you. I thought of

57

you when the Festival asked me to stand in but there was no time to find your number.'

What could she say or do? Give him her card? Too obvious.

'Did you fly from Prague? I visited the city once, with my parents. It's lovely.'

'I'll give you my card and then, when you come again, you can call and maybe I can be your guide.' Now it was he who sounded unsure of himself.

He took a card from his pocket and handed it to her and, at the touch of his hand, her heart began to race again. She was blushing. Dash it. What was happening? Quickly she picked up her water glass and drank.

'You have a card, Miss Crawford?'

Damn. How gauche. He must think me a fool. 'Yes, of course, and I'm Juliet.'

'Juliet. Quite perfect.' He took the card from her and this time she was delighted that there was no strange reaction when their hands met.

They had finished their drinks and her cake lay half-eaten on the plate. None of the courses she had ever been on had had a section on how to eat a heavily frosted cake elegantly while talking to a conductor you desperately wanted to impress. He was looking at her but making no move to rise and walk away. Should she be the one to move first? Did the old rules of etiquette – the senior lady present will signal to the other ladies and they will withdraw, leaving the gentlemen to their port – apply in a situation like this? In for the proverbial penny; after all he had suggested showing her around Prague: 'How much of the city have you seen, Karel? I mean, if you have an hour or two, I would be happy to show you my beautiful city.'

He stood up and he smiled again. 'You know, Juliet, I have been trying for some time to think how to ask you. I leave Edinburgh very early tomorrow having deliberately stayed an extra day to try to see some sights. I would enjoy very much to explore the city with you.'

She took him first through the gardens and as they walked she told him some of the colourful history of the city. They climbed up the paths away from Princes Street and she painted a word picture of the gardens in springtime when they are a riot of daffodils. They came out on to the Royal Mile and although the imposing bulk of the castle was so near she decided to take him down into the Grassmarket. 'This was for hundreds of years an agricultural market. Now it's full of trendy restaurants and designer shops but I still love it. See that cross?' she asked, pointing to a cobbled cross in the middle of the street. 'That marks the site of the town's gallows. Did they have gallows in Prague?' She did not wait for him to reply but hurried on. 'I want you to see the Flodden Wall; or wait, Karel, is it the usual things you want to see, the castle, the palace, etcetera?'

'I have seen castles and palaces before. The interesting, non-tourist places, something you can only see with a native.'

She smiled at him. 'I'm not actually a native but I have walked every inch of the old town, I think; another of those jobs one takes while waiting . . .'

'I know, for the break, the chance, the opportunity. But this you have now, Juliet. Such a beautiful name,' he said, with what could have been described as a flirtatious smile. 'But what is a Flodden Wall?'

'It was built in the sixteenth century to protect the city from the English. Flodden was a terrible battle where the King of Scotland was killed. He is reputed to have said, "It cam wi'a lass and it will gang wi' a lass."' She looked mischievously at him while she spoke and laughed at his expression. 'The King was James IV and he left a baby daughter who was Mary—'

He interrupted. 'Ah, the beautiful lady who was executed, but what exactly did you say?'

'Broad Scots is not one of your languages?' She knew she was flirting but did not care. It was so easy to be with him; for today she would forget that he was world-famous and remember only that he was an attractive man, someone with whom to spend a pleasant summer afternoon. 'He meant that his line, the Stuart line, started with a woman and he predicted that it would die out with his baby daughter.'

'It is a beautiful city, like Prague. When you come to Prague, Juliet, I will show you walls there and tell tales of kings.'

'Like good King Wenceslas?'

He smiled at her. 'Excellent. You know your Czech history.'

She smiled back. 'No, but I know my Christmas carols. You have heard of Robert Louis Stevenson?'

'Of course, and Sir Walter Scott and John Buchan.'

'Good God, the only Czech writer I have read is Ivan Klima.'

'But you must have read Václav Havel and Kafka. And you must also read Arnošt Lustig's *Lovely Green Eyes*. One day he'll get the Nobel Prize; you just wait and see.'

Juliet was delighted to be able figuratively to hold her head up. 'I'd forgotten Havel and Kafka for a moment and I will look out for Lustig, but I asked about Stevenson because I thought, if you have time, we could walk down or up, rather, to the Calton Hill. The view of the city from the hill was Stevenson's favourite.'

'I am at your disposal, Juliet, if you have time to spend with me.'

How easy he was to talk to; he had shed the mystical coat that marked him as the exciting and charismatic conductor and was now only – she almost laughed to herself – the exciting and charismatic man.

'I love showing the city to anyone who is interested.'

She took him up the steps that climb laboriously to Johnston Terrace and showed him the few sections of the old wall with which he was not impressed.

'It is an old wall, not very high.' He laughed at the expression on her face. 'Oh, poor Juliet, you love your city so much and I am not being the best of sightseers. Let us now go to see the view that the great Stevenson liked.'

Edinburgh is not a vast city and although the streets and even the pavements were crowded with noisy holidaymakers and Festival-goers, they were soon on the relative calm of Waterloo Place and Regent Road. Almost directly opposite the old burial ground and the huge edifice of St Andrews House they found the steps that lead up to the Calton Hill and its odd jumble of monuments. Karel walked up the steep steps effortlessly and Juliet tried to match his ability although her legs were beginning to complain about their unaccustomed activity.

They had walked past the observatory and reached the commanding structure of the National Monument, often known as Edinburgh's Disgrace, a memorial to the Scottish dead of the Napoleonic Wars, which was supposed to be an Edinburgh Parthenon; unfortunately money ran out after only twelve columns had been erected. They walked across the patchy grass up to the monument as Juliet explained its history and Karel saw that only the front and part of the sides of the design had been finished.

'This is a very sad monument,' said Karel as they stopped to look more closely at the unfinished work. 'It is a bit like life or even people sometimes. You see the front and it is very beautiful but underneath or on the back like this unfinished Parthenon, it is quite ugly.'

'I hope I don't know anyone like that,' said Juliet, who suddenly, in spite of the heat, felt a little cold.

'I hope you never do,' he said. 'Now, which way is the view of Robert Louis? There are so many lovely vistas; over there?' He pointed south-eastwards.

'No, Karel, turn north again, towards the city.'

He said nothing for a few minutes as he looked down at the long straight avenue of Princes Street dividing the old and new towns. Away in the distance stood the world-renowned Edinburgh Castle, proud in its towering splendour. He could see the gardens, a train snaking along the line that ran through them and, bizarrely, a little blue balloon that had escaped from some probably wailing toddler and now drifted this way and that on a summer breeze.

'It is very beautiful.'

'But Prague is more beautiful?' Juliet asked.

'It's different; some structures are older even than that great castle there but each city has much to offer. You have a date?'

The question was totally unexpected and Juliet's first reaction was to look at her watch.

He misread her motives. 'I'm sorry; I have taken too much of your time. I shall find you a cab.'

She laughed. 'Up here on the hill? I don't have a date, Karel. I only looked at my watch—'

'To see the time?' he finished for her.

'Yes, and no. I couldn't believe so much time had passed.'

'Almost seven o'clock. A good time for dinner. Will you have dinner with me, Juliet?'

She looked down at her clothes. 'Well,' she began.

'You look lovely,' he said quietly and his look made her blush.

'Thank you, and yes, I would like to have dinner with you.'

They walked down the hill and headed back towards the centre of the city. Cars, lorries, buses, bicycles, all flashed past them, the ancient lorries the noisiest of all as their gears complained at each stop and start. Karel stopped to watch one of the many pipers who stand and play on the city's street corners, seemingly unaware of the hordes who gawp at them or photograph them.

'In Prague our strolling musicians all seem to want to pretend to be Mozart. You should come in May; May is a month of music, from every window, in every church and concert hall.'

'And all dressed up as Wolfgang Amadeus.'

He grinned. 'Every one. Excuse me one moment. I had better ring somewhere although I'm sure my hotel will feed us.' He dialled a number, put the receiver to his ear and then covered the mouthpiece with his hand while he listened. 'French?'

She nodded just as he spoke and she waited, wondering, as women always do, if her casual cotton sweater and toning skirt would be suitable for whichever restaurant gave them a reservation.

'We are in luck,' he said as he returned the telephone to his pocket. 'The Café St Honoré. You know this place? A colleague recommended it; hungry musicians always know where is the best place to eat. This restaurant is very good and usually they are full but tonight there is a cancellation. This is a good omen, a delicious meal to end a perfect day.'

Juliet smiled but said nothing. It had been a lovely afternoon. What had they talked about? Scottish history and Czech, and they had, of course, discussed music, and art and galleries they had visited. They talked of books and writers, politics and the Prague Spring and the Jacobite rebellion and when they were silent it was because whatever they were gazing at needed no commentary. Indeed a memorable day.

They managed to flag down a taxi and arrived at the restaurant with a few minutes to spare. She excused herself and went off to do something with her hair and to put on some lipstick. It was all she could do. She had nothing with which to dress up her casual clothes. When she came back from the ladies' room there was a glass of champagne at her place and the waiter was pouring one for Karel who was standing waiting to ease her into her seat.

'To replace the energy,' he said as he lifted his glass.

She sipped. Delicious. She had been tired, pleasantly so, for they had walked miles, but hair brushed and lipstick reapplied, and, yes, a sip of champagne and she felt stimulated and relaxed at the same time. 'Is this what you drink after concerts? I must remember that.'

'I run after concerts. Then I go to bed.'

'Run?' Now she knew how he had managed to climb all those steps so easily all afternoon.

'Yes. It's how I relax. Unless there is a reception that it would be discourteous of me not to attend. And even after the reception, I run. Running clears the mind, and the head. Anyway, enough of me, shall we look at the menu and then we will talk perhaps of the plans of Juliet Crawford?'

Dare she tell him? He was not on the judging panel so there could be no reason not to.

'Come, Juliet, when you have finished this so fulfilling job what are your plans? I can help, maybe.'

Help from him was the last thing she wanted. She would do this on her own. 'You're very kind but I'm in a competition in November, in London this time.'

'Margarita Rosa Grey?'

'You know about her competition?' How gauche. He was a conductor. Of course he would know. 'Sorry, that was stupid.'

'No, not stupid. You had just heard about it when we met in the spring.'

63

She had forgotten that the competition had been mentioned. She blushed, wishing she had not brought it up for he had promised to see her there. She spoke quickly, hoping to blind him with new information so that he might forget whatever it was they had said at the Sheraton. 'I was fantastically lucky, thanks to my agent. I had a video recording – I'd had it made for a competition in Heidelberg – and just managed to get the application in on time. Two former teachers, one in Glasgow and one in Vienna, were sweet enough to write really glowing references. I almost stopped breathing until the end of June and then the letter came.'

'So wonderful a letter, yes. I have such a treasure too.' He did not remind her that both he and Alexander Stoltze had promised to provide her with references. 'And now you wait until November, is it not?'

She had just popped something small and delicious into her mouth and she swallowed it quickly. 'Yes, three fraught days, if I get that far. Twenty of us have been chosen. Monday, November 15th we have all been invited to rehearse with and conduct the Royal Academy of Music Ensemble, excerpts from works by Arriaga, Handel and Debussy. That's at the academy. Stage two is the following day and if—'

'When,' he interrupted. 'Positive thoughts, Juliet.'

She smiled. 'When' – she emphasised the word – 'I get that far, ten of us will be asked to conduct and rehearse with the academy's string ensemble in extracts from Tchaikovsky, Brahms and Bernstein. There will be three finalists and they will be able to conduct all day – all day, can you imagine? – with the London Symphony Orchestra at the Barbican and then the concert will be in the evening. It's open to the public.'

'And the music?'

'I pray I get that far because I actually know it all but, of course, so will everyone else: it's Mozart, Stravinsky, Britten and Shostakovich. Everyone does the Mozart, the overture from *Così fan tutte*, and we draw lots for the others. I'd love the Britten or even the Shostakovich. Sod's law says I'll get the Stravinsky.'

He did not ask who Sod was; perhaps he knew. Instead he twiddled with his wine glass. 'And the other pieces?'

'I am unfamiliar with the Arriaga but I've got the score and a few recordings. If I went to my parents I could spend every waking minute studying all the scores and listening to as many recordings of the pieces as possible but I prefer to try to stay here in Edinburgh. My flat mates help. They're all musicians and we have a pact. Anyone studying for an audition is waited on hand and foot. The flat's a mess when we're all studying – which, I have to say, is most of the time.'

'Tell me about your friends.'

Talking about Hermione, Gregor and Heather was easier than talking about herself, but she was still aware that she was doing most of the talking. He did tell her a little about himself, but only a little. After all, his career, his public life was common knowledge. Appointed to a post in his native Czech Republic at the age of nineteen, he had since worked with most of the greats, orchestras and conductors. She would not tell him that she owned every one of his recordings.

The meal was over: the wine was finished. Karel offered more, after-dinner drinks, coffee, but Juliet was aware that she had drunk more than she usually did and that she had told him more about her dreams and aspirations than she had ever told her parents, or Aldo or even Hermione who was the recipient of all her confidences. She felt suddenly as if she had been too open. This was a strange interlude, a day that would be looked back on by both of them with that puzzlement which is how we look at half-remembered things. Karel was already world-famous. She could not bear it if he thought she had been so friendly because of what he was. She held out her hand and he looked at her in some confusion.

'You live in this restaurant, Juliet?'

'No, of course not.'

'Then we will shake hands when I have taken you to your door.' But he took her hand and held it and she had the choice of pulling away like a teenager or letting her hand lie in his as they walked down through the New Town and into Stockbridge towards the flat.

Neither of them spoke as they walked in the lovely twilight through the city resplendent in its Georgian finery and at last they were at her door and she turned to look at him. She did not want the day, the dream, if that was what it was, to end. 'Would you like to come in, have coffee? My flat mates might be in, except Gregor who's playing in a late nightclub, but they'd love to meet you.'

'Hermione is the superb violinist and Heather the lyric soprano who will be great one day. And Gregor,' he finished seriously, 'the pianist who will, one day, be greater than Brendel?'

'No. Yes, he is, a pianist I mean, but he's a composer.' Shut up, Juliet, you're babbling.

'I would love some coffee, Juliet, and even to meet these very talented young friends.'

She opened the street door and they walked upstairs to the second floor. Their shoes echoed in the large, dimly lit stairwell, but there was no sound at all from the flat. Juliet opened the door and let him into the hall that was open on to the large living room. 'I'll make coffee,' she said and hurried into the kitchen. Could she run to her room and spray on a little light perfume? She had worn rosewater that morning but its delicate scent must have faded. No, she was not seducing him. Good heavens. She turned on the tap and filled the coffee pot. They would chat to the aroma of coffee beans.

Karel was standing in the large bay window looking down on the street outside but he turned when he heard her return and hurried forward to take the tray. 'Your friends are not here but I will meet them another time.'

She smiled and attempted nonchalance. 'Professionally, I hope you meet all three of them one day.' She poured the coffee and sat as far away from him as was possible but he stood up and brought his cup over to the sofa on which she was sitting. 'I have said something to make you nervous, Juliet? You are concerned that your friends are not here?'

What price years of education now. She felt gauche, a teenager who had somehow got herself into a situation from which she did not know how to escape. Escape? How melodramatic. She laughed and this time the laughter was genuine. 'No, Karel, although they would all love to meet you.' She sipped her coffee but was aware of him watching her. 'More coffee?'

In reply he put his cup down and then took hers and put it too on the table. 'Juliet, you are a very beautiful woman and I have wanted to kiss you since approximately twenty minutes past five this afternoon.'

'Twenty past five?'

'Or maybe twenty-five minutes past or maybe since you were in the café and too nervous to eat your delicious cake with Haken watching to see if you got some cream on your so beautiful mouth.'

'I have exquisite table manners and never get cream on my face,' she began, but got no further for he kissed her.

'Your lovely face does not need cream of any kind,' he whispered against her ear and then he turned his head and kissed her again. Their arms still around each other, they stood up slowly and kissed again. Juliet pulled away and looked into his eyes. She was insane; she had met him twice but somehow, as if she had no real control over her actions, she moved with him towards the hall, and then they were in her bedroom, and she was on fire with longing. She leaned against him, revelling in the strength of his arms, breathing in his smell, a mixture of soap and some faint cologne or, perhaps, aftershave. The skin of his face was surprisingly soft except on his clean-cut chin where a dark shadow was beginning to appear. And then there was time only to feel, to experience, as their clothes went tumbling on to the floor in haphazard piles. She could hear his voice but could understand nothing but his hands and his lips. She heard her own voice as it called out his name.

The sound of a door closing woke her hours later and she lay for a moment savouring her memories; then she stretched out a hand to reach for him but she was alone in the bed. She smiled. He had to leave early. She heard the shower and pictured him there under the waterfall. Naughty Juliet. She turned over in the bed hiding her face in his pillow. She fell asleep.

★   ★   ★

Karel had woken early, as always his body clock obeying the appalling demands he made of it. Edinburgh. What a beautiful city; it had cast a spell on him but he was wide awake now and in his own mind. He looked down at the girl sleeping in the curve of his arm. She was beautiful and he felt his eyes fill with tears as he realised how vulnerable she was. She had trusted him as a child trusts, slipping its little hand into the hand of father or mother as they prepare to cross a busy street.

This night, this love, amazing and fulfilling as it was, should never have happened, not now before she even had a chance to start her professional life. What needed to be done now, with the least possible embarrassment to Juliet, was minimise the damage. She was young but she was not a child nor was she completely inexperienced. Thank God he had told her of his early flight. She would not misunderstand and think that he was running away; he would write a note, not saying all that he would love to say to her, not yet – it was too early – but he would be fairly light, two consenting adults as it were. She would reply, possibly with a postcard of her Calton Hill and in a few weeks he would ring her from Heidelberg or London, maybe, and they would laugh and chat easily and agree to meet next time they were in the same city. She would not expect more and she would be able to focus on preparing for the next big competition.

He decided not to shower – she might wake – but washed and dressed quickly. Juliet sighed, stirred, and his gut tightened, not with lust or desire but with an unfamiliar yearning and regret, regret not only that he had lost control but regret that he could not simply slip back into her bed and take her in his arms. But he could not; it was unfair. For her sake, as well as his, he had to be strong. She was so young, so beautiful and, far above all, she was so talented. She should be, could be, great. Her career must come first. But if she allowed something so ephemeral – perhaps – as a love affair to sap her energies, she might well dissipate that talent and, more importantly, she might lose the will to succeed.

Later something wakened Juliet again: perhaps one of the other doors in the flat closing, or the front door. He had gone, left without waking her to say goodbye, to talk about meeting again. She jumped out of bed, grabbed her dressing gown and pulled it on as she ran along the corridor and into the living room. The cups were gone. Probably Gregor, who was almost compulsively neat, had tidied up. But when? No matter. She rushed out on to the landing and leaned over the iron balustrade just in time to hear the front door close with a sharp click of finality. She would not rush to the front windows. She did not return to the living room but went instead back into her bedroom where she sat and looked at the dishevelled bed where she had had the loveliest experience of her adult life.

Be rational and sensible. He said he had to leave early. She looked at her watch: 5 a.m. Where was he going, Prague, New York, London? She could not remember and what did it matter? What had happened between them was special. It had been the most beautiful day and night of her life and it had meant as much to him. He would call and tell her so.

But he did not.

6

'It's not much but it's something.'

'It's great, Heather; it's a job.'

Gregor was improvising at the piano and Heather was sitting on the sofa, painting her toenails. Had Hermione been at home, Heather would have painted her nails in her bedroom.

'My first since the *Messiah* during the Festival. I had hoped to start coaching them months ago.' Heather stuck her bare foot out and examined the pale blue polish on her toes. 'What do you think?'

'Your toenails are blue; I will assume that you are not having a heart attack and remain seated. It's perfect that the rehearsals are on my night off.'

Heather was applying her artistic efforts to her other foot but she looked up. 'I worried about that. You're not getting any time off.'

'Who needs free time at twenty-five? Tomorrow?'

'Yes, if you have nothing arranged.'

'I was going to stay here and play the piano until Mrs McDermott came in for hot chocolate but I could be talked out of it.'

They laughed at the thought of their elderly neighbour, who needed few excuses to invade the flat.

'Awful to have no one, isn't it, Greg?'

He padded on his bare feet over to the coffee table and poured her a third cup of tea. 'We don't know that she has no one. We know that no one visits her and that she loves to come in here, probably for the free food.'

'I think it's for the company.'

Gregor shrugged. His mother was not like Mrs McDermott, was she? But perhaps Mrs McD had thrown out her only child too. He refused to think that his mother might well be another old lonely lady in a few years' time. She was not fifty yet and she had a job; she also had a crowd of friends from her pub night. They were her family; they were the ones she liked to be with, to drink with and laugh with. Maybe he would send a Christmas card this year. He certainly did not want to see her, not after all the vitriol she had poured over him in the past, but he supposed there was no harm in sending a Christmas card. Control-freak Juliet would no doubt have their communal cards bought from the politically correct charity in plenty of time for Christmas. Busy she might be but what she saw as duty would be done. Made it easier for him: nothing to do but buy gifts for the girls and sign his name to the communal cards. Thanks to Heather and her amateur choir he would have the gift money. 'Jingle all the way.'

The next night he met Heather at the church down Leith Walk. What a barn of a place the hall was, with ghastly hospital-ward green paint, some of which was peeling. The few electric fires perched, for some obscure reason, high up on the walls. 'Don't they know heat rises?' he whispered to Heather as they walked in. Gregor was glad that Heather was friendly and bubbly, as well as exceptionally pretty. They would like her. He knew that if he had been on his own the evening would have been purgatory for everyone. He was simply not good at communicating but with Heather running it, all he had to do was sit at the piano, play some scales and a few hymns, maybe a Christmas carol, a doddle really.

'So, Gregor, Heather tells me you're a composer. Would I have heard any of your music?' Murray Thomson, amateur director of the very amateur choir, was standing beside him exuding bonho-mie.

Gregor loathed him on sight. Patronising git: there was some-thing about men like Murray that set his teeth on edge, made his skin crawl. 'I have done nothing since college and that was mainly experimental; I doubt that you would know any.' He tried to smile. The jerk was paying for the girls' Christmas presents.

'Have to say that the word experimental sends chills down my spine.'

Surprise, surprise. 'I'll play what you put in front of me.'

'I never thought you wouldn't, Gregor,' said Murray, who was standing close enough to Gregor to make him feel nervous. Schoolteachers used to do that to him sometimes, a scare tactic. It had worked then and it worked now. Murray went on although he had moved back a few paces. 'Maybe you could compose us a nice mass sometime. It would be rather special to have something composed especially for the St Sebastian Singers. Sounds good that, doesn't it? Well, must go and listen to our little songbird. Your girlfriend, is she?'

'Flatmate,' said Gregor automatically and wondered immediately if he should have said yes.

'Such a pity that decent sopranos are ten a penny.'

Gregor sat down on the stool before the ancient upright piano because he was feeling sick. He, who loathed and feared violence, wanted to punch the silly man in the face. 'Heather has sung at Scottish Opera.'

'Past tense, lad,' was the parting shot as Murray Thomson moved away.

Five gets you ten he's a bloody tenor, decided Gregor furiously. What a dichotomy Thomson was: on one side he seemed genuinely to love music – he was paying for this choir – but on the other hand he did too much point-scoring over not only his eager amateurs but also the professionals. Perhaps the choir was being sponsored to feed his ego. Well, wouldn't be the first time.

The next two hours were, for Gregor, of excruciating boredom. He played whatever Heather asked him to play and listened. It seemed that everyone knew at least one of the songs from *The Sound of Music* and Gregor, who had always liked the melody, felt, by the end of the evening, that he never wanted to hear 'Edelweiss' again. Quite simply the St Sebastian Singers murdered it.

'Fascinating that Sebastian was the first Christian martyr, Heather,' he said as she joined him to drink a blindingly hot cup of over-sugared tea during the break. 'I hope they're all praying to him like mad, or I will be before the end of the evening.'

'Don't be cruel. They're trying.'

'Very,' he agreed, and she left him to drink his tea in solitary splendour.

Heather began the second half of the evening by trying to show totally inexperienced singers how professionals learn to breathe. It did not go down at all well. They knew how to breathe, they told her; most of them had been doing it since before she was born. Eventually she admitted defeat and asked them to try breathing at home in front of a mirror.

'That way we'll find out if we're dead,' said the resident joker, Murray Thomson.

'You'll feel it in your tummy muscles,' Heather appealed to the women.

'One or two of us could do with a good old tummy workout,' sniggered Murray, 'couldn't we, Mrs Murphy, love.'

Will this nightmare ever end, Heather asked herself as she looked at the back of Gregor's bent head. Why wouldn't he turn and give her some encouragement? She would kill him when this was over, if it ever was over. 'Just remember to exhale too; otherwise you're not using all the muscles. Let's forget about breathing for now. Gregor, perhaps if you could give us a note we could hum.'

Gregor hit the F above middle C on the piano.

'I'll demonstrate, shall I? Mee, meh, mah, moh, moo. Right, now you try it.'

They did.

Please God, get me out of here. 'F sharp, Gregor, please. Mee, meh, mah, moh, moo. Your turn. Perhaps we should try a scale. Does everyone know what a scale is? Gregor, play a scale please. With me, class. Ah, ah, ah . . . Right, we'll leave that for tonight, but please practise at home.'

'We haven't done much singing,' complained another of the sopranos but Mrs Murphy stepped forward bravely.

'But this is all fascinating, love. Show us some more.'

But Heather had lost her nerve. 'I'll demonstrate at the warm-ups next week,' she said and tried to smile.

'If there is a next week,' moaned the grumbling soprano. 'I came here to sing and all we've done so far is sing a couple of songs from a musical and listen to you make sounds like a cat with its paws stuck.'

Several of the choir members started to argue, some wanting to listen to Heather, others expressing a desire to sing something, anything. Heather felt like bursting into tears. And then Gregor came to her aid. He played the first bars of the Wedding March very loudly. That stopped the infighting.

'What your extremely talented young teacher was trying to say is that the very first thing a singer needs to do is learn to listen. I'm going to play a scale, Heather will sing it, and you, all of you, will listen, not just hear her but listen to her. There is a difference in the meaning of those two words. Then I will play it again and you will sing it, making exactly the same sound as Heather makes. The first person to sound remotely like Miss Banner will get to choose the song you want to learn to sing. Right.' He played, Heather sang, and everyone, perhaps amazed that the extremely quiet young man at the piano could sound so forcible, listened and then they all did their best to copy her. They sang scales for five minutes and then Gregor stopped playing. 'Miss Banner, have you chosen your top student?'

Heather looked at her little choir. She knew that, for peace and harmony, she should choose Murray. 'Mrs Murphy,' she said. She was alarmed but not really surprised that the old lady chose 'Danny Boy', a fiendishly difficult melody for even the best of singers.

'What have you let us in for, Heather? I've seen more power in a dead battery than in that lot.'

'Most of them are lovely.'

'Pity they can't sing,' said Gregor and dodged her fist.

They were sitting on the top deck of a bus as it charged up Leith Walk. Heather was staring gloomily at the buildings they were whisked past. Gregor could see her face reflected in the glass. She looked sad. 'The Ave Maria was lovely,' he said, giving her an affectionate nudge.

74

She laughed and turned to him. 'I sang the Ave Maria.'

'Thanks be to God,' said Gregor and he was not joking.

'They are so awful. You know, Gregor, sometimes I think that people who can sing a bit but think they're terrific are worse than people who can't sing a note.'

'And now that we've covered the entire choir will we talk about the music they want to sing.'

'Don't be horrid. There are some lovely people, those old ladies—'

'The ones who should be commandeered by the army for bringing down enemy missiles? Just point your top A in that direction, madam.'

She turned away from him huffily. 'They're not that awful.'

'And your leading tenor was born with a pleasant voice but knows nothing about breathing or phrasing and has no idea what colouring means and has a reluctance to being told anything.' Gregor continued relentlessly. 'He's such a berk he might even be a soprano.'

'And his timing stinks,' said Heather, who was too upset even to notice that Gregor had tried to crack a joke at her expense. Sopranos were easy targets and learned to shrug things off.

'And he croons. I hate crooners. The basses are nice.'

'What's not to like about a bass? We have our work cut out for us, Gregor.'

'Hey, lady, I just play the piano. By the way, your tenor suggested that I might write a mass.'

'That was nice; shows he's keen.'

'Or deluded. He gave me the creeps.' Oily, that was the adjective he had been looking for all evening, and smarmy.

'Must say I didn't care for him either.' Heather pulled the hood of her coat up over her head. 'Come on, our stop.'

They clattered down the steps and out on to the pavement.

'The biscuits were good.'

'That was Mrs Henderson, the sort of frilly one. Great baker.'

'I couldn't hear her. Can she sing?'

'She was afraid to open her mouth but I have a feeling there's something there. She's never been encouraged to make a fool of herself. One or two of them, actually nine or ten are like that, uptight.'

'They need to learn humility; they have a kind of false pride. But some of them were listening to you, eager to learn from you. They're on the right track.'

She tucked her hand into his arm, mainly to encourage him to slow down. 'That's awfully deep, Gregor. It will take time and they do all love music. Murray Thomson wants solo parts: he wants to shine; a control freak, I think.'

'Then we'll introduce him to *Oberstleutnant* Juliet. Maybe she would come and conduct one night before she goes or when you're singing; you could ask her, Heather.'

'I want to do it on my own. You'll ask me to rope in Hermione next.'

'Wouldn't that be fun? We'd be a little orchestra, an orchestra of two and we would do our utmost to drown out that ghastly man.'

What had been fun was now serious and Gregor saw that he had been more upset by Murray Thomson than he had realised. But why? Apart from that smarmy over-friendliness at the beginning Thomson had stayed well away from him. He remembered that there had been one or two people like that at college. They neither said nor did anything except make him feel uneasy. 'Well, I'm just the piano player,' he said and laughed at Heather's look of surprise. 'Sorry, Heather, I was wool-gathering. It was a first time. You tried too hard. This isn't the Royal Opera House chorus.'

They were at their building and Gregor felt, as he always did, the warm pleasure of knowing that he was home and that the people with whom he lived accepted him as he was. 'If anyone had told me ten years ago that I would end up living with three gorgeous women I'd have told them they were crazy. But here I am.'

While Heather and Gregor had been at their first choir practice, Juliet and Hermione, aware that in a few short weeks their lives might change for ever, had picked up cartons of their favourite takeaway foods and had eaten them in the living room.

'Such decadence,' groaned Hermione as she lay back in her chair. 'Who will eat Chinese with you in London, Juliet?'

Juliet finished wiping her mouth and she too lay back. 'All the visiting soloists, I imagine, and conductors. No, they're big on fish suppers. Did you know that? I hear that the great and the good can be found before every performance queuing up at the nearest chippie.'

Hermione sat up straight. 'How absolutely fascinating. The last place in the world I would have thought to look. I shall make a point of it next time I'm short of toads. Who told you?'

'Oh, someone; Karel possibly.' She leaned forward and began stacking the empty containers. 'By the way, have you actually decided what you are playing at your posh wedding?'

'They asked for the *Poème*, Opus 25 by Chausson and the Mendelssohn Violin Concerto; that should be quite nice, don't you think?'

'Isn't the Chausson a bit morbid, a tad too full of Russian angst? Even the Mendelssohn's a bit sweetly sad, not a terrific choice for a wedding?' She piled the cartons together and carried them through to the kitchen where she put them in the refuse bin.

'I didn't choose the concerto, Juliet,' continued Hermione when she returned, 'and I love the *Poème*. Besides, I'm using it as an audition piece these days; got to get a job, be heard. Otherwise I might well end up as the world's greatest completely unknown and inexperienced violinist.'

Juliet attacked some sauce that had somehow transferred itself from the cartons to her pale yellow trousers. 'Bugger,' she said as she wiped. 'You should have gone to London; you had two offers.'

Hermione said nothing. There had been, at the time, an excellent reason for not accepting the London offers but they would sound, she felt, rather silly to someone as driven as Juliet and, besides, she was not quite ready to talk about her reasons. Perhaps she never would be.

'The audition, Hermione. Tell me about the audition.'

Hermione peered in a short-sighted way across the room at her friend. 'Thought that would interest you more than a wedding although you mustn't swear off men just because of Haken. What possessed you to jump into bed with him on a first date? You never do things like that; *moi*, sometimes; Heather, often as not; but you, with all your lovely scruples? I was surprised.'

Juliet stared across at her. 'It seemed right at the time.' She tried for lightness and decided that the tone was adequate.

Hermione uncurled herself and picked up her violin. 'The times I have felt the same and ended up in bed with a toad. Listen, cheerier things.'

She began to play and for fifteen minutes it seemed as if life itself stood still as the exquisite golden notes poured from the violin.

'Well?' she asked almost belligerently as her friend and flatmate said nothing.

'Oh, you spoiled it, Hermione, and by the way, you look like an angry sparrow.'

'What did I spoil, tell me, tell me?'

'Spoiled brat.' Juliet laughed. 'You should have gone to London. That was sublime and it's a lovely piece but not for a wedding. That exquisite long-drawn-out note at the beginning is beautiful but rather foreboding.'

'The family are philistines and know zilch about music. I suggested Brahms but, "Oh, no, darling; it has to be the Mendelssohn. One knows it so well." They've heard the first movement on Classic FM. Listen, I'll play the first movement.'

'Liquid silver,' said Juliet seriously when her friend had finished.

'God, how frightful. Juliet, I've just had a ghastly thought. What if they clap?'

'Pretend you were only going to play the first movement; take the cheque and enjoy.'

'Wish you were coming with me.'

'Don't be silly; your parents will be there. What are you wearing?'

'Mummy's doing the ghastly parent bit and so I shall have to be *un peu* restrained but I haven't quite decided. Daddy thinks my clothes are a hoot and Mummy knows he's always on my side so I really have *carte blanche*. I shall do Maid Marion, I think, but with a teeny modern twist.'

Juliet interrupted. 'At the moment you look more like Joan of Arc on her way to the fire, or at least the woman in that film, what was her name, Jean Seberg?'

Hermione ignored this levity and carried on, 'With lots of flowing chiffons and loads of bling.'

'Real bling?'

'Goodness, no. Let's go to London for a few days and raid Camden Market.'

'I can't, Hermione. I'm not ready for the competition.'

Hermione put her violin back in its case reverently. 'Mummy will go if I beg and if she's not busy, but it would be more fun with you.' She threw herself down on the sofa again. 'I know. I'll wait until you're ensconced in your London flat and then I'll come down and we'll go together.'

Juliet had returned to her score but she put it down again. 'Hermione, you still haven't told me about the audition.'

'The London Philharmonic.'

Juliet jumped from the seat and threw her arms around her friend. 'Oh, I knew it was just a matter of time. Oh, darling, you are so good, so talented, that Chausson just now was breathtaking; I'm so thrilled for you.'

Hermione did not return the hug. 'I lied. It's a tiny orchestra out in the sticks and the leader hates me already. She said something rather beastly about my personality – did I have none that I had to create one through a bizarre taste in clothes?'

'What a cow. Your clothes are beautiful; they just take a little getting used to.'

'Well, if the orchestra accepts me, and my clothes, she'd better start getting used to them.'

'You won't play in tweed and lace or is it leather and chiffon?'

'Very funny and no, of course, as part of an ensemble, I'll conform. I wore uniform all through school.'

Juliet looked at her questioningly. 'I know. Your father showed me some school photographs; in one, your blazer covers the hem of your skirt. You *were* wearing a skirt?'

'Of course,' said Hermione solemnly. 'I always wore a complete, if somewhat altered, uniform. My mother tried to turn that skirt down at the Christmas hols but I'd cut off the excess.'

'I wish I'd known you at school, Hermione. You must have been great fun.'

'I was but you would have stuck up your well-brought-up nose and had nothing at all to do with me.'

'You're right. Goody two-shoes; that was me. What fun I must have missed.'

Hermione got up and went over and perched on the arm of Juliet's chair. 'No, you did what was right for you and look where all your hard work has got you. You're disciplined, methodical, controlled; that's why I was so surprised that you jumped into bed with Haken.' She looked at her friend anxiously, afraid that she had gone too far. Juliet looked so stressed these days; she had stopped rushing to the telephone or to meet the postman and her eyes were tired and unhappy. No matter how hard she tried to disguise it, Hermione knew that Juliet had been affected deeply by her, what could she say – affair? – with the Czech conductor. One night was hardly an affair and yet one-night-stand was not the right expression for what Juliet had experienced. Hermione, who had watched her friend avoid relationships with perfectly respectable young men all through college, suffered for her. Juliet had little experience, so determined had she been to work hard, to be the best, to show her father that she was right and that he was wrong. And here she was now, ready to compete in a prestigious competition and part of her was suffering, full of doubts about herself and her own sagacity, her ability to make sensible decisions.

Juliet looked up at her and smiled. 'I'm fine, Hermione, focused. All that's on my mind now is winning the Margarita Rosa Grey competition. It's all I've ever wanted, to be a conductor: to be the conductor of a great orchestra. And you, my friend, funny clothes and all, will be my first soloist. Tell me more about this orchestra.'

Hermione got up. 'Let's go out for a walk. We've been cooped up here for days and you're beginning to look peaky.'

Juliet wanted to stay with her scores but was persuaded to grab a coat and follow her friend out of the flat and down the stone stairs.

The steps were quite narrow and in the middle of each one was a large basin-shaped dip where the treading of constant traffic had worn them down over the years. Outside a brisk wind was blowing and the struggle against the wind kept the girls quiet for a few minutes. Juliet reached into her pocket and pulled out a small red wool beret that she jammed over her hair.

'Short hair has its advantages,' Hermione laughed, tucking her arm into her friend's as they bent into the wind. 'Let's walk up as far as Ann Street and then down the other side. Maybe there will be some leaves still on the trees.'

The wind was determined to pull off every withered leaf still clinging on to branches and by the light from the street lamps they could see that the gardens in the beautiful New Town street looked sad, leggy chrysanthemums bravely attempting to hold their heads up as they were blown almost over by the autumn winds. In one garden late roses had given up completely and had allowed their petals to be stripped from the stalk and scattered to all corners of the garden like confetti at a summer wedding. A blue wooden gate creaked as it swung backwards and forwards on its hinge. Juliet grabbed the gate and closed it.

Half in fun, half in earnest, Hermione clutched at Juliet's sleeve. 'Gosh, you are brave. What if they were looking out of their windows and thought you a vandal? In a minute Edinburgh's finest are going to roll up and arrest you and then what will you do?'

'I closed a gate, Hermione; get a grip.'

'Gregor said you were a control freak. Maybe they like their gate squeaking in the wind.'

Juliet stopped. 'Gregor said that?'

'Oh, God, are your feelings hurt? He thinks you're wonderful but you are a bit of a controller; you do always know what's best for us.' Hermione thought quickly. She had been trying to cheer up her friend, not make her more miserable. 'And we need management. For four years you have organised us beautifully, Juliet. What will we do without you when you move to London?'

'I haven't won yet.'

'But you will, darling, you will.'

Arm in arm, they struggled back down the hill against the wind.

'The orchestra,' Juliet almost shouted into the wind. 'Tell me.'

'They're all "university women", frightfully intellectual,' Hermione shouted back, 'but they get some nice gigs, amateur choirs, physicists' dinners, that sort of thing, and they pay union rates. They need another violin and I was recommended, not by a friend of Mum, thank God, but by one of my teachers. It will look good on the old CV and there might even be some radio and television slots at Christmas. I think the Chausson piece will impress, and then Bach's Concerto in E; it's rich and agile and the slow movement melts, like chocolate sauce on ice cream, all soft and gooey.'

'And you will tell them that two London orchestras asked you to audition?'

'No, of course not. Daddy's a big benefactor; this lot don't know who he is or they're too intellectual to be impressed with anything as crass as filthy lucre. I want them to be impressed by my playing.'

'How could they not be?' yelled Juliet, aware as she did so that the thoughts going through her friend's brain were just like her own: the wish, the need to be accepted and valued as oneself. She was also aware that yelling into the wind was unpleasant and so she steered them home.

'You will come down to London, should I win?' she asked as they reached the street door.

'Try to keep me away, old chum.'

7

At last the big day had arrived. Juliet was in London where she would stay for the three days of the competition. Her hotel, she had told her mother, was very pleasant but now, sitting here at the Royal Academy, she had trouble remembering what colour the bedspread in her room was. She next tried to focus on the walls: were there paintings? She could remember nothing about the hotel at all. Must have been a breakfast room though, for her stomach, apart from providing a refuge for thousands of homeless butterflies, was behaving itself; no embarrassing gurglings. She decided to forget her hotel and concentrate on her fellow competitors.

They eyed one another up, some of them openly, others more discreetly. They could have been students of any subject, anywhere, each and every one wearing jeans and a shirt or sweater: apart from Juliet, who was wearing a vibrant emerald green silk, the colours were muted. One or two, the Americans, Juliet had met before, Bryony Wells in Paris and Forbes Johnston in Heidelberg. They were good and if the others were all of the same ability this was going to be a difficult competition. I wouldn't want to win any other way, she assured herself, and leaned back in her chair, feigning calm, to wait.

Those few moments were as much rest as she or any of the others would get for the next few days. Rehearsals were exhausting: the Royal Academy of Music Ensemble obliging. Twenty finalists rehearsed and then conducted the ensemble in extracts from the chosen music. The rooms seemed full of the sounds of music, hurrying footsteps, laughter, whispers and, quite often, cries of despair. The rehearsal rooms were hot and windows were opened to let cool air attempt perhaps to replace the volatile atmosphere. Juliet was nervous, her palms damp. She had not been able to rehearse a full orchestra in any of the pieces, a definite handicap. She let her mind go back to the flatmates who had tried, with the help of a few friends, to be a symphony orchestra: Hermione was the strings, Gregor tried to be the brass and Heather sang the wind. They had managed to rope in, on different occasions, a cellist, a flautist, some obliging violins and violas, and an extremely good oboe, but it was scarcely enough to reassure Juliet that the sound she heard in her inner ear was the same as the sound made by only four or five instruments and a human voice, lovely as it was. She was looking forward to the challenge though.

I know this music, inside out, and possibly backwards. What fun it will be to recreate it with a real group. There, that was positive thinking.

She would not be downhearted as she listened to the others talk of how supportive their orchestras had been in allowing them to practise for the competition.

'You're not adding to the discussion, Juliet,' said Bryony as she struggled to tie her thick dark hair into an obediently neat ponytail. 'Tell us how often you managed to conduct the pieces. Did you get to try the Usher Hall? I would adore to conduct in that place.'

'Actually, no, Bryony. I did almost all my preparation in the living room of my flat and never with more than seven in my ensemble but what a group it was.' She laughed at a memory of Gregor putting down his French horn, climbing over the sofa and running to become a double bass, sawing away manfully but at least coming in on time. No, the music she heard in her head had certainly not been the sound Gregor had made.

'My God, you poor girl,' said Bryony. 'How can you possibly laugh? My heart just breaks for you.'

'Very kind of you, Bryony, but I wouldn't have missed my rehearsals for the world.' She did not add that she had conducted the Handel while in Vienna; the Britten she had done in Glasgow. Only the Arriaga was completely new.

At the end of the day she waited quietly with the others in nerve-racking silence as the international jury completed their deliberations and then experienced euphoria at hearing her name called just after Bryony's as a semi-finalist. She did not feel too much of a hypocrite as she hugged the American. After all, just at this moment, she loved the entire world.

She walked back through rain-washed streets to her hotel, talking first to Hermione and then to her parents. 'I felt high the whole day,' she told Hermione. 'I had this picture of Gregor nose-diving over the sofa to become a bass and you skipping along from violins to violas to cellos like an Irish gypsy.'

'Irish gypsies don't skip between sections of the strings. At least I don't think they do. Anyway, Gregor and I are perfecting our nightclub act just in case we need to have something up our sleeves.'

'Any news today?'

'Juliet Crawford, you have only been gone a day and a half. No, Simon Rattle did not ring me today. Maybe tomorrow. Now ring your mother; bet she's sitting looking at the telephone.'

'Mum . . .'

'I knew you'd do it; I knew it. I never doubted for a moment.'

It seemed that her mother could tell from the sound of her voice but she still had to say the words. 'Mum, I'm in the semi-finals.'

'I know. I've been sitting here just staring at the telephone willing it to ring. I'm going to cry, I'm so happy for you and relieved. Oh, darling, you have worked so hard.' Juliet heard her sniff.

'Is Daddy there?'

'He's had to go out on a call. He'll ring you when he gets in. What are you doing now?'

'Walking back to the hotel.'

Her mother squealed in anguish. 'In London? Juliet, take taxis.'

'Takes too long, Mum, and I'm perfectly safe. The streets are crowded. Listen, I'm going to have something to eat; I'm starving, and then I'm going to sit up in bed reading tomorrow's music. I hope I'll be able to sleep after that. Last night I hardly closed my eyes.'

They chatted on for a few more minutes mainly about the other semi-finalists and Juliet put an end to the call as she reached an

Italian restaurant. A plate of steaming hot lasagne and a glass of very good red wine consumed under the watchful eye of a naked marble maiden entwined with ivy was exactly what she needed.

On the second day of the competition she found herself locked in the green room just as she was due to conduct the academy's string ensemble in an extract from a Bernstein work. She held the handle tightly and pulled; then she pushed, shook it and tried all over again. Nothing. Her heart was pounding as the adrenalin she should have been using to hype up her performance tore around her body causing her to feel sick, but it was not the nervousness that was necessary for a good performance but the rising hysteria of total terror. What if she could not get out? If she missed her turn would they disqualify her? At the very least they would think her unprofessional and incompetent. She shook the door as hard as she could and knocked with her knuckles. Nothing.

She looked round for help but saw nothing other than sagging leather sofas and a rickety water-stained table. Calm down, Juliet; the door is stuck. Someone will notice that you are missing and they will come in time. Please let them come in time. She opened her handbag and took out her mobile phone. Whom to ring? Whose number did she have? What difference did it make? Their phones were all turned off. Could she ring the office? What was their number? She would have to ring Directory Enquiries.

Dear Lord, this cannot be happening to me.

Upstairs they would be wondering where she was, asking themselves if she could be ill, or too stressed to appear. Bryony would say, would she not, that she, Juliet, had been perfectly composed and calm as they sat chatting in the green room.

'Damn it,' she almost shouted and tried the handle again. It turned obediently and the door was open. The corridor was empty. Nothing moved, not even the dust.

Dash, dash, double dash. Later there would be time to wonder, to ask herself questions about the door and its now seemingly perfect lock but for now she had to speed upstairs, thanking God for sensible shoes that allowed her to take the stairs, albeit noisily, two at a time. She reached the corridor, completely out of breath and paused for a second to recover. Damn, she could hear music. There should not be music – not without her.

Kazuhiko Shigetoku, very handsome and almost as broad as he was long, was on the podium. The jury, all men and all in business suits, expressions frozen, ignored her. Miserably Juliet slipped into the nearest chair and tried not to burst into tears. She forced herself to concentrate and to listen carefully to the young Japanese conductor, to give him the courtesy he would have been sure to give her but her mind continued to race. Was it over? Had she been disqualified?

She had to wait until both Kazuhiko and the ensemble had been dismissed before she heard her fate.

'You do realise, Miss Crawford, that if the conductor doesn't bother to turn up it is very difficult for the orchestra to proceed. Not that they are incapable of continuing without the genius on the podium.' The voice was scathing, the grey eyes hard and un-compromising. 'You have seen, I hope, that this ensemble has, at times, paid scant attention to what some of the competitors are doing; they are in fact making silk purses out of sow's ears. But if a rehearsal is called for eleven fifteen it is basic courtesy and professionalism for the conductor to lower herself to appear.'

Double ouch. 'Lower herself.' A remark like that really was below the belt, but how to answer such animosity?

'Perhaps we should listen to what Miss Crawford has to say.' Juliet's spirits lifted. She recognised the voice.

It was Alexander Stoltze. Juliet had not known that he was on the jury although the original panel had changed considerably because of illness and other emergencies; perhaps he had been called in at the last minute. He had not. He had come upon the competition during a courtesy visit to the academy but so great was his reputation that the jury had welcomed him to the rehearsals if not to their deliberations.

'Naturally we shall listen, Alexander.' The non-voting chairman of the committee was speaking. 'Miss Crawford, you do realise the importance of punctuality in these sessions. We have limited time, an orchestra that has to be paid and ten aspiring and – we hope – inspiring conductors to watch. Everyone's time is precious. Why were you twenty minutes late?'

His voice was calm and not at all hostile, almost avuncular, and Juliet turned to him gratefully. 'I'm sorry, my lord. I was locked in the green room.'

'Locked in – deliberately? I can't believe it. How could that possibly happen?' They were all speaking at once and now they were looking at Juliet and not all of the faces were friendly or understanding.

She would remain calm; everything depended on it. 'I didn't say "deliberately". Somehow the lock jammed and I could not open it.'

'How did you get out, my dear?' The voice was sympathetic.

Who was he? The professor, the English horn maestro, the Polish conductor? She did not know but she answered him gratefully. 'It just opened.' She knew how weak that sounded and wished she had some other answer but it was the truth and was all she could say. She heard the words 'girlish hysteria' and 'make allowances' and the even more frightening 'absolutely not'. So this was the end of the dream, a hysterical woman, probably suffering from premenstrual nerves – if she heard that old chestnut she would show them premenstrual tension – such a pity, obviously talented, etcetera, etcetera.

'Miss Crawford, please be aware that being late merely shows those waiting that you find your time more valuable than theirs. Since Mr Shigetoku was kind enough to change his time slot, we will hear you at 3 p.m. I'm sure you'll make every effort to be there.'

'Thank you, gentlemen,' she managed in as dignified a voice as she could dredge up and then she walked from the room, although her whole body wanted to run, to flee. They did not believe her and she wondered if she would have believed such an unlikely tale either. She would not return to the competitors' green room; she would go to the cafeteria, she would walk about in the dry, cold air outside, somewhere where there was no danger of being locked in or out, and she would make certain that she was waiting by the heavy door of the rehearsal room in plenty of time. She had left her coat in the green room and so elected to go to the café, which was quite quiet at that time.

Music is a powerful friend and Juliet was able to clear her mind of her embarrassment and her worries and focus solely on the pieces she was to conduct. At one point a voice she recognised broke through the wall of concentration and she looked up to see Bryony laughing with someone, a man, just at the door of the room. She dismissed them and returned to work, but a few minutes later the light was blocked by a figure standing right in front of her and she looked up, annoyed at the interruption.

Bryony stood there with a tray. 'Now, I bet you have no idea how long you have been sitting here. Look at your coffee cup; it's almost grey with age. Isn't that sad?' She put the tray down. There were two bowls of soup and two really appetising filled rolls on it. 'Life can be a real bitch, honey, but it feels better when the stomach is full.'

Juliet looked at her watch and then around the room, which was now almost full of people, eating, chatting in some cases: she had been so lost in her own world that she had been unaware of them. It was almost two o'clock; she had been here nearly three hours.

'Do I get to sit down?'

She jumped up. 'Sorry, Bryony, my mind . . .'

'I know. Maestro Haken said you looked so fierce he didn't dare disturb you. I told him what happened; I hope you don't mind.'

Haken. Her heart seemed to jump. Surprise, that was all, for he was in Heidelberg, wasn't he, or Prague? She would not ask. She did not care. Was he the man with whom Bryony had been laughing? She hoped not. 'This is kind of you, Bryony. I now have egg all over my face and hoped to redeem myself by shining in the Mozart, not that I'll get that far now.'

'Heck, they won't can you for being late. Not your fault you got locked in a room. Here, have a sandwich. I adore *ciabatta*, don't you?'

'Who told you I was locked in a room?'

'Gosh, honey, the entire college knows.' Bryony closed her eyes, the better to think. 'I don't know, Shigetoku maybe: one of the ensemble? Lousy thing to happen but it's not the end of the world. So you were a few minutes late.'

'Twenty.'

Bryony groaned in sympathy. 'That bad? Still, not like you were out buying Christmas presents; somehow you got locked in. No one can really blame you for an accident. Eat up, put on some lipstick and go wow them.'

In spite of herself Juliet laughed. The American was very kind; she would never have expected it of her and was angry with herself for making rash judgements. She finished her lunch and warmly thanked Bryony who brushed off her gratitude.

'Go freshen up in that loo over there. If you're not out in three minutes I'll send in the troops. Anyone special you'd like? Kazuhiko; he looks strong enough to break down a door – and cute too.'

Juliet laughed and did exactly as Bryony had suggested. Then she picked up her music and with Bryony's cheery 'Break a leg' ringing in her ears, went to the rehearsal room. No one commented on how early she was; no one commiserated about the morning's débâcle and she was able to put her heart and soul into her work. Did the ensemble really respond or were they doing their own thing and merely paying lip service to her efforts? She thought not for she knew, deep inside, that it had been good, all of them working together for the desired effect.

This was not Paris. There was no large gathering of the great and the good; that was reserved for the final. The semi-finalists sat on uncomfortable chairs in the rehearsal where each one had conducted, and waited.

The jury's deliberations seemed to go on for hours, much longer than the previous night. Feeling cold, although the rooms, with windows now closed, were beautifully warm, Juliet sat with the others and waited for their judges to reappear. At last the door opened and they were there. Kazuhiko's name was the first announced and Juliet smiled at him in congratulation. His willingness and ability to change places with her at the last moment had certainly helped this morning; she would be forever grateful. The second name to be called was Bryony Wells who ebulliently and characteristically hugged everyone near her.

'Please.' Juliet was praying. She could visualise her father's disappointed face when she failed yet again. She could hear his voice. 'You've given it a decent shot, Juliet. Now it's time to be sensible. Teaching, since you're much too late for medicine.'

'And the third finalist is . . .' Will the name ever come? It was like some ghastly game show where they know the name but deliberately spin it out for maximum torture. Please, please. 'Juliet Crawford.'

For a fraction of a breath she was stunned. She had believed, almost believed, tried not to hope. Then a small bubble of pure unadulterated joy burst into riotous exaltation. A finalist. She had made it into the finals even though she had a huge bad mark in the judges' mental copybooks. Others were congratulating her, the judges, the competitors who had not made the cut, Kazuhiko Shigetoku. Not Bryony? Yes, here she was with a bone-shattering hug. She had been outside in the corridor. Why? To stamp her foot in rage, to tell a friend who was waiting, to jump up and down in childish glee?

'Fabulous, Juliet. What fun it would have been to have had an all-girl final.'

'One day, Bryony.'

It was time to go, to ring her parents, her friends, and to get ready for the morning. As she walked through London she looked up at the starry November sky and, as if on cue, was rewarded by the sight of a falling star, a wishing star. Would she wish as she had done when she had been a little girl, wishing for curly hair or a puppy or a pony of her own, white, please, or black with a star on his forehead? None of those wishes had ever been granted; she would not tempt fate now. Still she smiled at the memory of the very earnest little girl she had been and she thought fondly of her mother who had filled her childhood with magic. Not caring at all what sophisticated London would think of a woman running like a tomboy, she picked up the skirts of her coat so that they would not catch in her heels and began to run.

First her parents. Her father, after all, had to alert his partners to the fact that he would be in London for two days. Her mother, every hair in place, lipstick freshened even though she was at home, would be telling all their friends, 'Yes, Juliet is in the final; we couldn't not be in the audience.'

Her mother, breathless, excited, answered the phone. 'Juliet?'

'Yes. I've done it. I'm in the final.'

'Oh, darling, that's wonderful. I never doubted for a moment. I even had my hair done. Wait, let me get Daddy.'

Juliet heard her calling and then her father was on the line. 'Well done. I'll look forward to the concert. You'd better win, Juliet,' he said jocularly. 'You know that Harry Wilson has promised to cover for me. He won't be thrilled to miss his golf game but, for you, he says he's prepared to make that sacrifice.'

'That's good of him. I'll certainly do my best.'

'How do you feel?'

'I was just so thrilled and excited but now I feel absolutely exhausted; it's as if there's a hole in my toe and everything is draining out.'

'Perfectly normal reaction. Have a decent meal and get to bed early. What are the plans for tomorrow?'

'Not completely sure; we meet the orchestra, check out the acoustics at the Barbican. It's so big, Daddy, seats over two thousand people. Millions were spent on the refurbishment a few years ago; seemingly the acoustics were so ghastly none of the big world orchestras would set foot in the place. Now they're clambering. You look up and these amazing steel reflector panels sort of hang there and it's fantastic the way the light catches them and changes, shimmers. Gosh, I so want to share it with you. But back to tomorrow. There will be last-minute rehearsals, photographs, interviews, but I do have some time to myself.'

She talked a little longer but was glad to terminate the call. Was it just that the adrenalin had gone, a natural reaction as her father had said after two stress-filled days, or had it anything to do with Haken, the concern that he might be there, somewhere in the auditorium, listening, calculating? Bryony had spoken to him and so he was in London and not in Heidelberg. Would he remember his promise? Why should he and why should she care? No doubt, like Maestro Stoltze, he just happened to be on business in London and why merely hearing his name should cause her to remember everything, the humour, the love and the humiliation, she absolutely did not know.

Determined to think of nothing but the final concert, she went to the narrow wardrobe in the tiny bedroom and took out the dress she had decided to wear at the final, if she got that far. She had agonised over the decision to wear a dress. What signal would her clothes be giving out? She had rejected Hermione's suggestion and instead of red, a colour that would be stunning with her hair and skin, she had opted for a long, but very modest dress in dark blue crepe. Around her neck she would wear a gold chain, a twenty-first birthday gift from her father, and in her ears she would wear stunningly beautiful diamond studs loaned by Hermione. She had not wanted to be responsible for such valuable jewels but Hermione had insisted.

'Something borrowed is good enough for brides: it's good enough for prize-winning conductors.'

'I'm not a prize-winning conductor.'

'Yes, you are. You won everything at college and you'll win at the Barbican but only if you wear these studs.'

Now Juliet looked at her dress, held it against her. She slipped out of her skirt and blouse and put the dress on, noting how easily it slid over her slender hips. The neck was low but modestly so, and the sleeves were long and comfortable. The style had been chosen so that it would be like a second skin; she could not possibly worry about material flapping around. The skirt was generous but not flared. In other words it did not outline her body, did not accentuate nor did it disguise her shape. It was, she decided, perfect.

I wonder if Kazuhiko is trying on his clothes. I very much doubt it. Am I doing the right thing by wearing a dress? What will Bryony be wearing? A dress, a skirt and blouse, tails? Sometimes trousers can look sexier than skirts. Damn it, damn it, I just want to be seen as a conductor not as a woman who conducts. Perhaps Hermione is right and I should have gone with red, saying, 'This is me. Accept it. I'm not playing token bloke blending in with the boys. I am a very good conductor who just happens to be a woman.'

She hardly slept at all, lying in the narrow bed watching patterns forming and reforming on the ceiling as the light changed outside and she played over and over the four pieces in the final, two of which she would have to conduct in eighteen hours, in fifteen hours, in twelve hours. At seven she got up, feeling irritable and edgy, and went to stand under the scalding hot water in the barely adequate shower stall. If she won, if she got a job with the LSO, she might just be able to stay at better hotels.

There, that in itself is an incentive to do well.

8

It would be a long day; she would eat breakfast calmly. It is interesting that, in moments of crisis, long-forgotten rules re-emerge. Mum's voice, not Dad's. Perhaps that was strange because he was the doctor, but she could not actually remember his ever expressing interest in his only child's health. Cobbler's shoes syndrome. But her mother's voice was very loud in her head. 'Imperative to start the day with a good breakfast, Juliet; doesn't have to be huge but has to be good.'

She sat in the hotel dining room, unaware of the speculative and admiring glances from two young businessmen and ordered. She drank freshly made coffee and tried not to think about the concert. Thoughts intruded. This time tomorrow it will all be over. The food arrived, beautifully presented – if only she were hungry. She could not eat, pushed the plate aside and drank more coffee. How angry her mother would be at her lack of appetite – and her father? She decided to retrieve her dress and head for the Underground.

The garment bag was not on the rack where she had left it; neither was her coat.

Do not panic. *Calmate.*

The door opened and the doorman was blown in just as she was looking for him. He was in his shirtsleeves and obviously cold. He must have been finding a taxi.

'Excuse me, my coat and my garment bag were just there on that rack. Did you put them somewhere else?'

He rubbed his cold arms. 'No, madam.'

'But they were here. To save time I brought them down before I went in to breakfast.'

'I'm sorry, madam; I know nothing about them. Let me check

the cloakroom. Perhaps one of my colleagues moved them. I'll ask.'

He hurried off and Juliet, trying desperately to batten down her rising hysteria, followed him. Losing control, a very unusual situation for her, would not help. He asked her to come into the cloakroom with him and she looked round quickly but efficiently. She thought she recognised her garment bag but when it was taken down and turned round it showed the name of a top London store, certainly not the one from which she had bought her dress.

'My coat is distinctive,' she said. 'The shoulders are light grey, the middle part is dark grey and the skirt is black. It's full length.'

He shook his head but whether it was because he had never seen it or could not visualise the coat from her description she had no idea. 'I'll ask the desk staff.'

She followed him back upstairs to the front desk.

'Oh, yes, a lady just telephoned,' said the receptionist in the kind of 'so everything's all right' voice that deeply irritated Juliet. 'She took it by mistake and will bring it back after her conference – around four, she thought.'

'Around four? Where is she now?'

'She's in conference.'

'Where?'

'She didn't say, madam. She'll bring it back as soon as she can.' The girl turned to answer the telephone, leaving Juliet standing at the desk.

Juliet took a deep breath. 'That isn't good enough.' She put her hand on the girl's arm to get her attention. 'What is her telephone number?'

The girl looked annoyed. 'She didn't say; she said she was switching it off while she was in conference so there was no point in giving it to us.' She tried to turn away again.

Juliet leaned over the desk. 'Deal with me now. Get me the hotel manager.'

The receptionist was extremely unhappy with that command but she did as she was asked and a few minutes later a tall thin figure came bustling along a corridor. 'I'm Henry Roebottom,' he said, holding out his hand to Juliet. 'What can I do for you, madam?'

'Someone has taken my coat and my evening gown from that rack there. She has just telephoned to say she picked them up by mistake and will bring them back this afternoon. That is unacceptable.'

'Of course, madam.' He turned to the doorman. 'Jim, get a taxi and go and get the items from the lady and bring them back here. I'm so sorry about this, madam, and I do hope you have nothing pressing for the next hour or so. Jim will be as quick as London traffic allows.'

Juliet covered her face with her hand for a moment while she tried harder to calm herself. 'Your unbelievably self-centred guest has refused to say where she is, merely that she is in conference, and she has turned off her mobile so that I can't ring her and tell her to do what she should have done in the first place – once she realised her mistake. She should have sent them back here in a taxi. I need the coat now since it is extremely cold out there and I need the evening gown long before this afternoon; I'm being photographed in it at two and if she doesn't get that gown to me in time I will be conducting the London Symphony Orchestra this evening in this.' She held out her hands so that he could get a good look at her very short skirt, very long boots, fishnet tights and oversized fisherman's jersey.

'Very nice, I'm sure, madam. I really don't know how to help you. We could ring every hotel in London where a conference is being held today.' He turned to the receptionist. 'Did the lady give her name?'

The girl shook her head.

'Jim?'

'I got a taxi for a blonde lady about an hour ago, sir. She was wearing a coat, long, I think, and carrying a dress bag.'

'Which taxi service?'

Jim shook his head. 'She was in a terrible hurry, sir, said the breakfast room was slow and so she was running late. I ran to the end of the road and caught her a taxi there. She pushed past me and into the cab: no idea where she went. It was perishing,' he finished apologetically.

'It's not your fault,' said Juliet quietly. 'I left the bags there, unattended; the initial fault is mine.'

'We do expect our guests to be able to leave coats unattended for a few minutes, madam. You have been out quite often this morning, Jim?'

'Yes, sir. People want cabs. Company phone numbers are impossible in the mornings and so I usually run to the corner, especially if the guest is a woman or elderly.'

Juliet closed her eyes for a moment to shut out the whole nightmare. She could not conceive of the mindset of anyone who would take someone else's clothes, even if by mistake, and then unapologetically turn their mobile phone off thus making it completely impossible for the owner of the items to make some frantic effort to be reunited with them. 'I might have been flying to New York this morning,' she said, 'or to Timbuktu. I hope madam has a state-of-the-art excuse.' She had been addressing the air but turned to the hotel manager. 'My name is Juliet Crawford and I can be reached at the Barbican.'

'Rest assured, Miss Crawford, as soon as the lady returns with your things I'll have them sent over.'

And what will we do if she doesn't get back in time? Juliet thought.

She went out into a bright but chilly morning and immediately wished she had returned to her room for another cardigan. The cold was piercing and reminded her of a winter long ago when she had tried to grasp an icicle with her bare hands. My gloves, my lovely gloves. They were, of course, in the pockets of her coat where she had deliberately put them in case she might inadvertently leave them in the dining room. She thought of Aldo and his lovely warm Glasgow voice. 'Positive thoughts, Juliet. Give me positive thoughts.'

She flagged down a taxi, reflecting wryly that London taxi drivers were unfazed by any situation. A woman wearing only a skirt and jumper on the coldest day of the year thus far was merely another eccentric passenger.

'Ugly old place,' said the cabbie later as he wrote her a receipt.

How that remark cheered Juliet. She smiled. 'You are so right but inside, my friend, it's beautiful.' That was not strictly true; the Barbican leaves a lot to be desired but at least, thought Juliet as she followed what one of her fellow contestants had called the 'Yellow Brick Road' – a painted yellow line – to her entrance, they are working on it. She went down three floors to the Waterside Café, aptly named since its huge windows looked over the lakes and, reflecting wryly that she drank too much of it, bought a mug of coffee. That warmed her nicely and, fortified, she headed off to the auditorium where she was to meet the other finalists and Mrs Melinda Wetherby, the contestants' liaison with the committee. How could she, *sans* dress, prepare for the day that might be the most important in her entire life thus far, a day that had not started too auspiciously?

'Negative vibes, Juliet; you're giving me negative vibes.' She heard the voice in her head and smiled. What a treasure is a good agent.

The first thing to do was to speak to the rather frightening Mrs Wetherby about the possibility of changing the time of the finalists' photo shoot. Unfortunately it seemed impossible to get her on her own. When Juliet did succeed in isolating her, Mrs Wetherby was not at all understanding. 'Change the time? We can't do that, Miss Crawford.' She looked not only unsympathetic but also absolutely astounded. 'How unbelievably unprofessional of you. This is a great opportunity; these photographs will be sent all over the world. Surely you have another dress?'

Feeling six years old and 'unbelievably unprofessional', Juliet shook her head. She had several evening dresses all happily keeping one another company in her bedroom in Edinburgh; there might even be a few more in Dundee and it was too late to make a frantic phone call to her parents.

Mrs Wetherby's mouth looked as if she had eaten lemons for breakfast. 'Itzhak Perlman is famous, among other things, for his attention to detail. I am quite sure that if he were ever in a small hotel in London he would eat breakfast with his violin.'

'If I owned a Stradivarius, Mrs Wetherby, I would breakfast with it too,' said Juliet caustically. 'And probably sleep with it,' she added under her breath.

'Is there time for Miss Crawford to buy a new dress?' asked Kazuhiko sensibly.

Even if there had been time, dress shopping was the last thing Juliet wanted to do. 'I'm very sorry, ladies and gentleman.' She managed a weak smile for the Japanese finalist. 'The person' – she would not say lady – 'who has mistakenly taken my dress promises to return it to my hotel by four. I will have it for the concert. That, I am afraid, is the best I can do.'

'I'm sure I have something that would fit, Juliet,' put in Bryony. 'I have another formal; I had a few days here before the competition and shopped. That would be okay, wouldn't it, Mrs Wetherby? I can go pick it up during lunch break.'

'Highly irregular.' Mrs Wetherby shot a look of pure venom at Juliet. 'We have never had this sort of thing before. You do know I will have to tell the committee. Yesterday you ruined schedules by being late and today you say that you have lost your dress.'

Mrs Wetherby did not cope well in a crisis. Juliet had had a teacher like her; everything that went wrong was seen as a personal affront to her and now she found that she was no more capable of dealing with the unexpected animosity than she had been as a child. 'I'm sorry; I need some air.'

She went out into the corridor and, to her chagrin, had to hold on to the wall for a moment as she felt herself begin to tremble. Several men were walking towards her and she straightened up. Damn, damn, double damn. Stoltze and – oh, God, no – Haken were in the group. What was he doing here? Even though Bryony had said that she had talked with him, Juliet had supposed him to be in Heidelberg or Prague, but he had promised. But that was before, before he showed what a jerk he was. She stared stonily ahead.

'Miss Crawford,' Maestro Stoltze greeted her. 'You are unwell?'

She managed not to look at Karel and smiled brightly at Stoltze. 'No. Thank you. Pre-final nerves; it's nothing.' She moved off and thought she heard them all wish her good luck; one voice added, 'Nerves are good,' but it was not a voice she recognised. Its message cheered her, though, and she walked along the corridor as if she had some idea of where she was going.

A minute later she heard Bryony calling her. To slow down, to wait. 'Rotten old cow. I had a math teacher like her in Junior High. Come on, we have some music magazine interviews. Try to get it together.'

'I'm fine, Bryony, thanks. Ever wanted to hit anyone?'

'All the time. Come on, smile. You'll look great in my dress; it's a raspberry silk, be great with your colouring.'

'Thanks. What are you wearing? I take it you're doing dresses too.'

'Kind of. I chickened out. I had a dress made, just in case, but the neckline goes down to the waist. Possibly a tad *outrè*, don't you think? I have a great skirt, black silk, with a black and white blouse, very pop art. Tell me about the one you're wearing tonight.'

'Very simple, blue crepe, not revealing except it hugs everything it should hug, but I hope it says, "Take this woman seriously."'

'Exactly. Hey, let's shake. We may not have time later. May the best woman win.'

'Kazuhiko's good.'

'Train your killer instinct, Juliet. You think for one minute he's saying you're a nice girl?'

Juliet looked at her and shook her head. 'He may well be, Bryony, and he's not the enemy; we don't have to impress him although it's always nice to make friends in the business.'

Bryony stopped. 'You know he saved your bacon yesterday, volunteering to take your slot so as not to waste time. You two got a thing going?'

'A "thing" as you call it with him or anyone else is the very last thought in my mind for at least ten years. I haven't got time.'

Bryony laughed. 'There's always time, honey. You just don't need to take the poor little lambs seriously.'

They had reached the green room and so there was no need for Juliet to find an answer.

It was later when they went up into the auditorium to listen to the acoustics that she had been forced to encounter Karel Haken. Almost three months since she had seen him; all that time with not one word to explain his abrupt departure. No, it was not abrupt; she had known he was leaving early from the airport but to leave without a word. She sighed. What had she expected? An affair across continents; a love affair ending when 'death us do part'? Her insides seemed to crawl with embarrassment. But he would get no satisfaction from discovering that she had fallen for him. Past tense. 'Had fallen', like a gullible girl who had been swamped by the charisma of the conductor and had endowed him with more virtues than he could possibly possess. Why she found herself thinking about him, remembering the feel of his skin, the touch of his hands, she did not know.

'Juliet.'

She stopped. She recognised the voice. For a second she closed her eyes. How to behave? She waited, long enough for him to know that she was working out her strategy, and then turned and looked at him coldly. 'Maestro?' She was pleased to note the slight look of unease in his eyes.

'I wanted to say how pleased I am that you are a finalist. Everything was excellent but the Brahms was an absolute delight. I wish you well tonight.'

Her heart was hammering and her mouth felt dry. Damn it, Juliet, you're letting him affect you. Cool it. She swallowed and smiled coldly. 'You're very kind, Mr Haken. If you'll excuse me?' She turned away and began to walk towards the doors. With all she had to contend with today, her reactions on seeing Haken were simply not worth worrying over.

'Juliet?' His hand was on her shoulder, forcing her to turn round. 'Why didn't you call me? What did I do wrong? If you didn't want to see me again, if you were angry you could have explained.'

'Angry? Angry, Maestro? Why should I be angry? Perhaps I just don't like being used, Mr Haken, and it certainly won't happen again. Let go of me.'

He dropped his hand but said nothing, just looked at her as if he were puzzled. After a moment he said, 'Used,' but Juliet was already walking away and did not ask herself why he should be puzzled. Had she asked she would probably have become even angrier but she would waste no more time on Mr Haken and certainly there would be no more sleepless nights. They had had a lovely day and a lovelier night and she was stupidly naïve and had thought it meant something. She shook her head as if to clear it of all extraneous material. This was it. Tonight was the final. She had seen him now, told him where she stood and so she had no further need to worry that she might suddenly see him and begin to wonder again just what she had done, what signals she had emitted, to make him treat her so shamefully. She blushed at her memory. Stupid stupid Juliet. Think of tonight. Think of the final.

Thank God he was not on the panel. She owed him nothing. He had not helped her through the elimination rounds; she had done it herself. She had been nervous but that was right; other contestants were too but how many of them, she wondered, had been apprehensive that a man over whom they had made a terrible mistake would turn up as he had once promised. Juliet laughed softly. Very few, if any, and she could not imagine Bryony losing sleep over any man, not if what she had said earlier was the truth. She looked at her watch. Her parents would have arrived in the city by now and were probably in a taxi from King's Cross. Her father loved trains. 'Gives me a chance to do nothing but read a book. Only civilised way to travel.'

Her mother found train travel a bore but she would tolerate it. 'Keeps Daddy happy, but my God, six hours cooped up in a box with nothing to do but look out of the window. Mind you, I do like having lunch on a train, very Agatha Christie somehow, isn't it?' And that ghastly inconsiderate woman would have brought back her dress and she would not have to wear Bryony's lovely but rather ill-fitting dress for the concert. She had worn it for the photographs: after all Bryony had been so kind.

The hotel had not contacted her by four thirty and so, as soon as she could get free, she ran upstairs and rang the front desk. No one had returned to the hotel with either a coat or a dress. For a moment Juliet panicked. How nice to be a man: Kazuhiko, like male conductors all over the world, was to appear in a black shirt and trousers. Should she want to, from which member of the London Symphony Orchestra could she possibly borrow the same outfit? She could not conduct properly in the raspberry dress; it was an evening dress, a dress for dinner and dancing under lowered lights or candlelight. What shops were there on any of the local streets? Aldersgate Street, Fore Street, Whitecross Street, Silk Street? She could not remember having seen a dress shop anywhere near the Barbican Centre, but in such an enormous central London area there had to be at least one and it had to be open and have the perfect dress in her size.

'Would Miss Crawford please come to the information desk on the ground floor.' The voice from the intercom alerted her the second time it repeated the request. Juliet almost burst into tears. Her dress. The lady, the lady had returned her dress. She almost flew back downstairs. She would forgive her; she would even invite her to the concert. Only the doorman was at the desk.

'I'm Juliet Crawford. Did someone leave something for me?'

'Yes, indeed. A delivery – just a few minutes ago.' He turned and took down a garment bag that was hooked on to the structure of his little booth. 'Here you are, Miss Crawford.'

Juliet's stomach plunged again. 'But this isn't my garment bag; it's from Absolutely Fabulous.'

'Yes, madam.' He looked at her as if he felt that she needed things to be explained to her in words of one syllable. 'The deliveryman came about ten minutes ago, the deliveryman from a shop called Absolutely Fabulous. He said, "This is for a Miss Crawford." Is there anything else, Miss Crawford?'

'No, sorry, I was expecting another delivery but this one is fine, a surprise, but fine. Thank you.'

She took the dress bag. Absolutely Fabulous: one of the most exclusive shops in London. Her parents? No, they knew she had a new dress and, besides, they could never afford these prices. Hermione? It had to be Hermione or her parents. What wonderful friends. Please, God, don't let it be scarlet.

It was a glorious blue-green and it was not from Hermione. At least it might have been but there was no card with it. Reverently Juliet removed the dress from the bag, stroking the fabric, enjoying the almost sensual play of the dressing-room lights on the fine material; this way green and that way blue. She held it against her, then put it down gently, carefully, as befitted its workmanship and hauled off her clothes. The dress slid over her head and down her body as if it had been made for her. The neck was low but discreetly so. It was a masterpiece of design. It appeared to have no seams but floated down from the neckline caressing her upper body but not emphasising her bust and then, as she turned to look at her back view, swirling out into a full skirt that yet lay calmly against her hips when she was still. The sleeves were long and neither too tight nor too loose, a perfect sleeve for a woman who wanted to conduct, and the hem was the fashionable handkerchief style. She twirled and turned in ways that she would never do on a podium and each time she swirled the handkerchiefs spiralled out so that her legs could be seen.

'Very sexy.' Juliet laughed. 'But you will be so discreet on the night.'

The dress was so simple yet everything about it said excellence: the fabric, the design, the fit. It had to be Hermione. If not her or her family then it had to have been bought by her parents as a special and most welcome gift. Still in the dress, Juliet rang the shop and told the assistant who answered that her lovely gift had come but that somehow the gift tag had become separated.

'There was no gift tag, madam. The gentleman who bought the dress this afternoon wants to remain anonymous.'

'A gentleman? But I have to know.'

'I can't help you, Miss Crawford. Even if I wanted to, I can't.

The gentleman paid in cash and I cannot tell you anything else about him.'

'Please, his age, his hair colour, something? Did he have an accent?'

'It was a foreign gentleman. Very *soigné*, you might say.' She stopped fearing she was being indiscreet. 'Enjoy the dress. It's one of the loveliest Madame has made.' There was a click, a definite end to the conversation.

The only men she knew who could not be described as '*soigné*' or foreign were her father, Gregor, and Aldo and even Aldo might, to a Londoner, be foreign with that idiosyncratic Italian/Glasgow accent that she often felt was put on every morning with his coat as he left his flat. But if *soigné* could be translated as sophisticated, elegant, urbane, then neither Aldo nor Gregor fitted the description, and she knew her father would never have dreamed of buying such a dress and he could never be mistaken for a foreigner.

Who bought it? Who cares so much? Oh, my God, could it be someone who wants too much? She thought of a face but discarded it. Stupid idea, Juliet. Never; it couldn't possibly be him. Whoever it is will tell me when he's ready to tell me, and right now I have too many other matters to worry about.

She wore the dress, the chain and the diamond earrings, enjoying their sparkle as the lights in her dressing room caught them. They really were quite beautiful. Dear Hermione. Juliet looked at herself and knew she looked good. The dress was elegant, easy to move in and, when she was standing almost still on the podium, would reveal nothing. Its simplicity set off the jewellery. But doubts set in. Will the audience think I'm there to sing? What if the judges don't take me seriously and the orchestra, this so wonderful and talented LSO, what will they think? I should wear tails. That's what they'll expect and it's a competition. My God, what if I lose because I offend someone. She threw open the wardrobe door. It revealed nothing more than the skirt she had been wearing all day and Bryony's raspberry dress. Bryony. Thank God: she too was wearing a skirt, and heels.

'Killer heels,' Bryony had said, 'to die for.'

Juliet examined her court shoes, then looked in the mirror. She liked what she saw. 'You look good, in fact – Absolutely Fabulous. Besides, my knight in shining armour deserves to see it and the critics can say what they damn well please.'

9

Her parents sent flowers with a card and, at the thought of them stopping on their way from the station to their hotel to send them, Juliet almost cried. How very sweet. She would treasure the card and, yes, she would keep a flower, for ever. They would not come to wish her well in person: she knew they wanted her to win as well as they knew that a show of parental emotion would only unnerve her.

Aldo did come to wish her luck. 'Wow, what a looker. That dress is exactly the colour of your eyes. Knock 'em dead, girl,' he said. 'I can hardly wait to see you standing up there on the podium at the Barbican. I can feel it, Juliet. Tonight is destiny.' He hugged her so tightly that she almost heard her ribs crack and left without another word. He had brought her a white rose and with trembling hands she pinned it to her bag; a pin would ruin the dress and he would see that she was wearing it after the concert.

She sat in the green room with Bryony and Kazuhiko and for once the auspiciousness of the occasion was affecting. Bryony and she said little after she had commented on the dress.

'Glad it turned up; not really how I pictured it.'

Juliet could have said the same thing. Bryony was indeed wearing a blouse and skirt as she had said but a jewelled belt encircled her waist accentuating her slenderness and somehow emphasising the swell of her breasts; her 'killer heels' also twinkled with jewelled straps around her slender ankles. She looked wonderful.

Juliet was the third candidate and she sat, first with the silent Kazuhiko, and then alone until the intermission when the others rejoined her.

'God, it was fantastic, Juliet. The audience is so receptive and the orchestra is divine. So far I think we're first equal, Kazu. Wouldn't that be a hoot, a three-way tie?'

'Unless Juliet outshines us both, Bryony. Good luck, Juliet. *Choi, choi, choi*, as we say in Japan.'

This was it. There was nothing she could do now but her best. She knew the music, knew exactly what she wanted to hear. All the months and years of training had brought her here to one of the finest concert halls in the world with one of the acknowledged great orchestras. Even if she lost, this night, this moment could never be taken away from her.

I am Juliet Crawford and tonight I am fulfilling one of my dreams. I am conducting a great orchestra in a great hall. She felt powerful and then her sense of humour kicked in as she thought of the weight of experience in the LSO. That is, if they'll let me.

Only one way to find out. Juliet stood up and shook out the skirt of her glorious dress and then she walked out into the corridor. The president of the panel of judges was there. He shook her hand, wished her well, and followed her up the stairs on to the stage of the Barbican.

'Your Royal Highness, my lords, ladies and gentlemen, our third and final finalist is a home-grown talent, Juliet Crawford.'

It had come. For her, this was it. Tonight she had to win or she would have no choice but to return to Dundee and her father's censure. She would be compelled to take whatever jobs she could get, for she could no longer, not at twenty-five for God's sake, be a financial burden on her parents. How still the hall was. It was so large and there were so many lights and hundreds of people there, sitting, hushed, waiting. Somewhere out there were her parents and dear Aldo – not Hermione who, for once, had a job for which she was being paid. The orchestra too sat still: quiet, ready. She walked to the podium, such a long, long walk across miles of stage, the handkerchief hem fluttering against her legs as she walked. Too late to remember to shorten her usual stride. Aldo said she had great legs: let them see them.

She was there. Up on to the podium. All her nervousness fell away as a cocoon falls away from the emerging butterfly; she was serene, sure that, at last, she was in the right place. How many of the world's best had stood here before her? All her heroes, giants every one. She looked at the orchestra. Dear God in heaven, every face was turned towards her, watching, waiting. She almost laughed with euphoria. She listened for a second to the expectant silence and then raised her baton. Again she prayed. Thank you. This is where Juliet Crawford wants to be.

When the music stopped at the end of her second piece, the symphony, there was a heartbeat of silence and then the audience applauded; the orchestra stood up and they too clapped. She bowed, she thanked the leader of the orchestra, and then she walked off. It was over. She refused to pin any hope on the orchestra's response. That had been quite lovely and she would treasure that moment of applause for the rest of her life, but the judges did not consult the orchestra. Only their own opinion mattered; they had watched her for three days; every moment of those three days would be taken into consideration.

Bryony, looking as white as a sheet, stood in the corridor with Kazuhiko. They tried to summon up smiles as Juliet herself did.

'Boy, you wowed them, Juliet.' Bryony was being brave but she was trembling.

'So did you, and Kazuhiko. We all did well. How could we not with such a fabulous orchestra?'

'The orchestra didn't give me a standing ovation,' said Bryony. The friendliness and kindness of the earlier part of the day seemed to have disappeared. 'Mind you, maybe they were applauding that gown. I'd have worn the raspberry one if I'd known your "simple" dress was a designer label.'

Juliet gasped at the malice in Bryony's voice. She had not deliberately lied about her dress but had described to Bryony what she had been intending to wear. It had not been her fault that her own dress had not been returned in time. Would she have worn it if it had been delivered? No. What woman alive would not have worn this glorious dress? The dress? How stupid. She felt sick. Who had bought it? What message might she have given just by wearing it? I didn't think. It was just so lovely, so generous. Oh, God, who bought this dress? She wished she could tear it off and throw it aside.

'They were congratulating the conductor, Bryony,' said Kazuhiko calmly. 'You were superb, Juliet. You are the winner by right. I offer my most sincere felicitations.'

'Oh, dear Kazu, I have never had felicitations before and thank you, but please, nothing has been decided yet,' Juliet began but the chairman of the judging panel was there to lead them back on to the stage where the dignitaries waited. Unlike the first time she had walked across it Juliet felt as if she were wading through mud. Her legs felt heavy, her heart was still beating wildly, and the palms of her hands were wet with sweat. Don't fall apart in front of a prince, please, Juliet, she told herself and then she was there, in her place on the stage with Bryony and Kazuhiko beside her. The audience, the orchestra, and the judges were all applauding them, and at last she was able to smile. It was over.

She tried to listen to the speeches, which seemed to go on for ever, although they were in fact very short. She peered into the auditorium looking for her parents but could see only rows and rows of white featureless faces. Even if it's Bryony, try to be dignified, try to congratulate her.

'Juliet Crawford.'

Later she tried to reconstruct that moment, tried to remember what she felt when she heard her name and realised that, at last, she had won a major competition, but she remembered absolutely nothing.

Over a late supper in their hotel dining room, Juliet's mother said that they had feared that their daughter was about to faint and as she started her excited chattering Juliet did as she had done countless times before: she sat quietly and let the tide wash over her. 'You closed your eyes, darling, just before you shook the prince's hand, but you curtseyed so nicely. And that gown, naughty girl. It must have cost a fortune. Daddy hopes you haven't been starving to pay for it. All three of you looked a bit traumatised coming on to the stage, you and the other girl more so, if you know what I mean. Mr Shigetoku doesn't give much away, does he? Bryony gave you such a lovely hug and that must have been hard because she was really good too, and the gentleman.'

Her father ordered champagne, an unheard-of extravagance. 'My daughter's worth it,' he said quietly and Juliet felt bathed in love as she saw, for the first time in her life, tears in his eyes.

I've done it; at last I've pleased him, at last.

They discussed the generous award which would not be handed over to Juliet in the form of a cheque but which would be administered by the competition in the way that would advance her career most effectively.

'What does that mean? What about your living expenses? Does this mean you'll get a job, a permanent position?'

How many times would she have to try to explain to her mother? 'Mummy, I've got six months, an absolutely fabulous six months working with the LSO. I'll conduct rehearsals, go into schools with the outreach programme, have the opportunity to work with and learn from the greatest conductors in the world when they visit here as guests. Perhaps they'll ask me to look over and assess new scores, or maybe even once or twice I'll be asked to conduct. Next year, who knows?'

'You mean you still don't have a job.'

'Of course I have a job. Mummy, we've talked about this. It takes years to make a conductor.'

'But, darling, there have been years.'

On the night that she had won a really prestigious prize she surely did not deserve to be made to feel guilty. Juliet looked around the restaurant, seeing people leaning close to each other, smiling, communicating without words. She heard the faint strains of violin music from a hidden CD player, the clatter of plates, quiet voices and sudden bursts of laughter. She could smell flowers, delicate. Discreet. Everything was normal, everything except Juliet herself whose every nerve ending was tingling. She wanted to plead, 'No dampers, please, not tonight.'

She told herself not to feel guilty. That was difficult when all the old school friends were advanced in various careers, and some, all named and noted by her mother, already married and, in some cases, starting families. How many times would she say that a conductor's career could take ten or even twenty years? How many ways were there to explain that there is a finite number of orchestras? In the main, most of them have a conductor. Where is the brand-new conductor to go? He or very occasionally she must prove, over months or years, that he has something to offer that this particular orchestra wants. Perhaps there is a record of prestigious awards and places in competitions which the Boards value. Even better, but extremely rare, is when an orchestra demands the appointment of a conductor as happened in Scotland with the appointment of the Frenchman, Stéphane Denève, to the Royal Scottish National Orchestra. Juliet knew that the entire orchestra had begged for Denève's next free date. How inspiring to be headhunted by the orchestra itself.

At last all the sleepless nights took their toll: Juliet could feel her eyes crossing, just as they had done on the few occasions that she had suffered from jet lag. Her parents agreed that they had an early train to catch and after promising to come home as soon as possible Juliet made her triumphant, if totally exhausted, way back to her hotel. The red light on her telephone glowed to alert her to recorded messages. First she had to get out of her clothes, her beautiful dress that she would keep for ever. There were a number of messages for her, three of them from Hermione. Juliet punched in her friend's number at once.

'We're sitting here, all three of us, waiting to be told.'

'I'm sorry, my best of friends, too much partying. I won.'

She listened to shrieks of excitement for some time until Gregor took the phone. 'We know,' he said bluntly. 'I knew you would be held up and so I looked it up on the Internet, especially since you were too busy with princes of the blood royal etcetera to bother with us.'

He was teasing, of course, and, after he and Heather had congratulated her, Hermione said, 'By the way, Maestro, or is it Maestra, did you wear the studs?'

'Yes, Hermione, I looked absolutely stunning.'

'Good, Ma will be delighted that they have been unjinxed.'

'Unjinxed? Hermione, what have you not told me about these earrings?'

Hermione laughed and Juliet prepared herself. 'Are you sure you want to know?' asked Hermione. 'You're not wearing them now, are you?'

'No, they looked slightly OTT with pyjamas. Tell me.'

'Do you remember Nigel?'

Nigel? Juliet thought back through the long list of toads in Hermione's love life and, at last, with a sinking feeling, remembered Nigel. 'Hermione, are you telling me that my earrings are the same ones that you and said toad were wearing at your twenty-first birthday party?'

On the end of the line she could hear Hermione convulsed with laughter. 'Yes, I never actually told you that Mummy gave them to me, did I? It was more a question of her utterly refusing to wear them again after she saw one of them in Nigel's hairy nostril.'

'That is so revolting.'

'Ma's words exactly. The other one, of course, was in my delightful little nose. They have been cleaned, Juliet.'

'You are utterly horrid, Hermione, and I will never speak to you again,' said Juliet and hung up. Despite herself she went over to the mirror and looked very closely at her ear lobes but there was no sign of anything untoward, no redness or swelling. Still, she soaked two cotton pads in cologne and held them to her ears for a few minutes and then she started to laugh. How typically Hermione. Friendship with her was never dull.

Sure that she would not sleep, she got into bed and prepared for all the events of the past three days to replay themselves in her head. They did not. She had a vision of Hermione's mother's aghast face as she had discovered where her beautiful diamonds were being worn, laughed softly, and fell asleep.

The next morning she was awakened by a call from the front desk. Flowers were being delivered. She jumped out of bed, showered quickly and ran downstairs. After her experience of yesterday the staff could not do enough for her. Her dress had been brought back, too late to be of any use, and with no apology from whoever had taken it.

'I will have a bottle of our finest champagne sent up to your room, Miss Crawford, with our congratulations and our apologies.'

'Thank you, but I'm returning to Scotland tomorrow. I can stay tonight, I take it. There's so much for me to do in London.'

Mr Roebottom smiled. 'You are the hotel's personal guest tonight. Enjoy the rest of your stay.'

Juliet thanked him, asked that the flowers that had arrived be taken up to her room and then went into the breakfast room. What a different feeling from yesterday when she had been so fraught. She wondered if she looked like a prize-winning conductor but caught a glimpse of herself in a mirror and realised that she looked exactly as she had looked the morning before, if a little less preoccupied. She ordered an enormous breakfast and then sat drinking orange juice while she waited for it. Now was the time to let the astounding result sink in. I've done it. It's beginning; at last my career is beginning. Make a list, Juliet. Things to do. Buy some new clothes. Find a flat. Move out.

At the realisation that the time had come for her to leave Edinburgh she almost lost her joy in her achievement. I'll miss them all so much. But it's time. We'll just have to promise not to lose touch.

'Miss Crawford, there's a call for you. Several messages have been left but a Mr Aldo needs to talk to you right now.'

She had left her mobile phone in her room and, annoyed at her stupidity, thanked the receptionist and hurried out.

'Good morning, Maestro. Did no one tell you never to turn off your phone especially after getting your face plastered all over the papers? The interest is overwhelming, lassie, so eat up your porridge . . .'

'Boy, how Scottish we are today. Who's calling, Aldo?'

'Everybody. I'm on my way to City to catch a shuttle. I'll ring you later. Have a good day, girl.'

He disconnected and she finished breakfast and returned to her room.

She had never seen so many flowers and especially not in November. Bouquets and baskets arrived all day, every colour imaginable, reds and yellows and blues and pinks, some sweet-smelling, others relying on their outrageous beauty and with no perfume at all, many from friends but flowers had been sent by people Juliet did not know except by reputation: conductors from all over the world, a few of them women, together with theatre managers, orchestra leaders, both men and women. She wrote down all the names, determined to write a note to each and every one although looking at some of the famous names she wondered if she would even be able to discover an address to which to send them.

She was sitting in the middle of the floor, almost swooning from the heady perfumes from some of the more exotic offerings, when there was a knock at the door and, without thinking, she called, 'Come in.' Karel Haken opened the door and stood on the threshold, looking down at her sitting there in her sea of blossoms, yet more flowers, tiny white rosebuds, in his hands. He was the last person she would have expected to see.

'I also brought a little vase,' he said as she sat still, feeling slightly stupid and very embarrassed. 'You will need everything that will hold water. The sink is good but I even used the waste basket which was not, of course, a basket but made of some type of metal.'

Still she said nothing but she did get to her feet, the carpet she had created of the gaudy papers that had wrapped the flowers rustling and crackling under her feet, and Karel went on, 'You were sensational, Juliet, and never has a conductor looked so lovely. What an inspired choice, to wear a dress, I mean. The papers are full of it too.'

'Yes, I know,' she said. 'Some journalists gave more inches to my dress than they gave to my conducting, but thankfully, so far, only one has taken the "Juliet plays the gender game".'

'Ignore nonsense,' he said, holding out a broadsheet she had not yet seen. 'I like this one that says the Margarita Rosa Grey competition has a genius for launching future stars. They title it, NEW JEWEL IN THE CROWN.'

That galvanised her and she stepped over two bouquets to take the paper from him. 'What?' She stared at the offending headline and then read through the article and Karel stood quietly inside the door, the flowers in his hand. She lifted her head from the paper, said crossly, 'For goodness sake come in and close the door,' before going on to finish the article. She did not see him smile as he obeyed. She continued reading and then crushed the paper and looked at him as if in some surprise. She looked at the flowers which he was now presenting to her, took them, held their simple beauty up to her face for a moment and said, 'Thank you. I thought you were the bellboy; he's been up and down like a yo-yo.'

Now it was Karel's turn to look puzzled.

She tried to work out an easy way to explain. 'That's colloquial,' she began. 'Oh, never mind. Why are you here? I was rude to you yesterday. I assumed that would be enough.'

'To make me go away? Yes, normally that would be sufficient but you said something strange and I thought I have to talk to Juliet, just one more time. I leave after Christmas, you know, to return to Prague and I will then be in Malta and back to Heidelberg, and in the middle of Heidelberg Edinburgh, this time as myself, not in place of anyone.'

She had no idea what he was trying to say and so she fussed with the flowers, trying to find a space for them. The only available space seemed to be on the table beside her bed and she did not want to put them there. Damn it, she thought. I don't want his blasted flowers at all.

'Tell me what you want to say. Or was that it? You think I have an interest in your itinerary?'

He flushed again and held out his hands as if in supplication and then dropped them back to his sides. 'I'm sorry to have bothered you, Miss Crawford.' He put a small packet on the table with the flowers. 'Arnošt Lustig,' he said. '*Waiting for Leah*. You will like.'

She let him reach the door. 'Karel, wait. The flowers are lovely;

thank you; and thank you for the book – that was thoughtful. What was it that you wanted to ask?' She could not believe that leaving a woman, with whom one had just spent the night, without a word, was a Czech custom but she would allow him to explain if that was what he meant to do. After all, her life as a conductor was just beginning. If she was lucky she need never be in the same hall with him again; she could afford to be generous.

'You said that I had used you but, you know, when you completely ignored my note I felt that I was the one who had been used.'

'That is low. Your note. You know perfectly well that you got out of my bed and disappeared out of my life. Did I pay you well enough for the expensive dinner or are you hoping to collect something else? I looked everywhere for a note, a message, a telephone number. I sat by the phone for days hoping that you would call.' She turned and picked up the little vase and the flowers and managed to curb the impulse to throw them at him. 'Get out, get out and take your flowers with you. I hope I never have to see you again.'

Karel looked at her and had she been less angry she would have seen the genuine despair in his eyes. He took the flowers from her, dropped them, complete with water-filled vase, in her waste-paper basket and walked out, closing the door very quietly behind him.

Alone in the room Juliet stood looking at the door. 'Damn him, damn him,' she sobbed. 'Why do I let him ruin everything?'

10

With the rather feeble excuse that there were too many ends to tie up at the flat, Juliet went to Edinburgh before going home for Christmas.

The four friends sat for hours talking and making and discarding plans. Juliet was moving out in January and since she would be gone for at least six months Hermione would need to find a compatible fourth person to rent her room.

'I'm much too busy to do anything before January,' said Hermione. 'You're the only one of us who isn't working at the moment, Juliet, and with Christmas coming and most of us away, there just isn't time to look around.' She looked at her friends. 'Unless anyone knows someone who's looking for a place?'

'I might,' said Heather, 'but it's too early to say.'

'Love rearing its ugly head again?' teased Hermione. 'You don't mean you think Peter what's his name from the BBC might want to move in? Making plans, are we?'

Heather almost simpered, which made all three of her friends want to shake her. 'We have been seeing rather a lot of each other.'

'Not again,' groaned Gregor. 'You've found real love at last.'

'Just because you can't find anyone,' teased Heather but Juliet was dismayed to see a look of real pain cross Gregor's sensitive face.

Later, when Gregor had gone to the theatre and Peter had come to take Heather out, she asked Hermione if Gregor was in love with Heather.

Hermione prevaricated. 'What makes you think he might be?'

Not even with Hermione could Juliet speak about that sad expression. 'Nothing really. It's just that he spends so much time with her; he plays for this choir she's coaching and he was always running after her when she missed phone calls.'

Hermione was lying on the wooden floor, just off a very worn but rather lovely Caucasian rug, stretching her spine. She would not have been pleased had her friend told her that she looked all of twelve years old. She rolled over on to the carpet and focused on Juliet. 'He's a lovely human being. Do we see so few that we find Gregor's nurturing odd? He plays for me and look how much he helped you. How many sections of the orchestra was he?'

'I get your point but I'm worried. What if Peter what's his name moves in?'

'Not my problem and not yours either, but I should think Gregor might like a bit of male company.'

A sound of knocking made them both look towards the hall. 'Blinkety blink blink.' Hermione scowled. 'It's dear old Mrs McD. I promised she could come in and hear all about the competition. Put the kettle on while I let her in or should we ply her with alcohol?'

Juliet who – although sometimes exasperated – was actually fond of their neighbour, and, of the four friends, probably the most aware of Mrs McDermott's living conditions, was also the most practical. 'Gosh no,' she said as she got up. 'We'll never get rid of her.'

Mrs McDermott was still sitting in the living room and was finishing her third cup of tea when Peter brought Heather back. 'Dear Heather,' she said, 'and her lovely young man. I could have just one more cup, Hermione dear, while we all catch up.'

Heather introduced her to Peter who refused all offers of refreshment. 'No thanks, we're awash as it is, Hermione, but I'll stay for a minute while Heather tells you all her plan.'

Mrs McDermott was visibly and audibly excited at the thought of a plan but Juliet and Hermione, knowing Heather well, were more cautious.

'Come along, tell all,' said Hermione, sitting down beside Mrs McDermott and smiling widely at Heather.

Heather took Peter's hand, as if for comfort or perhaps encouragement. 'All right, straight in. This is all terribly exciting but I need you all to help. Juliet, I want you to conduct my choir at the concert so that I can sing, and I'd like Hermione to play a solo. Gregor will play for you and the choir of course.'

Juliet pushed her heavy brown hair off her forehead and stared at her in amazement. 'You have to be joking, Heather. I have absolutely no experience conducting singers; I don't know the music and even worse I don't know the choir.' She looked at Peter and could see, quite easily, why Heather had fallen for him. He was big and broad and had a very nice rugged face although, at the moment, it looked rather misunderstood and discontented.

'You could sight-read the music and make it terrific, Juliet,' said Peter, which was kind and – just possibly – true. 'I'm going to try to get it broadcast over the Christmas period. We're always looking for local interest stuff and, with the fabulous *Messiah* broadcast, that would give Heather two opportunities to be heard in less than two weeks.' He was smiling now and animated. 'Great chance for her – and the rest of you too.'

'Heard. By whom? Who listens to the radio at Christmas? Everyone is out frantically trying to find presents, or delivering them or buying mountains of groceries and frozen turkeys, and standing for hours in the post office waiting to post last-minute cards that won't get there before Easter.' Hermione stopped for breath.

'You are funny, Hermione dear, but I listen to the radio all day, and if I knew my favourite people in the whole world were going to be broadcasting I'd be glued.' Mrs McDermott looked at Peter. 'It won't get in the way of the dear Queen, Peter?' she finished anxiously.

Peter ignored her and, without realising it, immediately lost any respect Juliet and Hermione might have had for him. 'There are remote places in these islands that depend on radio, Hermione; huge audiences, believe me.'

Hermione squeezed Mrs McDermott's hand. 'I'd never play when the Queen was talking, Mrs McD. Don't worry.' She smiled gently at the old woman but her face when she turned to Heather was decidedly frosty. 'Why the sudden request for help?'

Heather, thought Juliet, is very lovely and she has played the pretty girl card all her life and will probably continue to play it when she's Mrs McD's age. She looked at the old lady as she too sat smiling and holding Hermione's hand – just as Mrs McD herself continues to use it.

'It was Gregor's idea really, a bit of a joke probably, but the first day when we went down to see them he said, "You should ask Juliet to conduct for you and you should sing and Hermione should play."'

'Too many "should" for Gregor.'

'But he did,' said Heather, 'and it could be lovely and such great networking for all of us.'

'Date?' Juliet was looking at Peter who flushed.

'Christmas week possibly, probably, but naturally it would be pre-recorded.'

'Fee?'

Heather jumped in before Peter could answer. 'Golly, Juliet. Peter is doing us a favour.'

'Peter, my dear child, is trying to fill his schedule – extremely cheaply.'

At that Peter jumped up and walked over to the door. 'That's unfair. I was trying to do something nice for Heather, and you lot. Nice little angle. Four fabulous musicians, old college chums, flatmates, and now that you've won the Margarita Rosa Grey competition, Juliet . . .'

'Even more bankable.' Hermione smiled sweetly.

Heather got up and flounced over to Peter. 'We talked about this before you won, Juliet. I've worked really hard with this choir for pennies. Gregor has given up his one night off every week to play for us; I thought you would want to help him – he speaks of you so highly. Who knows who might be listening and even if no one useful or important is, we're still building up a fan base for the future.'

'Spoken like a true professional,' said Juliet.

'Are you being sarcastic?' Sweet little Heather was beginning to show her claws.

'Realistic. Now since I'm free until Christmas I have no real objection to helping out but if I'm going to do it, I have to do it properly and that means talking to Gregor about the music and taking the remaining rehearsals. What about you, Hermione? Will you play something cheery and Christmassy?'

'I haven't said I'll do it yet. I'll talk to Gregor.'

'Are you girls squabbling?'

They had almost forgotten their uninvited guest. 'No, Mrs McD.'

'Good, then if Gregor's not here, perhaps this nice young man would walk me to my door.'

'Now was that a very astute way of getting rid of an unwanted man or what?' Hermione laughed as Peter escorted the old lady out.

'Silly old cow,' said Heather. 'I get really tired of seeing her sitting in the living room night after night.' Now Heather, like Peter, looked aggrieved and misunderstood. Were she to see her face when in such a mood she might well be more careful.

'Chill, Heather. She's a poor lonely old woman who is not here night after night.' Hermione curled up in her favourite chair. 'There are still lots of things to discuss but we'd best wait for the weekend so that Gregor can have his say. Be an angel and put a CD on, Juliet; music to clean one's teeth by.'

'How about the *Messiah*?'

'Very funny. Is Peter coming back, Heather?'

'Why on earth should he? He doesn't live here.' She stood in the doorway, her eyes filling with tears.

Hermione jumped up and went to her and Juliet stayed where she was, kneeling on the floor, sorting through compact discs. 'Come and sit down, Heather. I meant nothing; just interest. I suppose it's inevitable that one of us would get seriously involved.' They all turned as they heard running footsteps on the stone stairs. 'He has come back.'

Heather hurried over to open the door just as Gregor put his key in the lock.

'That's service.' Gregor, his pale cheeks red with cold, looked round. 'All my girls. This is nice. Were you waiting up for me? Are we having a council?' He flopped on the sofa where Hermione was now ensconced. 'Squash up, mate.'

Gregor was in great spirits, having been helped with last-minute backstage work by a member of the chorus in the opera that the theatre was staging. 'Wonderful bloke. He happened to be late leaving the dressing room, saw me carting boxes, and pitched in to help. So here I am, ladies, all yours.'

Juliet looked at him, seeing how young and attractive he looked when he was animated, but she said nothing.

'We could talk about New Year's Eve since Gregor's here?' Hermione looked round.

'Fine. I don't care what we do,' said Heather and then immediately added a clause that proved that she cared very much. 'But we must see the fireworks and we have to walk along Princes Street and up the Mound and listen to all the bands and see all the crazy people.'

'We'd be the crazy people if we go out on to the streets of Edinburgh on Hogmanay. Have you any idea how many people from all over the world will pour into the city?' asked Gregor.

'Hard to tell but it will be at least one hundred thousand if previous years are anything to go by.'

'Fabulous,' said Heather and Hermione almost simultaneously and Juliet laughed at their enthusiasm.

Hermione banged on the table beside her. 'All right but first let's have a lovely dinner here. It will probably be our last.' They all looked sad for a moment as realisation of the changes in their lives sank in and so Hermione went on quickly. 'You said something about your cousin visiting, Heather?'

They chatted for some time about the menu and other guests. Heather had forgotten to ask if her cousin could bring her boyfriend. She also broke the news to Gregor, who did most of the cooking, that these guests were both vegetarian but he took the news in his stride.

'It's supposed to be freezing at the end of the month,' said Juliet, 'but who trusts weather forecasts? We'll have dinner, walk up to Princes Street, possibly the Mound if we can manage it, watch the fireworks, sing "Auld Lang Syne," and back down to have a glass of bubbly with Mrs McD – and pudding if we haven't had time.'

Heather shrieked and jumped up out of her chair. 'Damn damn, double damn. We can't go up to watch the fireworks. We have to have tickets. I've been so busy with the choir . . .'

Juliet, with her usual efficiency, had ordered tickets before she left for London and she now produced them. She looked down at the envelope. 'Our last New Year's Eve together; rather sad really.'

'Just our last one as flatmates, Juliet,' said Hermione. 'We might spend a New Year together in Austria or New York. Our friendship isn't ending.'

Juliet looked at the others. Instinctively she knew that it was already different. It saddened her to realise that she was more despondent over leaving this flat, this group of people, than she had been over leaving home. She shrugged. This was life: meeting and parting, making an effort to keep relationships working.

Hermione snuffed out a low-burning candle that had been filling the room with a perfume more redolent of the American south than Edinburgh in winter and stood up. 'I'm off to bed. First thing tomorrow I have to go out to Liberton to rehearse with the orchestra. Did anyone know that Liberton was originally Leper's Town? Thought you'd all like to know that.' She was halfway to her bedroom when she stopped and came back. 'Gregor, I've just had a fabulous idea. Simon, our conductor, has hinted that he'll slip in a solo for me at our big New Year concert. Why not write me something, a New Year bagatelle, a study of some kind?'

Gregor looked up from the list he had been compiling. 'I can't compose to order, Hermione, but thanks for thinking of me.'

'Your beloved Mozart composed to order all the time, old chum. You have three days.'

Gregor smiled at her departing back and turned to Juliet. 'Here's the shopping list for the Hogmanay bash. Plenty of time to do it after Christmas but best check that there's enough money in the box?'

They all turned as they heard the exquisite sound of Hermione's violin from her bedroom.

Heather grabbed her coat from the chair where she had thrown it when she came in. 'Quick, remind her of the time. We'll have the awful Mrs McDermott back on the doorstep in a minute.'

Gregor was left sitting alone on the sofa looking at the door through which his three flatmates had gone. 'Heather's becoming an absolute cow,' he said softly. 'And if that's what love does to a rather nice human being, count me out.'

Since he was indeed a decent young man he did, as usual, accompany Heather to her next rehearsal. Juliet did not. The choir's permission would have to be asked. The hall was less cheering than it had ever been and since the outside temperature was lower, the antiquated heating, although struggling bravely and loudly, had lost the war against the invasion of cold air. Any heat from the inadequate radiators that were set into the walls immediately flew straight out of the many tall, narrow windows that lined the two longest walls of the room. Gregor longed for a few panes of stained glass to soften their austerity. The warmth from the choir's welcome, however, more than made up for the chill of the building.

The members, who had improved immeasurably from the standard of their first meeting, were thrilled to discover that there was a chance that the mighty British Broadcasting Corporation might record their Christmas concert for a later broadcast.

'One other thing,' Heather said when they seemed to have digested this exciting news. 'With your permission I plan to ask some professional musicians to help us out, lend some weight as it were.'

'You mean real singers, Heather?' asked Mrs Murphy.

Heather pretended to groan and hid her face in her hands. 'Mrs Murphy, you are real singers. Remember? No, I'll sing a solo as I promised, but I thought too that since Gregor and I have a friend who is a real conductor we would ask her to conduct and that would free me to sit with the sopranos.'

'Add a little gravitas,' interrupted Murray Thomson.

'That wasn't how I was thinking, Murray.'

'But your voice will disturb the balance.'

Gregor shot Heather a warning look; she was about to explode. She took a calming breath. 'Good point, but it won't.'

'She's a professional, Murray. Singers do something funny with their voices when they're singing with lesser voices, don't they, Heather?' The contralto had plucked up her courage to speak.

'Colouring, Collette; it's called colouring and I'll demonstrate later. For now how about a look at your new music?'

Most of the choir held the music that Heather handed them as if it were the finest vellum. Heather, as a finale to their concert, was going to have them sing the Amen Chorus from Handel's *Messiah*.

'What about the other musicians? Or is it just this conductor, Heather?'

'Sorry, no. To add variety I hoped to ask a violinist, a wonderfully eloquent player.'

'How exciting.' Several choir members were thrilled, twittering and chattering like nesting birds.

'Oh, I love the violin; heard Yehudi Menuhin in a school hall right here in Edinburgh for sixpence once when we had sixpences.'

'So exciting that she's out of a job like the rest of you, Heather?' Murray was unhappy, it seemed, with the rest of the choir's animation. 'I'm not financing a charity for indigent musicians.'

'No one had asked you for money, and, as it happens, Juliet, the friend I've asked to conduct, has just won an international competition' said Heather triumphantly, 'and will be conducting the London Symphony Orchestra next year.' She tried not to look at Murray as she spoke; for the moment it was enough to have deflated him. 'What do you think, people? If we want Juliet, she's prepared to come in tonight to listen to us.'

The consensus of opinion was that the choir would welcome the input of a genuine conductor, especially since it meant that Heather would sit with the sopranos, at least two of whom knew that they could keep in tune and on key only by being close to her. They listened as she rang Juliet.

'Right, she'll be here in no time.' She did not tell them that Juliet was in a café on the same street. 'Very exciting to think we can sing this, isn't it?' Heather went on, flourishing her copy as Gregor played the orchestral music softly as a background to her voice. Sometimes he deviated and played all four voice parts at the same time and she found herself noting, not for the first time, what a gifted musician he was; she tried to make a mental note to tell him how much he was appreciated. Somehow she had not been properly appreciative of any of her friends lately. 'I wouldn't even consider this if I didn't feel that you are all, each and every one of you, capable of singing it, especially with a recording crew there, but we'll have to work really hard. Okay?' She saw the solemn and, in some singers, excited affirming nods. 'Great. I knew you wouldn't let me, us' – she gestured towards Gregor – 'down. Right. We'll do this as if we were all, are all, professionals; that means that we will sing the difficult parts slowly before we even sing through the whole piece. Musicians often, possibly always, play this way too. Isolate the tricky bits, master them, and then it's a doddle. Willing to try?'

Again there were solemn nods. They had come a long way in a few months; there was not nearly so much questioning of her methods; all except the truly self-opinionated understood that Heather knew best. She did still have a few argumentative doubters, of course, like Murray Thomson, but Heather was beginning to understand that sometimes he argued just because he liked the sound of his own voice, and, although she listened politely, she now rarely paid any attention to him. To give him his due, he seemed perfectly happy with this arrangement; all honour satisfied.

'Singing should never be mechanical,' she continued. 'The phrasing must be there at the beginning, not added on as you would put whipped cream on top of a piece of cake.'

'Only one problem, love,' said the imperturbable Murray. 'The whole thing is difficult so you might as well start at the beginning and continue to the end.' Having had the last word he settled down to work.

*   *   *

Juliet was a success, possibly because she told them that she had not conducted a choir since her final year of elementary school. Perhaps too the aura surrounding the LSO had wafted its way north across the Cheviot Hills and, for a moment, had settled on this little choir.

'Thank you, Juliet.' Heather hardly knew what to say to thank her friend. 'They grew as singers just with you in the room.'

Juliet laughed. She had found the choir extremely amateurish and so anything she said would sound like a criticism. She took refuge in what she knew to be a truth. 'You two have worked so hard with them, Heather. Probably your sitting with the sopranos helped more than anything. What did you think, Gregor?'

He nodded even though they were walking along a street at after ten o'clock. 'Did you notice that she also made a fabulous tenor in the amens?' He nudged Heather laughingly and she moved away crossly.

'I'll do anything to get their performance broadcast.'

The actual performance in the local church went better than anyone, including the choir, although possibly with the exception of Murray Thomson, had envisaged. They had not felt it right to sell tickets but a donation had been requested from those attending and the money collected would be shared equally between the church and a charity.

'Can't help liking old Murray when he does things like this,' said Heather as they stood drinking mulled wine and eating mince pies after the performance. 'And he's asked me to continue in the spring. Up for it, Gregor?' Her face lit up with a joy that they all noticed. 'Here's Peter.'

Her boyfriend's arrival allowed Gregor not to answer. Seeing her euphoric with success and love was hardly conducive to saying, 'Not in a million years.' He would think of a more politically correct answer during the holidays. 'Well, Peter, got a weekly slot for us?'

Peter took him seriously. 'Wouldn't I love to have that power? Thank you all, though. I hope you'll be pleased with the broadcast and with your publicity. We did manage to get two critics in tonight and though they will probably devote their inches to Heather's voice and Hermione's playing . . . oh, and yours, of course, Gregor, they might find something positive to say about the choir. But you do understand we're working on the four professionals, best friends, working with inner city amateurs' angle.'

'God help us all,' said Juliet *sotto voce*.

11

Hermione rang Juliet on Christmas Eve. 'There's a letter for you from the LSO. I've had it a week, sorry.'

Juliet was interested only in the content of the letter. 'My God, open it and read it to me.' She waited, hearing the clear sound of paper being torn, of paper being removed from what was left of the envelope after Hermione had summarily dealt with it. Then silence. Why was she taking so long? 'Hermione, whatever it says, read it to me. I can handle it.'

'If you're sure; you're not going to like this.'

Juliet thanked God that she was not a singer, as she would have ruined her throat for ever with the force of her yell. 'Hermione.'

'Heaven's sake, Juliet, you've destroyed my ear. I was only trying to think of the best way to tell you—'

'What?'

'That your dishy conductor is going in to a hospital for a knee replacement operation in January and so will be unavailable to be your mentor. Wait for it. "After due deliberation and much consultation we have managed to acquire the services of Karel Haken, the brilliant young Czech conductor who, I am sure, needs no introduction." It finishes off with lots of "how wonderful he is" at everything and how lucky you are to be his pupil.'

Oh, please, God, it can't be him. You can't do this to me. I slept with him and he discarded me. Please, God, please. Inside she was whimpering. 'Shit,' she said through gritted teeth. As soon as she had uttered the expletive Juliet looked surreptitiously around the hallway where she was sitting on a carved oak chair hoping that neither of her parents had heard her. 'Swearing – on Christmas Eve, Juliet?' She could see the solemn disappointed faces.

'Very impolite, Juliet,' said Hermione. 'Shall I post it?'

'Please. Oh, blast it, Hermione. This I do not need.'

'He's a jerk, Juliet. Remember.'

That was when Juliet remembered what Karel had said. There had been a note. Why would he lie about something that could be so easily disproved? She would have to talk to her friends; she had to know for sure. 'He came to the final as he promised; he went to a lot of trouble.'

'Juliet, he's attracted to you; why wouldn't he be? You're a lovely woman and you speak his language.'

'Czech?'

'Don't be facetious; conductor-speak. By the way, do you plan to listen to yourself on the radio?'

Juliet thought for a moment, her mind still full of the news of Haken's secondment to the London Symphony Orchestra. 'Conductors don't make a noise unless they impale ghastly tenors with their batons, and I seriously considered that. What a horrid little man. Murray Thomson, I mean. Is he gay, do you think?'

'Because he's horrid or despite it?'

Juliet played with the telephone cord before answering. 'I suppose that was a stupid question. I don't like him; he's odd. He seemed to me to come on both to Heather and to Gregor.'

'Maybe he likes them both; he doesn't seem to have bothered Heather, perhaps because she has eyes only for the luscious Peter. Let's not worry about it, although I don't think she plans to continue with the choir; too many other things up her sleeve.'

Juliet traced the pattern of the hall carpet with her foot as she talked. 'But she was so excited about being asked to continue. Surely she's not leaving those lovely people in the lurch. They were so appreciative of her work and you have to give her enormous credit – it could not have been easy to get a completely inexperienced group of wannabe singers to that level. Gregor's not taking them on, is he?'

'God, no. He only played as a favour to Heather. One of the sopranos baked him biscuits, but apart from her they infuriated him. He's not easy to please, our Gregor.'

'He seemed pleased with that fellow in the chorus at the theatre. Oh God, Hermione, what am I thinking? Forget I said that. Where is he spending Christmas?'

'At the flat. I told him to invite his mother; she can have my room.'

'I didn't even know he had a mother. How awful; all these years and I've never really spoken to him about his family. I thought . . .'

'What? That he'd sprung from the head of Zeus? It's not that Gregor's ashamed of his mother: she's ashamed of him; but one day—' She stopped. 'Juliet, do you think he's told her he's playing the piano on a Christmas programme?'

'Best mind our own business, Hermione. Is there really time to get the letter to me before New Year?'

'Shouldn't think so but I'm willing to try. I'm awfully sorry.'

'It's not a problem. You've given me the ghastly news; I can wait to read it.' She thought for a second. 'Be an angel and fax it. Have a super Christmas and love to Chloé and Sebastian. I'll see you in Edinburgh – when?'

'I'll have escaped by the 30th. It's our last Hogmanay together. Let's make it fabulous.' She paused for a moment. 'Juliet, what did you mean about Gregor and the fellow in the chorus?'

'Nothing. It was nothing, just glad that Gregor had made a friend. He's always so alone.'

Juliet woke early the morning after her conversation with Hermione. She was thrillingly aware that it was Christmas Day and that every Christmas Day in her twenty-five years had been magical. Up early, breakfast in front of the Christmas tree, a church service with all her favourite carols, perhaps a walk in the snow. Juliet laughed. When did we last have snow at Christmas? I'm twenty-five and I'm making up nostalgic Christmas-card Christmases. The house around her slept on, still, hushed, but it was not the usual peace of a house where everyone slumbered on quietly, but more that utter quiet that in childhood had augured the first winter snowfall. Perhaps the world outside her bedroom window was dressed in white. Juliet stretched her legs, straightening her toes, trying to find a cool spot on her linen sheet. That habit too she had brought from childhood. She would find a chilly place, allow her foot to grow colder, just for the sensual pleasure of pulling it back into lovely, comfortable and comforting warmth. This morning the quality of her duvet and the efficiency of a modern central heating system defeated her. She laughed again. 'Masochist. Now will you brave the dawn to see if there is snow?'

The blue-grey world outside showed only traces of a heavy frost but the sky felt heavy, as if, in just a moment, hosts of snowflakes would come drifting down to line the leafless branches and to fill the hole in the trunk of the thick old sycamore whose roots were destroying the boundary wall. Juliet felt a childlike stirring of anticipation but her feet, now chilly on the polished wood floor, reminded her that it was not yet six and that she should return to bed. She would lie for a time, listening to the soft cooing of the pigeons that were already perched on the guttering around the roof above her bedroom window – poor pigeons, were they cold on Christmas morning? – and then surprise her parents with tea in bed.

She had tried to dismiss the contents of Hermione's call from her mind; already she had stared at the fragile fax paper so much that the words had begun to blur as she read them. She vowed to dismiss Karel Haken from her mind but his words haunted her and she had to try to discover the absolute truth before she went down to London. With the way things stood it would be virtually impossible to work not only creatively but naturally with him and, in the privacy of her little down-filled cocoon, she admitted that she really wanted to find out that he had told her the truth. Was it possible that he had indeed left a note or was it merely that she wanted to believe he had? Whatever had happened to her on that glorious summer night had marked her, stayed with her, echoed in the silence of this perfect Christmas morning. She had to be rid of him. As soon as Christmas was over and she had returned to Edinburgh, she would ask her flatmates if any one of them remembered seeing a note. She wished she had spoken to them when she first returned in triumph, for it had become more and more difficult to get them together in the same room.

Although they had made initial plans for New Year's Eve the final details were bound to need a war council.

And I'll talk to them then, before we even begin to discuss Hogmanay, or I'll never get a chance to ask.

Juliet rolled over and buried her head in her pillow. She groaned. If only I didn't feel that my entire life depends on what I find out. But she refused to wonder if she was worrying more about her private than about her public life. She routed Karel out of her head, got out of bed, took a deep breath, pulled on her rather tired old college dressing gown – that would have to go, not nearly grand enough for a fully fledged conductor – and went to make surprise tea for her parents.

Juliet's mother was not happy that her daughter intended to go back into Edinburgh before New Year's Eve. 'Darling, I want to take you shopping for clothes. After-Christmas sales? Great bargains?'

Juliet put the last breakfast cup into the dishwasher as if it were made of the finest porcelain and then slowly she straightened up. She had thought this conversation might happen and had hoped to avoid it. 'Mum, I want to hit the Edinburgh sales: more choice. Why don't you join us one day? You, Hermione, me?'

Lesley was in a dilemma. That her daughter had a friend whose mother was an Honourable was a source of continuing delight, that Hermione's parents deigned occasionally to invite Juliet's parents to dinner or drinks was a pleasure that had never diminished with familiarity, but she pushed all that aside. Her daughter was going out into the big, wide world and she could not bear it. 'I love dear Hermione, Juliet; you know that. But is it wrong for me to want to spend some quality time with my only child? It's the beginning of your professional life, darling, and you won't belong to me any more. Couldn't we have a day by ourselves?'

Juliet sighed and sighed again as she thought of the amount of sighing she had done lately. Her mother was becoming even clingier as the day of her daughter's leaving for London became ever closer. Even though she had been away from the family home in Dundee almost permanently for the past ten years and knew that her mother should be quite used to her absences, she understood the older woman's anxiety. That did not make the situation easier. 'Mum, we've had a wonderful Christmas, more than a week *en famille*, and hours of mother-daughter quality time but now I want to spend Hogmanay with my friends. It's Edinburgh, street parties, lots of fun and it will be my last time with my chums.'

Lesley suddenly looked crumpled. 'Friends are always so much more important than mere mothers.'

Juliet hardly knew whether to laugh or cry. She decided to do neither. 'I won't dignify that, Mum. Besides, I need some new clothes and there will be great sales at the beginning of January. I'd love it if you joined us for that. Let's have a lovely girlie lunch at Harvey Nicks and you could help me choose some eveningwear.' She did not want her mother's advice, which she had stopped taking, in so far as clothes were concerned, several years before, and she could see battles ahead. Both her mother and Hermione had very definite views which they aired at the slightest opportunity and Juliet felt that she was perfectly capable of choosing the correct clothes for her lifestyle all by herself. Mind you – she thought again of her mystery dress – she would never have tried that gown on in a shop, and not only because she was quite sure she could never have afforded it. A mystery man knew what suited her better than she knew herself. She felt a tingling all over her body and hoped her mother could see no change. She concentrated on the dress – shubette, whatever that was; man-made surely – how beautifully it hung and how cleverly cut and tantalising the handkerchief hem was. She sighed again but this time at a lovely memory and wondered when or if she would ever know which wonderful man had bought the dress. Who was he and why had he not come forward to take credit? He had to be wonderful, since if he were not, by this time surely he would have asked for some kind of payment. No, this knight in shining armour was truly altruistic, a word that could not possibly be used to describe her mother.

The week had been pleasant but several times Juliet had caught herself looking at her own family as if she were an outsider and it had seemed that sometimes she walked on eggs, tentatively, unnaturally, almost as if she were acting a part. She was the dutiful daughter and she had learned her script faultlessly but there always seemed to be something missing in the relationship. Her father had never laughed at her errors of judgement as Hermione's did. She tried to remember that lovely moment after the competition when her father had bought the champagne; how wonderful she had felt then. She sat down beside her mother on the sofa.

'Mum, I love you. You're my mother and will always be my mother. Isn't that enough? I have several friends; I will make even more as I grow older but you're the only mother I will ever have. Now, I'm going in to have a party with Hermione and the others – possibly the last Hogmanay we will have together – and if you want to shop with me do come in for a day. Hermione loves seeing you.'

Gregor did not; in fact he wasted very little energy at all thinking about Mrs Crawford. He knew she did not consider him good enough to be her daughter's friend and he, in turn, considered her not nearly good enough to be Juliet's mother. To him, Juliet was another such as he, a changeling who had somehow been left in a home where she could not possibly be understood. Heather, on the other hand, had seen a marked improvement in relations with Juliet's mother as she became a better and better singer, but, like Gregor, she did not judge Juliet by her mother's character flaws; she would not join the shopping expedition simply because she had far better things to do.

'I'll think about it,' Lesley said to her daughter, 'but you know I hate driving in snow.'

'It isn't snowing and if it does, take the train.'

'You know I hate trains.'

Dr Crawford stopped at the door of the very lovely French provincial kitchen. 'Will we see you before you head south, Juliet?'

'I don't think so, Dad.' Juliet went to him and they hugged.

'Ring us when you surface on New Year's Day and if you're out at a party, keep an eye on your drinks.'

'Sure, Dad, we'll probably just walk up the Mound to see the fireworks and then party at the flat. We'll be fine.'

'Say hello to everyone for me.' And he was gone but she felt warm and cherished. Things were getting better.

Since it was an absolutely beastly day with a cold wind roaring around Edinburgh looking for trouble, she was delighted to see Gregor and Hermione at the station to meet her. She greeted them warmly. Why was it that hugging friends was sometimes so much easier than hugging parents?

'I told Dad we were going out to see the fireworks; hope it warms up a bit.'

Hermione and Gregor hooted.

'What a tender flower it's become since it got an almost real job,' teased Hermione. 'Wear a vest.'

Juliet smiled. Some things – and people – never change. Gregor proved that by the enticing smell that was emanating from the kitchen when they arrived.

'I'm doing a nice roast for supper.'

'Mercy, Gregor, we have all eaten too much over Christmas. Let's have a salad.'

'Nonsense,' argued Gregor. 'We are fast losing all our old traditions, all our old recipes. British food is the best in the world.'

'Is that why you have pasta six days out of seven, you old hypocrite?' Hermione interrupted.

He ignored her. 'This halcyon existence we are living will be over in the blink of an eye; so together we will be traditional. We will prepare and eat British food and then we will make music.'

'Does it have to be English too?' asked Heather, who was preparing a French song cycle that she would be singing with the chorus at Easter.

'Very funny. Now, Juliet, your face is tripping you. You should be fairly exuding *joie de vivre*. Let us charge our glasses—'

'For the nineteenth time,' interrupted Hermione.

'And then Juliet will tell all.'

Juliet looked at their well-loved faces. How she would miss them, even if she would not miss Yorkshire pudding and perfect roast potatoes. 'I think I may have misjudged Karel Haken.' She had meant to couch it less aggressively but there, she had stated it quite baldly.

Heather smiled at her over the rim of her wine glass. 'Don't you mean you hope you have misjudged him?'

Hermione and Gregor looked at her in surprise. 'Aren't we catty? Just because you seem to have found the love of your life doesn't mean the rest of us are aching to jump into bed,' said Hermione.

Heather blushed furiously and began to protest and Juliet stood up. 'We're behaving like ten-year-olds. Do you want to hear my concerns or not?'

All three nodded and put their knives and forks down.

'For heaven's sake eat and don't spoil this lovely meal. It's just that Karel came to my hotel room the morning after the competition. The day before I had bumped into him in the corridors at the Barbican and I was beastly to him and he wanted to straighten it out.'

'Wonderful,' said Hermione. 'I should jolly well hope you were beastly to him. Don't be sorry for him, Juliet. He behaved badly.'

'He said he left a note.'

The words dropped into the pool of expectation around the table and disappeared and then they all spoke at once.

'What a liar.'

'You looked everywhere for a note.'

'Some men will say anything.'

Juliet let them speak until they had exhausted themselves. 'The more I think about it and his face when I yelled at him, the more I believe him.'

'Perhaps he's practised at being poor little misunderstood man,' suggested Heather. 'Stock in trade as it were.'

'No, I think I would know when someone was lying.'

'I turned the place upside down, Juliet. I was just going to bed –

mea culpa, mea culpa – when he left.' Her already pale face became even whiter and she put her hand to her mouth as if to stifle a cry.

'Why, Hermione? Why didn't you ask on the day? I can't really remember but we did hear him leave, or did we hear him in the shower?'

'I heard him in the shower,' said Juliet. She looked at Gregor's face. 'I didn't?'

'I don't think he showered, Juliet. Hermione was out with one of her toads and we met in the street: almost three. I tidied up, put the glasses away when I made Hermione some tea. We chatted for ages – she always gets a second wind in the wee small hours – and then I had a shower – scene shifting, dirty work. Apart from Hermione wittering on about her toad and how God-awful he was, the flat was quiet; we didn't even know if you others were back. No one checked.'

'Witter, witter, witter. That's what you said, Gregor.' Hermione looked as if she were about to cry. 'Witter, witter, witter.'

Juliet looked from one to the other and to Heather who obviously had no idea what was going on. 'And? Hermione, tell me.'

'Oh, God, Juliet, when Gregor went to have a shower he asked me to write a note for the milkman.'

Juliet was almost sure that she knew what she was about to hear. 'And?'

Hermione started to cry and Juliet went to her and put her arms around her. Heather said nothing but looked on with mild curiosity and Gregor turned his back on all the emotion. 'Tell me. You wrote the note, didn't you?'

'Yes, milk and apricot yoghurts, your favourite. Oh God, oh God, how could I have been so stupid?'

'Tell me.'

Hermione gently disengaged herself from Juliet's arms and stood up. 'I forgot. I meant to do it right away but I was the teeniest bit squiffy and I forgot. Later something woke me, the door possibly – I am closest to the front door – and I remembered. I didn't want to let Gregor down – he doesn't often ask me to do anything – and so I got up. The kitchen was fanatically neat, no old envelopes. Oh, Juliet, there was a piece of paper – a sheet folded over and' – she thought frantically – 'there might have been a name on it. It was on the lamp table beside the sofa in the living room. There was writing on one side. It never occurred to me, oh, please believe me.'

Gently Juliet put her hands on either side of Hermione's face. 'You're as blind as a bat without your glasses. You didn't see my name, anything at all?'

'I never thought for a nanosecond that it was a note. I never thought.'

Several emotions went rampaging through Juliet: anger, frustration, joy, misery. He had left a note. What had it said? Had he wanted to see her again? Did he ask her to ring him, email? Had he said, 'It was great but there's no future?' She wanted to howl like a banshee but here was Hermione, her dearest friend, looking so miserable, Hermione who gave so much joy in so many ways. She took a deep cleansing breath. 'Just as well I rarely see the milkman. Cheer up, old chum. Now I can speak to him. We'll sort it out.'

But how?

By seven o'clock on New Year's Eve, the flat was full of the smell of roasting venison, vegetarian stuffed peppers, bread baking, vanilla candles, and the myriad scents of holly, moss, ivy and whatever other greenery Gregor and Hermione had found on their raid of friends' gardens and allotments and then fashioned into arrangements that would have cost a fortune in any reputable florist's. For once the music was not supplied by one or other of the friends although Heather's lovely voice occasionally sang along with the choir from King's College. Apart from the dining room where the several electric lights were all blazing, the lighting was subdued, but the armies of candles that marched along the mantels and window ledges bravely fought and won the battle with the encroaching darkness. The eight-foot-high Christmas tree was a symphony in silver and green, decorated as a surprise by Gregor, and its dozens of tiny silver lights twinkled like stars in a dark sky.

Mrs McDermott sat in front of it, her first glass of champagne in her hand, and wondered.

'You're a good boy, Gregor,' she said, 'and one day you'll get your reward.'

'Thanks, Mrs McD, I'm glad you like it.'

'Oh, I didn't mean the tree, dear, which is lovely but all Christmas trees are, aren't they?' She sipped her drink and sat quietly, her eyes still gazing at the tree, seeing who knows what. She was not left in peace for long because all the flatmates and the guests joined her and if the tree had reminded her of happier or possibly sadder times, she soon seemed to forget as she joined in with the others.

Juliet looked around the room as they ate and drank and laughed, as the crackers were shared and the funny hats worn and silly pictures taken that would be treasured for ever. 'I wish it could be like this always,' she said to Hermione.

'Well, it will be, old chum. We'll remember it but it has to change, Juliet. Where will we all be at this time next year? Promise to ring me.'

'And me,' said Gregor. 'And you, Mrs McD, will we ring you too next Hogmanay?'

Mrs McDermott was a little tipsy and she almost leered at him. 'If you can, dear boy. If you can.'

'It's time to go,' said Hermione, 'if we want to be on Princes Street by midnight; who thinks that together we can fight our way up the Mound?'

There was a raucous shout from the flatmates that Hermione assumed was affirmative. 'We're off to see the fireworks, Mrs McD. Have fun with the telly – and the champagne, you naughty girl.'

On the street the flatmates and their visitors were caught up in the general euphoria of a city in party mood. Revellers, some of them already well on the way to inebriation, called to them or even attempted to join them as they walked four abreast towards Princes Street. It took much longer than they had anticipated, so densely packed were the roads and pavements; the happy crowd was of every age and, it seemed, from every country.

'Please, you take my picture for my mother?'

They lost track of the number of times some youngster pressed a camera into their hands with the same smiling request.

'I love this,' yelled Hermione as they posed several young tourists so as to have the best possible view of the castle in the picture, 'but we'll never get up the Mound at this rate. Did you hear that; there are at least seven stages with top acts. Super fun. Come along.'

'You're too wee to fight crowds,' said Gregor. 'The crowd coming down the Mound will sweep you along if they don't step on you. Let's check out everything first.'

'He's heard reggae.' Hermione laughed. 'Please God we can't get near or we'll be stuck there all night.'

The joy of fireworks is that they burst in the air and so, no matter where they stood, they would get a good view. Music was everywhere; there were solitary musicians on the street – for this night only, a pedestrian precinct – there were pop bands and singers in the gardens, and some enterprising fiddlers had even got themselves on to the giant Ferris wheels. Someone was playing a penny whistle and Heather began to sing along and the others joined in. A crowd gathered as Heather's lovely voice rose effortlessly over the cacophony around them and then someone asked her to sing something in French. She stood for a second looking quite stunned and then, with a clear, heartbreakingly beautiful voice, she began.

Her three friends stood watching her and saw that tears were streaming down her lovely face as she finished. *Chagrin d'amour dure toute la vie.* The pain of love lasts for a lifetime.

'Really lovely, Heather,' said Gregor. 'Is that in your French song cycle?'

'Such a weepie, isn't it?' said Heather as she blew her nose. 'Gets them going every time.' There was no time for her to say anything else as people began to turn towards the gardens in order to see the fireworks.

'Damn, the screen's failed at this end of the street,' groaned Hermione. 'What time is it? I don't want to miss it; Juliet?'

'That was lovely, Heather,' said Juliet, who was wondering if

Heather had really been feeling for herself the sentiment of the song. She dismissed it. Peter had almost moved into the flat, had he not? 'Stop panicking, Hermione. Quick, hold hands everyone. Three, two, one,' she yelled with the crowd around them. 'Happy New Year.'

The ring tones of her mobile phone woke her early on New Year's Day. Juliet groped on the bedside table and then remembered that she was not in her own bed.

'Answer the bleep-bleep thing,' came muffled tones from under the duvet.

Frantically Juliet reached under the pillow. 'Dash it, Hermione, lift your head.' She rolled her now unresponsive bedmate over and recovered the phone, looking at the little clock on her radio at the same time. Eight o'clock on New Year's morning. What philistine was ringing her? 'Hello.'

'Juliet?' The voice, even though it was slightly nervous, was unmistakable.

'Karel?' She sat up quickly.

'It is the time to wish the Happy New Year, no?'

Where was he? Prague, Heidelberg, Malta? Had someone not told her that he might conduct the young Maltese tenor, Joseph Calleja, in recital at the little theatre in Valletta? Not that she was keeping track. Such things were everyday chatter in the music world, who was where and doing what. 'Happy New Year, Maestro.'

They spoke together across the wires. 'Karel, I wanted . . .' 'Juliet, I think I . . .' 'Sorry, you first . . .' Both together again.

'Where are you?'

'Vienna. I wanted all my life to attend the New Year concert in the Golden Hall, and this year I am here. And you, what do you do today? You are with your family?'

If she were with her family she would be watching the New Year concert from Vienna's exquisite golden concert hall – but not so early. 'Sort of. I'm in Edinburgh.' She was stupidly nervous. 'Karel, it's so good of you to ring me. I owe you an apology.'

Hermione's note to the milkman had to have been written on his note. 'Karel.' She spoke quickly, anxious to get it all out. 'I never saw your note. When you were here with me. I never saw it. A friend thinks she used a piece of paper that was on a table to write a note to the milkman. You did leave it in the living room?'

'The milkman has it?' The voice was redolent with scepticism.

'I think so. Karel, it was an accident; my flatmate . . .' She looked down at the small lump under the covers that was Hermione. 'She wouldn't hurt a fly so it wasn't done on purpose but she's blind as a bat without her glasses.' She smiled. He could think what he liked: it was the truth.

'How stupid, not you, Juliet, or your friend, but me. I was leaving and you were asleep. I needed to say something or maybe call from the airport and I wrote quickly. As I put it under the lamp I knew I should take it in your room but I had closed the door and you were asleep.' He laughed, a brittle, sad, not at all merry laugh. 'I wanted to wake you but . . .'

He stopped and she listened for a moment. 'Karel, Maestro? Are you still there?'

'I don't think too many milkmen have notes from me; I sure hope not.'

'What did it say?'

What should he say? She had not seen it and so he could say anything, but he remembered her on the night of the final: she had been exultant, mesmerising, a beautiful, talented woman exactly where she should be. He could not now tell her what being with her had meant to him. 'Oh, nothing too important,' he said lightly. 'It was a nice day; maybe we could do it again sometime, that sort of thing. And here we are, going to work one with the other, right? A great chance for you, Juliet, and nothing should interfere. That's what you want too, yes?'

'Of course, Karel.' She was getting the brush-off, nicely but still that was the message. What a nice way to start the year. 'Thanks for calling. I hope you enjoy the concert. I usually watch it. Goodbye.'

She pressed the disconnect button just as he spoke and quickly pressed it again but he was gone and so she could not find out if she had actually heard him say, 'I wish you were here.'

'Happy New Year.'

Juliet looked at Hermione emerging. Her purple hair looked wilder than ever; she had not taken out any of her studs and her face was hot and red. Juliet laughed. 'Right this minute, old chum, I can't imagine anyone I'd rather be waking up with.'

'I'm not going to share the sentiment. My wish list is legendary. Leonardo di Caprio, Brad Pitt . . .'

'Good heavens,' said Juliet as she got out of the bed. 'Pretty boys. Grow up. I'm off to make the first coffee of the year.'

'Make enough to sober up Mrs McD. I hope she hasn't been sick in your bed.'

'Thanks for the thought,' said Juliet as she pulled on her dressing gown.

When the coffee was perking and its wonderful aroma was permeating the apartment she went into the living room to open the windows to air the room. To her surprise they were already open and the room was quite chilly. She closed them and it was then that she remembered that Gregor, who had given up his bed to one of Heather's friends, was supposed to be sleeping in there. She looked around almost as if she expected to find him on the floor but he was not there and so she returned to the kitchen where Hermione joined her.

'Gregor's up already. Wonder where he went.'

'No idea.'

'Want to tell me about the phone call?'

Juliet poured herself more coffee and then stood up. 'Not important. You heard me say Karel before you submerged? He did leave a note but it sounds as if it was a brush-off. Not nasty – just, let's take it easy. And now that we're working together we should put work first. Sounds good to me. Now, I'm off to get dressed.'

She had just turned off the shower when a terrified shriek rang out. Hauling on her dressing gown and grabbing a towel she hurried out, wrapping the towel around her wet hair as she did

146

so. Heather's young cousin, Fiona, was sobbing in a chair while a bemused Hermione looked at her, taking in the pink bunny slippers and the pyjamas over which Winnie the Pooh clambered. 'Am I drunk or is she wearing what I think she's wearing?'

'Stop that noise at once,' said Juliet sharply, and immediately Fiona was quiet. 'Now calm down and tell us what happened.'

Fiona tried but sank into her seat snuffling and sobbing. Juliet and Hermione looked at each other and laughed. Whatever had frightened her could not possibly be too serious.

'Sorry, Fiona,' said Hermione, 'but that yell was enough to wake the dead and no one in this flat – but us – heard it.'

'A man,' sobbed Fiona. 'I've slept with a man.'

'Haven't we all, darling,' murmured Hermione, ignoring Juliet's glare.

Juliet wondered if the girl was having some sort of crisis of conscience to start the New Year as she keened on, 'I'm ruined, I'm ruined.'

'Let me get you some coffee, Fiona, and your dressing gown. It's too cold for just pyjamas.'

'No matter how cute the bunnies are.' Hermione could not take the situation seriously.

Juliet hissed, 'Behave,' and hurried off to Heather's bedroom where Heather was still sound asleep. So too was Gregor. She looked down at them for a moment, picked up the first dressing gown she saw and went back to the kitchen where Fiona was sobbing quietly into the mug of coffee that Hermione had brought her.

'Fiona, are you worried because you slept with a man last night?'

The girl sobbed afresh and nodded. 'I promised, I promised, and now I'm ruined.'

'No, you're not. Calm down. Gregor doesn't count.'

Fiona looked at her. 'But he's a man.'

Juliet turned to Hermione, who had said nothing, for help. 'I'm not about to teach this child the facts of life and you're being no help. Fiona, Gregor hasn't hurt you.' She turned back to Hermione. 'Did you open all the windows to air the living room last night?'

Hermione frowned. 'I have no idea but I could have. I hate the stale smell of wine and food, probably did it automatically. Why?'

'It must have been freezing in there so very sensibly poor old Gregor went looking for a source of warmth. From where he's lying, snoring like all get out, by the way, he must have slipped in between them from the bottom. That way neither of them could push him out. Very sensible manoeuvre and very clever for someone who had as much to drink as he had last night.'

'But why didn't he come in to us? He knows us.'

'Then that's probably why he didn't. For God's sake, will you reassure this girl that her virtue is intact before I slap her? Put her in your bed and let her sleep it off. We still have to deal with Mrs McD.'

'Sorry, Juliet. You're right. Come on, Fiona, maybe you had a touch too much of the grape last night. Have a nice nap in my bed; you'll feel lots better when you wake up. Juliet's father wanted her to be a doctor. Did Heather tell you that? Just as well she's not; absolutely no bedside manner.'

Juliet looked after them. How like Hermione to get the last word. She was chilled, although she was now dry, and wanted to get dressed. She found Mrs McDermott sitting on the edge of her bed, pulling on her stockings.

'Who screamed?'

'It was nothing, Mrs McD, a misunderstanding. Would you like some coffee?'

'I've taken up enough of your time, Juliet, besides having you give up your bed for me. I was perfectly able to go back to my own flat, you know.'

'I know but we were all a bit tiddly last night.'

The old lady straightened up. 'You're a good girl, Juliet.' She took Juliet's hands and held them in a very tight grip, so tight that Juliet winced as her fingers were crushed together. 'Happy New Year, my dear; it's going to be a wonderful year for all of you. Don't forget us altogether when you go off to London.'

'I won't. I'll come back often.'

Mrs McDermott released her hands but she continued to look at

Juliet very seriously. 'That's what you think now and you mean it. But circumstance has a habit of getting in the way. For circumstance exchange job, opportunity, men.'

'Least of my problems. Tell you what. I'll send you a postcard every now and then. Let me make you some breakfast.'

'I'm still enjoying my venison. Better get dressed before you catch a chill, Juliet. I'll let myself out.'

Juliet got dressed and went back to the kitchen. She needed more coffee. Hermione was standing by the sink.

'Be an angel and get down a mug or two, if you want some; that is, if lifting your arms over your head won't cause any undue loss of blood to the brain.'

Hermione reached up. 'Were I completely sober I would be able to tell if what you have just said makes any sense.' She turned to find the mugs but not before she had stuck her tongue out, awarding Juliet with a view of her stud.

'Yuck. Aren't you supposed to take that thing out at night?'

'Couldn't find my tongue last night, or was it the wee small hours?'

'You found your mouth with a champagne glass often enough.' Juliet shovelled sugar into the mug she handed her friend.

'That's automatic,' said Hermione as she sipped the strong, too sweet coffee. 'Finding one's tongue on the other hand requires minute motor skills and delicate fingering.'

'How about a bacon sandwich?'

'Dear God, Juliet Crawford, you're supposed to be my best friend; you swore in blood.'

'I am. Every soldier I have ever dated, and their number is legendary,' Juliet exaggerated, 'assured me that bacon sandwiches the morning after the night before soak it all up.'

'I don't have the constitution of a bloody great grenadier.'

'You do quite well actually, considering your size.' Juliet had begun to prepare breakfast but stopped, spatula in hand, and began to laugh. When she was calm she wiped her eyes and moved some bacon slices in the pan. 'Had you ever in your wildest imaginings conjured up a New Year's morning like this?'

12

A new year. Apart from her first real job, the official beginning of a career that she hoped would take her, not only to every great concert house in the world, but to the very top of her profession, the coming months would bring her a new home, new acquaintances, some of whom might become friends, and new experiences. There would be sadness – after all, she was saying goodbye to her closest friends – but there would be joy too, the joy that was obtained by doing something to the best of one's ability. Thanks to their telephone conversation on New Year's morning she knew where she stood with Karel Haken; they would have a superb working relationship since they had laid to rest any ghosts that might still be hanging around unwanted like mist on Scottish hills. She felt free, energised, excited. Now was the time to get ready. In less than two weeks she had to be in London – at least they had found a flat for her – and all ends in Scotland must be tied up first. Today the end to be tied was replenishing her wardrobe, a bore but necessary.

Hermione was prepared, even anxious, to trawl the department stores with her. Unlike Juliet she loved shopping even if it was for someone else.

'Is your mum coming in, Juliet?'

'No, thank God. It's too cold. Two of you telling me what and what not to wear is one too many.'

'Wouldn't be a problem, darling. I'm much more forceful than your mama and besides, all I need to say is, "Oh, Juliet, Mummy would adore you in this," and she would capitulate.'

'Are you being nasty?'

'A tiny bit. I love your mama, Juliet, but she is funny.'

'Criticism not allowed,' said Juliet in the voice that meant, 'This far and no farther.'

'Sorry. She makes the best raspberry jam in the entire world.'

'I know. Now I'd best make a list so that we don't run round in too many circles.'

'You're shopping with your auntie, Juliet; this is a military campaign, *mon ange*.' Hermione looked around to make sure that she had everything she needed; all Juliet would need was a chequebook and a credit card. 'By the way, where did Heather sleep last night?'

'I don't care: none of our business. Come on, I need to get busy.'

'Right. What will you wear during the day, rehearsing, talks with orchestra members, board members, conductors?'

'I'll rehearse in jeans and shirts; everyone does.'

'And you'll make creative decisions about what to wear on the podium. Unlike the men who can wear the same old suit till it falls off, you can't wear the same gown every time even though it's gorgeous.'

'As far as I know I won't be doing any important conducting; what I have is fine.'

'Then let's find something fabulous for your private life. Come along, Harvey Nicks and Jenners, here we come.'

The designer room at Jenners lovely department store invites the shopper in with its plush carpeting, its pale walls, and the light that pours in from the many tall windows. Hermione began to go along the racks of designer suits, all on sale. 'Interviews? How do you want the media to see you?'

'If they interview me when I'm working they'll find me in jeans or in evening dress – and no, I still haven't decided about that. Off duty, something smart, elegant, classic.'

'God, Juliet, you sound exactly like my mother talking to her dressmaker. You're twenty-five years old; you may have an old man's job but you needn't look like Derby's idea of Joan. We want hip, modern, boho. Turn the establishment on its ear. You may be the first and last female conductor of a great orchestra before the whole thing is replaced by a synthesiser . . .'

Juliet, who had been in a buoyant mood, stopped, her euphoric bubble bursting around her. 'Don't even joke about that.'

'It isn't a joke. You've been reading so many scores lately that you haven't had time to listen to debates on Radio 3. It was pointed out that many American orchestras are in debt; British ones are being moth-balled. Debate. Is an orchestra merely a romantic anachronism existing solely to provide employment for talented musicians?'

Juliet held up for inspection a short-skirted suit in lime green. 'You are kidding me? I don't have enough problems with gainful employment? Now you tell me that there won't be an orchestra for me to conduct in what . . . ten years' time, twenty, or is it even less than that?'

Hermione took the suit. 'Lime green is too last year. This now?'

'That's a ten,' Juliet pointed out as she looked at the label on a very pretty pale pink suit with a faux fur collar on the jacket.

'And so are you. Trust me, miss, I was an eight, I am an eight and, God and chocolate willing, I will always be an eight: you are a ten. It's all in the cut, Juliet. Numbers are merely a guide.'

'My boobs will never be covered by that jacket. I hate accentuating them.'

'They're your finest asset, apart from your legs and, by the way, your conducting skills. Now, I'm going along with not highlighting them when you're on the podium – don't want elderly wind instruments to fall over – but otherwise you have to make the best of everything you have.'

'I have to be a little circumspect at the beginning, Hermione; I nearly blew getting the job. I want to keep it.'

'Fine, but you had decided you were making a stand immediately. This is me, a very feminine woman who just happens to be a brilliant conductor. How do you like them apples, boys?'

'I'll try the suit.'

In less than an hour Juliet found herself standing in a dressing room surrounded by lovely clothes that Hermione had persuaded her to buy. She looked at herself from all angles in the strategically placed mirrors and was not sure that she liked what she saw. Hermione and two sales assistants stood looking at her.

'You looked wonderful, miss. You've no idea how lucky you are to have your own personal stylist with you.'

Juliet glared at her 'personal stylist' who grinned back at her.

'She looks fab, doesn't she, ladies? Big problem with some of my clients; they just do not have a realistic picture of themselves.'

Juliet examined herself in the mirror as the sales assistants nodded solemnly. On her head was a Cossack-style cap into which all her hair had been tucked; she was wearing a long, loose black tunic over black trousers which were in turn tucked into her own long leather boots. A wide leather belt was fastened not around her waist but much lower across her hips, so that the bottom of the tunic stuck out like a short frill. Cross-laces kept the belt fastened exactly the width of her hips, and over the tunic she had slipped on a soft cashmere cardigan in raspberry. The right and left fronts of the cardigan had not been buttoned but were tied in a loose knot. 'I look like the missing extra from *Dr Zhivago*.'

'But fab,' said Hermione. 'What a pity there isn't a perfume to go with them – Dr Zhivago, sensuous but sensitive.' She turned to the assistants, who obviously thought her quite wonderful, and smiled. 'She'll take them all, ladies, and do you happen to have that cardie in green? Mix and match, Juliet. Your flat sounds as if there's scarcely enough closet space for two evening gowns and a winter coat – did we look at coats? – and so you have to have clever clothes.'

'Aqua,' put in the assistant, proffering a cardigan.

'Great, an entirely different look for – wow – twenty-nine pounds ninety-five. Wasn't that simple? Now, Juliet, let's pay the bills – the pink suit is a good-luck pressie from Daddy – and then I'm not moving another step unless it's towards the restaurant. Let me treat you to coffee and a ridiculously fattening cake.'

'No cake; we ate too much over the holidays. Besides, one ounce and the belt won't fasten. Have you any idea how many times you have uttered the words "let me treat you" in the past few months?

I'll buy and you may have cake. I'm only going to be gone a few months and I'll come home as often as possible.'

Hermione stopped still in front of a rack of seriously reduced designer dresses but she was uninterested in the clothes. She was, for once, quite serious. 'No, darling, you won't. This is the end. Your first contract. I'm thrilled but it will be followed by another, perhaps abroad, Prague, Heidelberg, Boston even; that's what you want, isn't it, to be the first woman in the history of conducting to become music director at one of the great American symphony orchestras.'

'I'm prepared to work a few years first,' said Juliet dryly.

'And I'm not hanging around either. This has got to be my year. Heather will certainly spread her wings too. We have to face facts.'

'You haven't mentioned Gregor. Is 2005 going to be the year for him too?'

Juliet was laughing and then she saw that Hermione was not sharing her humour. In fact Juliet could almost swear that there were tears in Hermione's eyes. She finished writing the cheque, winced a little as she did so, and handed it to the cashier. 'Hermione, what's wrong? Is Gregor all right?'

'Damn it, I suppose I'll have to tell you, talk to you. Let's get that cake and, believe me, you'll need the energy provided by large layers of chocolate.' She waited until Juliet had been thanked profusely and had picked up all her bags, and then, heavily laden, she headed as quickly as the surging crowds would allow her towards the lifts. Juliet, thoroughly alarmed, hurried after her.

'Hermione, tell me.'

'Not here.'

She was so unlike her usual sunny self that Juliet forbore to argue and stood silently while they waited for the lift, and she remained quiet while the ancient machine spirited them upstairs. Only when they were sitting with coffee did Hermione return to Gregor.

'You remember when Heather's silly little cousin was here?'

Juliet nodded.

'You remember that Gregor very cleverly slipped in between them in Heather's bed to keep warm, poor lamb?'

'Of course I remember. What are you trying to say, Hermione?'

'You remember we laughed at that silly mummy's baby when she howled that she'd slept with a man and you said it was only Gregor, and he didn't count, an innocuous fairly funny remark, I thought. You only meant that Gregor wouldn't assault anyone, that he was merely finding a reliable source of heat.'

'Hermione, just tell me.'

'He thinks he might be gay.'

Juliet almost dropped her cup. 'We've known Gregor for four years; we've been living together for two years. He dates you and Heather. He's rather keen on you.'

'No, he isn't. He adores you but he says he realises that that – sorry – is probably because even when we were first together, he recognised your genius. Yes, he thinks you're a genius, the one of the four marked by the gods. And he doesn't date Heather or me. He might see a film with us or go to a dance or a party but we don't date and we never ever have any physical contact.'

'Yes, you do. He's always wrapped around you.'

'Because I'm his friend, Juliet, his big sister, his port in the storm. He has never once made any advances and although I sometimes thought it a little odd it never occurred to me that he's like that with every female. He really, really loves us, you and me and Heather but we don't . . . light any sparks.'

'But that's because he's so used to us.'

'I considered that, even thought he might be being noble and, yes, he was unused to us when we all moved in together and, at first, I thought he was quite keen on Heather. She's so unlike you and me.'

'Unlike as in we're pushy and demanding and she's girlie and soft and . . .'

'Exactly, and the problem is, the poor lamb has been worried about it for years and hasn't known what to do.'

'When did he talk to you?'

'Yesterday. It must have taken some courage.'

'What brought it on or out? Has he met someone who interests him, excites him, someone at the theatre?'

Hermione cut off a corner of her cake and then squashed it flat. 'Very satisfying,' she said and then added, 'I don't think so although . . .' She stopped ruining the cake and looked directly at Juliet. 'Do you remember the night the fellow on the Scottish Opera chorus helped him? He said then that he felt wonderful, that it was more than just blokes helping blokes. He says he felt something he'd never felt before and he desperately wants to feel it again.' She looked down at the cake as if unable to look at anyone, even Juliet when she said, 'Physical desire. He says he knows, and has known since secondary school, that he's different from his friends. At first he thought that it was merely that his overwhelming love of music was pushing everything else out but he saw other boys in college falling for girls, having their first experiences, affairs. We can have no idea of how hard life has been for him: no family money for lessons, no family understanding of music. He saw us and loved us and he tried; how he tried.' Her eyes filled with tears again and instead of angrily brushing them away, as Juliet had thought she would, she let them fall. Large tears welled up in the corners of her eyes and Juliet watched them hesitate for a second as if caught suspended by an eyelash and then they rolled over and ran down her face.

Juliet had hardly ever seen Hermione – Hermione the invincible – in tears and was helpless to act in the face of such sorrow. For it was sorrow. Hermione was totally silent, no sobbing, no retching, no whimpering cries; never before had Juliet felt so absolutely useless. What could she say? What should she say? She had known several gay classmates over the years but she had only ever been asked to accept, never to moralise or attempt to explain or comfort. Was she being asked to comfort? She cast around for something, anything to say, hoping that the right words would come. 'Hermione, it's not the end of the world. I mean, if he is gay, if it's right for him, it's not the end of the world,' she repeated, and then, since Hermione only looked at her with abject despair, added, 'It isn't, is it?'

'It is for me,' said Hermione quietly.

The tears had stopped flowing in such a relentless stream.

Hermione took a handkerchief from the pocket of her minuscule black lace skirt and delicately tidied her face where escaped streaks of mascara painted her pale cheeks. 'I tried to seduce him; I've waited and waited and on the 6th it was just the two of us. Heather was somewhere, you had taken Mrs McD to some Three Kings Concert and Gregor had a night off. We made a huge salad and had some wine and I thought, This time he has to say something. I threw myself at him, Juliet, and he was horrified and then upset, for me, and for himself but I was so embarrassed that I fled and it was only last night that he cornered me and we talked. How about that, Juliet, darling, at last something Daddy can't buy for me?'

'Hermione, I'm so sorry. I just don't know what to say. I never suspected. You have so many dates, so many toads, and all the time . . . Has it been all the time? Why didn't you talk to me?'

'I fell for him the first composition class I took with him. Oddity factor, I told myself; a bit of rough, someone from, if not the wrong side of the tracks, at least tracks that Mummy wouldn't want to know about. He's so clever and intense and funny and he looks like an elf, at least I think he does – rather tall perhaps – and he's so vulnerable and kind and . . . oh, he's just Gregor and there's no one in the whole world like him. Now he wants to leave and he can't, Juliet. He likes the flat and us, and he could never afford the same kind of living arrangement. Will you talk to him?'

'I'll try but it seems that, now that all this has come out, your feelings and his own self-doubts – he's embarrassed too, don't you think?'

'About possibly being gay? How can you not know? And if it's my embarrassment that's bothering him, I'll get over that. Do I look like someone who is easily embarrassed?' She smiled at Juliet with eyes suspiciously bright.

'You look devastating as always.' Juliet stood up, picking up her carrier bags as she did so. 'Come on, we'll go home, have some dinner, normal evening, then we'll have the usual fashion show and we'll – shock, horror – still be trying on things when Gregor gets home. A bottle of wine – you can go to find one in the kitchen, taking an inordinate amount of time and I'll speak to him. God knows what I'll say but I'll think of something. You were struggling through *War and Peace* to impress him?'

'Yes. Some good it did me. One day he said he never saw me reading anything other than what he called "cheap thrillers". Thought I'd try to impress him. Don't think he even noticed.'

What was there to say? They headed out of the department store and Juliet flagged down a taxi. 'This suit deserves a taxi,' she explained to a surprised-looking Hermione as she held up one of her bags.

'Such a pity the committee didn't just hand you a nice cheque. I know, I know, don't tell me how eminently sensible and helpful everyone is being. I'll miss you and if Gregor leaves too—'

'He won't, Hermione. You'll leave him, you know, because this is your year too, remember.'

'But I would take him with me. I always thought I would take him with me.' How sad she sounded.

They were quiet as the taxi sped through the New Town, each busy with her own thoughts. Juliet was almost as nervous as if she were appearing before a judging panel. Gregor gay? Or, possibly what was even worse, Gregor unsure of his sexual orientation. Just what was the right thing to say? In fact she had to say nothing because Gregor saw through their elaborate subterfuge.

'Hermione's told you then, Juliet.' He was curled up in his favourite old chair, his red hair standing up all over his head as if in mortal terror, each strand heading in a different direction, escaping.

'She's afraid that you'll leave.'

'How can I stay? Before she was just my chum, my dearest friend. Now . . .'

'Can't you pretend it was the wine?'

He laughed like a boy, a delightful sound and Juliet found time to note it and hope that Hermione heard it too and took heart from the joy of the sound.

'Hermione under the influence? She's got a concrete stomach and—'

'The family liver,' Juliet finished for him.

'I couldn't bear to cause her unhappiness or embarrassment, Juliet. Every time she sees me she'll see herself being rebuffed and it wasn't her.' He blushed, an ugly red blotch that spread across his white skin. 'It was what she wanted that was rejected.'

'She's not the first woman or man to be rebuffed,' said Juliet. 'She'll get over it, but she won't get over losing your friendship.'

'She won't lose that. I'll always be her friend but, perhaps for a time, it would be better if I moved out.'

'Gregor, I'm moving out. She'll have to get someone to take my room but in the meantime she'll be alone with you and Heather. We can't all leave her at the same time.'

He stopped and jumped up as Hermione came back with a bottle of wine and three glasses. 'Hermione, I'm pooped; I'm off to have a shower. See you both in the morning.'

'But I want you to see my new clothes, Gregor.'

For a moment he was angry. 'Because gays are so good with clothes? Give me a break, Juliet.' He stopped at the door and smiled at them, the old Gregor again. 'Sorry, but you know that I have absolutely no interest in clothes. I'm sure they're lovely and I'll see them another time. Goodnight, girls.'

Hermione held up the bottle and Juliet shook her head. 'It'll be fine, Hermione. Let's just give him time.'

13

The foursome had dinner together on the night before Juliet left. Hermione had brought along a toad – possibly to show Gregor that she was perfectly all right – Gregor had invited Mrs McDermott, but Heather, looking pale and rather drawn, was alone. Peter, she explained, was working late.

'Should I invite Mrs McD to take your room, Juliet?'

Juliet tried to gauge whether or not Hermione was serious. 'You're joking, aren't you? She's lovely as a guest, even as a nuisance who turns up seventeen times a week when you least want her, but living here? She would drive you crazy.'

'Gregor has endless patience; it's Heather who gets shirty.' Hermione selected two bottles of wine from the rack under the sink. 'I'll take these in for Geoffrey to open.' She returned a minute or so later. 'What do you think of the Peter not coming?'

'Nothing. He has odd hours; on the other hand we haven't really seen him, in the flesh as it were, since the recording. And she sang that "Plaisir d'Amour" as if she felt it.'

'Callas was like that, according to my godmother; everything she felt inside came out when she was singing.'

'That accounts for the strident top notes, does it?'

'Nasty. Is that salad ready yet? I don't want to leave the pale and wan Heather alone with Geoffrey for longer than I must.'

Juliet refused to comment beyond reminding Hermione that, in a second, Mrs McDermott would arrive. 'And she's much more likely to swallow the poor man whole.'

'There's a picture. Now come on, our last dinner. Who knows when we will be together again?'

*　　*　　*

Next day all three of her closest friends accompanied Juliet to Waverley Station and less than ten hours later she was sitting forlornly in her unfriendly flat, at first sight a cold concrete box that had been found for her by someone on the committee. Its main value was that it was part of the Barbican complex and very close to the music centre. Juliet would have no excuse ever to be late for work and would have no transportation costs or worries. 'Right, start as you mean to go on. Unpack. Get some life into this place, a photograph here, a painting there, flowers everywhere, candles and music.'

She had a meeting with Karel on her first day and she was terrified. What could she say? She had apologised for accusing him of lying but she could not help feeling that having had a physical relationship, albeit for one night only, with her boss was hardly the ideal circumstance in which to start the most important training of her entire career. She dressed carefully and conservatively: a calf-length tweed skirt with a tailored shirt, plain tights and flat black shoes. Her make-up she limited to a discreet pink lipstick and she made sure that she smelled only of her lightly scented soap. In any event she need not have worried. He was seated at the piano when she entered and he stood up immediately, his hand held out in greeting. He was almost casual, in jeans and a shirt and tie, but the sleeves were unbuttoned and rolled up. He looked good.

'Juliet, I think we may say Juliet and Karel when we are together, yes. Welcome to the London Symphony Orchestra and to this wonderful centre.'

So easy, so civilised. They spoke of their respective New Year celebrations for a few minutes and then he invited her to sit down at the table and, when she was seated, he sat down opposite her. For several minutes he went over the plans for her time with the orchestra.

'One other matter, Juliet. The orchestra has decided to do a benefit for the United Children's Charities; it will be on the second Saturday of February and so we have only a few weeks to prepare this and we must still honour all other commitments. You, Miss Crawford, are going to be thrown into . . . the swimming pool?'

'The deep end, I think.'

He smiled and for a moment her heart beat faster; his face changed so completely when he smiled. 'Thank you,' he said. 'The deep end. It is impossible for me to conduct everything and everyone who has volunteered to appear although we will have other guest conductors for the concert itself.'

He reeled off a list of names of singers, instrumentalists and conductors that made Juliet stifle a gasp. So many people whose prodigious talent she admired would be in the concert and – was he saying it, had she understood correctly – she might be allowed to conduct some of them in rehearsal?

He was still talking and she pulled herself together quickly so as to miss nothing. 'No need to make notes, Juliet. It is all in this folder. I will leave you to read everything and then when we meet tomorrow we can discuss any problems you may foresee. For now, perhaps we can spend a little time just talking about this great art form we both love. For instance, a question that most reporters will ask you. Can you remember when you knew that you wanted to become a conductor?'

'Oh, yes. My godmother took me to an orchestral concert when I was eight. Alicia De Larrocha was playing a Beethoven concerto and I think Aunt Sarah thought I would want to emulate her. I did love her playing and still do but it was the conductor I admired most. I don't remember who it was, the usual conductor of the Scottish National, I suppose, and easy enough to find out, but I thought he was the most magical, wonderful man I had ever seen.'

'And you don't know who he was? Poor man.'

'Appalling, isn't it? Those were the days when I thought the conductor was God and that the orchestra were helpless without him. I believed he told each instrumentalist when to play and that if he didn't "point" at an instrument it wasn't allowed to participate.'

'And it is not like that? You shock me.'

They laughed together and she realised that he was working very hard to make her feel at ease.

He went on. 'When did you discover that conducting is colla-boration with the orchestra?'

'At school: I was perhaps fourteen or fifteen. I had decided to take a piece more slowly than it was marked, for effect; I could hear it in my head and it was beautiful, but the school orchestra – some of them – paid no attention and the result was chaos.'

'We have all been there. This orchestra is superb, Juliet; you know that. Each and every one probably knows the pieces you will work on far better than you know them yourself. The leader is a more than gifted musician and they can take their lead from him but they will listen to you and discuss your ideas with you.'

'I'm looking forward to the experience immensely and I am very grateful for the opportunity.'

He looked into her eyes but she dropped her head so that she would not meet his gaze. She wanted to read nothing in his eyes and even less did she want him to read anything in hers. This was far too important; many hopeful and talented conductors had applied to enter this competition and she had won. She owed it to all those who had not succeeded as much as she owed it to herself. She would work hard and she would do well. Everything else was incidental, unimportant. She prayed that he would not mention their abortive relationship. Her prayer was not answered.

'Juliet, I hope that working with me will have no awkwardness, no added stress; we can put it behind us, yes?'

'Of course, Maestro. I've forgotten it already.'

For a moment he made no reply and the atmosphere felt strained and heavy. Then he looked up and smiled, a smile that moved his mouth but did not quite engage his eyes. 'Good. You know that I am available at any time if you have a question or a problem. We will meet together once a day anyway but at other times, I am here.'

'Thank you.'

'I will introduce you to the orchestra later this morning. For the next few days I want you to read, to study, to watch and to listen. Conducting means knowing every single detail, every note; it means being able to dissect the piece and put it together again; it means getting one day to the stage where you are not relying on the orchestra to play the right notes. Can you compose?'

164

'I've taken classes but no, that's not a strength. Working with Gregor, my flatmate, was insightful; he looks at a piece very differently.'

'But he is in Edinburgh and you are in London.'

'He plans to visit; all my friends do.' Once he had wanted to meet them or so he had said. She would not remind him. 'Have you any general suggestions, Karel, any pointers?'

He stood up and perforce she had to do the same; the interview was over.

'Let us walk to the studio and look at the music.'

She went with him to the door, assuming that he had decided not to answer but he had been thinking. 'Pointers, suggestions, nothing is more important than what I have already said. First step, study the score at home, for when you first see a piece you do not see the detail, the seed from which the flower grew, you see the flowers, the whole bunch and you must take it apart and smell the different scents and be aware of the feel of every petal. Do you understand, not just the overwhelming beauty of the bouquet but how it was constructed, put together so that that blue flower can only be beside that pink one? It would lose its individuality beside the red.' He looked directly at her again. 'Am I losing you?'

She shook her head with a smile and he looked away as they reached the elevator. He pressed the call button.

'Then you rehearse with all this knowledge in your mind, the rhythmical connections, the dynamic connections, the intervals, and, for me, I want to think I am aware of what the real genius, the composer, wanted. Learn the music inside and out. Be yourself, not a clone of any other conductor. To understand such and such a conductor you must know – intimately – the piece in the way in which he or she does. So far for your age and more importantly for your experience I think you are doing very well. You have, we all agree, the ability to go as far as you want if you are prepared to work. In the meantime I would suggest, politely, that you get rid of unnecessary motions, do away with gesticulations that only distract. Sometimes you allow the fingers of your left hand to – how can I say it?' He made a rippling gesture as one might if one were trying to show the movement of waves. 'What is it for, this little wobble? I remember sitting in Carnegie Hall in New York once and overhearing a lady in front of me say, "Good God, I never saw anyone conduct with his knees before." And that alerted me to what was annoying me about the conductor; he swooped, he swayed, he bent from the waist and sometimes from the knees, almost ravishing the first violins if I may be so crude. Poor first violins: conductors breathe garlic fumes their way and sometimes even throw sweat all over them. I think about my knees every time I stand on a podium and I pray that I am the only person in the auditorium aware that they are even there. I do not wish them to intrude. Do they intrude?' He looked comically down at his denim-covered legs.

She was frantically trying to see in her head a video of herself conducting. Did she make gestures? Did she sway? Did her left hand wobble? Surely not. His knees, did they intrude?

'I have never been aware of your knees, Maestro.'

'Thank God.' He smiled and for a second moment he was the Karel of Edinburgh. 'Your beautiful dress, Juliet. Do you plan to wear it again?'

What an odd question. 'I'm glad you liked it. And yes, I'll wear it; it's very special for many reasons and I won in it. Is there something wrong with it? Could you see my knees?'

'I was unaware of your knees,' he said enigmatically as he held open the door. 'Now let us look at some of the music and discuss it before we go to meet the orchestra properly.'

The room was large and airy but not so clinical as her new flat. It was the mellow golden wood that half panelled the walls that added warmth. Two large tables of much darker wood stood side by side against one wall and their tops were buried under piles of music. It was at once frightening and exciting and Juliet felt her breath catch in her throat. This was it. She had begun. She looked at Karel. 'Thank you,' she said.

He smiled. 'A lovely moment, yes?' he said, as if he understood what was going on in her mind. 'Juliet, I have one piece of advice and I think, extrapolating from what you said, that you knew this even as a young inexperienced girl. You will only produce the sound you want if you can hear it in your head a fraction of a second before the orchestra plays it. Good luck.'

So began the most intensive week of Juliet's life. Merely finding her way around the Barbican was a nightmare. The first meetings she attended were almost terrifying in their intensity. She was to become increasingly grateful for the briefing notes, for so much ground was covered that she was sure she would never remember the half of it. They went over the orchestra's schedule for the time that Juliet would be with them. She was glad that she had done her homework and was aware of the LSO's world-famous educational and community programmes and she was honestly excited, not only by winning the competition but also by the opportunity to participate in all the orchestra's endeavours. No trainee conductor could ask for a better start; she pinched herself rereading the names of legends whom she had stood in line for hours to hear. And now she would be working with and for them.

Every evening of her first week she went back to her flat and lay down fully clothed on the bed in an attempt to ease a throbbing headache. College had been a nightmare: so many places to be, too many things to remember, so many new people to meet; lecturers, fellow students, but out of that had come Hermione and Gregor and, later, Heather. Now this new experience made her recall those first terrifying undergraduate days. She found the Barbican Centre totally incomprehensible; it was like some vast concrete warren. But with the work she was at ease. Every moment was exciting. Would she ever stop waking up in the morning and saying, Dear God, thank you? I'm here where I want to be, where I need to be. Would she ever take her work, her life for granted?

'I hope not,' she groaned, rolling over on her bed and immediately felt better. The headaches would go. It was exactly what she had suffered in her first term in Vienna, speaking and listening to a foreign language that she only basically understood. Her poor tired brain had been unable to cope and had rewarded her night after night with a splitting headache; they had gone eventually because she had learned German. The preparation for this new experience far exceeded the preparation she had had for total immersion in Vienna.

She opened her eyes and looked at the stucco ceiling, her very own stucco ceiling, at least for several months. She looked at the walls, not exciting, but there were her prints, one of which was William McTaggart's, *Where the Burnie Runs into the Sea*, which in one form or another had hung in her bedroom since she was a small child. Next to it there was Raphael's *Madonna of the Pinks*; she had put all her small change into the collecting box at the National Gallery once when she had visited the exquisite work, surprised by how much its beauty had affected her. Slowly she got up off the bed and wandered into her handkerchief-sized living room. She had been delighted to discover that the sofa became a bed, not large but big enough for Hermione, or Heather, or even Gregor should he want to visit. She could imagine neither her mother nor her father sleeping there but she knew contact with her flatmates was a priority. They could not be allowed to disappear out of her life. In the first few weeks she rang their mobiles more often than she talked to her parents. She felt guilty, especially as her mother would ring if she left more than forty-eight hours between phone calls home.

'Tell her you're all growed up, Juliet,' advised Hermione. 'Explain too that every minute is busy with real life. It's for their own good, being cruel to be kind, etcetera. Believe me, parents almost always have to be told when they need to take a back seat.'

'I ring you more often than I ring my mother.'

'Snap. Of course we talk to each other more. We understand the stresses. Parents are happier with the joys. It's their revenge for nappies.'

Naturally the first thing Juliet's mother said when next she telephoned was that Juliet was not to be afraid to tell her if there were any problems, any worries. 'I know you're out in the world, darling, but you're still my little girl and I worry. You haven't mentioned any young men.'

'Mum, I haven't had time to draw a breath never mind bag a man. For the next few months I am part of the London Symphony Orchestra; these will be the most important months of my entire life. There's no time to waste on dating.'

'What about your conductor; he's young, isn't he? Is he married?'

'He's my boss, Mum, completely off limits.'

'You're twenty-five, Juliet. The only young man you brought home during the past five years is that Gregor person. I'm glad that you're away from his influence but I do wish dear Hermione had moved down with you. She has so many contacts.'

Juliet did not know whether to be more amused by the idea of sweet, kind, funny Gregor as an influence or the thought of herself using any of Hermione's exalted contacts. She had dated friends of Hermione, several times, and some of them, non-toads, were very pleasant but not one had touched her heart. She was not ready. For a fleeting moment she remembered lying in Karel's arms and she drove the thought away. That had been madness. Did they not say there was madness in midsummer? She would get over it; she had. Even the shock when she heard that he was to substitute for the conductor who had originally been supposed to mentor her had faded without so much as a faint bruise.

She was not immune to him. She had discovered that at her first rehearsal meeting with the orchestra. She had met them all casually on her first day but this was the first working meeting. Karel had been standing on the podium, facing the music, his back to the door and so had not seen her arrive. He was wearing a dark green shirt and black corduroy trousers and soft black suede loafers. The orchestra too were very casually dressed and Juliet in her first day outfit of neat skirt, blouse and loafers felt decidedly overdressed. But then she was the new girl; she was the one who had to make an impression and she had argued long and hard over what to wear. Casual but smart for the first few days, she had decided; time enough for boho chic. To overdress would be wrong but this was her work, her office as it were, and to be underdressed could have been seen as insulting. One of the cellos was wearing a skirt. Juliet smiled in her direction, Bless you, cello, but the cellist did not return the smile.

Panic raised its ugly head. 'They don't want me.'

Stop panicking, Juliet, she's probably short-sighted and if she hates the sight of you, so what? Win her over; show her once again that you can conduct.

But oh, the joy, the relief when the girl did in fact take out her glasses and perch them on top of her head while she waited.

Karel became aware of her and turned. He smiled. 'Miss Crawford, welcome. Ladies and gentlemen . . .' He needed to say no more. The members of the orchestra got to their feet as Juliet walked across the floor to the conductor's stand. Karel began to clap and they followed his lead. She was welcome.

His shirt was open at the neck and she could see some black curling hairs just above the last fastened button. She felt that she was staring at them and tried to look away. She had never seen him so casually dressed before. Even that day in Edinburgh he had been wearing a tie until . . . She wished she could look away.

'To work. We have had several meetings with Miss Crawford who now knows exactly what is going to happen over the next few months. She will be observing but she will also take some rehearsals and eventually some performances. She will also be involved in our family workshops; I see some smiles.' He stopped and turned to look directly at Juliet. 'How are you with six-year-olds, Miss Crawford?'

He was waiting, damn him, for an answer.

'Fantastic,' she lied since, as far as she was aware, she had never met a six-year-old.

Did he know? He smiled again and she could not stop herself from smiling back. It was her first day, her first rehearsal as a real conductor; she was prepared to smile at the world. If anything had existed between them she had destroyed it and really it was better so. He was effectively her boss. Never sleep with the boss and never accuse him of lying unless you are very sure of your facts.

Being mesmerised by hairs on his chest surely showed only that all her instincts were alive and well. They were young; they had been attracted to each other. It was over.

Wonderful. Time for music.

14

'Well, hello, beautiful.'

Juliet looked up from the score. A very good-looking young man in an extremely expensive cashmere coat was standing in the doorway, his head bent to make sure he did not strike the lintel as he entered. She looked behind her just in case someone else had come in while she had been absorbed. Then she smiled. 'Hello, yourself.'

He came forward, hand outstretched, and she had no choice but to shake hands. 'Are all Americans as friendly as you are?'

'Where beautiful women are concerned, yes, even if they are sopranos.'

'And do they all spout as much rubbish?'

He pretended to reel back clutching his heart. 'Ah, fair cruelty. That's my best chat-up line and it's worked every single time I've used it.'

'Perhaps it failed because I'm not a soprano.'

'That would account for it. A mezzo?'

'A conductor.'

He came forward again and rudely took her score out of her hands. 'Hot dog. A lady conductor.' He examined the frontispiece. 'Wellesz. Symphony Number One. Don't know him.'

'He was Austrian. Forcibly exiled in England after the Anschluss.' She held out her hands for the score and he gave it back to her. 'His music is very beautiful.'

'I'll believe you. In fact I'll even listen to it since you're conducting it. Where have you been all my life?'

Juliet had put the music back on her stand and was studying it, or at least pretending to study. She groaned. 'I was beginning to find you charming.'

'The chat-up line?'

'Yes. Overused in, so they tell me' – she pretended to think – 'the 1950s.'

He refused to be cowed. 'Have you had lunch? No, good. Then let me take you to lunch and you can tell me all about being a lady conductor.'

'I never said I was a lady.'

He laughed. 'You're smart. A conductor of the female persuasion. Hot dog. If that isn't a contradiction in terms. Come on. You can even tell me all about what's his name, Wellesz.'

'I'm working, Mr . . .'

'Lyndholm, Erik. And you're not working. You're having a delightful sparring match with me and so you'll need food because I am persistent. It's Minnesota; the winters sure encourage people to hang on in there.'

She knew who he was – now that he had said his name. She had heard him sing at Covent Garden, the count in *Il Trovatore*. Today he was clean-shaven and so she had not recognised him but she warmed to him. He was like a great puppy, anxious to please and be pleased, and she especially liked that he had not taken it for granted that she would know who he was.

'You're in the benefit?'

'Yes. *Figaro*'s best bits and the duet from *Don Carlos* – if they can replace the tenor in time.'

'You want him replaced?'

He laughed and it was a very baritone laugh, rich and warm and full. 'Hey, lady, there isn't a baritone alive who doesn't want the tenor replaced, and the sopranos, come to think of it. But seriously, no, his wife went into premature labour this morning and the poor guy is, as we speak, running to the airport.' He stopped smiling and looked at her very seriously. 'Will you please tell me who you are so that I can ask you, very nicely, to have lunch with me?'

'My name is Juliet Crawford and yes, I'll have lunch with you, but very quickly. Understood?'

'Yes, ma'am,' he said meekly.

Juliet picked up her coat, leaving the score on the stand, and went with Erik to the door of the rehearsal room. When had she last had lunch with a man who was neither her father nor Gregor? Dinner with Haken had been in late August and it was February. She had decided that there was to be no emotional involvement but lunch with an attractive man was not involvement. She would eat lunch, and she did indeed feel hungry, and then she would say 'thank you' and 'goodbye'.

It did not quite work out like that. Erik Lyndholm was an amusing escort. He was also extremely attractive and his speaking voice was almost as engaging as his singing voice. He was a good listener and Juliet found herself talking to him and laughing with him as if they had known each other for much longer than an hour. She looked at her watch. Almost four. She jumped up from her seat. 'Erik, do you see the time? I'm late.'

He stood up too, gesturing to the waiter as he did so. 'You're not conducting this afternoon?'

'That's beside the point. I have a job and that involves learning and studying on my own as well as with my colleagues.' She almost ran to the door. 'Goodbye, Erik; it was fun.'

At the door she was forced to wait for her coat that a waiter had taken and hung up. A typical February sleet was lashing any pedestrian misguided enough to venture out on foot; to brave the storm without a coat would have been foolhardy. The coat and Erik arrived together. 'I'll get you a cab.'

'No, I'm faster on foot. Thank you again.' She began to run but he was pounding along beside her and she was glad of his bulk which protected her from the full force of the wind.

They arrived at the stage door, windblown, wet, dishevelled and walked right into Karel Haken. 'Maestro,' said Erik, 'what a pleasure, but if you don't need to go out, don't. The snow's coming in from Minnesota.'

'From Norway, I think you will find, Mr Lyndholm. Miss Crawford, I had waited to see if you wanted to talk over the Wellesz but I see you have been busy.' There was the slightest hesitation before the word busy and that rankled with Juliet who had been prepared to apologise.

'Extremely, Maestro. I trust you did not wait long.'

But Karel merely bowed his head slightly and walked past them into the worsening storm.

Erik held the door open for Juliet. 'Frosty,' he said. 'Doesn't he like women conductors?'

Perversely Juliet found a need to defend him. 'He's mega supportive, Erik. I think he has a right to be annoyed if he'd made an effort to find someone to help them, and then found they had taken a long lunch. I mustn't keep you any longer either.' She held out her hand but, to her surprise, instead of shaking it, he pulled her forward into his arms.

'Dinner? At eight?'

She pulled herself back. 'Whoa, cowboy. Lunch was lovely, Erik, but I have a lot to do and will be working this evening.'

'You have to eat and I want so much to see you again; we've hardly begun to get to know each other.'

'And we don't need to do it all in one day. I had a lovely lunch, Erik; and yes, I would like to see you again but today I'm working.'

'Work I understand. Let's exchange cell phone numbers.'

They wrote down contact numbers and Juliet did not step back when he reached forward and kissed her. After all, he meant nothing. For men like Erik, kissing a woman goodbye was as automatic as paying the bill in the restaurant. The stage door opened behind Erik and she saw Karel blown in with flurries of snow. He turned and walked out again. Juliet would not allow herself to wonder if he had disliked what he had seen.

'Well, pooh to you, Santa Claus,' she said as she entered her studio. She had first made that remark at the tender age of four when her mother had tried to correct a naughty behaviour by telling her that Santa Claus was watching her. She had used it all through her life in an attempt to appear braver than she was but why she would want to make a show of bravado before Haken she had absolutely no idea.

'You are teasing, Araminta.'

Hermione had been surprised to have a Sunday telephone call

from her agent. She could not remember when they had last spoken; there had been communications every few days for some months after Hermione's graduation but in the past year Hermione had initiated all correspondence and then she too had given up. No one in the musical world was interested, it seemed, in yet one more young, albeit extremely talented, violinist.

'No, it's quite serious.' Araminta's voice trembled with suppressed excitement. 'Fidelio Recordings are offering you this unbelievable contract. Hermione, I have been an agent for over twenty years and believe me, this is the first time a record producer has contacted me on a Sunday. You're hot. You'd be a fool to turn it down.'

Hermione had had several glasses of champagne the evening before and was feeling just a tad fragile but she was in full control of her faculties and, especially since her agent had been of singularly little help in the time since she had graduated, she wondered if perhaps Araminta was not quite in control of hers. 'Why do they want me? When did they hear me play, surely not at the January concert?'

'I sent them a tape of the audition you did for the Philharmonic. You thought that I hadn't been working for you, didn't you, and, by the way, I did tell them about the Fullerton-Smythe wedding. It seems – and I hope you didn't know this, because if you did you should have told me – that the impresario, Godfrey Pickering, is Sally Fullerton-Smythe's godfather.'

'I didn't know; they're friends of Mummy. But what difference does it make?'

'For heaven's sake, Hermione, when Pickering hears you play he'll want to sign you up. Violinists are the new Callas. Think of that delightful girl, Nicola Benedetti. Pickering lost out on snapping her up. Pity I didn't contact him last year; your first CD could be out already.'

Hermione sat down in the little chair by the telephone; she could feel the first stirrings of excitement. A contract with a reputable recording company – what fledgling violinist would even think of turning it down? 'Araminta, I want to play. Isn't that the way it goes? I get a job, a solo somewhere, maybe a recital, and people hear me and like the sound or, and this is a big or, I win a fabulous competition as Nicola did, and then recording contracts follow. This is the wrong way round. I have done nothing worth anything since I graduated; I'm a complete unknown.' She desperately wanted this to be a dream come true. She could feel it; she could taste it. Fidelio Recordings. 'Oh, God, Araminta, I can't believe this. Tell me it's true.'

'Of course it's true. And remember, when you graduated, with all honours possible, two orchestras offered you a place.'

'Because of my father.'

'For heaven's sake, Hermione: how many times do we have to go over this? That is not the case, you stupid girl. It doesn't hurt having a father who is a known generous patron but it means diddley squat if you've got a tin ear. Now for the love of Mike say yes so that I can call him back.' And get back into bed with two aspirin, was what she added to herself. Araminta had partied until four, had fallen into bed at six and had been wakened at ten. Her head ached, her mouth felt as if it were lined with sandpaper and her stomach rebelled forcefully against everything that she had put in it during the past ten hours; she wanted oblivion. But oblivion would be even sweeter after negotiating a fantastic contract. She waited, fingers crossed.

Hermione was confused. A record contract, the culmination of months, years of study, hard work, any artist's dream, it was within her grasp. But recording artists surely had to have built up a repertoire. At this stage, she had barely looked at many of the great concertos, never mind played them; some of them, she was perfectly sure, she had never even heard. Several great names rushed into her mind: Itzhak Perlman, Yehudi Menuhin, Jascha Heifetz, Fritz Kreisler. What would they say or advise her to say?

'Araminta? Repertoire? Mine is very limited.'

'They're not expecting Joshua Bell, for God's sake. Think, Hermione, you're young, very attractive, distinctive, and you play like an angel. Your first disc will launch you. Television will grab you. Film-makers will want you and that publicity can't be bad.

Great conductors will ring. You'll learn as you go along just as you're doing now but you'll be paid for it. Anton expects you to play the things you know best on this first disc and then together you'll discuss what you should learn for the second and so on and so on. Speak. Please.'

'I'd be a fool to say no, wouldn't I?'

'Frankly, yes. What will I tell him?'

'I want to ask my father.' Hermione, like Araminta, had her fingers crossed.

'You're twenty-five years old: you need to call Daddy? The record industry can't support too many classical artists. Think.'

'Yes. Say yes.'

Araminta whooped with glee and terminated the call. Hermione found that she was sweating; the palms of her hands glistened and she could feel moisture on her nose. The telephone in her hand was wet and she hastily put it down and grabbed some tissues from the square box on the table.

What a fool she had been. She had said yes, and she should have said no. It was totally ridiculous to sign a record contract at this stage in her career. What career? Ninth violin in a second-rate orchestra. She should leave the orchestra where she was learning nothing and she should ring Araminta back and ruin her Sunday.

She picked the telephone up, wiped it with a Kleenex and dialled. 'Daddy, you'll never guess.'

15

'But how are things with you? Have you conducted anything yet? Are you allowed to do something at the benefit? I'm coming down for that, by the way, and my parents – Daddy has a zillion seats – and Gregor.'

Two days after her call from Araminta, Hermione had telephoned Juliet and discussed the proposed contract. Her parents had been all for it. 'After all, darling, Araminta knows the business best.' Juliet had reservations but had not discussed them with her friend; after all, was it not too late now?

'I can't wait; that will be fabulous.' She went on with their conversation.

'We're staying with Daddy but we'll try to get over to see your dear little flat. I'll bring champagne and we'll bless it. Now, you haven't answered one of my questions.'

'I've forgotten them.'

'Acerbic wit. Men, conducting? How goeth both?'

'Great actually. I've met a really yummy American, a baritone. He's gorgeous in that sort of bright and breezy American way: great teeth, fabulous haircuts, and Armani suits, understated elegance. Lovely voice and he's very naughty.'

'Fantastic.'

'Not that kind of naughty. He's in the benefit but he's singing at the Garden so will be here for a while which is great. Funny old business, Hermione: meet someone and two weeks later he's on the other side of the world. Having a career in the arts isn't awfully conducive to successful relationships.'

'Rubbish. Look at the army. Daddy was in the Guards when they married. Mummy says she still goes weak at the knees thinking of him in full Christmas tree order.'

Juliet forbore to remind Hermione that her father had abandoned his army career and his dashing uniforms within two years of his marriage. 'Hermione, I've just remembered something. What happened with Heather and the two auditions? Did she go to the auditions?'

'Yes, I was fearfully jealous; the sun was blazing in Montpellier. Didn't she tell you? Half the time I think she lives in Never-Never Land. Anyway, the English National says her voice isn't right yet, maybe in two or three years and she's waiting for the French to ring. It's between her and a young Russian. Rather exciting. This is *the* year, Juliet.'

'Wonderful. Tell her I'm thrilled. Now I really must go, Hermione. Tell me what happens with the contract; it's terribly exciting.'

Juliet wondered if she might ask Karel for advice. Would he advise such a young and inexperienced instrumentalist to sign a contract that seemed to tie her down for several years? Since she and the senior conductor were working well together and chatted naturally during breaks she plucked up courage. Finding herself for once alone with him she plunged in. 'Karel, Maestro, may I ask you something unconnected with the programme?'

He looked up from the score he was marking and smiled at her; he looked tired. She had not noticed that earlier. She was exhausted every evening and he was working even harder.

'If I can help, I will.'

'What would you advise an inexperienced artist who, out of the blue, is offered a phenomenal contract with Fidelio Recordings?'

His eyes narrowed. 'A contract with Fidelio? I know several musicians who would be forever grateful for such a contract.'

Reading between the lines, Juliet decided that he meant that the musicians were experienced. 'But an untried musician?'

'Would not be offered such a contract. Are we talking about you, Juliet?'

'Me?' She laughed. 'Good gracious, no. Picture me, alone in a recording studio, baton in hand . . .'

'Looking totally delightful,' he said and turned away as if embarrassed.

'And totally stupid without one musician to conduct,' she said quickly to make light of the remarks, for both of them. 'It's my friend, Hermione.'

'The violinist with the purple hair and, what else did you tell me, the earrings in her nose.'

'Studs.'

'The studs in her nose. I must hear this paragon for myself.'

Hear Hermione. Oh, if he would. 'She's good, won every prize at college; auditioned for two orchestras and was offered places by them which she turned down.'

'How strange.'

'Her father is Sebastian Elliott-Chevenix.'

'Ah, I see, but surely she knows her father's money means nothing to those orchestras.'

'They accept plenty of it.'

'Possibly, but, even so, it would not buy a place for his daughter.'

'We have tried to tell her that and now she has been offered this contract, I think so that she can be signed up before someone else signs her.'

'You're joking; because of money?'

'Because she's good. You would tell her not to accept?'

'Absolutely. It will stifle all natural creativity. Instead of trying to learn a piece for sheer pleasure she will struggle to learn to fulfil her contract. This happens too often to young musicians, singers too. She is pretty, with her purple hair and the . . . studs in her nose?'

'Very.'

'I fear that her youth, her beauty, her talent, will be exploited. You know sometimes the record companies decide what an artist will play. That's not good. First she should learn to become totally independent and that, I think, means years of learning from different masters, not adapting to what the record company says the public want. A great artist influences the taste of the public: she's doing it the wrong way around. You should talk with Maestro

Stoltze when he comes for the benefit. He has agreed to conduct when Maestro Rostropovich plays. In the meantime, suggest that she look at the career patterns of other violinists, Tasmin Little as an example or maybe Julia Fischer, both very talented and very pretty, and neither one has either purple hair or a stud in her nose.'

Juliet, who had mixed feelings about both the studs and the hair, now came firmly down on Hermione's side. 'She wouldn't be Hermione without them and they don't affect the way she plays.' She had also noted that Stoltze was to conduct Rostropovich. She hardly dared say those names and now it appeared that, even if she did not meet them, she might be likely to watch them work together. What bliss.

'And that, the playing, is all that matters.'

'Exactly.'

He grinned at her. It was not a smile, more mischievous some-how, more endearing and she was quite sure that he had no idea how young he looked. 'How would you like to sit in when Maestro Rostropovich is here?'

Her heart began to thud. Mstislav Leopoldovich Rostropovich. To be in the same rehearsal studio as the great cellist and con-ductor, perhaps to be asked to do something in some small way . . . 'I'd kill for the opportunity.'

This time he laughed, a joyful sound that made her want to laugh too. 'I do not think we need go to such extremes. Now, spend the rest of the day preparing for your school visit and I'll see you here tomorrow at ten sharp; a great deal to squeeze into the next three days.'

She no longer needed to lie in a darkened room for half an hour or so after she left the offices or rehearsal rooms. The headaches were gone but the pace of the work was so intense and often so exciting that she was exhausted. Her cure was to fill her bathtub with hot, delicious scented water and to half sit, half lie in it with a glass of red wine until the stresses of the day slipped away as softly as the bubbles slipped away from her body as she moved in the water. She would sip her wine slowly and then, when it was finished, she would lie like a beautiful boat becalmed in a harbour until the temperature reminded her that it was getting late and that she had not yet eaten.

The falling temperature or the strident ringing of the telephone.

She got up, wrapped a towel around herself, and went into the living room. 'Hello.'

'Hi, beautiful, have you eaten yet?'

Erik. To lie or not to lie. 'No, and I'm extremely hungry.'

'Hey, what a coincidence. Me too. Fancy a steak and a bottle of good red wine?'

'Singers shouldn't drink when they're working. Conductor-speak.'

'You can have most of it. Fawning-male-speak.'

'It's a deal.'

'Pick you up in ten minutes.'

'Twenty.' She did not tell him she was undressed; she preferred that, if possible, he not think about her body. On the other hand she found herself thinking that a bubble bath with Erik might be quite fun.

In exactly nineteen minutes and thirty seconds the buzzer on the main door announced his arrival.

'I need thirty seconds, Erik. I'll be right down.'

'Very funny. Don't I get to see your apartment?'

She pressed the button to open the main door. 'That depends,' she said and hung up, leaving him standing in the foyer. At least he was inside; he was a baritone and had to keep warm even if he was from Minnesota which, inadequate geography lessons seemed to have told her, was a frozen waste for several months of the year. She was, of course, quite ready but took her time turning out lights, checking her lipstick. She was excited and it felt good; verbal jousting with Erik was harmless and fun and it was so wonderful to be away from the frenetic activity of the past week.

He smiled and held out his arms when she appeared and she allowed him to kiss her. His face was cold as were his lips on her cheek; he had not tried to kiss her mouth. Fifteen love to Erik.

'You look great. It was well worth the extra thirty seconds.'

Thirty love. 'We're going to the Smithfield Market. On the top floor at Smith's there's a great restaurant. Do you know it?'

'I don't know London very well at all and it would never have occurred to me that one could eat at Smithfield Market.'

'Shame on you. London is the neatest place, full of surprises.'

Juliet agreed and longed for time to explore on foot, the best way to discover a city. Erik, a frequent visitor, knew the city well and, to Juliet's surprise, he did not head for the Underground but took her arm and walked, unerringly, to their destination, which was not far away. Erik had reserved a table and they were seated almost immediately. A few minutes later they had ordered – they had not chosen to look at the menu – and an opened bottle of red wine was on the table with some excellent bread.

'Are you in London often, Erik?'

'Not so much as I would like. My agent tries to get me something here every year. Don't get me wrong, I love the Met, it's my operatic home, but I really felt I had made it when I sang here first; a tiny part, but who cares? I called everyone I knew to tell them and several people I didn't know.'

'For instance?'

He pretended to be hurt. 'You don't really believe I actually called complete strangers? I did tell people unlucky enough to get stuck in elevators with me – captive audience. Mostly they were thrilled for me although one guy said, "Great, buddy, but did you happen to catch the Packers' result?" Philistine.'

'And did you happen to catch whatever it was?'

'Absolutely. Football is my other passion. You didn't think I got these shoulders doing breathing exercises?'

She had thought very little of his shoulders having been too busy trying to adjust to her new life but she looked at them over the top of her wine glass, noting their breadth and the excellent tailoring. They, the shoulders, were definitely worthy of more thought. Behave yourself, Juliet.

'Don't do that,' he said and for a second she thought she had spoken aloud.

'Do what?'

'Look at me speculatively with come-hither eyes.'

'I was merely assessing the value of exercise,' said Juliet as two large plates on which rested perfectly done steaks were placed before them. 'Dear Lord, they don't expect me to eat all that?'

'I did tell you for serious meat-eaters, but you can take a doggie bag.'

'No dog.'

'Neither do ninety-five per cent of the people who ask for one. It's a euphemism. Now tell me all about your work. When do I get to see you on the podium?'

'Maybe soon, maybe in six months, maybe never. It depends on how I impress Maestro Haken.'

He waited while the waiter refilled their wine glasses. 'A delicious piece of gossip for you, Juliet?'

'Gossip? Don't you know the three rules to observe before imparting gossip?'

'No, and I don't care. The gossip sheds a light on the frozen Czech. Rumour has it that he's having a fling with the beautiful Bryony.'

Juliet sought to control her face. 'I hope they'll both be very happy. When do you go back to the States?'

'Are we touchy? You're not interested in the maestro, are you?'

'Don't be silly, Erik; he's my boss and you know that sort of liaison very rarely works. If I wanted to be bitchy I might say that his interest could never really have been in her conducting.'

'Ouch. Boy, stay on my side, Juliet.'

Ashamed of herself and her overreaction, she sipped the wine. 'I was, wasn't I? Bitchy? And I'm wrong; she's a very good conductor. Besides, didn't I hear she's working in Melbourne? But never mind them. Tell me all about you and Minnesota and why you wanted to become an opera star instead of a linebacker.'

He was quite happy to talk about himself and so they abandoned any speculation about a relationship between Bryony and Karel, and Juliet relaxed; she certainly had no wish to spend an evening with an extremely attractive and interesting man speaking about another one.

The night was crisp and clear as they left the restaurant and cold enough for their breath to form before them as they walked, still talking. 'In Minnesota,' said Erik, 'it's dangerous to talk outside. Breath freezes solid and people have been known to fall over it as it piles up on the road.'

What nonsense he talked but he was fun and Juliet was enjoying herself immensely. She allowed him to hold her hand as they walked; it felt right.

'I'd love a coffee,' he hinted as they arrived at Juliet's door.

'Too late. I have a meeting with Maestro Haken at ten and preparation to do before that. Your fault for taking me out to dinner.'

'Can I come in for five minutes?'

'Absolutely not.'

'Juliet, you have just exactly the right amount of sternness; you'll make a great conductor. Violinists will tremble.'

She ignored that.

He looked down at her and Juliet looked back at him. He certainly was good to look at. He put his right hand very gently under her chin, bent down and kissed her very gently on the lips.

'That was nice,' he whispered. 'Think I'll do it again.'

Juliet found herself leaning towards him. It was very pleasant; she did not at all mind being kissed a second time.

'Off you go to bed, Maestro,' he said and stepped away from her. Game, set and match to Erik.

16

He had known. It was obvious from his expression. He was not surprised. Dash it, thought Juliet angrily, one step forward, two steps back with this relationship.

She was working with the woodwinds when the door opened and Bryony stood there in the doorway, looking a million dollars as Erik would say: skin-tight suede jeans, a see-through blouse with a ruffled front that attempted – feebly – to preserve decency, at least three coats of mascara or was she wearing false eyelashes? Her shining dark hair was tied up in a ponytail that any seven-year-old would have loved. Bryony Wells, it appeared, had been given permission to sit in on some of the classes. Damn it. Erik was obviously right: Karel Haken, the iceman, was involved with Bryony Wells. Not that she cared and she certainly would not allow an extra person watching her to affect her. She would be civil. 'Hello, Bryony. I had heard you were in Australia.'

'I was and it was wonderful but then a friend' – she managed to inflect the word with all manner of innuendo – 'managed to talk management into allowing me to audit some sessions. I won't upset you, will I?'

Juliet managed to laugh. 'Gosh, no, Bryony. It'll be fine.' She was extremely proud of that lie.

During a break Karel joined her at a table in the Waterfront Café. He did not ask but merely put his coffee cup down on the table and slipped into a seat. His face was troubled and, just for a moment, he had difficulty meeting her eyes. 'I was not told, Juliet. This morning there she was and I could not argue with her credentials.'

Her heart lifted. At least he had not organised Bryony's

appearance. She put her spoon carefully into the chocolate at the top of her cappuccino and folded it into the coffee. 'Miss Wells's presence is unexpected, Maestro,' she said. She put the spoon down and looked up. 'I expect that, like me, she is here to learn.' She was quite pleased with how she was handling this. Bryony had no right, no right at all, to sit in on her coaching sessions.

He looked at her, a guarded expression in his eyes, and then smiled. 'From you she will learn a great deal, I think, and not all about music. Life around you is not dull, Juliet. If you wish I will leave you to relax but I had hoped for a few minutes to discuss your ideas for the Shostakovich.'

'Please do.'

They had scarcely begun before they became aware that someone had approached their table.

'Hi, I hope I'm not intruding.' Bryony, mineral water in hand, was smiling down at them.

Had she a tail, Juliet decided, it would be wagging.

'We were discussing Miss Crawford's interpretation of the symphony.'

Without invitation Bryony sat down beside him.

She must be really sure of herself, thought Juliet, as she waited in vain for him to say something. But it was Bryony who spoke.

'Wow, I'd love to listen in. I won't say a word, if that's okay with you, Juliet?'

Juliet wanted so badly to yell, 'No, it's not "okay with me",' but she did not. What purpose would be served by having open animosity between two participants on the programme? She could not quite bring herself to be totally charming. 'Should you not ask permission from the conductor, Bryony? But if it's fine with you, Maestro, Miss Wells's input could be illuminating.'

Bryony did not, in fact, contribute to the discussion but listened avidly and then walked back with them to the elevator. There Karel excused himself and the two women entered the elevator together.

Juliet decided to try to find out who had negotiated Bryony's presence. 'It's really none of my business, Bryony, but I'm interested in Mrs Grey's feelings about having us both working with the orchestra at this time.'

If it is possible to flounce petulantly in an elevator, Bryony did it. 'It's nothing to do with her. She financed the award; she does not run the orchestra and they can allow anyone they want to sit in on rehearsals. That's all I'll be doing, just listening.' She looked at Juliet's face and laughed. 'I get it. You want to know if Karel sneaked me in. Oh, poor Juliet, ask him or aren't you sure enough of him yet?'

Unfortunately the door opened and disgorged them just at that moment and so there was no time for Juliet to reply. She thought a lot though as they waited for latecomers. 'Aren't you sure enough of him yet?' If Bryony were indeed involved with Karel surely she would know that Juliet was not. And if Karel, the conductor, had not authorised Bryony's presence, who had? And did that unknown person think that Juliet and Karel were personally involved? Could Karel have told anyone of the one-night stand, which was what she had taken to calling what had been for her – and for a moment only – a very special time? Surely not? He did not seem the type of man to brag about his conquests. How do I know what type he is? Maybe the entire orchestra knows about us. Bittersweet? Yes, that day was bittersweet and in six months this whole experience will be too.

Castigating herself for allowing Bryony's presence to get under her skin so obviously, Juliet got back to work and lost herself in what really mattered – her interpretation of great music.

There was no time to worry about anything outside the orchestra for the next few weeks. Life was lived at a fever pitch as everyone prepared for the Saturday evening benefit concert. So many world-famous 'names' had offered to participate that it was almost impossible to put together a well-balanced programme. Faces that Juliet had previously seen only on record covers or on television wandered in and out all week long. Each night she was almost too tired to ring her parents but too stimulated not to want to share with them the events of the day.

Her father took to listening in on another telephone as his wife's excitability increasingly exasperated him.

'Rostropovich,' she would exclaim. 'You actually spoke to Mstislav Rostropovich. Richard, listen to this. Juliet spoke to Rostropovich.'

'Why don't you come down? Hermione and her parents are coming and Gregor.' Fleetingly Juliet wondered why there had been no mention of Heather. 'I know it's sold out but I might be able to do something. Maestro Haken did ask.'

'We can't drop things at the last moment, Juliet. This dinner party has been arranged since Christmas.'

'Come down soon then.'

'We will. But what about this young man you're seeing? Will he be there?'

'Yes, he's singing.'

'Lovely. Did you hear that, Richard? Juliet's young man is singing.'

'I'm not deaf and he's not "Juliet's young man" yet. You'll let me know when he is, dear.'

Juliet was glad to hang up, wondering as she did more and more often lately what it was that kept her parents together. They were so different and seemed to spend less and less time with each other as the years passed. Was that what marriage was like, exciting for a few years when each partner could not see enough, hear enough of the other, and then gradually calming down as each became more used to the other's presence, habits, good and bad, annoying quirks of personality, even endearing traits? Or did what had once been endearing and charming eventually fade into insignificance, or, what was worse, become a source of aggravation? But how can anyone on the outside judge?

Juliet shrugged, decided to remember to ask Hermione about Heather, and took herself off to bed.

The benefit was a resounding success and although Juliet was not called upon to conduct any of the items on the programme, she did take some of the rehearsals.

Karel stopped her as she was leaving the Barbican the evening before the concert. 'I would have given you a spot, Juliet,' he said. 'But too many famous conductors offered their services.'

'Thank you, Maestro, I didn't expect a spot. It will be a thrill just to listen to the concert.'

'You're good enough. Don't think that you are not. There are glowing reports from some of your rehearsals and not only from the orchestra who are on your side anyway, but from one or two of these great artists. I'll be glad when it's over and we're back to normal. I feel that you have been rather neglected.'

'Neglected? No, Maestro, that's the last word I would use. I've loved every second of the rehearsals and look forward now to the performance.'

'Me too. You know some of my childhood idols are here. For me this is also a thrilling experience. We will be very busy tomorrow with the dress rehearsal. You have a new dress?'

'What on earth for? I shall wear my lucky dress.'

'I thought girls liked new dresses for special events?'

'Who will even notice me, Maestro? I'll wear my dress.' She wondered fleetingly if she would ever find her generous benefactor. The final, the dress, the unknown hero, all seemed to have faded from her mind, so involved had she been in her new life.

He smiled as he belted up his overcoat. 'Oh, you will be noticed, Juliet. Now, get a good night's sleep because tomorrow will be a revelation to you.'

And it was. Juliet had thought the pace of life frenetic before. By four o'clock on the day of the concert she reflected that her working days must, in fact, have been fairly calm. Someone had just handed her a paper cup of coffee and she realised that it was the first time she had stopped since early morning. She wanted to lean back in her chair and close her eyes but something told her that that would not be a good idea. Imagine being found sound asleep, mouth open, by a visiting celebrity. Would it be better to be discovered by a pianist, a violinist, or a conductor? She gulped the hot coffee. I'm so exhausted, I'm irrational.

The best course of action was to go outside for some fresh air and so Juliet, feeling distinctly below par, grabbed her coat and headed for the lake.

The tinny strains of 'La Donna è Mobile' from the mobile phone in her pocket sobered her up. It was Gregor who had arrived with Hermione and her parents for the concert.

'You should see this bedroom, Juliet. Talk about conspicuous consumption. Carpets you sink to your knees in. Three armchairs, tables from some French whorehouse; you know the kind of thing, all curly bits and some of it blue. The bed's big enough for eight marines.'

It was good to hear him. Why she should think he might have changed in a few weeks she did not know but just hearing him cheered her. 'You're going to move out then? You can have my sofa.'

'No thank you – this time. How can I discuss inequalities academically if I have no knowledge and/or experience; I'm putting this down to research. I'll tell you all about my personal bathroom later. Hermione and her mum are being completely remodelled as far as I can see and Seb's been on the phone since the plane touched down. How are you? Frazzled?'

'That's a good word.'

'Listen, I know you're busy but we wondered if there would be time before the concert for us to see you and your des res?'

'I'd love it. I've got a few things to do here and then I'm rushing home to shower and change. Any time after five would be great; I have to be back at six though.'

They arranged to meet at five thirty and, feeling much more energetic and relaxed, Juliet finished her coffee and set her mind to finishing her last few tasks. Nothing impeded her but she still needed as much time as she had been given to get ready. For a moment she envied Hermione who had spent the afternoon being cosseted but only for a moment; it was far more fulfilling to help one of the world's greatest violinists find the cafeteria.

Hermione, with green hair, and matching fingernails – which highlighted the bling that adorned her fingers and wrist – breezed in carrying a bottle of very fine champagne and a plate of *pâté de fois gras*. She hugged Juliet and then ran around the tiny apartment like a small silver firefly, opening doors, and exclaiming, 'It's fabulous; how exciting.'

Since the whole apartment would have fitted in the living room of Hermione's own flat Juliet was not sure that fabulous was the correct adjective but she appreciated her friend's wholehearted enthusiasm. She looked at Hermione who was stunningly lovely in a silver shift so short that it was barely decent, and shoes in silver and green with impossibly high heels. 'Why the green hair? Your dress is lovely, but how can you walk on those heels?'

'Manolo Blahnik, aren't they lovely,' was the inadequate answer. 'Come along, Gregor, the champers. Doesn't Gregor look handsome? Mummy was quite prepared to put up with his old jeans and his velvet jacket; but behold, a vision.'

'You do scrub up well, Gregor,' agreed Juliet, taking a glass from the unfazed Gregor. 'Karel wants to meet you both.'

'That's why I bought a real dress,' said Hermione, 'but why Gregor conformed I have no idea.'

Gregor smiled and Juliet noted that 'scrubbed up' Gregor was an attractive young man. Even his wild red hair was in some semblance of order.

'Least I could do for your mum,' he said, 'just in case the green hair, green fingernails and the indecency of your skirt upset her too much.'

Juliet felt warm inside. They were her two dearest friends and it was obvious that they were back to their old selves.

'Rinse your hair tomorrow with what's left of the champagne,' suggested Hermione to Juliet as they made their way over to the auditorium, 'or is that supposed to be beer?'

They were to meet, together with Hermione's parents and their other guests, backstage after the concert and Juliet left them at the front door and slipped round to the artists' entrance. She would not sit in the auditorium but would stay backstage; there were plenty of tasks for her still to perform.

The performance began exactly on time, in itself a tremendous feat of teamwork, and Juliet knew where they were only by the magical sounds that occasionally drifted or flew to her. Once or twice for a few minutes she was able to stand in the wings and actually watch part of the performance. From where she stood she could see the audience and she gloried in the rapt expressions. She held it in her heart, a night to remember, a memory to hold fast in some small secret place, to take out when needed on cold unhappy days when only sublime music could supply balm to wounds.

It was over. Some of the world's greatest musicians had descended on London, worked their magic for the benefit of thousands who had never heard their music or their names, and departed, except for those who stayed for a reception in their honour. In the crush Juliet found Erik and introduced him to Hermione. His pleasant but predatory eyes rested on her appreciatively.

'I was looking forward to purple hair,' he said.

'Green's the new purple,' said Hermione solemnly and Erik pretended her remark made sense.

'And you say she's a good violinist?' he asked Juliet when Hermione had flitted away.

'I think she has greatness and I want to introduce her to Karel. Have you seen him? Tall men are extremely useful in overcrowded rooms.'

He grinned sardonically at her. 'Glad to be of assistance, ma'am. He's over by the window with Maestro Rostropovich and Bryony. God, that girl is predatory.'

'She won't get anywhere there. Why doesn't she trust to her talent?'

'Time. There are quicker ways than hard work to the top of the ladder. Who's the good-looking young man with Hermione?'

'Gregor.'

'Is the hair real?'

'Absolutely.'

'You have the most fascinating friends.' He neatly lifted two glasses of champagne from a tray carried by a hurrying waiter. 'Here's to you, my dear. By far the prettiest conductor in the room.'

'That is not a compliment. Go grab some egg rolls or something while I speak to Hermione's parents. They're over there beside the pink flowers.'

'Heck. Mr Moneybags. You do have interesting friends. I go but I shall return.'

Juliet did not reach the Elliott-Chevenixes. She was intercepted by Karel who wanted to introduce her to various people in her role as winner of the competition. The evening went on, a kaleidoscope of colour and taste, scents and sound. Exotic blooms disgorged their perfume into air already heavily laden with a cocktail of expensive perfumes. Clinking glasses, voices trying to make themselves heard, shouts of laughter invaded the memory of the exquisite melodies that had poured from fabled instruments in a steady stream of golden memory. Introductions were made, 'Maestro, may I introduce . . .' 'Miss Crawford, I have the honour to introduce . . .' 'Juliet, meet. . . .' Lights from candles and chandeliers shone on jewels, on dresses, on medals, on hair black as polished jet, yellow as summer corn, green . . . Juliet felt her head swimming with exhaustion, too much champagne and not enough food.

'You look faint, Juliet. Are you all right?' It was Karel, his eyes, his expression concerned.

'Merely hungry,' she said honestly. 'Erik disappeared hours ago to find some Chinese egg rolls but he never returned and I've decided that the mixture of those lilies, fearfully expensive perfume and aftershave is something I can well do without.'

'You will learn to ignore it. It's one of the few downsides, like overwork. Me, I dislike all the chattering voices; they sound like hens in the farmyard. Now, follow me. I will beat a path through to a tray of delicious chicken fillets, much easier to eat than egg rolls.'

She felt much better after some solid food. 'How did you know this was here, Karel?' It was the first time for some weeks that she had used his Christian name but neither of them seemed to notice or care.

'Because I hid it. I spent three years starving at receptions; during the third year I kept my eyes open and so now I take precautions. You see how much you learn, Juliet.'

They were interrupted, of course, by Bryony and then by Hermione who was leaving with her parents.

'But I looked everywhere for a girl with purple hair,' said Karel.

'Today I'm into green.'

He looked at her and smiled. 'It is very . . . good, but will you do me a little favour?'

'Of course, Maestro.'

'When you come to play for me will you please remove the nail colouring?'

Hermione examined her emerald-green nails and looked at Karel and smiled. 'Whatever you say, Maestro. What about the hair?'

'I can become used to green. You will come down?'

'I'd be honoured.'

He bowed. The gesture meant 'the honour is mine'. 'Juliet will be in touch,' he said.

He watched Hermione walk easily across the room on her ridiculously high heels and Juliet watched him. She saw Hermione turn and wave at the door but she was not quite sure to whom she was waving.

'She is quite something, your friend, Hermione.'

'She is indeed,' said Juliet and smiled.

'I met Gregor, by the way. He seems a very serious young man. Is he composing?'

Gregor serious? But perhaps he was in different company. We all wear many masks. 'I would suppose composers compose, Maestro. I really don't know.'

'Tom Redpath seemed very interested in him. Do you know him?'

'Is that Sir Thomas? I've heard of him, of course.'

Karel looked at her very seriously. 'What have you heard?'

There was something about the way he spoke. It seemed to Juliet as if the crowded room had suddenly become quiet. Voices were hushed; laughter did not bounce from the walls, even the filling and refilling of glasses happened silently. 'What do you mean?'

He was not looking at her but across the room, lifting the hand that held the half-full glass, with which he had walked twice across the floor, as if in farewell to someone who stood for a moment at the doors. 'Exactly what I said. What have you heard?'

'That he is very wealthy. That he could have been a concert pianist, or a painter of note, or a prize-winning poet, but that he chooses to play dilettante.'

'He also has beautiful gardens at each of his many homes.'

She knew he was not telling her everything. 'And?'

'He picks up and drops young talent if it does not conform to his interpretation of their visions. I would not want your friend hurt.'

'Why not? What is he to you?'

'Because he is your friend, Juliet,' he said seriously, his mouth very close to her ear, 'and I would not have you hurt.' He moved back slightly. 'Tom might well commission something if Gregor . . . interests him enough, and he will pay generously. But the commission might never be produced. The money will be paid but that is not enough for the Gregors of this world.'

She decided to concentrate on Gregor and not what he had said about her or how her senses had reacted to his closeness. 'No, it isn't. Why shouldn't it work?'

'It might. Why should it not? Usually Tom likes . . . sponsors singers; there are more of them than there are composers, I suppose.' He changed the subject. 'You will enjoy a full day off tomorrow, no extra rehearsals. Won't that be pleasant? Have you plans?'

Juliet smiled in anticipation. 'Yes. I'm seeing Hermione and her parents for lunch, and then there's an exhibition at the Royal Academy. I don't care what it is; it will just be so lovely to have a day off.'

'Indeed. Ah, forgive me; I have some goodbyes to say. It was a superb concert, Juliet. Thank you for all your hard work.'

And he was gone, moving easily across the room from group to group, shaking hands here, and kissing a powdered and perfumed face there.

Strong hands circled her waist and a voice breathed in her ear. 'If

I told you that I have just picked up a Chinese takeaway, would you let me see your *pied à terre*?'

Juliet turned in Erik's arms. His face was cold and so he must indeed have been out in the cold night air.

She smiled up at him. 'Spare ribs?'

He nodded affirmatively.

'How do I know you're telling the truth?'

'Three packets of soy sauce in my breast pocket.'

She checked. 'Okay, you have a deal.'

17

'Hello.' Juliet had been awakened from a deep sleep by the sound of her telephone. The ringing sounded to her, in her groggy state, as if it were desperate, despairing, almost sure that it would not be answered.

'Juliet. It's me, Heather.'

Grogginess fled. Since Juliet had come down to London Heather had never once contacted her and she had made a mental promise to question Hermione during her visit, but there had been so many other seemingly more pressing issues to discuss. 'Hold on a sec.' She sat up and switched on the lamp on the bedside table. The clock informed her that it was barely two o'clock. She had been in bed for less than two hours. 'Heather, I'm here and awake. Is everything all right?'

'No,' mumbled Heather and then burst into tears and Juliet sat and tried to decipher the sense between the hiccups and sobs and occasional clear words. One that was as clear as a sunny day on the Riviera was the word pregnant.

'Heather, try to calm down. It's all right, I'm here and I'm listening. Did you say you were pregnant?'

More sobs and then, 'God, Juliet, you're the only one I can turn to; you've always been the practical one, the unemotional one, the flatmate we all depend on. Tell me what to do.'

Tell her what to do. Juliet, trying to digest being 'the unemotional one', had absolutely no idea. What did a woman do when she discovered that she was pregnant? Announce the good news to the father probably, or to her parents or both. From the hysterical outburst it seemed as though Heather had done neither or had done both with appalling results.

'Heather,' she began gently. 'You have told Peter?'

Further prolonged sobbing.

'Heather, please speak to me. What did Peter say?' She could not say, 'The baby is Peter's, isn't it?' No, she could not say that to a friend and surely Heather had been seeing only one man for the past few months, from the day when she announced breathlessly that she had found, finally, the perfect man.

'He doesn't want to know.' There was a silence broken only by a loud sniff as if Heather were trying to pull herself together. 'He's married, Juliet; the bastard's married.'

Juliet closed her eyes for a second as if to shut out the sorry and oft-painted picture. 'I'm so sorry, Heather. What about your parents?' Juliet had met Heather's mother once or twice while they were in college – Heather's father had seemed always busy with his farm – and she sympathised with them and with her friend. Such news would be difficult for them to handle, but surely only at first; Heather was their daughter. They would help. And dare she mention Heather's brand-new contract with the Opera House in Montpellier? She wished she could remember which dates Hermione had told her were in the contract.

'You saw Fiona's reaction to Gregor sneaking in to get warm? Magnify that a million times. The disgrace will kill them. I can't tell them and I can't ever go home unless I, unless . . . Oh, God, oh God, Juliet, that's an even worse sin.' She began to cry hysterically again.

'Heather, Heather, try to stay calm; don't talk about sin. If there is any, it's Peter's, not yours. I take it you never knew about his wife?'

There was no answer but Juliet, having seen Heather receive telephone calls many times, could almost feel her head shaking vehemently from side to side. 'Heather, listen, you can't deal with this on your own and certainly not while you're upset. What did Hermione say?'

'I haven't told her. She's not really a sympathetic person, you know, but, of course, you wouldn't recognise that; I imagine she'd say, "Get rid of it if it's a nuisance, darling."'

How could Heather have lived in Hermione's flat for two years and speak of her like that? Juliet wanted to slam the receiver down and leave the girl to get herself out of the mess. 'She'd say that about a rash,' she said coldly. 'Not about a baby. I take it you haven't spoken to Gregor either?'

'I thought about it but he's been awfully busy lately. I never see him. I think he's composing, seriously, I mean. I hope so.'

'That would be super but it doesn't help you just at this time. You couldn't tell Fiona?'

'She's too young and she'd tell every member of our entire family.'

Juliet was beginning to feel helpless. 'You have been to a doctor?'
'No.'

The mood lightened. 'Perhaps you're just late; it often happens, too much work, stress.'

Heather was quite calm when she answered. It was as if she had aged during the length of the telephone call, as if perhaps, frightened and alone, she had been going through things in her mind. Now that she had said them out loud to another person she was finding the maturity to deal with them. 'Juliet, it's almost March. I told Peter I thought I was pregnant just before the New Year. How late can you be without being pregnant?' She laughed, a harsh joyless sound. 'Joke, Juliet.'

Juliet had seldom felt less like laughing. 'You should have said something earlier. We're your friends, Heather. New Year's Eve, "Plaisir d'Amour", you knew then and you were unhappy.'

'I couldn't say anything; it would all have come spilling out and, besides, I didn't know about the wife then. He's shocked; he'll take some time. That's what I thought.' She was quiet for a moment and then in a much calmer voice, said, 'What am I going to do?'

'See a doctor tomorrow, today; that's the first thing, and tell Hermione and Gregor or let me tell them. You need support. Heather, if you're too far on you won't be able to . . . you can't . . . It's too late for a legal abortion,' she finished starkly.

'I am the world's most selfish woman, Juliet. My career has just started and now I can kiss it goodbye but that option never

occurred to me anyway.' She sounded very firm and very dignified. Juliet had never liked her more.

She thought quickly, mentally trying to run through her schedule. 'Look, can I ring you later? I have to see the diaries, the
schedules; my mind isn't working too well.'

'I'm sorry. I just couldn't think . . . I was so desperate but it
doesn't seem quite so awful since someone else knows.'

'No, don't worry. I'm pleased that you thought I could help.
Tomorrow morning, you know what I mean – I'll check the
schedules and see if I can get a few days off. Now that the big
benefit is over work might not be so frenetic.'

'I never asked you how it was going. I meant to ask Hermione
but the time or the mood was never right. Everyone seems to be
busy just now, except me. I hardly see Gregor these days.'

'Don't worry about anything. Listen, promise me that you will
try to sleep now and then, when you see her, tell Hermione;
honestly, Heather, you should know that she's only flippant about
flippant issues. And you must make a doctor's appointment. Will
you do that?'

Heather promised to talk to Hermione first thing in the morning,
thanked Juliet, apologised for calling so late, and then hung up.
Juliet turned off the bedside lamp and fell back against the pillows
expecting to fall asleep immediately but she was still half awake,
her mind frantically seeking solutions when her alarm clock jolted
her again.

It was not the clock. It was her telephone, and the caller was
Bryony. 'Juliet, *mon ange*, you're over an hour late.'

Juliet, holding the phone in one hand, threw aside the sheets and
got out of bed. 'Bryony, what time . . . why . . .?' She looked at her
watch. Nine o'clock. Damn, damn, damn.

Bryony was still chattering, oozing sympathy. 'The maestro
asked me to ring you – to see if you were ill. He said he couldn't
think of any other reason for you to be an hour late for a scheduled
meeting. Have you got someone tall and gorgeous there, you lucky
girl, someone perhaps of the baritone persuasion?'

Did the woman know how stupid she sounded? Or, thought

Juliet sadly, is it just that I am a million years older than everyone else? 'I'll be there in five minutes, Bryony. Thank you.'

'Oh, take your time. I promised him I'd run over the list of scores he'd asked you to check. Byee.'

Had she ended with anything other than 'Byee', Juliet might have felt, if not kindly disposed towards the American, at least not openly hostile, but the silly word infuriated her and she hurried into her shower, scrubbing at her skin as if she were scrubbing Bryony, not a fulfilling experience.

It took more than five minutes to get to the auditorium. She would have been better to take the time to have some coffee, since she definitely was one of those who do not function well without that early morning stimulus.

Karel, in a long-sleeved green polo shirt and dark trousers, was on the podium but he was leaning over talking to a seemingly awestruck Bryony who looked up at him adoringly as he spoke.

'There are difficulties inherent in binding together musicians from different countries, differing experiences, schools. For example, when I do this' – he pretended to make the gesture for 'let's begin' – 'a Russian or a German will be early and an Italian will be late.' He chuckled.

Juliet fumed. Is he flirting? So what?

'Every time?' Bryony was incredulous. 'Gosh, Maestro, doesn't the poor conductor have enough problems?' Her eyes seemed to be gazing into his. Was he looking down into her cleavage? Juliet decided that she hardly cared. Seen one, seen 'em all was her philosophy.

Karel went on with his tuition. 'No, no, it is not a problem once the foreign musician has worked with Stoltze or with Maazel or with Rattle. Musicians learn very quickly. This sound for him, that for her, and they produce.' He looked away from the inviting valley that was bounded on either side by multicoloured silk chiffon ruffles as he saw Juliet.

To Juliet, hypersensitive, his face appeared to change, to become cold and remote. 'How very kind of you to join us, Miss Crawford. You worked so hard last week that you feel you deserve a little free time? Hardly professional. I had hoped to ask you to conduct a schools' concert next Thursday but Miss Wells has graciously agreed to fill in. Now, if you would be so kind, if you are not too tired, to make some telephone calls for me in my office – the notes are on my desk. We' – his gesture seemed to embrace, not only the orchestra, but Bryony – 'will continue with this rehearsal.'

Juliet felt her face grow pink. The orchestra members seemed suddenly terribly busy with their instruments, several taking refuge in turning them upside down in an attempt to empty them. (Of what, for God's sake? They had barely been taken out of their cases.) Bryony smiled at her in the most innocent fashion imaginable. Juliet could not have spoken had her life depended on it but turned and left the room. 'How dare he?' she hissed through gritted teeth as her fingers curled into the palms of her hands until the nails threatened to split the skin. 'How dare he treat me like a naughty ten-year-old? And how dare he give Bryony a job that should have been mine? Bryony has no right even to be here.'

She did not go immediately to the great man's office to make telephone calls like some PA or, God forbid, social secretary; she went instead to the nearest café and drank two cups of very strong black coffee. If he's waiting for me to simper and flutter my eyelashes, he'll wait a long time. Damn it, damn it. I have worked so hard and today I'm late. I was late during the competition but that was because . . . why was it? I could not get out of the green room. Someone locked me in there. I'm sure of it and I'm not paranoid.

The coffee, or perhaps, taking into consideration its strength, the mere act of sitting down drinking something, calmed her, and she managed to laugh at herself. I am not paranoid but I'm behaving as if I were.

She bought some yoghurt, not apricot unfortunately, and made her way to Karel's office. Was it in her remit to make business calls for the senior conductor even if they were business-related? Perhaps it was childish to take refuge in her dignity and refuse to do it. She decided to make the calls; some were fairly mundane but one or two were to German houses, which put her hard-won command of German to the test. She continued stoically until her own mobile rang.

Again it was Bryony, Maestro Haken's other cut-price secretary, to tell her that the maestro would like her to return at once.

'He's going to run through that Shostakovich piece you've been working on, Juliet, and, my dear, please don't get mad because I'm only trying to help. You were obviously mad as hell leaving the rehearsal – the orchestra was so embarrassed – and that's not good. Anyways, honey, hope you're calm and collected and – professional, now.'

With a supreme effort, Juliet succeeded in staying calm. 'It's kind of you to worry,' she managed, but took extreme pleasure in pushing the disconnect button much more severely than was strictly necessary.

She hurried back to the rehearsal. Karel was among the orchestra, talking to a group of the brass players and did not immediately acknowledge her. There was no sign of Bryony. Juliet took her usual seat, her spirits rising as she acknowledged sympathetic smiles from several of the musicians. After several minutes when Karel had not returned to the podium, the leader coughed, possibly to alert him and he turned. Perhaps he had finished what he wanted to say. He saw Juliet and came forward.

'Take your place, Miss Crawford; overtime this week is not an option.'

Trying not to be hurt, Juliet moved to the podium. Damn it, she'd been sitting there like a bump on a log while he chattered but she would not allow anyone to see that she was rather more than discouraged by Karel's animosity. She was late. She was usually early and she had apologised. What more did he want? She took a deep calming breath, which did not work, and opened the score. She looked at it, quickly reading the first few lines. She picked up her baton, a particularly nice one, a graduation gift from Hermione's parents. The orchestra were waiting. She looked at them and, steadily, each and every member looked back at her. The leader smiled encouragingly and adjusted his violin on his shoulder. He was such a fine violinist and a really gifted leader.

What was she to do? How had it happened? The score had been perfect that morning, hadn't it? She looked at it again. Her music was new and therefore the paper was white. This score was yellowed, cracked: there were finger marks on the corners, which were, in some cases, curled from having been turned down. The score was marked, in pencil which had faded or been rubbed out as the conductor had changed his mind, or in green ink – ink because the owner of the score was satisfied with his interpretation and would not change. Who used green ink? Certainly not Karel who used a pencil.

She closed the score and put the baton down again.

Not everyone was annoyed; some obviously found her chagrin funny. She determined that never ever would she laugh or even smile at the discomfiture of a fellow human. She wanted to cry but that was what silly weak women did in moments of crisis and she was mature, a professional, and just because things were going from worse to unrecoverable, that was no reason to fall apart at the seams. So, she had been late; she had been taken to task in public as if she were a fourth-former and she was annoyed, both with Karel for playing schoolmaster and with herself for being late, especially since this time it was definitely her own fault. But to be rebuked like a recalcitrant child . . . it was unforgivable. To have him behave like a father with a four-year-old. 'You were naughty and so you can't have a treat; someone else shall have it instead.' Damn it, damn it. Why was Bryony allowed to be there? Secretarial work. How dare he? And now this. I can't believe this is happening. Who is doing this?

She took a deep calming breath. Forget it, Juliet, get a grip. You can do it.

Again she looked at the orchestra, waiting there, poised, ready to play whatever she asked them in whichever way she asked them to play. She opened the score and closed her eyes – to stop her seeing what she had already seen, or in the futile hope that it would all have been a terrible mistake? No, this could not be happening. This was deliberate malice. The front cover of the score read quite clearly, Shostakovich, Symphony Number Nine, but after reading a few lines Juliet knew without a doubt that a certain Wolfgang Amadeus Mozart had definitely composed the music inside. Certainly the cover was the original one of the music that she had bought in Edinburgh – there was her name in the top right-hand corner – but the pages inside had been torn from an old score and substituted. She could see glue traces on the pages. What on earth was she to do?

Wing it, Juliet. You know this symphony; for weeks now you have gone over it again and again. You can pretend that you are following and just conduct from memory. You can do it.

One or two members of the orchestra were stirring, moving restlessly, aware that something was very wrong. Juliet breathed deeply and raised her baton and the music began. The beginning of the first movement was not too awful; she was even able to make a few sensible remarks, but towards the mid section she lost the way completely and the orchestra, sensing that everything was not as it should be, played without her. She did not dare look at Karel and eventually, since she could not bear to pretend that she was conducting, put her baton down. Under the direction of the first violin the orchestra continued to the end of the first movement and then they too stopped. Juliet gathered up the music and got down from the podium. She looked at Karel who was studiously avoiding her.

'Ladies and gentlemen, shall we take a break? Miss Crawford, if I may see you in my office, now.'

'Of course, Maestro,' she said with as much dignity as she could muster and walked from the room.

He was just behind her and caught up with her before she reached the lift but he said nothing until they were in his office and the door was closed.

'I thought, I believed, that this opportunity was the most important thing in your life, Juliet, but today – what manner of professionalism have you displayed today? You were late and I was annoyed, maybe a little too much, but this exhibition . . . A first-year student at a third-rate music school could have made a better job of the beginning of the symphony, but to stop, to let the orchestra just get on with it, without even to try to direct, what has happened to you?'

'Are you finished?' Juliet asked and she was too angry to cry. Tears would come later.

'For now. You wish to explain?'

'Why, why should I even try? Your whole body language says you have already made up your mind. You spoke to me as if I were a naughty child in school. I was late and I'm sorry. This time it was my fault and I apologised, but to be humiliated before the orchestra in this way. To be given secretarial work. That, Mr Haken, was insupportable.' She turned as if to go. 'To save you firing me, I'll go. I'm sure you'll be much happier with your protégée, Miss Wells, in my place, although, strictly speaking, I think you'll find that Mr Shigetoku's marks were higher. But perhaps you don't let little things like that worry you.'

He was across the room before she reached the door and he pulled her round to face him, his hands gripping her forearms. 'What are you talking about, to go, to go where, and Miss Wells, what are you saying about Miss Wells?'

She shook his hands off. 'You're losing your command of English. I know about you and Miss Wells. I have known for some time. Half the orchestra does too, I should imagine, but your private life is nothing to me. I will resign, Maestro Haken, and will send a letter of apology to the committee.'

'It will not be accepted. To resign because you are proven to be incompetent or unprofessional will only make the panel of judges look foolish; you will stay, Miss Crawford, and you will complete the course, and' – he grabbed her again by both arms so tightly that she winced with pain – 'you will be a success. Do you hear me? Tell me, Juliet, tell me. Why were you unprepared today?'

Unprepared? She would not think of anything but his willingness to think her lazy and incompetent. Anger pulled her from his arms. 'Look, Maestro,' she said, thrusting the doctored score against him so forcefully that it would have been impossible for him to look at even if he had wanted to do so. 'Someone has pulled out the score and inserted music by Mozart. Look at the colour of the cover and the music inside. See? Different. And my own score – the Shostakovich – is covered in my pencilled notations.' She glared at him. 'Well, Maestro,' she challenged, but just then there was a peremptory knock on the door, which opened to admit Margarita Rosa Grey.

'Karel, *querido mio*, and dear Miss Crawford. Forgive me, but I am in London for one day, and would love to audit a rehearsal. You will permit, Maestro, and you, Miss Crawford, you will allow?'

What could they say? To deny their sponsor was totally out of the question. 'Of course, madam,' said Karel as Juliet tried to calm her breathing, smile sweetly and look as if she had not been on the verge of punching the senior conductor.

They left the office together, Juliet still with the vandalised score under her arm. At the door of the auditorium Karel took it from her.

'We had decided that you would use my marked score, had we not, Miss Crawford?'

Juliet had almost forgotten that she had promised to attend the opera in which Erik was starring, that most human of all operas, Mozart's *Le Nozze di Figaro*, *The Marriage of Figaro*. She had read the reviews, *a tour de force* for the young American's first Figaro and was rather ashamed that she had forgotten her promise so easily. During the performance she sat in her pink suit in the really good seat that Erik had obtained for her and tried to listen as if he were a complete stranger and not someone who had shared her bed.

There were several curtain calls and, with a little personal pride, she watched Erik bowing on the stage and then made her way backstage. As always it took several minutes to freshen up, retrieve her coat, and then walk through the crowds to the stage door on Floral Street. Inside the first set of glass doors anxious opera-goers stood clutching programmes, compact discs, photographs, even flowers. The second set of doors was jealously guarded by the doorman who stood there chatting with the receptionist but keeping a watchful eye on the line of fans. No one would be allowed into the inner sanctum unless he had his or her name on his list. Juliet edged her way past the line trying to avoid catching anyone's eye.

'Miss Crawford for Mr Lyndholm,' she said quietly to the doorman when she opened the door.

He looked at the large visitors' book on the desk. Over his shoulder she could see her name halfway down rather a long list and she smiled. Erik was saying goodbye in style.

'This way, madam.'

Juliet followed the doorman through yet another set of doors. An imposing figure in a glorious velvet cloak with a huge fur collar stepped back to allow her through and she gratefully thanked one of the world's finest basses for his courtesy. Then she was hurrying down the wooden ramp to the dressing rooms. Erik's door was open, mainly because no one could breathe with it closed, so many friends were there. The doorman smiled and left her, hurrying back up the ramp to guard the doors as Cerberus is said to guard the gates to the underworld.

Erik, already showered and changed, was holding court. Expensively coiffured and coutured women hung on his every word; some of them were quite lovely and, for a moment, Juliet found herself wondering what he saw in her. Oddity value, she decided, it's the *cachet* of the job. She smiled; her heart was not at all dented, and that was when Erik saw her and, abandoning the adoring throng, bustled his way towards her.

At last the fans – or was it worshippers – had gone, and they were alone. Erik looked around his dressing room rather sadly and then pulled Juliet into his arms as if for comfort. 'I hate saying goodbye to this place.'

'It isn't really goodbye, it's *sayonara* or *arrivederci*.'

'Still hate it. Know why I was so late getting down?'

'Were you?'

He put his hand across his eyes as if to shut out pain. 'Oh, cruel Juliet, you didn't even notice. I was an age. All my corporates were lined up outside the locked door like schoolboys outside the headmaster's office. But, tell me, why was I late?'

'You were bowing to all the silly women throwing flowers?'

He held her a little away from him and looked into her eyes. 'Silly women?'

'Some of them are, don't you think? I was in Vienna a few years ago, Domingo and Baltsa singing.'

'Pretty good?'

'Not their most shining hour,' said Juliet with some feeling. 'It wasn't the singers' fault – it was a ghastly production. Anyway, some middle-aged woman threw the tenor some flowers and they landed in the orchestra pit. I can still see her in her silver lurex pant suit and her carefully coiffed hair climbing into the orchestra pit like a ten-year-old after a football. Silly exhibition.'

'You're too severe. She wanted her hero to see her flowers.'

'Why? So they could strike up a friendship and live happily ever after? Get real. She could have impaled herself on a valuable instrument.'

He began to laugh and hugged her again. 'I'm sure you don't know what you just said. But collecting flowers was not why I was late. I walked all around the stage. The auditorium looks sad after a performance. It's as if it's been used and discarded. From the stage you can see papers, programmes on the floor, and tonight I swear there was an ice-cream tub under a very expensive seat. I always say, "Thanks, you were great."'

'What a romantic.'

'Just wait, Madam Conductor. You can scoff. You'll get to know an auditorium; it will tell you its secrets, the places where sound disappears and the places where it can bounce back even better. It's impossible to be indifferent to an auditorium; some you'll love, some you'll hate. But heck, my last night in London and I'm starved.'

His last night. She had forgotten; in such a short time she had become used to Erik in her life that she had not thought that, of course, he was not based in London. His home was New York. It was really silly to become fond of anyone quickly. She pulled out of his arms. 'Then we'd best find somewhere to eat.'

'You can't do a clever little supper at your place?'

'Not one of my many sterling qualities. I think there's a tin of beans.'

He had his coat on and wrapped a long multicoloured scarf around his neck. 'Garish?'

She looked carefully. 'No, anyone looking at it and you would say, Isn't that sweet; his grandmother must have knitted it for him.'

'My niece gave it to me for Christmas; she's eight.' He turned off the lights and they walked together along the corridors of the almost empty house.

Juliet decided not to ask him about his niece. Swapping tales of the family was for people whose relationship had a future, not for people who might not see each other for months, even years. 'You said there was a party. There will be food. Or Bertorelli's is right across from the stage door: trust me, they do a fabulous linguine.'

'Tonight I think I'd prefer the beans.'

Two hours later he was gone. The tin of beans still sat in solitary splendour in the kitchen cupboard but a half-empty bottle of wine stood on the kitchen table. Juliet would be annoyed when she saw it in the morning, for drips of wine had rolled down the neck and continued on down the sides and had somehow formed a ring on the polished wood, wood that did not belong to her.

She sat in the bed where Erik had been and thought about getting up to put the lock on the door but decided against it. He would call her from New York, he had said. He would be in Europe later in the year; they would meet then. A few hours, he had said, and we can be together, maybe Paris, maybe Madrid; it's so easy these days. A few hours: she looked at her watch. He had been here only a few hours and once again, it had been lovely. Am I in love with him? Am I devastated that he has gone? No, I'm hungry and a little sad, but certainly not devastated. How different it had been . . . once . . . no, that was over: she must destroy those memories. She considered getting up to open the beans and decided against it. Best to go to sleep. It would be fatal to be late again for work. Her last thought before sleep was that she had completely forgotten to telephone Heather. Some friend.

18

Heather and a baby. He was thrilled but, at the same time, rather annoyed with himself for not knowing until she had told them a tad fearfully after her late night tearful conversation with Juliet. Hermione had had no idea either, but she said if Heather hadn't had the decency to throw up at the crack of dawn every morning as all the books said pregnant women did, then she, Hermione, could not be blamed for being unaware of the pregnancy. Heather had put on no weight, and was that not one of the first signs, after the morning sickness business? Did their breasts not get bigger and surely the tummy should look a little rounder? Heather was as flat as a board. Or was she? It seemed to him, now that he was consciously thinking of it, that perhaps she did look a little plumper. Or was he imagining things? What fun it would be to have a baby in the flat. He certainly would be happy to take his turn babysitting. He thought he might be quite good at it. There had always been someone in the housing scheme anxious to unload a baby for a few hours so that they could nip off to the pub or the pictures. He bet Heather's experience of babies and babies' parents was not so rounded as his. What a funny little group they would be, Hermione, Heather and a baby, and him. I'd love to have a baby, he thought, someone to love unconditionally; at least that was the way he would love. But at this moment, just having found out about the baby, if he were Heather he was quite sure he would be absolutely terrified. He did not think of physical pain for he had little experience of it. His pain had usually been mental. Harder to deal with? He shrugged. He had no answer. What a lifelong responsibility, even if you sloughed it off as some people – his mother for instance – did. But Heather had sobbed that she would have the baby, that she did not believe in abortion, and that her career could wait, Montpellier could wait, Covent Garden could wait. Covent Garden had not actually been begging for her to appear but if they did this year, and they might, they would have to wait. Hermione had said that Heather was welcome to stay on at the flat.

'Actually be quite handy to have a regular house sitter if Gregor and I are off hither and yon. But see what your parents say. They'll want you to come home.'

Heather had not been sure of that. 'More likely want me to go to one of those ghastly convent places where they make you scrub floors until the baby is born and then they take it away. No one will take this baby away.'

She had looked quite fierce until she started weeping again. He could not handle gallons of tears and snotty noses and so he had patted her shaking shoulders and gone off to seek solace in the library. 'But I'll help, Heather. I'm sure I was changing nappies at eleven; no end to my talents.'

Juliet jumped out of bed when the alarm sounded and took a shower as hot as she could bear it. She looked at her watch. Almost six. She would ring Hermione who would not mind being wakened. But first she would make instant coffee – no point in facing Haken without artificial stimulus. She noticed the disfiguring ring while she was scraping butter on to a piece of rather overdone toast.

'Damn, damn, damn.'

Washing did not improve the mark and certainly did nothing to dissolve it. She finished eating the toast with one hand while she hauled on jeans and boots with the other. Then, coffee mug at hand, she dialled a very sleepy Hermione. 'I'm sorry, but you can go back to sleep, can't you?'

'Not today,' wailed Hermione. 'I have a meeting about this recording deal. Juliet,' said Hermione, sounding suddenly very wide awake, 'it's six o'clock, are you all right? Have you had a battle with the gorgeous Czech?'

'He's not gorgeous. He's quite ordinary actually and yes, I've had several battles with him recently.' She was going to tell Hermione all about them when she remembered that Karel had loaned her his own score, with his markings, and with it she had impressed the sponsor of her award, so much so that she had been heartily embraced by the wealthy Mexican philanthropist. 'I knew it, I knew it. All the time I wanted you to win. I could feel it in here.' La señora had struck her cashmere-covered breast rather forcefully. 'I don't' – she pronounced it 'dunt' which made Juliet want to laugh – 'interfere during your classes, me, no, I stay away, but as soon as you are finished, you will come to Acapulco and we will talk, yes?'

'No, actually he's got me an invitation to live the high life in Acapulco but I'll tell you all about that later. I needed to talk to you about Heather.'

'She told us. Poor kid. She really fell for that swine.'

'Has she made a doctor's appointment?'

'Yes, tomorrow or is that today? It took a few days. Gregor's going with her for moral support.'

'How did he react?'

'React?' Hermione sounded puzzled. 'He didn't. Possibly he looked slightly embarrassed for a millisecond and then he was a supportive friend again, even told her he could change nappies. Methinks the nuts and bolts had not occurred to her. She does want you when she confronts her parents, though. Can you get a few days off? You must be due something?'

'I haven't had an opportunity to speak to Haken; things have been a tad hectic. I'll tell you all about it later but today I'll look at the schedules; I may be going to Paris to watch some rehearsals. Will you tell Heather I'm sorry I wasn't in touch yesterday and I'll ring her this evening?'

They rang off, Juliet had another piece of toast which was not quite so badly incinerated as the previous one, a second mug of coffee, and was in the rehearsal room thirty minutes before anyone turned up. She had hoped to find her doctored score so that she could show it to Karel – there had been no time yesterday since

Mrs Gray had taken him off with her when she left – but it was not in the room; possibly Karel had locked it in his office for safe keeping.

The orchestra assembled in dribs and drabs, one musician, then three together, another solitary cello, and then suddenly the room was full, as if the remainder of the orchestra had needed the courage afforded by numbers and had herded together like lemmings to thrust themselves together into whatever the day had to offer. Several carried paper cups of coffee from brand-name coffee shops, and the rich dark smell struggled to impose itself on the mixed odours of humanity.

Karel and Bryony arrived together. If Erik telephoned, when Erik telephoned, she would tell him that it looked as if the gossips were correct, even though Karel had seemed surprised by her accusation. She was furious with herself for losing control during their argument; now he knew that she listened to gossip and yet she had vowed to be the consummate professional and at the first sign of trouble she had reacted like a fishwife. She would give him nothing to worry about from now on.

It was mid-afternoon before she could ask him about her Shostakovich score and about getting a few days off. She hoped he did not remember having challenged her with being late to make up for some of the extra time she had given to the benefit. She would ask about the score first. He had to see it; probably he had already examined it. 'Maestro, may I have my score back, if you've finished with it, that is?'

He seemed genuinely puzzled. 'Your score, Juliet?'

'You took it from me, Maestro, when you very kindly loaned me your own score yesterday while I conducted before Mrs Grey. We were outside the auditorium. You took the score.'

He considered. 'You're right, of course. Now what did I do with it? I must have left it here.'

'I thought so too but I've looked everywhere and it's not here; could you have taken it to your office?'

Again he was quiet, deep in thought. 'I am trying to see myself and I see that I took the score but what I did with it, I have no idea.

Throw it down on a table, no. Maybe before Mrs Grey came I would have tossed it on the desk or a table but I took it at the door and so I brought it here and here it must be.'

They readily established that it was not. 'This is a puzzle. My memory must be wrong and obviously it is in my office. We can go there right after this next meeting unless you have something to do immediately afterwards.'

'No, nothing. There is one other matter, Maestro. I need to go home for a few days. Can you tell me when it would be convenient?'

'Your parents are well?'

'Yes. I meant home as in Edinburgh.'

'Ah, the lovely green and silver girl. I should like very much to hear her play.'

He could not possibly be angling for an invitation, could he? 'I'm sure Hermione will come down to audition any time you ask her, Maestro.'

Did he look disappointed? Was she risking blowing Hermione's chances with the conductor? No, he's not petty. Is he?

'Then we shall look at the schedules when we look for the score.'

And she had to be content to wait until the business of the day was over.

Bryony tagged along with them to the lifts. 'Anyone going for coffee?'

Juliet said nothing. It was up to Karel to speak.

'We have some business, Bryony; perhaps another time.'

She was expansive. 'Sure, it's just that that meeting went on so long and talking takes more out of me than conducting. I'll pop along to the Waterside, relax, have a coffee, maybe a glass of wine. I'll be there a while.'

'Afraid I have to shop, Bryony,' said Juliet. Nothing would persuade her willingly to meet Bryony socially. 'My cupboard is bare; down to my last tin of beans actually.'

The lift arrived at her floor; Bryony breezed out with another 'Byee' and so Karel was spared saying anything. They continued to Karel's office but there was no sign of the score.

'This is very strange, Juliet, and perhaps . . . no, I was going to say disturbing but that is melodramatic. Maybe I have a cleaner who—'

'Is a secret and unknown but superb cellist and she stole the score because Shostakovich sounding like Mozart is something phenomenal and she is going to study it and reveal it to the world.'

He had absolutely no idea what she was talking about.

'Sorry, it's just so ridiculous. If you don't see the score you have only my word that the pages had been switched.'

'I don't need to see it, Juliet. I believe you.' He looked down at his highly polished shoes and then back at her. 'I overreacted yesterday and I should never have asked Bryony to take the schools' concert but I can't change it now. I'm sorry.'

Juliet looked at him, saw dark curling hair at the open neck of his short-sleeved polo shirt. The pain of remembering what had been was so overwhelming that she almost closed her eyes. 'It's fine, Maestro. I was late; I won't be again.'

For a moment he looked as if he might say more but perhaps the expression on her face stopped him. 'Thank you. For now, we will consult the schedules and find a breathing space and also a time to hear your friend who should not accept this recording contract. It's bizarre; even if she is the greatest young violinist in twenty years – and if she is, why has she not been snapped up before this? – she cannot possibly have a repertoire. Sorry, not my business. Here, the schedules . . .'

They spent some time looking at the next few weeks that were full of pencilling in and crossings out. 'Awkward. See, here I want you to go to Paris with me; an overnight will do it. I have arranged some work for you with Paris Opera; that's in April but we must arrange before; they are very keen. We'll choose a day when the orchestra is quiet.' He turned pages, read them, turned them back again. 'Go this weekend and you can have Monday; that's the best I can do until May.'

'Thank you, Maestro.' Would Heather consider speaking to her parents so quickly? At least she was going to see her but, if her own parents heard that she had a weekend off, they would expect her to stay with them. Not this time. Heather came first. They would just have to travel to Edinburgh to see her.

She had forgotten Karel.

'You look very fierce, almost as angry as you looked yesterday when you yelled at me. I know, you are hungry. I am hungry; you are hungry. We could go somewhere very quick and then there would be time for grocery shopping.'

So easy to say yes. On the surface it sounded so simple. They worked together; they could go and have a meal together. It happened all the time. But he was the person who would write all the reports on her in a few months' time. His remarks, his sentiments, could affect her entire future. But she had just been confronted with something that she did not want to explore. Better not to be with him for a while, until she had schooled her thoughts and her emotions. 'If you don't mind, Maestro, I'll do my shopping; that will take ages. I really did mean one tin of beans.' She tried to smile brightly to show no offence was meant. 'Then if I'm going home this weekend there are several calls. But thank you.' They had been sitting at the table where the schedules were laid out and Juliet stood up. 'Someone went to a great deal of trouble to vandalise my score, Maestro Haken. I really want to find it.'

'Believe me, so do I.'

She took the night train to Edinburgh. She could have asked to be allowed to leave a few hours earlier so as to catch the four o'clock but she wanted to ask no more favours and, besides, she could catch up with preparation and so be ready to start bright and early on Tuesday morning. Karel was in the foyer as she left and he stopped talking to his companion to raise his hand in farewell. 'Have a good weekend, Miss Crawford.'

She smiled and waved to him and heard, 'Off to Scotland.'

'Lucky girl.'

'She deserves a break.'

What else he said, if anything, was lost as the doors closed behind her but the remark buoyed her up and after she had made sure that she had absolutely everything for the weekend that she had meant to take, including an exorbitantly expensive box of Turkish delight for her former flatmates, she took her newly purchased score of Shostakovich's Ninth Symphony and began laboriously and joyfully to mark it. She went over her first conversation with Haken about the piece.

'An inspired choice, Juliet. Shostakovich, Symphony Number Nine in E flat Major. Why?'

'Because it's cheeky. Shostakovich is so naughty and he gets away with it. Everyone thought he was going to do a Beethoven, something grand and triumphant; Stalin was waiting for it, and he's such an ego that he doesn't realise that he's being parodied in it. The Maestro could have ended up forgotten and frozen in some gulag, and he knew that – he wasn't unaware; he's no not-of-this-world composer scribbling away untouched by what's going on around him. That's what's so fabulous. He's defying Stalin and so, in its way, look' – and she had pointed with her pen to the first lines of the opening Allegro – 'listen to that. Isn't it fun?'

Karel had smiled. 'I never thought of the maestro as naughty or – what did you say? – cheeky. These are words I would not use but you're right. Bravo, Dmitri and bravo, Juliet, or is it correct to say brava?'

'A bit twee,' said Juliet and almost laughed at the expression on his face.

They were still no closer to finding either the score or the person who had doctored it. It was definitely no part of any prank that members of the orchestra might have participated in. There was only Juliet's word that a trick, a rather nasty and unpleasant one, had been played. She wished she had shown it to him as soon as they had entered his office. Had she done so they might not have spent all that time yelling at each other.

The journey up to Scotland was unremarkable. She lay in the hard little bunk with its stiff white sheet and its inadequate blanket and tried to read but although the book gripped her she was afraid that the little bed did not. She felt as if at any moment she might be hurled out of it on to the floor. Possibly that fear was in the minds of the train staff who had perfected hospital corners that kept the sheets so tight that not only was it impossible for the bed's occupant to move, breathing too became difficult. Juliet got up, hauled the covers off and lay down again and was surprised but pleased to find herself still in the bed and reasonably warm as a knock on the door heralded her cup of coffee. She left the 'health bar' alone. They pulled into Edinburgh's Waverley Station almost on time and she hurried out to the corridor. It was much too late for a panoramic view but she never tired of seeing even a small part of Edinburgh come into sight.

It was a cold, clear day as she stepped off the train, looking up at the great bulk of the castle. *Nemo me impune lacessit.* She said the words every time she arrived: *Wha daur meddle wi' me?* Who dares to meddle with me? Not me, said Juliet as she felt her heart singing with joy. Was there anywhere in the world a more beautiful capital city? She avoided the taxi rank: there had been little exercise in the past weeks and so she set off up the unbelievably windy steps to Princes Street. At the top she stopped and turned to look beyond the gardens to the slopes leading up to the castle. Already they were covered in strong green shoots, daffodils, thousands of them; in a few short weeks the hillsides would be yellow and there would be the pink blossom on all the trees. Tiny little yellow primroses would perhaps be already in bloom along her parents' driveway, and under the white rhododendron there might just possibly be a small rare pink one, but nature guarded her pinks carefully and some years she did not share. If it were not for Heather she might carry on further north to Dundee to find out. Spring in Scotland; she would miss it this year.

Hermione, in her pyjamas, answered the door and drew her in with a big hug. 'We're all here, but the others are still sound. Gregor was out late and so we'll leave him for a while. Let's have some breakfast and catch up and then we can take Heather some tea.'

'Tea?'

'Pregnancy is a strange thing. She was perfectly fine during the first, what do they call it, trimester, and now that it's over and all the other pregnant mums are rejoicing at being rid of morning sickness, Heather is finding all kinds of things that turn her poor little stomach: red wine, smell of anything frying, coffee.'

'I don't suppose any of those are good for her,' said Juliet, seating herself at the table in the kitchen.

'But Gregor and I aren't pregnant and unless we get up earlier, we have the same regime.'

Juliet laughed. 'You did switch the toaster on, didn't you? I'm starving.'

'I thought I had,' said Hermione, putting the switch down. 'Another symptom, I'm told, of pregnancy. Here, have some yoghurt.' Six cartons of apricot were taken out of the refrigerator and put down in front of Juliet. 'Gregor is resident midwife; there is nothing, it appears, that he does not know or is not prepared to find out. Just as well someone is welcoming this poor little sprog.' They heard the doorbell and automatically looked at their watches. 'Damn it, that has to be Mrs McD and even earlier than expected. In a moment of weakness I told her you were coming. Let her in, there's an angel, while I start the eggs. She doesn't know about the baby,' she finished as a warning.

Juliet went to the front door and welcomed their neighbour.

'I was watching for you,' Mrs McDermott said. 'I was hoping that you weren't too grand now that you're living in London.'

Juliet reassured her and brought her into the kitchen. The old lady seemed tinier, frailer than she had been at Christmas, but her hair was as freshly and as badly dyed as it had ever been. She accepted coffee and cereal from Hermione and sat down. 'We hardly see Heather these days, do we, Hermione dear, or Gregor. That boy has become a recluse since he went down to London to see you, Juliet. Heather's singing or teaching almost every day. Did you know she's taking that church group again? No wonder she's beginning to look washed out.' She stopped to eat and Juliet looked at Hermione.

'Is she taking that group?' she asked. 'I thought she turned them down.'

'She did – twice – but nothing else came in and the money's regular. Gregor's still playing for her and I fill in when he's busy.'

'What good friends you all are, looking out for one another.' Mrs McDermott sounded sad and Hermione leaned down and hugged her.

'But you're one of us, Mrs McD. One for all and all for one.'

'You're a good girl, Hermione,' said the old lady, patting her hand. 'Now sit down and eat your eggs – yes, I'll have just a spoonful – and Juliet can tell us all about London. Is it terribly exciting, Juliet? Your postcards don't talk about anything besides your work.'

Probably since neither Heather nor Gregor appeared even after the second pot of coffee was empty, Mrs McDermott reluctantly left. Seconds later Heather and Gregor, wearing the dressing gowns that Juliet had seen almost every morning for years, were at the kitchen door and Juliet found herself, for the first time in all their years of friendship, jumping up to give Heather her chair, even though Heather actually looked better than she had looked at Christmas.

'She's healthy as a horse,' said Gregor as he stuck four pieces of bread in the toaster. 'Great to see you, Juliet. I have loads to tell you. But first things first. When are you going to see Heather's parents?'

Juliet looked at Heather who seemed to be fascinated by watching the progress of the toast. 'Heather, I have to travel back on Monday. Let's go today. I'll rent a car; easier to get to the Borders.'

Heather jumped up to snatch the toasted bread; feverishly she began to spread it thickly with butter.

'Feeding two?' asked Hermione and Heather burst into tears.

Juliet glared at Hermione who looked puzzled. 'It's all right, Heather; she's trying to be funny.' She patted Heather, aware that her ability to nurture and soothe was not a cleverly honed skill, and shooed Hermione out. Gregor picked up his toast and his mug and went too. 'You look fabulous and you've seen the doctor. What did he say?'

'*She* said yes, you're pregnant; I wasn't sure about dates and so she thinks the baby might come early June or late May.'

Juliet looked at her stomach, which still seemed as flat as it had ever been, and Heather saw her and laughed ruefully. She opened her dressing gown and it was obvious that she was several months pregnant.

'I was pulling it all in, bad for the baby. I've promised not to wear a panty girdle again, except for today, Juliet. If you take me to see my parents today – I can't go down so obviously pregnant, I just can't. My father will, oh, God, I don't know what he'll do.'

'Haven't you got anything loose, or you could borrow one of those flowy dresses from Hermione?'

'I'd have more chance of getting into something of yours. Have you a long cardigan with you? I'll wear that.'

Gregor, now dressed in jeans and sweater, but with his red hair still in disarray, poked his head in. 'I'm going to rent the car, Juliet. You two can't go by yourselves. I'll drive and wait outside while you talk to Heather's dad.'

'Is that okay with you?' Juliet looked at Heather who was opening a carton of yoghurt.

Heather nodded towards Gregor. 'It'll be nice to have you there.'

'I'm not coming,' said Hermione who had squeezed in past Gregor. They all knew that Heather's parents disapproved of their daughter's friendship with the daughter of people who, for some mistaken and wholly inexplicable reason, they called Parasites and Blood Suckers. 'I thought I'd stay at home, keep the fires burning, have soup ready when you struggle back.'

Juliet was still worrying about confronting a man whose own daughter had no idea how he would react to an unexpected pregnancy. Her own father would probably hide successfully whatever he was really feeling and would talk instead about how stupid and foolhardy were young people who were told everything there was to know and still believed nothing until it actually happened to them.

Gregor managed to hire a Renault Clio in a nice cheery red. 'It's not red,' said Heather. 'Aren't they all called after wines, claret or burgundy or something?'

'Who cares? Let's get going.' If they were going all the way almost to the border between Scotland and England, having what could possibly be a long and distressful talk with Heather's parents, followed by a long drive back to the security and sanctity of Hermione's beautiful flat, Juliet wanted to be on her way. Nothing could possibly be gained by wasting time. Get it done and get it over – face the music.

The bright early morning had been replaced by a rain-soaked city. As always, weekend traffic in and around Edinburgh was busy and no one said anything until Gregor had negotiated his way on to the road that swept down towards the Borders. Once they were away from the trailing skirts of the city their mood, if not their outlook, brightened. Rain-washed hills were somehow not so depressing as substantial rain-soaked buildings, which, to Juliet, always seemed to look sad. Fat, wet sheep huddled against masterfully wrought dry-stone walls and Juliet found herself wondering if there was a limit to the number of sheep that could be supported by one field. Snowdrops powdered slight slopes and if their journey had had any other purpose Juliet would have asked Gregor to stop so that she might pick some to carry with her. She remembered how cool the white petals would feel against her cheek, how their faint scent of woodland and earth would wipe away the smell of travel, but she glanced at Heather and realised that she saw nothing of this beautiful countryside. Poor girl, what did she see: the interruption or perhaps the end before it started of a successful career, or did she see only the faces of her parents as she gave them her news? They stopped once, ostensibly for coffee but really so that the very nervous Heather could use the loo. Juliet found her in there, tears pouring down her cheeks as freely as rain poured down the nearby hills.

'He'll kill me,' she sobbed and threw herself into Juliet's arms.

'I won't let him touch you,' Juliet comforted her, and wondered what she could possibly do to restrain a furious father. 'And besides, he'll probably be much more understanding than you think he's going to be.'

He was not.

Heather's father was as rugged as the hills around his small farmhouse. On a bright sunny day the picture made by the stone farmhouse with its dark green door and window panes set down in a neat, mostly vegetable, garden against the dark brown of the low-lying hills would have been lovely, a view for a tourist to photograph. Several picturesque rivulets of water ran down the hill directly behind the house, draining into a small burn or stream that flowed to the east of the garden. Water, Juliet decided, always adds to a view.

'Looks pretty, Heather. Lots of fish in that stream?'

Heather tried to pull herself together as they walked down the path bordered with overgrown lavender plants. She shrugged a non-committal answer to the question. 'Ducks,' she said. 'Mainly mallard.'

'I'm off for a walk,' Gregor called, 'and then I'll sit in the car. I have some work, so take all the time you need.'

Heather turned a white face towards him. 'Don't go far.'

'I'll stay in the car. I'll come if you need me.'

A little melodramatic perhaps. 'Go for your walk,' said Juliet. 'Nothing's going to happen.' She tried to picture herself in Heather's shoes and just could not. She had been at odds, as far as career options were concerned, all her life with her own father but never in a million years could she see herself being afraid of him.

Heather's parents were short and stocky and as solid as their house. As always Juliet wondered where the golden Heather had come from. Mr Banner stayed by the fire and merely nodded to acknowledge Juliet's presence; her mother was friendlier, and after she had given her daughter a quick hug, put out her hand in welcome.

'I'll make a wee cup of tea,' she said. 'And by the looks of you both you could use some scones.'

Heather rushed to help her mother while Juliet sat and tried to engage Mr Banner in conversation. At last Mrs Banner and Heather returned with the tray. Juliet watched Mrs Banner shakily pouring tea into cups that were obviously from the best set; they were small and fine with a gold rim around the bottom and the top and outlining the handle. Full-blown pink roses bloomed on each side of the cup and surrounding the pinks were golden roses with golden leaves. Old Foley, she almost said aloud, for her grandmother had had such a set.

She thought fleetingly of the ever-hungry Gregor out in the car but never the less she enjoyed the strong tea and the large homebaked and surprisingly light scones. 'Your own butter, Mrs Banner?' she ventured and saw a look of scorn on Heather's father's face.

'Tesco,' he said abruptly.

At last tea was over and Heather and Juliet jumped up to help clear away the dishes. Heather was trembling and Juliet pressed her hand and smiled in what she hoped was an encouraging way.

Mr Banner made the confession, if not easy, possible. 'You have something to tell us, Heather. I hope you haven't given up teaching that church group – the Lord's work for a change.'

'No,' Heather began. 'No, actually I'm coaching them again; they're getting better. The sopranos are soaring ever upwards.' She laughed at her attempt at lightening the atmosphere and dutifully Juliet laughed too. 'Making a joyful noise, Daddy,' she said almost desperately and then, without pausing, launched into her story.

Her father sat quietly while she stumbled through and then stood up; the room felt full of menace and Heather backed towards Juliet who actually found herself looking around for a weapon. 'Whore of Babylon,' was how Mr Banner received his only child's news and at that the sobbing Heather joined her mother in hysterical weeping.

'Mr Banner, please,' Juliet began.

He looked at her, his eyes full of contempt. 'Singing? Singing for a living?' He spat into the fireplace behind him where a feeble fire burned.

The old cups had made Juliet feel some kinship with Mrs Banner but she pushed it away since the downtrodden woman obviously agreed with her bullying husband in everything he said.

'Singing in the kirk on a Sunday was what I wanted. How proud we were, every Sunday, her with her best coat on and her hair brushed so that it caught the light when she moved in the kirk, and then she would sing and we were that proud. Lovely voice for praising the Lord but no, she had to get her head turned. And now where has it got her? All that money wasted and her with no job and no husband.' She began to wail again.

'Quiet, woman; it's all your fault for turning her head with the silly television and the sillier magazines you read. Well, there's no place for you or your bastard here, Heather.'

Bastard. Juliet looked at him and saw that his face and his body language were as solid and immovable as the bleak hills outside. Until he had said that word she had been almost as afraid as Heather, for never in her life had she been in circumstances like these. But that word did it. 'Bastard? How dare you, Mr Banner. How dare you spout all that rubbish about praising the Lord when you yourself are totally without Christianity? You should both be ashamed of yourselves. Perhaps I don't attend a church very often but I'm perfectly sure I read something about "Suffer the little children to come unto me." And nowhere was there a word about only those conceived in holy wedlock.'

Mrs Banner screamed and Heather, although she looked taken aback, stopped sniffling and put her arms around her mother. 'Mummy, Mummy, it's all right. She didn't mean it.'

Later Juliet was to regale Hermione and Gregor with the story, assuring them that at this point she had almost believed she had stumbled on some madhouse. 'The scream made the hairs on the back of my neck stand up,' she said. 'You think that's just something hairs do in Gothic novels, don't you, but it happens. It was the phrase holy wedlock, I think, according to Heather anyway.'

Gregor had wiped tears of laughter from his eyes. 'No, it was "conceived". People like the Banners spell sensitive words like that out or use senseless euphemisms such as "in the family way".'

'It's all that's sensitive about them then, because they threw us out – literally. I don't think I heard "and don't darken my door again" but I may have. By that time I was gibbering as much as Heather.'

'You should have seen them, Hermione,' Gregor had finished the story. 'Heather could barely walk and Juliet was half-carrying her down that wee path. I'd been counting the number of Brussels sprouts still growing on all the leggy stocks in the garden, then the door opened, Heather and Juliet sort of fell out, the door slammed and the curtains were pulled, swish, swish; they must be on rings for I could hear it. I was hoping they'd go flying right off the rail.'

'Poor Heather; she kept sobbing that she would pay all the money back and her father was yelling about how could she possibly earn anything since she had no skills and would soon have her brat, and her mother was going on about not being able to lift up her head at the Rural, whatever that is. I was trying to be dignified and tell them that Heather would be perfectly fine with us and her father told me I was pretty useless too. "Can you bake scones like these?" he yelled at some point and of course I can't. Does an inability to make scones show in one's face, by the way? Whatever, it certainly confirmed my uselessness.'

'Perfectly good scones can be got at any decent bakery, Juliet. Dash it all, I wish I'd been there.'

Juliet looked at the tiny figure with green hair, at the large silver links that circled her hips, possibly in an attempt to anchor the various tops she was wearing to the long leather skirt. 'The only thing that kept me sane was thanking God that you were safe at home,' she said with a great deal of feeling.

'Devil's spawn,' said Gregor as he removed his shoes and put his feet up on the table. 'The idle rich,' he explained in answer to both Hermione's and Juliet's looks of enquiry.

'My family are rich, if you must use that dreadful word, simply because they're not idle.'

'Keep your green hair on.'

Heather, in pyjamas and dressing gown, appeared at the door just at that moment and all three jumped up to bring her in. She had gone straight to bed when they had arrived back at the flat, utterly exhausted both physically and emotionally by the events of the day. She had spent, Gregor had counted, exactly thirty-one minutes and forty-three seconds with her parents.

She looked at them, her eyes sunken in her head, and red from weeping, but there were no tears left. 'I thought he'd be angry,' she almost whispered, 'but he's my father. I thought he'd let me stay.' She pulled her pink, little-girl dressing gown more tightly around her. 'I'm sorry but I have no idea what to do now.'

It was Hermione who took control. 'You're going to have dinner,' she said. 'No, don't panic, *mes amis*, I did not cook it but a chef we all know and love and who has sworn me to secrecy made a few of our favourite things. This is your home, Heather, and we are your family and you will, of course, have the baby here. Gregor, be an angel and open some wine. I'll get Heather some milk.'

Heather argued, talked about applying to the welfare system, explained that she had earned very little since she had graduated and could see no way in which she could earn for the next few years.

'Pay me back when you're at Covent Garden,' said Hermione. 'In the meantime I told you it would be wonderful to have someone looking after the flat when the rest of us are away.' She picked up her glass. 'One for all and all for one. Now, quick, those sauces won't wait.'

19

It felt good to be back in the Barbican Centre. How strange that in such a short time it had come to mean so much to her. Previously she had loved the Usher Hall in Edinburgh; that, she had said, was her favourite concert venue. But now? Things had changed. This great centre with its wonderful music, its apartment buildings with their blue gates and hanging baskets of flowers, its lakes and gardens, would always have a very special place in her heart. She rushed on Tuesday morning to get in early.

Karel was already in the room when she arrived; he looked up from the score he was studying and smiled at her. 'Good morning, Juliet. Did you have a pleasant weekend?'

Where to begin? She took refuge in polite nothingness. 'Lovely, thanks; hillsides covered in snowdrops and sheep.'

He stood up and removed his brown leather jacket and hung it on his chair back. 'Always so hot in here, no? Your journey sounds delightful; in the Czech Republic one does not see too many sheep or cows but perhaps I didn't look in the right places. I shall go in Scotland again one day and look for all the little fat white sheep.' He smiled at the thought.

'Actually, the ones I saw were depressingly grey, rather bedraggled because of the rain.'

'Oh, Juliet, you are destroying my picture of bucolic pleasure.' His face was solemn but his voice was laughing and she smiled back. 'There was a call for you on Friday, by the way, not important enough to spoil your weekend, I thought.' He picked up a piece of paper and handed it to her. 'Jeffrey Forbes; he wanted to come tomorrow to interview you. I asked him to wait until Thursday until you have conducted the schools' programme. You will conduct, will you not?'

What of Bryony? How had he paid her off?

'I can hardly wait, Maestro, for the concert, not for this journalist. Why does he want to talk to me?'

'Because you are newsworthy. Now let us begin.'

'Maestro.' He was standing in front of her chair, tall and just broad enough, his dark hair sprinkled with grey. She had not known that he was in the country but that meant nothing; conductors crisscross the globe like ocean currents.

To her surprise he kissed her. 'You permit an old friend?'

'I'm honoured, sir.'

Maestro Stoltze smiled 'Pooh. Among friends there are no maestros, only Alexanders and Juliets. I have been hearing wonderful things about you.'

From whom? Karel? Did he have nice things to say? He would be honest, would he not? 'Thank you. Sometimes I think things are going very well, and other days . . .'

'We all have off days. Music goes missing; we have to be in so many places we mix up appointments. Don't worry; it's easier when you have an assistant. Now, Juliet, I came down to the bowels here to take you to lunch.'

'But, Maestro.'

'No argument. A maestro's prerogative. Besides, I have cleared it with Karel who is, I am sure, very jealous.'

'More likely he is wondering just how many long lunches his assistant intends to take.'

'The young American is a charmer, is he not? Understandable. You are a woman first, a conductor second.'

She was not sure whether or not she agreed with that. Was she not a woman who just happened to be a conductor or a conductor who just happened to be a woman and, if they were about to argue semantics, she could plead, quite rightly, that at this particular moment and for the rest of her time with the London Symphony Orchestra she was absolutely conductor before anything else, before woman, daughter, friend. She said nothing though. How did a neophyte conductor disagree with one of the most important people in the business? For the moment she would keep her thoughts to herself.

'Let's go up to the library floor. Searcy's Restaurant is quite excellent. The best of British but with a French twist. Perhaps you have been before and would prefer to go outside?'

'I've been bringing a sandwich, Maestro . . . Alexander; there is so much learning to do.'

They had reached the restaurant, a large high-ceilinged room with almost a wall of glass looking out over lakes and gardens. 'And it never stops; that is what is so exciting about the life you have chosen, Juliet, or the life that has chosen you, for it is that way, is it not?'

They stood for a moment at the entrance and for a second she wished this were her father speaking. How wonderful if he could understand as Alexander did. How much older than her father was he, or was he younger? She had been in the habit of thinking of conductors as older men, André Previn, Sir Colin Davis, her favourite, Daniel Barenboim, and even he was only in his early sixties, not at all old in today's world. She would look up Alexander's birth date in the library.

'What are you thinking, my dear? Your face tells me that your mind is a million miles from this delightful restaurant.'

She was young enough to blush furiously. 'No, it is in the restaurant, but, to be totally honest, I was wondering just how old you are, unbelievably rude, I know.'

'Not at all. I am fifty-two, and in the prime of my life.'

'Absolutely.'

'More than twice as old as you are, Juliet, but today, here with you, a very beautiful young woman, as my luncheon companion, I feel twenty-five again.'

She laughed and he laughed with her.

'Shall we stand here all day?' he suddenly called to the restaurant manager who hurried over immediately.

He refused the first table, which surprised Juliet as it seemed perfectly fine to her, but graciously accepted the one right beside it by the windows, and, waving the manager away, pulled out a chair for Juliet. They sat down and were handed the menus.

Alexander smiled at Juliet. 'So, Juliet, isn't this pleasant? We can have a glass of wine,' he said and gesticulated with his hand to the waiter who had been waiting politely for the great man to be ready to order. He did not ask what she preferred but ordered two glasses of Pouilly-Fuissé and Juliet, who would much have preferred a red, was delighted that he had not ordered champagne. 'Now tell me all about the course. Is it as rigorous as you hoped it would be or too demanding, not demanding enough? Are you enjoying the outreach programme? Was the benefit exciting? How I would have loved to be there but one can be in only one place at a time. There, enough questions for a start.'

Juliet was able to say, truthfully, that the programme was as much, and more, than she had hoped it would be. She told him all about her first weeks and the heady excitement of meeting several world-famous musicians during the benefit rehearsals, but did not mention Bryony at all, and Karel only as much as was quite necessary.

'Maestro Haken has been exceptionally kind; nothing is too much trouble. He had a right to be angry when I took an extra long lunch break with a friend.' Her mind raced. What had he said? "The young American is a charmer." How did he know? But she must get back to the conversation, 'That I hadn't meant to is beside the point but he had come to help me – and I wasn't there. Justifiably annoyed, I should say.'

The wine was put in front of them and Alexander gallantly lifted his glass and toasted her. 'To you, to a long and distinguished career. Now let us order.'

When their orders had been taken he went back to what Juliet had been saying. 'Karel never mentioned your lunch date, Juliet; I would surmise, therefore, that he was not annoyed.'

How wonderful if that were the truth.

They sat chatting and sipping their perfectly chilled wine until their choices arrived.

'A huge difficulty for the young conductor is lack of age and experience. For instance, it is very, very important to know a composer's entire output. You must compare and contrast and see the maturation and recognise the seeds of the flowering genius. But a twenty-five-year-old cannot possibly know intimately every work by say, Smetana, and if by some odd chance they did know it all, then they could not possibly know anything at all by anyone else. Age is a strength for the conductor; his powers wax with maturity. Karel says you have an amazing ability to think into your selected composer's mind but he agrees with me that in five years you will be one hundred per cent better and in ten, my God, my dear Juliet, where will you be in ten years?'

'You are flattering me, Alexander. In ten years' time I may well be teaching little girls to play the piano. I have made so many mistakes.'

'But of course. The orchestra would be very surprised if you did not. They are on your side. I have spoken with several of them and to a man, or woman, they admire your ability to be totally honest. It is quite exciting for an orchestra who are used to being conducted by elderly paragons who believe all their publicity to find someone who says, "I'm sorry, I can't really tell why that note is wrong. I just know it doesn't sound right. It's not clean." Is this your biggest problem, intonation?'

'I'm told that I take things too quickly, but, yes, intonation is a minefield. I believe I have a good ear. I can tell when a chord is wrong.' She bowed her head. Should she confess to what she saw as an almost fatal flaw? Would he help her? Could he? She lifted her head again and looked at him with troubled eyes. 'I try very hard. I really do but – I can't always tell which instrument is hitting the wrong note.'

He gave a shout of laughter and at once looked much younger than his fifty-two years. 'What is it they say in this delightful country? "Join the club." Were you always in a hurry when you were a little girl? Hurry with playing the piece. Hurry with learning what took even the sublime Furtwängler years to learn. This is where you are training your ear, Juliet. Just think, say that one day last week you told a flautist that his note was too low when he knew that yes, it was wrong but probably too high. He will be angry that his note is wrong but pleased that you recognised it, that you could

236

hear its imperfection. So now you know that you heard a wrong note and that it was high, not low, and so you listen to the sound again in your head and say, "The flute is too high." It takes years of listening to one hundred and twenty instruments all playing together for a conductor to sharpen his skills. The best conductors are those who can listen, really listen.'

'You make it sound so easy.'

'Time, Juliet. It is on your side. Now tell me how nice your lamb is.'

The food was excellent, as was the service, and Juliet was rather surprised that Maestro Stoltze had been impatient and, at one point, almost rude. She had thought that his charm was an integral part of his psychological make-up but it seemed he used it or not at will; she was disappointed. The restaurant was elegant in its simplicity but Juliet would have preferred that the single flower on the table had been chosen for its scent rather than for its looks. She decided to relax and enjoy the meal. Alexander was at his best with her and was a delightful companion; he seemed genuinely interested in her experiences as a fledgling conductor and was full of possibly apocryphal tales of his own beginnings. He made her laugh; he made her feel feminine, and intelligent, and, more importantly, accepted.

'We must do this again, Juliet,' he said as they headed for the lifts. 'In fact, I am going to Covent Garden on Friday evening and would be delighted if you would come with me. It's a ballet although I'm not sure what but I'm told this phenomenal young Cuban, Carlos Acosta, will be dancing. Three times I have tried to see him dance. Tell me that you too are an aficionado.'

She loved ballet and had not been out since Erik had left for New York. He telephoned often but that was not quite the same. She was lonely. An evening at Covent Garden, and in the company of a sophisticated and worldly man, would be wonderful. She told him so but not quite in those words.

'Good. Then give me the address of your little home and I will pick you up at, say, six. And not, I think, black tie. We will blend.'

Juliet almost skipped back to the studio. Not black tie. Hermione would be delighted that she was to have another chance to wear the little pink suit. Juliet was feminine enough to wish that she still had the diamond studs to wear with it.

Much later that night as she lay in a bathtub full of hot scented water she found herself again wondering how Alexander had known that she had had a too-long-lunch with anyone; she was, now that she thought about it, quite sure that she had never mentioned his name.

'No glamorous dress today?'

'For a schools' concert?' Juliet looked at Bryony, who had decided to let her resentment of Juliet's position with the orchestra show. The past few times they had been in the same room she had been barely civil and if eyes can be said to smoulder, hers certainly had. Juliet found herself wondering why Bryony was there when it seemed to bother her so much that Juliet had won the competition; surely watching her all day must rankle.

'You really are amazing, Bryony,' she said. 'I think, if our positions were reversed, I would want to be miles away.'

Bryony laughed heartily. 'Golly, Juliet, whatever for? You of all people should know that the best man – or woman – doesn't always win.'

Juliet said nothing but her mind was reeling. What on earth did Bryony mean? She merely smiled, went on checking that the music in her folder was the music she was going to conduct, the music the orchestra was going to play, and that she had the notes for what she had planned to say to the children. If Bryony wanted her to react she would not indulge her. She remembered the dreadful feelings she had had after the Paris débâcle but if one allowed feelings of grievance to take root then they would only grow and choke any creativity. That had been a hard-fought lesson.

'You're not going to conduct Mozart dressed like that?'

Juliet looked down at her ensemble, long peasant shirt, low-slung belt, high boots into which her embroidered jeans were tucked, and managed to laugh. Her confidence in her outfit was a tad dented. Was she wrong to dress so differently? Would the teachers accompanying the pupils think she had lost her mind? No. But if they did, so what? She was trying to communicate in her own way. 'Actually, no,' she said at last. 'I have the most fabulous felt hat. Mozart was trendy; he would love it, and, what's more important, so will the youngsters.' She closed her folder and without another word walked out, closing the office door very gently behind her.

Karel was walking along the corridor towards her. 'Good, Juliet, I was just coming to find you. Will you join me for lunch? There are still some details about Paris we have to discuss.' He took it for granted that she would agree and turned and walked back towards the elevators. 'No glorious dress today?'

She looked at him quickly but he was smiling. 'For a moment there I thought you really expected me to be formal.'

'You look wonderful. In honour of the Moussorgsky piece, I suppose.'

'You don't know much about fashion, Karel. This is called boho and is *le dernier cri*. I actually hadn't thought of the music at all; I was merely hoping to show our audience that classical musicians aren't stuffy. Wonder what Mozart would say?'

They had reached the lifts. 'He would be speechless,' said Karel and with an enigmatic smile ushered her into the elevator.

The concert went well; there were, in fact, several quickly hushed wolf whistles from a row of teenage boys when Juliet stepped on to the podium but they settled down to enjoyment of the music. For the young conductor it was as perfect as a concert can be. The orchestra responded to her and the school-children seemed to be receptive to her discussion of the music, several extracts from music by Moussorgsky, Sibelius and Mozart.

'Well done, Maestro,' said Karel when he met her in the corridor. 'There are dozens of very angry young men on buses leaving the Barbican right now.'

Juliet stopped, the smile draining from her face. 'Angry? Why? What happened? I thought it went well.'

Did she imagine that he began to reach out his hand as if to touch her? 'It was superb. No, I heard several angry young men –

and women – saying they wanted to get your autograph but their teachers hauled them away. Your inbox will be inundated. Just wait and see.'

He was right. Next morning Juliet was almost swamped by emails, and several of them were from girls who had loved her clothes but had hoped to see her in the dress that had caused a storm at the competition. 'Blinkety blink, damned if you do and damned if you don't. So help me, next time I'll wear a sack.'

'That really would cause a sensation.' She had been so busy reading her emails that she had not heard Karel come into the office. 'May I see?'

She scooted her chair over so that he could see the screen. 'Wonderful, thirty-five messages, some from children who have never been in a concert hall before. This is fantastic, Juliet. And, no, it's not about your clothes: only a few. You're seeing the ones that say, "You should have changed into something more romantic for Mozart." Actually, speaking personally, I find *Doctor Zhivago* extremely romantic.'

She would not take him seriously. 'Very funny, but you're right, ninety per cent are talking about the experience, the sounds, their feelings at being in a concert hall. I hoped they wouldn't really notice the clothes, just notice that I wasn't wearing tails.'

'We never wear tails for informal school programmes. Jeans. Next time I'll wear a hat. Look at that. "You are so trendy. Way out." What does way out mean?'

'I have no idea,' she lied. 'Now I have to get ready for that interview.'

'Not before you see the review.'

She jumped out of her chair. 'Review? What review?' She almost grabbed the paper from his hand. 'Did they like it? Did they hear the music, hear how fantastically wonderful it all sounded?' With growing anger she read the review and handed him back his newspaper with a muttered, 'Sorry.'

'It's very important for us to get such good reviews of our educational programme, Juliet. This is very positive.'

'Is it? Not a "and the music was quite nice," or even a "Karajan she ain't." Just "Juliet is the jewel in the orchestra's crown." How bloody corny and patronising, and not even original.'

'You are angry, Juliet, but this review is about the concert. He is applauding your ability, and yes, he mentions a rather unusual outfit, but so what. In any art form it takes time to build up a reputation. I think you will always be called the Jewel but it will be because you are a jewel, a wonderful conductor. Me, I think it is rather nice.'

She looked at him and she was still too angry and ruffled to see the warmth in his eyes or to notice that his face was even thinner than usual or that he looked tired. 'No one makes patronising avuncular remarks about you, Maestro.'

'Avuncular? Oh, the uncle. No, they don't, but the world is not a fair place, Juliet. When I was growing up in Omolouc times were hard; not so hard as for musicians like Maestro Stoltze, but hard. When I would complain my mother would say, "Wicked, thoughtless boy, there are starving children in Africa." Why do you laugh?'

'Oh, Karel, mothers all over the world are the same, except in Africa, perhaps,' she added soberly. 'But I too was shamed by starving African millions. My father says his mother always said China: "There are children in China would be pleased to have that meal," was what she used to say. Very well, I will try to see this in a positive light and now I will go for the interview.'

'Don't antagonise the man before he opens his mouth, Juliet. Walk softly.'

'That's a quote, Karel, and the second half is "and carry a big stick".'

She smiled at his look of surprise and whisked herself out of the room. She hurried to the green room and got there just before the journalist, Jeffrey Forbes, was shown in. She remembered Karel's suggestion that she be sweetness and light, and so she offered him a seat which he took and a cup of coffee which he did not.

'I have no objection if you have a cup while we're talking, Miss Crawford, but I can't do two things at the same time.'

She smiled, poured herself coffee and sat down. She noticed that he was looking at her legs, which were almost completely hidden under a calf-length tweed skirt.

'Clothes are important to you?'

'Yes,' she said calmly. 'They avoid embarrassment and chills.'

He smiled sourly. 'Very droll. Perhaps you could tell my readers when you decided to become a conductor, Miss Crawford.'

What did he want her to say, expect her to say, and how would he print her reply? Would he tell his readers her answer showed a desire to dominate or would he find it charming? She decided to tell the story more or less as she had told it to Karel. 'I was eight years old. In fact it was a birthday treat. My godmother, who had given me a piano for my birthday, took me to a concert in the Usher Hall in Edinburgh. Alicia De Larrocha was playing and Aunt Sarah had high hopes that I would be enthralled and eager to emulate her. I was bewitched and, yes, with the playing which as always was outstanding but I couldn't take my eyes or my attention off the conductor. Strangely enough I have no recollection of who it was. I told my parents when I went home next day.'

'And you have never hesitated, deviated, never thought, even once, that you should have taken your godmother's advice and become a pianist?'

'Not for a second. I love the piano. I enjoy playing, listening to great pianists even more but I had to be a conductor.'

'A power complex?'

She had thought that remark, which she had expected, would have been phrased a tad more delicately. 'Possibly,' she said calmly. 'I know that I never think of it as power, of being in control, especially since a bolshie orchestra will soon knock the stuffing out of anyone they think is playing above their weight. If I were a concert pianist I could show only my interpretation of how I think the piano score should be interpreted; I would try to think myself into the head of the true genius, the composer, but still I would have control only over my own interpretation, my own playing. As a conductor I read the music for every instrument. I study, I listen, and then I come to several conclusions; next I try to put the overall picture in place, to create this one magnificent whole; the flutes should sound just so, and the bassoons and the violins, etcetera. Next I try to create, with the help of twenty, forty, one hundred superb musicians, the magnificent whole. I suppose one might say the conductor has an overview . . .'

'A divine overview, Miss Crawford?'

'God alone is divine.' It was a put-down but he merely smiled and she went on. 'An overview of how I feel the piece should sound. I present it to the orchestra and hope that they will agree.'

'And if they don't?'

'It's called patience, Mr Forbes, and understanding. Many of the brilliant musicians with whom I work were playing and interpreting before I was even born. They are usually willing to listen and even to be swayed. If they don't agree, they tell me; they tell the leader, that's one of his reasons for being there, and we discuss it.'

'Some nuts are hard to crack though.'

She smiled at him. It was a beautiful smile and she knew it. It was part of her arsenal. 'Indeed, but none of the hard nuts, as you call them, are in my orchestra.' She stood up, the interview over. He could write what he damned well pleased.

'But I haven't asked you questions about the difficulties inherent in being young and a woman and, dare I say it, sexy?'

'Pretend you did,' she said as she walked over to the door. She stood there, holding it open for him.

'My readers,' he began.

'Will be fascinated, as always, by the depth and breadth of your interview.' Again she smiled a truly beatific smile as he walked past. His hand, with his notebook, touched her breast – by accident? – and when she closed the door she leaned against it and closed her eyes for a moment while she counted slowly to twenty. Not well done, Juliet, my dear. You let the smarmy sexist pig get to you and make a note to self: Do not stand within striking distance. She looked down at her sweater and took off the matching scarf. Attractive and trendy but in the green room she felt too hot. She could still feel his hand on her nipple and she rubbed at it with the scarf in the hope that it would go away. What am I going to say to Karel? That I didn't like Forbes, that I had a gut instinct that he was leading up to questions that I feel are nothing to do with music?

She went over to the CD player and idly rifled through the discs until she found a favourite, a truly lovely piece of Mozart, a cantata written for the Vienna Society of Musicians in 1785. As the disc started she heard the exquisite poignant sound of solo wind instruments, one after the other, each more beautiful than the last, leading in and then completely surrounding a glorious tenor voice. They caressed the sound, spoke to it, answered it. A moment of silence and then the allegro, the voice dominant but the winds vying with it, and then deciding to work in glorious partnership, equals, one showing the finer points of the other, until, the voice silent, the instruments swept to a definitive close.

A te, fra tanti affanii
Pietà cercai, Signore.

To thee, when in so much anguish, I looked for help, Lord.

Works every time. Thank you, Herr Mozart. She switched off the music system, reflecting that a great tenor voice is certainly a gift from God.

Then she went back upstairs. Hermione would have handled that creep better. Maybe I should have purple hair.

Later that same night she was in the front row of a box at the Royal Opera House watching seemingly weightless dancers soar through the air and, instead of watching in wonder, she found herself wondering how Alexander Stoltze had known that her vandalised score had gone missing.

The altered music had never turned up and nothing had been said about it. This week work had gone on more or less as before except for yesterday and Juliet's first public performance, for it had been a public performance, although the audience consisted of schoolchildren. And very discerning they were too, decided Juliet, ignoring for a moment the odd protestation of undying love or the wishes that she had worn that dress and so looked more like a 'real' conductor. Karel had also finalised the details of her trip to Paris and her heart beat with excitement at the thought of returning to the scene of what she saw as her worst humiliation – the competition where she had failed to make the final. Now she would be returning, not to conduct, but to observe, not as a mere conducting student but as the winner of the prestigious Margarita Rosa Grey competition. Karel was to accompany her for the first visit but on the second visit he would stay only one day.

'I would love to be there the whole time, Juliet. Paris is an enchanting city and I go as often as I possibly can but' – and here he had treated her as an important member of the team – 'we cannot both be gone at the same time.'

If only it were true: if only she were a really important part of this great orchestra. How wonderful that would be. A small part of her thought too for a mad moment that to be in an 'enchanting city' with Karel would be very pleasant.

Don't be stupid, she told herself ruthlessly. Any city is enchanting in the right light.

'Are you unwell, Juliet?'

She had completely forgotten where she was and Alexander Stoltze was leaning close to her, his expression concerned.

'No,' she whispered. 'It's just so wonderful.'

She kept her mind firmly in the great theatre and fixed on the flawless artistry being exhibited on stage by dancers including – they were thrilled to see – Carlos Acosta, but eventually it was all over and they joined the hundreds of ballet lovers who queued for coats, talking, laughing, uplifted by the spectacle. Most spoke of what they had just seen but Juliet heard a few voices, 'Isn't that Stoltze? How exciting. So this is what conductors do in their spare time.'

If Alexander heard them he gave no sign but helped Juliet with her coat and ushered her from the theatre out to where his limousine was waiting. No taxi worries tonight.

Juliet was young enough to appreciate the luxury of a chauffeur-driven car; she would tell Gregor all about it for the naughty pleasure of hearing him rant and rave about the haves and the have-nots. Some day he would be a rich and world-famous composer. She fully expected him to turn up to openings on a bicycle; that also saved greenhouse gases.

The great car slid quietly away from the kerb and purred along towards Juliet's apartment building.

'I'll escort you in, my dear,' said Alexander when they arrived and although she assured him that the building was completely safe he insisted on walking to her door with her. She was rather nervous and, as if he sensed it, he kept well away from her, and then walked with her along the corridor near enough to be escorting her but not close enough to touch her. She relaxed and that is when he put his arms around her and kissed her full on the mouth.

She had been nervously expecting something but was still taken completely by surprise and although she did not respond she was so surprised and dismayed that she did not reject him and so he kissed her again and at that she pulled herself free. 'You misread my signals, Maestro,' she said. Inside she was in turmoil. Had she been sending signals? Surely not? Or was he so used to being fawned over that he was conceited enough to believe she would welcome his advances?

He laughed and it was genuine laughter. 'Bravo, Maestro. You are a very beautiful and desirable young woman and you cannot blame a man for trying. Come, come, Juliet, you gave no signals at all, my dear. You are in no way to blame. Now goodnight; it has been a most pleasant evening and I trust my precipitate action has not spoiled our friendship.'

'Are we friends, Maestro?'

'But of course.'

'Then will you tell me who told you that I had a late lunch with Mr Lyndholm and who told you that music went missing during one of my sessions?'

She had disconcerted him and it was obvious that he did not like the experience. 'Karel,' he said after some thought. 'He is my protégé, you know, and his career, his ranking, his opportunities are very important to me, like a son. He discusses everything with me. No doubt he told me during one of our briefings.'

He had already told her that Karel had said nothing about her taking a long lunch and gut instinct told her that that statement had been the truth and that Maestro Stoltze was lying now. But why?

She managed a fairly normal smile. 'Of course. I should have thought of that. Goodnight, Maestro, and thank you.'

20

Gregor opened his eyes to find that for the third time this week he had fallen asleep without undressing. That meant too that he was lying on top of his bed and explained why he was cold instead of deliciously warm and comfortable. He had to get into a routine. This working until the early hours of the morning and then walking home to save money was not doing him the slightest bit of good if he woke tired, hungry and cold. He had absolutely no idea of the time since the room was dark and he rolled off the bed and went to the window to open the curtains. He could not remember closing them and so realised that Hermione had probably closed them for him so that the heat from his single radiator would not escape. 'I love you, Hermione,' he said, 'but not in the way you need. I'm sorry. God knows I'm sorry.' He pulled open the curtains but instead of looking at his watch he stood, spellbound, and looked at the sky.

Only Michelangelo could have done this or did he mean Turner with his mastery of light? The sky, as he pulled aside the curtains, was grey with the faintest hint of a dawning rose edging the clouds as a girl often edges the opening of a dress or jacket in a contrasting shade but, as he watched, the entire width of sky outlined by his bedroom window was set alight. Just as a match set to paper and dry kindling in a fireplace will suddenly burst into glorious flame running along the sticks, consuming them with ease, so too did the master painter devour the grey of the night sky. Great swirls of red, frail wisps of pink and eddies of gold and grey enchanted his tired eyes and suddenly in his head he heard music, triumphant, glorious.

He hurried to his desk for manuscript paper and knelt there at the window scribbling furiously as if the music were being dictated to him; it was original, held no echoes of any masterwork, no Beethoven or Grieg, no Debussy or Stravinsky. This was pure Gregor Morrison.

The bare branches of a great sycamore were outlined against the wakening sky that seemed to attempt to devour them, but still they waved in the slight breeze allowing the glorious flames to rush past them. Gold, rippling like the surface of a pond in the warm breeze of a summer day, overtook the red, the pink, the grey. Gregor laughed aloud and scribbled furiously, black dots and lines, swirls and curves, clambering over page after page of his paper.

The sky had paled; the beautiful dawn had gone, replaced by a weak sun in a pale grey sky. 'A sour day,' his mother would have said, his mother who had been so proud of her clever son, the first member of the family ever to get to university, but who had washed her hands of him when he had fallen willing victim, as she saw it, to the demands of classical music. She had delighted when her untrained child had sat down at the battered upright piano in the miners' hall and played immediately anything that anyone hummed or whistled – after all, had his precocious ability not brought in a few bob and the odd pint? But this refusal to study something useful, his refusal to learn a proper trade, was unacceptable. She would be embarrassed, after all her noisy pride in him, to discover that he was barely scraping a living working in a menial job, one that was scarcely much cleaner than the one that had killed his father.

'Gregor?' Hermione, in a comfortable pale blue jogging suit, was at the door with a mug of coffee. 'Can I come in? Are you all right?'

He tried to stand up when he heard her but his legs were cramped and he staggered. 'Damn it, cramp, pins and needles. I've been kneeling for hours. Thanks, Hermione,' he finished as she handed him the coffee, which he drank gratefully right there on the floor by the window.

'I thought you were sleeping off a massive night; didn't hear you come in last night.'

But he was not listening, once more deep in his composition.

'Why not have a shower and I'll make you some breakfast.' He said nothing. 'Gregor, the street outside is full of naked women; it's a parade.'

'This is good, Hermione, good.' He was shaking with excitement as she took the sheets of manuscript paper from him and began quickly to read. He said nothing as she turned over page after page but his eyes never left her face as he tried to read in her expression just what she thought of his work.

When she had finished she said nothing but put the music down on his bed, the only uncluttered surface and then crouched down and hugged him and they stayed like that for a moment. 'And you didn't think you were capable of composing something for me for that New Year concert. You have to learn to value yourself. Gregor.'

He smiled. 'I'm glad you're the first to read it, Hermione,' he said at last. 'It had to be someone who understands.'

'Have you been up all night?'

'Only since dawn. Must do that more often; it's mind-blowing.'

'So's your composition. Let's play it.'

'It's too raw; the structure and form aren't right yet and I have to score it but it's playing in my head, Hermione, and it's the best I've ever done. I can hear it all, the strings, the woodwinds, the triumph over darkness; that's you, the solo violin. I want to roll this up and hide it under my shirt because it's so beautiful and I want nothing to hurt it, no critic, no conductor, no sodding expert.'

'No one will hurt it, Gregor. I can hardly wait to play it and soon – won't it be fabulous – you can have Juliet conduct it. But for now, how about some breakfast or some lunch?'

He was rolling up the sheets. He could not let them out of his sight. As he followed Hermione into the living room, still rubbing at his protesting muscles, he began to realise just how hungry and tired he was but oh, this joy, this fulfilment; it was exactly as he had felt it years before when he had composed his first piece for piano; he had been the greats all rolled into one, Mozart, Beethoven, Liszt, Bach, all of them. He was one with them, an immortal among immortals. Such is the arrogance of youth. The feeling had lasted until he had actually begun to study music and, at first, had been terrified of the gap between an untaught boy who could play by ear on a badly tuned piano, and real genius. Bach was his god, if he believed in any god at all, and *The Well-Tempered Clavier* the most brilliant book of music. He had absorbed the pieces, making them part of him and had striven just to approach the foot of the throne on which the masters sat. The great Mozart could sit and scribble down the melodies dancing in his head and not one note would have to be changed. The sublime Beethoven, on the other hand, edited umpteen times, never satisfied. Were these scribbled notes, tentatively named 'The Triumph of Light over Dark', were they ostentatious, presumptuous? No. For at last he, Gregor Morrison, had composed something that would one day, after a great deal of work, be worthwhile.

He smiled at Hermione. 'Hermione, I wish,' but he could not go on. He wanted to tell her that he wished, with all his heart, that she could be his inspiration, his muse. She would play the solo, of course; that was definitely for her.

'Are you ready to show it to Sir Thomas?' She put a plate of lavishly buttered hot toast on the table in front of him.

Gregor thought about Tom, this unexpected but long awaited answer to so many unspoken prayers, who had, so suddenly, come into his life, structuring it, forming it as he would attempt to do with his composition. 'No. I'm not sure . . .' He tried to analyse his feelings: excitement, anticipation, euphoria, gratitude. No, he would leave analysis to the experts. 'It's so wonderful to be taken seriously,' he finished.

'We have always taken you seriously.'

Was she hurt? No, not Hermione. 'I know and that's great.' He took an enormous bite, chewed and swallowed it and then looked around. 'Where's Heather today, by the way?'

'Recording. The chorus is doing something. *Dream of Gerontius* perhaps. Afraid the weekend's sport sort of knocked that out of my head.'

He smiled. 'Poor old Heather. Isn't it odd? My mother would sympathise with her but she threw me out because I wanted to be a musician; Juliet's father has a face like a sour plum because she's not a doctor and your parents, who should be the ones with all the hang-ups, are great.'

She unfolded her left leg from under her and curled up on her right leg. 'I'll tell them you approve; they'll be enchanted.'

He grinned. 'Heather,' he said. 'Thank goodness she doesn't have those early morning sickness things. Can't you just see the chorus master's face if right in the middle of bar seventeen . . . ?'

'Thank you, Gregor. No need to draw a picture. Damn, I promised to get Mrs McD for coffee. Can you go and pull something decent on and I'll get her, and remember, no word of the baby.'

He got up obediently and, taking his toast with him, went back along the hall to his bedroom. He could tell old Mrs McD about his composition. She was a funny old bird. Whatever anyone said, she did come to see them because she loved music and, although there were enormous gaps in her knowledge, she also knew and appreciated a great deal. He found himself wondering about her life, her family. She told them nothing but then did they ever ask her about her past? Maybe she would tell them. And they should tell her about the baby. If Heather, as seemed likely, was going to have her baby in Edinburgh and it was going to live here with them, their neighbours would be certain to find out; better to tell them before the event. Still, the baby was Heather's and, although she was involving them all, even bringing Juliet back from London to help her, announcing its imminent arrival was her business.

Mrs McDermott looked as if a puff of wind would blow her over. Hermione was so struck by how rapidly the already slight old lady was losing weight that she commented before she could stop herself. 'Mrs McD, you're skinnier than I am and I'm half your height. Aren't you eating? Aren't you well?'

'I'm fine. Hermione dear, I'm not happy with green; the purple was so you.'

Hermione twirled. 'Think so? To tell the truth I'm giving my poor old head a breather, letting it go until this wedding and then I shall colour co-ordinate. But back to you. Gregor, don't you think Mrs McD is too thin?'

Gregor had just come back from his bedroom – fully dressed, for him – in old jeans and a polo-necked shirt that had seen better days. He looked at their neighbour and he could see, as Hermione had seen, that she had lost considerable weight that she could not afford to lose. He sat down beside her and took her hand. 'Not feeling well, Mrs McD? Lost your appetite? Will I make you some of my world-famous scrambled eggs and then we'll have a recital?' He looked up at Hermione. 'A brand-new work by that man about town, Gregor Morrison, never before heard; in fact, Mrs McD, I only started it this morning.'

She clapped her hands with glee and held them tightly together in her lap now that Gregor was standing. 'And there's a part for a purple-headed paragon?'

'Absolutely, but eggs first, and then you will have to be very kind, for not one note has been played yet, and it's not scored, but I've just realised that I can't wait to play it myself. I have a sponsor: can you believe it? When we went to see Juliet, a man introduced himself . . .' He seemed to realise that he was talking feverishly, excitedly, perhaps too much. There was too much happening too quickly. 'Anyway, we're talking about financial backing to give me time to create. I faxed him some of my college pieces and he liked them, said what the teachers said, they showed promise but were immature.'

'I'm so pleased, Gregor; this is going to be such a wonderful year for all of you. Now let's hear what you've done.'

'Food first.'

Maestro Stoltze disappeared out of Juliet's life as serenely as he had entered it. Flowers were delivered to her flat a few days after the ballet, and the card accompanying them said that he would be in Prague for several weeks and would contact her when he returned. She found herself being glad that he had not sent them to the offices; for some inexplicable reason she wanted neither Karel nor Bryony to see them. She looked at the flowers and knew that she did not want them in her flat. They had no scent, an unforgivable sin in a flower as far as she was concerned, and since she was trying to be totally honest with herself, she wanted no reminders of Alexander Stoltze, neither of his arrogant presumption nor of his undoubted charm. Were she in Edinburgh she would have taken the flowers along the landing to Mrs McDermott but apart from a few people in her building to whom she murmured Good morning or Good evening if they met in the halls she knew no one to whom she could give them. She rang Hermione. 'I have a huge bouquet of forced flowers on the kitchen table and I don't know what to do with them. I'd give them to Mrs McD if I was at home.'

'Remind me to ask you why you want rid of them but I was going to ring you. Mrs McDermott isn't very well. She had a heart attack yesterday, right here in the sitting room. Gregor was marvellous – there is no end to his knowledge – and seemingly he kept her alive until the ambulance got here. She's in the Western and don't worry too much, she's already fussing about getting home.'

'What do the doctors say?'

'Just that it's not her first heart attack, and that she's seriously undernourished; obviously she doesn't eat properly.'

'You can't think that the only time she eats is when she comes to us?' Juliet was thinking rapidly, reasoning, remembering.

'No idea; they weren't too keen to talk to mere neighbours, but you know, Juliet, I went along to her flat to get nightclothes and washing things and it's full of really lovely furniture. I can't swear to it, since I'm no authority, but it looks as if there's a very rare cabinet in the sitting room, a Venetian *lacca povera* bureau cabinet, and if it's genuine my mother would kill for it. There's also, again if it's real, a very dirty Lalique Pour Homme perfume bottle on a table. You know the thing, looks a bit like the spirit of Rolls-Royce. The rooms are fearfully dark though, curtains drawn in every room . . .'

'Mummy does that to stop the sun bleaching things.'

'Mine too but not every curtain in every room and not twenty-four hours a day. I pulled one to get some light and the dust almost choked me. And they're rather special too; I'd need to look in daylight but they seem to be hand-embroidered panels sewn on to dark blue velvet, quite lovely. I've seen some like them in a country house somewhere.'

'You would have.'

'Ouch, Juliet. National Trust property; Mummy haunts them to see what they're doing with gardens.'

Juliet, who had been standing up at the kitchen sink when she decided to ring Hermione, pulled out a kitchen chair and sat down. They had befriended Mrs McDermott but they had laughed at her, surely never patronised her, but they had not done nearly enough. 'Sorry, Hermione, I just can't take it in. Living with lovely furnishings but undernourished. Our poor old neighbour hasn't been living in squalor?'

'I think squalor is filth and rags. This is amazingly neat but it's dusty. I only looked in the two drawers she told me to look in and I felt badly enough about that, I can tell you, and there isn't much, fairly basic undies and nighties, but clean. She has a lawyer from quite a posh firm and they're contacting him to find out about relatives.'

Juliet had never thought of relatives; Mrs McD had never mentioned anyone, never thrown a remark such as, 'My daughter used to do that,' or 'My sister liked these,' and they had always, as they thought, respected her privacy. Where is the fine line that is drawn between respecting privacy and nosiness? It is so fine as to be invisible. 'Does that mean,' she began hesitatingly, 'golly, Hermione, it doesn't mean that she's . . . dying or anything like that?'

'No. At least I don't think so. It's protocol. I'll ring you when I speak to him; I plan to ring him tomorrow and find out what else we can do. She's rather weak but insisting that we're not to trouble.'

'I'll send some flowers.'

'And a postcard; she loves your postcards, usually brings them in to show us.'

They talked for a while about Heather and Gregor, about why Juliet wanted rid of an expensive gift of flowers, about getting Hermione an audition with Karel, and when the call was over Juliet went back to preparing her evening meal but she had lost heart and decided to save the barely prepared food for another night and to go over to one of the restaurants at the Barbican. She had changed from her smart – I am a conductor and to be taken seriously – outfit and was wearing her oldest and most comfortable jeans and an enormous sweater. She thought for a moment about changing again and decided against it. She would be highly unlikely to meet anyone at this hour; this was a night off for the orchestra. There was a piano recital, which would be very well attended, and she could get lost easily in the crowd if she hit the restaurant at the interval. She always felt like a grazing animal at the Waterside Café, a not unpleasant feeling; wander this way to look at and perhaps construct a salad, this way to see if anything hot appealed, then that way if a glass of wine was needed, back that way to get some tea, oh, and back over there again to see if they have their yummy apple pie and then at last to the till. Except at concert intermissions it was usually easy to find a table and she did so now, even managing to find one of the sought-after tables that looked directly on to the terraces and the lake. She set out her meal, realised that she had forgotten to pick up cutlery and went back to find some, carrying the tray with her. Karel was standing in the line and in the process of paying his bill.

He smiled and she saw that his eyes lit up with pleasure. 'Juliet, oh, don't say you are finished?'

'No, I haven't started; I forgot a knife and fork.'

'Good, then we can eat together – there was something I was going to talk to you about tomorrow – but perhaps you are eating with friends.'

'No, I'm alone.' Her friends were in Edinburgh. She had made no friends since coming to London, except Erik perhaps. Who in this mad business had time to make friends? She was delighted to be surviving. She wondered what he wanted to discuss; the school concert probably.

'Something is wrong, Juliet, you look a little stressed,' he said as they moved to the table. He put down his tray and took off his heavy overcoat as he spoke.

'You've very perceptive, Karel; perhaps that's what makes you such a good musician.' She tried to smile as they sat down, the legs of their chairs scraping in harmony. 'Snap.'

'Snap? I do not understand.'

'It's from a child's card game. We have almost the same meal and so we say "snap".'

'Snap,' he said. 'Now what is wrong?'

She told him all about Mrs McDermott and forgot to ask him what he had wanted to see her about.

'And yet Hermione says her home is full of beautiful furniture? The elderly can be odd sometimes. My father had an aunt who lived like a peasant, a tiny house, no carpets, no paintings on the walls. He used to drive once a week to the country to take her food and in the winters coal and wood. When she died they found money, many, many crowns and even hellers – this is before the euro, you understand – in envelopes all over the house, behind the clock, in a milk jug, and yes, under her pillow, the equivalent of maybe twenty thousand pounds. The old can sometimes become strange; she had lived through so much famine and political troubles, perhaps she was just being prepared. Maybe your Mrs McDermott is like that.'

The idea of Mrs McD stuffing the odd fiver into an envelope was so ludicrous that Juliet laughed with real pleasure. 'Oh, you've cheered me up no end. No, nothing like that is going on. She's still very interested in her appearance, you know. It's rather bizarre – she dyes her own hair rather badly – but we think she prefers to spend money on that rather than on food and the flats are fearfully expensive; if she owns it, well and good, but there are still all the taxes and upkeep, and if she rents, poor lamb, that's where the money's going.' She looked over at the inroad he was making in his dish of curried chicken. It certainly smelled enticing. 'I hope your father got his just reward.'

He looked puzzled and then his face cleared and he laughed. 'His just reward. The money; all those grimy, soiled notes that smelled of coffee beans or potatoes or even soap. He did it because she was his father's sister and he knew his father would have

257

wanted it. That was his reward, if he needed one. Just as well since his cousin, the aunt's son, came, collected the money and a few bits and pieces and went away. He did not wait for the funeral. Not much love in that family.'

'Where is your father now? May I ask?'

'Of course. He lives where he has always lived, in Omolouc; he is on the music faculty of the university and I am glad he does not have to make hundred-mile round journeys with coal and logs. By the way, his instrument is the violin and you have reminded me of Hermione. Ask her to call me and we will arrange an audition.'

'Thank you. She is good.'

He smiled at her again and she found herself remembering how amusement made his face change completely, the rather cold austerity disappearing under laughter lines. 'I trust your professional judgement, Juliet, which reminds me of what I wanted to discuss. Let me get some coffee and we can sit a little longer?'

'Yes, of course, thank you.'

When he returned with two mugs of coffee he began with no preamble. 'We want you to conduct the first half of the concert on Saturday evening. I am in Manchester recording a radio programme and it will be convenient for me if I don't have to worry about missing planes. Is that good with you?'

She was stunned. To conduct the orchestra in a real programme in the Barbican. Never had she thought she would be allowed to do it so early, if at all. 'Yes, of course,' she managed. 'Thank you.'

He shrugged. 'You're ready and you know the pieces; you can take the rehearsal tomorrow and Friday. You have the school concert on Wednesday so unfortunately you won't be free to take a rehearsal then but two should be enough. We'll talk tomorrow and if there are problems we can discuss.'

He walked to her building with her but, unlike Alexander, he did not enter. 'You are safe inside, yes?'

'Of course. Thank you. Goodnight.'

He waited till the glass door had closed behind her and then he turned and went quickly across the courtyard and when he was out of sight she forgot all about being mature and sophisticated and ran for the door. Someone just might hear her if she yelled yippee in the corridor.

Her telephone was ringing as she reached the flat and immediately she thought guiltily of her parents, still hurt and angry because she had not visited them during her quick trip north. She picked up the receiver, expecting to hear her mother and so was perhaps rather more effusive than she would normally have been.

'So you have missed me?' It was Erik.

'I thought you were my mother.' She sat down; conversations with Erik were apt to be lengthy. 'How are you?'

'Good. Do I sound like your mother or, my God' – she could just see him hamming, slapping his brow with his hand – 'the poor woman doesn't sound like me?'

'Don't be silly. Where are you?'

'Berlin, so it's almost bedtime and I'm so alone.' She said nothing and so he went on. 'I'm recording Mahler's *Des Knaben Wunderhorn*. I have to fly back to the States Sunday but thought we might get together for dinner Saturday, if you're not already engaged.'

'I can't fly to Berlin for dinner.'

He laughed. 'How very British but don't worry; I thought I could pack up Saturday, fly to London then catch the New York plane from there.'

'Lovely. That would be lovely.'

'Great. I'll call Friday; should know my schedule better by then.'

He hung up and she stayed where she was, thinking. It would be fun to see him; he was good company and she liked him. The evening would be very pleasant. There would be no surprises, no sudden moves for which she was unprepared. No hidden agendas with the Eriks of this world, thank goodness.

Her reaction to his call reminded her again that she needed to soothe her mother's hurt feelings and so she dialled her parents' number.

'Mummy's at her yoga class,' her father told her.

Juliet looked at her watch. 'At this time of night?'

'They go for coffee afterwards. It doesn't make much sense to me, calming herself down with yoga and then drinking coffee for an hour or so afterwards. She'll be back in half an hour, give or take, and I'll ask her to ring you. What are you up to?'

'Everything's going well, actually which is why I wanted to ring Mum. I've got two concerts to conduct this week. Oh, darn it. How stupid. I've just accepted a dinner engagement for Saturday and that's the night of the second concert.'

'Awkward.'

'Not really. I'll ring him back. Perhaps we'll be able to have a late dinner – depends on one or two things. Daddy, is Mum still annoyed that I didn't see you both the other weekend?'

'Yes and no. She doesn't want to think she's not the most important person in your life; she knows it will come but she doesn't want to accept it.'

'I had to help Heather.'

'On the Saturday.'

'Don't you start. I felt that Heather needed me more than Mummy did. Of course, I would have liked to get home but I couldn't this time and I don't want to be made to feel guilty if I don't see my parents every time I visit Scotland.'

He ignored that. Perhaps he did not want to believe that his attitude sometimes made his daughter feel guilty. 'Tell me about your dinner date.'

'Erik Lyndholm.' She explained how Erik planned to break his journey from Berlin back to America.

'Sounds serious.'

She could picture him. It was almost eleven o'clock and he would still be wearing a tie and he would probably have on a jacket. She tried to remember when she had last seen him in an open-necked shirt. Did he potter in the garden without a tie or was it during the last holiday that the three of them had been on together? She could not remember when that had been.

'No, he's only a friend.' She felt sad when she said that, for it was true. Erik was a friend but he would never be anything more. Was there even a point to their Saturday dinner? Of course there was, just as long as Erik knew the ground rules. 'Dad, when did we last go on holiday as a family?'

'Good lord, I have no idea; when you were at school probably. Does it matter? We went to Paris or was it California?' He was beginning to sound desperate.

'Bet Mum knows but thanks for not remembering, Daddy, because I can't remember either but it certainly wasn't California because that was to visit Disneyland and I was twelve at the time.'

'We went to Barcelona and you were sixteen, Juliet,' her mother informed her when she rang later. 'I remember that it was our last holiday together because you refused to go anywhere with us after that; you said none of your friends went on holiday with their parents.'

Recognising the tone of ill usage Juliet thought quickly. 'Thanks for being so sensible about it, Mum. All lovely things come to a natural end as we move on. It's that lovely piece in the Bible. "To everything there is a season . . ."' Holidays *en famille* had got past their sell-by date. She could almost feel her mother gathering herself together to explode and hurried on. 'I wish Heather's parents were as sensible as you and Dad. She is quite distraught and that can't be good for her.'

'She shouldn't have got herself into such a mess in the first place, not in the twenty-first century.' Mrs Crawford was silent for a moment and Juliet could hear her breathing. 'You're not trying to tell me anything, Juliet?' she asked at last and Juliet started to laugh which was not the sensible thing to do.

But when she had eventually made peace with her mother it was too late, she decided, to ring Erik because it was an hour later in Berlin. She would try to catch him before his recording session started in the morning but his mobile was turned off when she tried to reach him as she walked to her office. The day was full, not a moment free to ring him, but it was a satisfying day. She felt that she worked well with the orchestra and that, although Karel was not effusive in his praise, he was pleased with her. The whole atmosphere of the rehearsal studio seemed light, happy and productive.

'You look like the cat that's got the cream.' Bryony had been allowed to do nothing all day but listen and she was unhappy. Her lovely face looked sulky but in an instant she had brightened and was smiling. Karel had returned from taking a telephone call in his office.

'You're neglecting me, Maestro,' she almost pouted. 'I sat all day long praying that you would let me take the orchestra for just a few minutes.'

'It wasn't possible today and won't be this week, Bryony. Remember I have to write reports on Juliet's progress and how good would it be if I had to write: "Unfortunately Miss Crawford was not given sufficient rehearsal time with the orchestra." '

Juliet tried to look as if she had gone deaf and Bryony laughed. 'Heavens, Maestro, I wouldn't dream of insinuating myself into Juliet's time. You're right; she needs as much practice with the orchestra as possible.' She moved closer to him and looked up into his eyes meltingly. 'My understanding was that I too would be allowed to do some work. If not I had better fold up my little tent and steal away.'

Juliet stoically examined the score in front of her although the notes were running together and were completely indecipherable, so incensed was she by Bryony's remark. She refused to look either at Karel or at Bryony. Surely he would remind the American that she actually had no right to be there.

He did not.

21

Juliet managed to talk to Eric on Friday evening. 'I'm so sorry that I had forgotten about the concert, Eric.'

'Sorry, heck, honey, I take it as a compliment. You are so looking forward to an evening of my charms that you forgot you were conducting a fine orchestra. What's to be angry about?'

'You're very sweet, so perhaps next time.'

'This time. Look, Juliet, I had my manager change my ticket and you're conducting the overture, right, and then the maestro will be there. I'd love to see you conduct; we could eat afterwards. If you want to stay for the rest of the programme, fine. Otherwise we could stay till the intermission and then skip out. You don't really have to hang around after concerts, do you? Plenty of time to do a post-mortem Monday, right?'

'I suppose so, Eric; it's just that if his plane is delayed . . .'

'I get to see you conduct the whole concert. It will be a pleasure. No worries, Juliet. You just think about looking beautiful for your fans and don't worry about me. I'll be there.'

'I'll leave a ticket for you.'

After they had disconnected she thought about 'looking beautiful' for the concert, never mind any fans. She did not want to think about her appearance but here it was again. What was she to wear for the concert? She had talked about having a black A-line skirt made to wear with a white blouse.

'God, no, Juliet.' Hermione had been adamant. 'You'll look like a Victorian governess; a starched white blouse and black bombazine skirt. A gold pocket watch pinned on that rather splendid bosom of yours and you'll be ready to audition for *Mary Poppins, the Opera*.'

That left the dress from someone unknown and her more modest but still very attractive blue dress that she had originally bought for the competition. She stripped to her bra and panties and tried them on one after the other, whirling and twirling in front of her mirror. Her conclusion was that both were lovely and that she wanted to wear the Absolutely Fabulous dress again but, lest any reviewer in the audience should write in his – or her – newspaper that poor Miss Crawford had only one dress to her name, she decided to wear the blue.

She changed her mind two minutes before she was due to leave for the concert hall. After all, this was her first real concert, and she needed all the reassurance she could get. With a slight pang of regret, she slipped the blue dress back into her tiny wardrobe. 'I will wear you,' she said, 'but not tonight.'

Heather rang her while she was changing in the conductor's dressing room. 'I wanted to wish you luck. Are you at the Barbican yet?'

'I am sitting in my underwear in a chair that has been sat on, possibly, by every great conductor in the world.'

Heather laughed. 'Hope something rubs off on you and who knows, Juliet, ten years down the line some neophyte conductor will say the same about you.'

Juliet was almost positive that the chair would not be in existence but she thanked Heather. 'And what about you? Any decisions? Plans?' She wondered if she should mention Heather's parents. Surely they would be over the initial shock by now.

'I've had an email – can you believe – an email from Peter. The toad is afraid I'll be in touch with his wife. I won't, of course, although sometimes I think it would be kind to tell her what a swine her husband is.'

'Perhaps she knows.'

'Perhaps, but if she does I don't want to add to her hurt. Enough of the person from the BBC. At least I have the job in Montpellier which means work for December. Isn't that fabulous?'

'I'm thrilled for you, Heather. I really am, but what will you do about the baby?'

'Take her with me, of course. I told them I was pregnant and would have a small baby and guess what they said?'

'Your problem, not theirs?'

'Sort of. They said that it has even been known for sopranos to sing virgin princesses while *enceinte*, and so long as my voice isn't different, they expect me to handle childcare like any other professional. And since I won't be pregnant but – possibly – nursing, it should be fine. Gregor, bless him, says he'll come over and babysit if I can't get anyone else. Isn't he a star?'

'Yes, he is. I haven't heard from him in a few days.'

'His boyfriend came up on Monday and whisked him off to an estate near East Linton.'

The room began to swim around Juliet and she closed her eyes for a moment. 'His boyfriend?' she said at last.

'Oh, come on, Juliet; you can't be that naïve. This Sir Tom fellow: you surely don't think he's interested only in Gregor's composing?'

Juliet still felt faint. 'He has to be interested in his work, Heather; it's just too cruel if he's not.'

'He's interested, Juliet, but he's interested in Gregor, Gregor, the very attractive young man. He arrived on Monday, stayed at the Balmoral, as one does if one has money to burn. Hermione invited him for drinks and, so help me, he kept eyeing Gregor as if he couldn't believe his eyes, and Gregor's different around him, not so abrasive, softer, just as funny but he looks at Tom for approval the way he used to look at you. Mrs McD was here too and that was something to write home about. I'm surprised Hermione hasn't told you all this.'

The way he used to look at you. 'Heather, I'm so pleased about the contract but I must dress; wouldn't want the leader of the orchestra to find me in my best Janet Reger undies, would I?'

She sat for a moment going over the conversation in her head. Gregor involved with an older man, albeit a very rich and cultured man. Oh, please God don't let him get hurt. Did he look to me for approval? I never knew. Did I give him what he wanted, needed? God, friendship is a nightmare. No, Juliet, life is a nightmare and friendship is one of its many joys. Gregor is a friend; ergo, Gregor is a joy. Now put your dress on.

It was time. The auditorium was almost full: only an empty seat or two here and there. The lights were up and so was the buzz from the crowd: murmur, murmur, laugh, laugh; she thought she could hear the crunch of a sweet wrapper or a sweetie paper as they were called in Scotland, someone with a tickle who was determined not to interrupt the music with coughing. 'Bless you,' said Juliet, 'and if you do have to cough, don't hold it until a break and then explode and ruin everything.' Where was Karel? In Manchester? In the air above London? In a taxi? Who knows? He had not telephoned but he had sent her freesias, freesias whose lovely perfume was filling her dressing room. She had bent her face to them, inhaling their perfume, redolent of sun-kissed days in the south of France; not that she had spent many sun-kissed days in the south of France but she had seen freesias, glorious buckets full of freesias on her one and only trip to Marseilles and somehow their perfume always took her back. Karel? Do I want him here? Yes. No. If he does not come I have to conduct the concerto and I have never conducted a concerto in an actual concert before but it's the violin and I'll pretend it's Hermione and I will not be terrified. Gregor. Gregor and Sir Thomas. Please let it be right for Gregor. Is Erik here? Dear, uncomplicated Erik.

The orchestra was on stage; she loved the sound of their tuning. Lovely, lovely sound, promising all manner of glories. The leader went past, shaking her hand, wishing her well as she did him, rapturous applause; he was a great musician and popular. Her turn now. Were they as expectant, as nervous, as keyed up as she was? She smoothed the dress. The fabric caressed her, sensuously, gently; the handkerchief hem fluttered around her ankles, now hiding, now revealing. She faced the light and, her heart absolutely full of joy, walked towards it, to face the music.

There was more than polite applause. Karel's absence had been relayed to them and so they had known it was to be the competition winner, the apprentice, the conductor who had conducted a schools' programme with her hat on; they were welcoming her, Juliet Crawford.

She stood motionless, waiting for absolute quiet. She fixed the sound she wanted to hear in her head, lifted her baton and from then on was aware of nothing but the search for perfection. The orchestra worked with her, watching her hands, her face, reading her gestures, her instructions, her prayers, and answering all of them. Somewhere near the theatre, Karel sat in the car that had brought him from the airport and listened to the broadcast of the concert and then the outburst of applause for the orchestra and for their young conductor. Then he picked up his mobile phone and dialled.

'I'm still in the car,' he said truthfully, 'but should be there for the symphony. Please ask Miss Crawford to conduct the concerto.'

He finished the call and sat on. Her first concerto; she had conducted it with the leader playing the solo part and had been in the auditorium for the rehearsal when he himself had conducted with the renowned soloist. How would she manage? Make or break time. He wondered what she had chosen to wear. The Radio 3 announcer had merely announced the elegant Miss Crawford; he would not sully Radio 3's listeners' ears with a description of a dress, and Karel smiled, imagining Juliet in the dress she had worn for the final.

'Albert, find a Starbucks and we'll have some coffee; then I'll sneak in during the concerto.'

In the theatre Juliet found that she was not at all terrified when she heard that she was to conduct Beethoven's great violin concerto, a well-known and popular work. Rather she found that she was relishing the opportunity. She was calm and composed; she found herself wondering where Karel was and if Erik was there and had seen the overture but these thoughts were unimportant and she banished them easily. All that was important was Beethoven; the soloist would be superb and so she must not let him or the orchestra down. She went up on to the podium and made a modest bow. They had expected Karel and some, most no doubt, would be disappointed but the soloist was the same and she went off again to bring him on. He shook hands with the leader and then stood near the podium facing the audience, his head down. The hall held its collective breath; the orchestra waited, the conductor waited. Then the great man lifted his head, smiled at her and lifted his bow.

For a split second Juliet wished that she could sit somewhere with her eyes closed simply to listen. The maestro was superb; he made the violin paint a picture in glorious sound. She saw a Regency buck swagger down a great Viennese boulevard. How he bowed to the ladies, how he lifted his lorgnette to examine something in a window, aware that the ladies continued to look at him, so grand was he, after they had passed. Juliet almost laughed. The third movement already and she had been aware of nothing but the fact that the sounds in her head were, if anything, being surpassed by the wondrous ribbons of light pouring from the stage. Oh, Hermione, you should be here. Attention, attention, don't let it wander. Keep in control; her heart seemed to soar with the notes from the violin as it talked with and to the instruments of the orchestra. Silence. Silence for a second and then the hall erupted in frenzied clapping, stamping of feet. The soloist went out and came back, went out and came back and Juliet went with him. Neither of them spoke; there are moments where words are unnecessary. He hugged her spontaneously and naturally and then she led him back again and he, great man that he was, bowed to her and led her forward to receive the audience's accolades. She included the orchestra and then, finally, having lost count of the bows, the soloist returned, played a cheeky little encore and left the stage.

Juliet went with him and all the adrenalin deserted her and she almost staggered. The orchestra were around her, congratulating her, but, at last, she was alone and was able to sit down and calm her now trembling legs. There was a knock at the door and it opened to reveal Bryony. 'I thought I'd come, get you some coffee. You must be on cloud nine after that performance.'

'You're very kind, Bryony,' said Juliet, accepting the coffee. 'It was wonderful but with—'

'Oh, of course everyone realises that the soloist carried you.

268

Karel and I sat in the car drinking Starbucks and listening, commenting of course.'

Juliet almost spilled the coffee on her dress. 'You and Karel?'

'Yes, we were here the entire time. I don't actually say he was expecting you to blow it but no doubt he'll go over your mistakes on Monday. Well, he's changing for the symphony so I guess the big night's over. Byeee.'

Juliet put the coffee down on her dressing table and looked in the mirror at her face, which was now drained of all colour. He had sat in his limousine listening to the concert; he had been there the entire time and with Bryony.

No, damn it; don't let Bryony get to you. If he was there and had thought for one moment that I could not conduct the concerto he would have come in. There must be another reason why he stayed outside. Remember, you misjudged him once before.

Another knock and there was the leader. 'Fantastic, Juliet. Thank you. Karel is here but he sends his congratulations, says he heard most of it in his car, and he'll see you at the party afterwards. Okay? I have to rush.'

He was gone. A party? Never. Damn it, where was Erik? She pulled on her coat, picked up her bag and went out into the corridors. She would see if Erik was hanging around outside. Several minutes later, having ascertained that he had indeed picked up his ticket but was not outside the auditorium she went back to stand in the wings. From there she could see the orchestra and, on the podium, Karel.

He was, as always, immaculate, the white tie and tails sculpted to his body, his dark hair shining in the many lights above him. It was long enough to fly around as he moved but beautifully disciplined and fell back exactly into place. She could see beads of sweat on his nose and forehead and had a sudden urge to wipe his face. Karel. Had he sat in his car with Bryony? What had he said? That he was sorry that he did not have enough power to have Bryony there on the podium instead of Juliet? Had they laughed together as they sat in the warm darkness drinking their coffee?

I don't care. She could feel a tear begin to trickle down her cheek and she lifted her hand to brush it away. No, she had cried enough over Karel Haken. Oh, God, what is happening? Does being in the presence of genius act as an aphrodisiac? Juliet could feel her heart pounding and her blood running. She knew that if anyone touched her she would burst into flames and disintegrate before their eyes. Her palms were sweating, her cheeks felt hot and there was a bead of sweat running down between her breasts. She tried to clear her mind of all negative thought, to concentrate on the music. Mozart is the genius, Mozart, not Karel, but surely Wolfgang Amadeus would be excited by the sound this conductor was drawing from this symphony orchestra, great as the orchestra was. Every musician seemed to be breathing as one, thinking, listening as a single unit. The charioteer was in his chariot and all the horses obeyed every slight command of his hand, his head, his body. It was sublime. She wanted to strew petals at his feet as he walked across the stage and when everyone else in the hall burst into applause she burst into laughter.

What a time to discover it. What a time to admit that it was Karel who set her senses on fire as no other man did, as only he had ever done. What a time to realise that she loved him, had loved him since Edinburgh, and would always love him. Her laughter turned to tears and as the conductor left the stage and walked into the wings he saw Juliet running frantically for the stage door.

For a moment he stood, his hand out as if to call her back and then he turned and walked back to share the applause with the orchestra.

Outside, Juliet had run almost slap into Erik who had been coming round to the stage door to try to find her.

'Hey, honey, what's wrong? Being so damned good just got to you?' He ignored her silence and hugged her, patting her on the back as if she were a frightened child. 'You were great. I hope there's something in the papers tomorrow before I leave. I should write it myself and send it in. "Brilliant young conductor knocks the socks off the audience in the Beethoven violin concerto." How does that grab you?'

She pulled herself away. 'I had a little help.'

He smiled. 'I noticed. It was fantastic and so was the overture, one of my favourite pieces.' He looked closer at her face. 'Are you all right, honey? Anyone I should slug?'

She laughed, feeling better already. 'You are a tonic, Mr Lyndholm. No, everything's fine. I think the emotion of the whole thing just got to me.'

'What did the maestro say? Pity his plane didn't stay so late you had to conduct the symphony too.'

'I'd be like a wrung-out dishcloth. Aren't I in a feeble enough state with the first half?'

'That symphony was sublime though. The whole concert was great; worth every penny, if you know what I mean.'

She looked up at him and smiled. He looked like a world-class American baritone, tall, rugged, handsome, clothes just that little bit more than Madison Avenue. 'That coat has to be Italian.'

'The suit's Italian, the coat is, in fact, British. Superb tailors over here. Now,' he said, tucking her hand into his arm, 'where shall we go eat and yes, my recording will probably win a Grammy, thanks for asking.'

'Oh, Erik, I'm sorry; so much happened tonight, it went out of my head.'

'As long as I didn't go out of your head. We could go to the hotel at the airport, unless you know of someplace else we can get a really good meal this late. When did you last eat? I had breakfast and something disgraceful on the flight across. It looked like two dead white squares with a dead yellow square stuck inside it, revolting, and somebody needs a lesson in making coffee.'

Coffee. Starbucks. Karel and Bryony in a car drinking good coffee and murmuring comments about the quality of the music. Until Erik had said coffee she had been about to tell him that she was sorry, she had really looked forward to seeing him but she felt too drained, she would not be good company. That was changed.

'Tailoring we do, Erik, sandwiches – we need a little work, and the airport hotel sounds great. I have my party dress on. The world deserves to see it.'

*   *   *

Taxis seemed to appear out of nowhere when Erik was looking for one; it was almost as if he conjured one up when he needed it. In no time at all they were standing at the door of the hotel dining room and the maître d' – more elegant even than Erik, if that were possible – was assuring them that, yes indeed, he had a perfect table.

Juliet sat down and looked around the spacious room. Along the side wall with its tall windows was an elevated area with several occupied tables and an amazing number of thriving green plants. More tables and potted plants were lined up in the centre of the room and then a wooden balustrade enclosed a long table, which carried the most adventurous and eclectic combination of hors d'oeuvres Juliet could remember seeing anywhere.

'Secret is not to eat too much,' warned Erik who had been studying the wine list. 'Damn, this list is almost as long as the score of *Walküre* and almost as heavy.' He looked across the table at her. 'You look sad, honey. Problem?'

Juliet laughed and shook her head. 'Not unless trying to choose is a problem.'

Erik closed the wine list and, with exaggerated fatigue, set it down on the immaculate white cloth. 'Don't look round but if you tire of me there's an entire table of businessmen behind you who agree that you and that dress are an unbeatable combination.' He took her hand and ran his finger lightly across the palm and on to her wrist. 'You really are something, Juliet. I can't tell you what seeing you up there on that podium did to me tonight. You were wonderful. You're talented and you're beautiful and you are so very sweet.'

Perhaps if he had not mentioned the effect that seeing her conduct had had on him the evening might have been different. Juliet had begun to relax and the light touch of his fingers had promised to rekindle flames that had been banked down, but now, instead of Erik she saw Karel, his hair damp against his head as he stood before the orchestra drawing from them that inspired and subtly shaded performance. She tried to smile, tried to regain the feelings of a few short moments before. She accepted Erik's suggestions for wine, she gave a wonderful performance of studying the menu and even managed to order an entrée; almost feverishly she chatted. When would Erik return? He had mentioned *Die Walküre*, the second opera in Wagner's Ring Cycle. Would he consider adding Wagnerian roles to his repertoire?

Erik toyed with his wine glass and looked at her gravely. 'Maestro, something tells me you're making conversation. Let's go choose some hors d'oeuvres, let the evening proceed. It will only go where you want it to go.'

Juliet looked at him and her eyes were sad. 'Erik,' she began.

'No, don't say anything. This is me, Erik, and you don't have to pretend with me. I think you are one fabulous lady, Juliet, and I have to admit that I got real excited seeing you up there tonight and I wanted you more than I have ever wanted you. You belong there, just as I belong on a stage. Sometimes that pretend world is more real than the real world; I like it there and I was getting to the stage of thinking maybe it would be nice to share it with a beautiful woman – preferably one with a cute Scottish accent,' he added, showing that even in stress he could summon up his proverbial good humour, 'but you have some baggage. It's not just business with you and the maestro, is it?'

Juliet looked at him and wished that she could forget everyone and everything and throw herself into his arms. What was wrong with her that she could not fall in love with this totally lovable man? God, Juliet, what more do you want? 'There was something, last year. I thought I had got over it; we never spoke of it and we worked really well together but things . . . are a little out of control and I don't know what to do. Oh, Erik,' she said sadly, her lovely eyes swimming with tears, 'I don't want to care and I want desperately to finish my apprenticeship.' She stopped. This was no way to behave. She stood up and he stood too. 'I have to go, Erik. I'm so sorry about' – she waved at the table – 'the food and . . . oh hell, here come the entrées.'

'I'll get you a cab.'

'No, no, please. I can manage. I'm so sorry.'

'I can eat both. Remember the little white sandwich.'

They stood for a moment looking at each other while the waiter stood with the plates and tried to pretend he saw and heard nothing.

'I'll ring you,' she began.

'Sure, sometime when you're in New York. We'll do lunch.'

Juliet fled and did not see Erik take out his wallet and hand the waiter a note. 'Sorry, we lost our appetites. Room 351. I'll take the wine.' He tried to whistle 'La Donna è Mobile' as he left the dining room but managed only a few notes.

22

Driving rain: it was almost horizontal and it was grey. Grey is such a wimpish colour, not bold enough to stand up for itself, it merely limps apologetically along. Vainly the trees rushing past outside the window tried to haul themselves up straight, attempted to push their green branches into and above the cloying grey mist, but flowers and grasses merely kowtowed and lay down before the onslaught. Juliet knew that if she were to gaze out at the rain much longer the little bubble of intense excitement inside her would join the grass to lie meekly down and be drowned. And then the decision to look or not to look, to read or not to read, was taken out of her hands, for the train had plunged into the tunnel and she could see nothing.

'Wow.' She had not expected it, not quite so quickly. Was she under land or was she already under water? Was the full weight of the English Channel at this very second pressing down on her head? Would it find a tiny fissure, a crack, a gaping hole?

'Nervous?'

'No, of course not; an overactive imagination.'

'Let's walk to the buffet car and have a snack. By the time we have eaten, we will be in the sun again.'

She stood up, moved out of her very comfortable chair, and, trying to look like an experienced Eurostar customer, walked behind him towards the buffet car and there she found another nice surprise. The buffet car was French and so, instead of a paper cup full of hot water and a floating teabag, she found a glass of drinkable red wine and an absolutely delicious goat's cheese sandwich. *Vive la France*. She forgot the rain and the mist and the English Channel just there above her head and remembered that she, Juliet Crawford, was on her way to Paris, a welcome guest of the Opéra de Paris. The bubble in her stomach remembered too and began to procreate with gay abandon so that she feared that she might just leave the ground and float away on a cloud of euphoria. And all this before she drank the wine.

'This is pleasant, no?'

How little he knew. 'Yes, Karel; it was a really lovely idea, to travel this way.'

'I thought we could talk together. There is never time in the office; so many people around all day with questions that have to be answered immediately and I don't think you even allowed me to congratulate you for last Saturday's magnificent concert. I looked for you, you know, to take the last bow with me.'

Several of the bubbles burst as Bryony's mocking tone superimposed itself on Karel's voice. Had she picked him up at the airport? Don't think, Juliet. 'You were very kind to allow me to conduct the concerto. No one could fail with such a soloist.'

'But of course they could.' He stopped and she thought she saw a faint pink tinge on his cheekbones. 'It was your time, Juliet, an opportunity, and you took it and succeeded even beyond my expectations.'

'You thought it might not go well?'

'You should know me better than that. One of the world's greatest ever violinists deserves the very best an orchestra can give. I knew you were capable – if I did not return on time.'

'But you did, Maestro.' Her tongue, as always, moved faster than her thought processes. She had decided never to speak about the concert, merely to accept any censure that he chose to give but he had only said that the evening was an unqualified success and that she should look for more conducting opportunities in the next few months. 'I believe you sat outside drinking coffee in the limousine while the concert was going on.'

He put his glass and his goat's cheese sandwich on the little table in front of him. 'I sat outside a coffee shop for five minutes, Juliet, and I was then driven to the Barbican where I watched the finale of the concerto from the wings before going to my dressing room to change from jeans to tails. In the car I made an executive decision while I was listening to the opening piece. I don't owe you an explanation for my decision, which was made, I thought, in your best interests. Enjoy your wine.'

Had there been another seat in the carriage she felt he would have got up and left her. She sat in her comfortable seat, feeling suddenly bereft and completely alone although she could almost feel his body beside her. She forced herself to eat every bite of her sandwich which now tasted like cardboard but she could not drink the wine, and all the time her mind worked. He had deliberately waited outside the theatre to give her a chance to shine, not to fail. He would not risk his, or the orchestra's reputation by allowing an inept musician to conduct the Beethoven. He had given her a chance and she had listened to Bryony's words of poison and instead of thanking him graciously – what had she done? Bryony. Bryony who wanted her position, Bryony who had been there just before Juliet discovered that her score had been vandalised. Had she been around when the door of the green room had mysteriously locked and then unlocked itself? No, she had been in the auditorium at that time, or had she? She tried to sneak a look at Karel's profile, austere, remote, controlled. She could sense his anger or could she? She did not seem to be much good at figuring him out.

They were out of the tunnel. Light, the light of northern France burst through the windows and Juliet tried to forget the last few minutes by sitting back and trying to enjoy the countryside as it swept past. She saw differences immediately. The land was so tidy and it was vast. On previous trips to France she had flown in and flown out, not the best way to see a country. Now, leaning back in a very comfortable seat, she was able to watch farms and villages fly past. It was not exciting, after all trains do tend to travel in the most accessible route possible and that usually means flat, and flat can mean dull. But it was not dull: it was France.

'It can only be *la belle France*.' His voice broke the silence and gratefully she turned towards him.

'Amazing, isn't it? The farmhouses say, I'm French, the fields, everything.'

'Juliet?'

Her heart seemed to flip. What was he going to say? 'Yes,' she said, her jawline tense.

'I want you to promise me one thing. Will you do that?'

'Of course, Maestro.'

'Then believe that I have now, and in the past few weeks, only your best interests in mind. It is good for my reputation too if you do well, you see. It reflects on me; after all, I am the substitute, not the first choice.'

'You're too modest, Maestro. I watched you conduct the symphony: it was a revelation.'

'And so reflects well on Maestro Stoltze.' He stood up. 'I will get some coffee for us. Drink your wine, Juliet, or wait until tonight and we will taste some of Paris's finest.'

He was smiling down at her and so she handed him the untouched wine glass. 'Coffee would be lovely.'

They had scarcely finished the coffee before the train pulled in to La Gare du Nord and Karel lifted their overnight bags down from the rack. 'Usually I walk. I adore walking in great cities but' – he looked at her shoes with their narrow heels – 'the Métro will have us at the opera house in no time. *Bienvenue à Paris*, Juliet.'

Paris. It was raining, rain that seemed determined to wash every stain from the buildings and the streets and even from the people crazy enough to walk about in it. Karel looked at his watch as they came upstairs from the Métro. 'Can you run in those shoes?'

Juliet nodded and, to her surprise, he grabbed her hand and pulled her along through the driving rain. The wind tore at her hair and the rain slapped at her, stinging her cheeks and making them, had she but known it, rosy and red. She could see nothing and decided to trust herself completely to Karel and closed her eyes against the relentless onslaught of a spring storm.

'Watch the kerb.' He had known that her eyes were closed and she opened them for a second and jumped across a large puddle and landed on the pavement and then stopped, as she always did, in awe as she saw before her the sumptuous building that incorporated the opera house. Her eyes took in the great series of provocative lamp-bearing statues, the mighty columns, the steps where she had picked her way through the friendly French students. No one was sitting there today. No birds pecked in self-importance among any crumbs that might have been left by picnickers, although she did retrieve an empty bedraggled paper bag that blew listlessly across a step.

'Sacrilege to leave litter here.'

He agreed but hurried her on and up the steps to the doors. 'You have about three minutes to comb your hair.'

Juliet looked down at her legs and almost shrieked. 'Look at my legs. I'll have to change my tights.'

'As always you look delightful. Go, but meet me here in . . . two minutes.'

It took more than two minutes but Juliet went into her first meeting in Paris with her wet hair neatly tied back and her legs and shoes clean and elegant. Everyone spoke excellent English, which was just as well since Juliet's French had not improved greatly in the past few months.

'You need to work on your French,' said Karel as they took a taxi to their hotel after the meetings. 'Tonight, at dinner, one of our hosts, Etienne Duprez, will refuse to speak English. I have never really discovered how much he understands – every word, I'm almost sure – but he refuses, for whatever reason, to speak English. How is your German?'

'Ich spreche ziemlich fliegbend Deutsch; I'm fairly fluent. Remember, *Ich habe ein Jahr in Wien studiert* – I did study for a year in Vienna.'

'Gut gemacht.' He answered her in German. 'Well done. He speaks fluent German and will probably forgive your lack of French but that is something you could think about during the next month: some coaching in French. It will be useful later on too so it's not just for this two-day visit to Paris. And for now, a quick shower, a change of clothes and then a superb dinner.'

The dinner was magnificent and Juliet managed, she hoped, to win over the non-English-speaking board member. Most of the conversation, which ranged from war in the Middle East to the future of orchestras, from global warming to the chances of the French rugby team in the Six Nations championship, was, as a kindness to Juliet, in English, but she dived deeply into the great well where she had once been assured that everything she had ever learned was stored, and managed to pull out French vocabulary that she had no recollection of ever learning.

'Two days of total immersion and you will be perfect,' Karel assured her as, very wearily, they made their way back to their hotel.

'I'm sure.'

'No, you're a natural. I'll take you to Prague . . . to conduct, of course, and in no time you will be able to speak Czech.'

The taxi drew up at the hotel entrance and Karel paid the fare and helped Juliet out. 'I like your pink suit,' he said. 'That, and your German, certainly won over Monsieur Duprez. I think you will have a lovely time in Paris. April in Paris.'

The cab had driven off and they were still standing as if loath for the evening to end.

'It snowed once when I was in Paris in April. I was so disappointed.'

'This year it promises to be everything the songs say it is.'

'You add weather forecasting to your talents, Maestro?'

He took her arm and they walked slowly, side by side, into the foyer, across the soft, deep pile of the carpet towards the lift. He pressed the button and still they stood quiet as they watched the little light tell them which floor the expected but rather rickety lift was passing. It arrived; the gate creaked open. For the length of a heartbeat neither moved.

'Goodnight, Juliet. Breakfast at seven?'

'Seven.'

She stepped into the lift and the door closed, leaving Karel standing outside. 'Goodnight, Karel,' she whispered.

Upstairs in her lovely bedroom with its French provincial furniture she sat down at the delicate, feminine dressing table and looked at her face in the mirror. She looked different but what had changed? Were her eyes brighter? Good French wine. No, you were very careful. Was her mouth softer? The wine again, Juliet: you're merely feeling less stressed. She smoothed the pink skirt and thought that her left thigh tingled; in fact the whole left side of her body felt strange. '*Les moules*,' she decided. 'Shellfish can be dodgy.'

She looked at her watch: so late but an hour earlier in Edinburgh, and Hermione, if she was in at all, would be wide awake.

'I'm in Paris.'

'Lucky you. With someone exciting, I hope. Your baritone, *peut-être*.'

'No, I wasn't very nice to him, Hermione, and he is the sweetest man. We are no longer an item, if we ever were one.'

'Tell Auntie Hermione all?'

Juliet could almost see her curling her legs up under her, getting herself comfortably into a position that to anyone else would be a contortionist's torture. 'I arranged to meet him for dinner after the concert; then I had to conduct the concerto . . .' She stopped, remembering again the heady excitement of knowing that the sounds in her head were, if anything, being exceeded by the sounds the soloist was producing. 'It was sublime, Hermione, one of those golden moments that you just pray that nothing will spoil.' She eased off her ridiculously narrow, high-heeled shoes and rubbed one aching foot against the other.

'And something did?'

'Yes, and no.' She remembered her euphoria, remembered sitting in her dressing room as if she were surrounded by the lightest and most colourful of bubbles and then Bryony . . . 'I watched Karel conduct and everything came blindingly together. I saw how far I still have to go, what a genius he is, and how much I . . . bloody hell . . . how much I still care and then, all I could hear, instead of the applause, was Bryony's voice seeping poison into my brain, telling me . . . or allowing me to think that he and she . . . Oh, hell, never mind. I ran. I'd forgotten about Erik and I bumped straight into him and he was so . . . normal . . .'

'Normal can be nice. Dull, maybe, but nice.'

Juliet laughed. 'I thought, To hell with them, Bryony and Karel, and I decided to have dinner with Erik and then, I was wearing my beautiful dress, the mystery one, and I knew I looked great and I knew Erik was going to want me to stay with him and I was going to stay.'

'And when it came to the bit, you couldn't.'

'Just as the waiter arrived with the most delicate sea bass.'

'You didn't think maybe you should finish your dinner? Sea bass is very expensive.'

'Don't joke. I just knew that he deserved more and I deserved more or perhaps I didn't deserve anything and I got up and left. I just left. I mumbled, "Sorry," and left. Can you believe me? Madame Sophistication, the jewel in the orchestra's crown.'

'Darling, you behaved very well.'

'He broke his journey home to see me and I left him right in the middle of—'

'The fish course?'

'This is serious,' said Juliet a tad frostily.

'Of course, it is, but it's not a hanging matter. If you're not in Paris with Erik, you're there with Karel.'

At the mention of his name Juliet found herself again assaulted by that delicious feeling as if her very limbs were melting and knew that, more than anything, she wished he were with her now. Where had he gone? His room was on the same floor. 'Yes, meetings at the Garnier. We fell out on the train. He'd just bought me some wine and it all spilled out, not the wine, my belief that he had hoped that I would blow it, and he . . . He closed down; it's as if he locks himself in somewhere and his body is there beside you so that you can feel his leg against yours but he's not there.'

'You didn't do an Edwardian comedy routine and throw the wine at him?'

'Don't be silly. I left it.' She could hear Hermione laughing on the end of the line. 'I'm glad this is such a source of amusement.'

'I'm seeing poor Europe strewn with the remains of beggared men and the wine they woo you with; I take it you left the *vin ordinaire* in London too?'

'There was nothing ordinary about it at all. I hope Erik consoled himself with it. I'd better go to bed; an early start tomorrow.'

'Don't you dare disconnect. What's happening in Paris?'

Juliet melted again. 'Oh, Hermione, it's purgatory. He's funny and charming and it seemed as if we were friends again; we walked as if we were joined at the knees and we stood and said nothing but it was such intense silence, palpable, electric and then, just when I was ready to offer anything, he said, "Goodnight."'

Hermione made odd noises that could only be construed as deep thinking noises and then she said, 'None of my toads were Czech, unfortunately, and there were no conductors among them but I think all systems are go. Just be yourself, Juliet, don't shy away. Give him a chance.'

'And what if he doesn't take it?'

'He will if he wants to badly enough. What did you wear tonight?'

'The pink suit.'

'Oh, great choice for Paris, but more than time we went shopping again.' Hermione stopped and then spoke seriously. 'It will be fine, Juliet; there are still a few months to work on him. I'm coming down in a couple of weeks, by the way. Did he tell you? He's an angel. The wedding is the 12th and so he'll fit me in that week.'

Juliet lay back on her bed: she was absolutely exhausted. Emotion is so much more tiring than hard work. She looked at the prints on the opposite wall. Monet's, but scenes of London in the fog or was it smog in those days? Somehow she had not expected to find pictures of London, even if by the great French impressionist, Monet, in Paris. 'Can you stay?'

'Absolutely. What fun. I'll curl up on your tiny sofa, be good as gold auditioning for the maestro and then we will have FUN.' She said the word as if it had capital letters. 'I want to go on the London Eye, a bit twee and possibly, what do you think, a tad disappointing. I mean, it's not very high, is it, but it will be quite an original way of seeing the city. And I want to walk across the wobbly bridge.'

'I don't think it wobbles any more; that was the whole point.'

'Then I shan't come down at all. Go to bed, Juliet, darling, and tomorrow – tomorrow will be wonderful.'

Juliet sat on the bed for several minutes holding her phone and remembering the conversation and thinking about Karel and even of Bryony. No, she would not think of Bryony whom she was quite sure she understood. I won't let her upset me, she decided. She has an agenda shared by someone else but whatever it is and whomever it is I shall be professionalism personified.

Pity really that Bryony was not in London to see it. She had gone when Juliet and Karel returned next day. An opera company in Hungary had asked her to work with their senior conductor and naturally, 'I couldn't possibly turn down such a good opportunity.'

The message had been left for Karel, not for Juliet, but he shared it with her when the orchestra was taking a coffee break and so they were alone in the rehearsal room, much too busy to take time for coffee. He was as he had been on the journey back from Paris, not remote, but somehow untouchable; he was consummate professionalism made flesh.

And that's the way I want it. If there is something still between us Karel does not want it and I know I must concentrate on learning, learning. There is no time for anything else. Maybe when my time here is up, maybe . . . Right now I must concentrate on not putting a foot wrong, on absorbing everything that Karel and the musicians are willing to teach me, on impressing him and the orchestra, and oh, what joy to be rid of Bryony.

23

Gregor sent a text message. 'What do you know about moles?'

Juliet, who had just stepped out of the shower and was rubbing her hair dry to the soothing sound of masterfully played 'Goldberg Variations', inhaled the aroma of freshly ground coffee, took a large swallow, and sent back a cryptic, 'Nothing.' A second message came: 'Don't be facetious.'

She drank more coffee, generously spread a piece of rather blackened toast with apricot jam, noted that where food was concerned – and music – she was definitely in a rut, wrote back: '*The Wind in the Willows*?'

The third message said, 'Not good enough. When can I talk to you?' She texted that she would ring during the morning break, and she kept her promise. 'Gregor, I have a masterclass in thirty-two minutes and nineteen seconds with one of the most exciting conductors in the world. I cannot handle moles, or anything else, at this point. What on earth are you talking about?'

'On earth; that's very funny. Moles, Juliet, but bless you for calling me; I knew I could depend on you.'

'You can't depend on me, Gregor. I haven't the slightest idea what you're talking about, and, apart from *The Wind in the Willows*, I know zilch about moles. I do know they can't talk.'

'How droll. Juliet, Tom's letting me live at his house. You know that, don't you? Hermione brings you up to date?'

Juliet did not answer immediately. Tom. Did Gregor know how his voice changed when he said that simple monosyllabic word? It was true then, what they had suspected, what Gregor had agonised over. 'Are you happy, Gregor?'

Now he sounded surprised. 'Happy? What on earth does that

word mean? I'm content; I'm at peace with myself. I'm happy living with you girls and I'm moving back after Easter – for a while anyway. I'll be there for Heather, no matter what happens in my private life, and that brings me back to the damn moles. Tom is coming back this weekend and I woke up this morning and the lawn is covered in molehills. How did it happen? Where did they come from and how do I get rid of them? This is my sponsor's lawn we're talking about. If Tom is angry, Juliet, God knows what will happen. It's not the money or living in a house like this – it's my life. Help me.'

Juliet sighed. What would he say if she sobbed back, I have just realised that I am still in love with someone who sees me only as a student whose possible success could look good on his résumé. It's my life, help me. But she did not yell because that was not her way. 'As far as I know I have never in my life seen either a mole or a molehill. Do you trap them somehow?'

'My God, Juliet, what's happening to you? That's barbaric.'

'I didn't say kill them. I said trap them, humanely, and set them free, preferably in someone's else's garden.' Her humour was not appreciated.

'I thought I could depend on you.'

She groaned. 'I'll ask around but don't expect an answer immediately.' She left the green room reflecting on how like Gregor it was to contact the one of his friends who was furthest away and therefore least likely to be of any help. Or was it just that in their years together at college he had become used to asking for her help and she had become accustomed to giving it. I love you, Gregor, but find your backbone and why didn't you ask Hermione? The Elliott-Chevenixes have, no doubt, already fought and won the battle of the moles. By this time she was pounding up the stairs heading to the auditorium and hoping that she would not meet Karel.

He was alone in the room seated at the table and studying a score. He was wearing surprisingly scruffy jeans and a dark green cotton crew-necked sweater; his thick dark hair had fallen forward over his face and, as she watched, he pushed it back with a suntanned hand. Strange that she had never noticed the tan before.

He had seen her; she could not back out until someone else came. 'Hello.'

He raised his head and looked at her and for a moment there was real warmth in his eyes. Then they became cold and grey as the unseasonable sleet that was ferociously hurling itself at the windows, but he spoke warmly enough. 'Juliet. You look a little worried. Is there something about the music perhaps; the Shostakovich?'

'No, it's moles,' she blurted out.

He looked puzzled. 'Moles, the little animal who makes the mountains in the gardens?'

'Sorry, it's nothing, so trivial.'

He was on his feet now; she could feel the energy emanating from him. He was always either very calm or almost hyperactive. 'But it cannot be nothing if it concerns you. Nothing is trivial if it affects the work. Are you able to put this worry out of your mind while you conduct the Brahms Serenade?'

She bristled. 'Of course I can. I am a professional.'

As if in opposition to her tenseness, Karel seemed to relax. He smiled. 'A very young professional. Sorry.'

She glared at him, making him inescapably aware of what she was thinking. Thirty was not, in her mind, so very much older than twenty-five.

He looked down at his hands for a moment as if hoping some answer would be found there. 'Juliet, all I meant to say is that even for a very experienced conductor, real life can intrude. We don't want it to do so and over the years we learn some . . . avoidance techniques. I, for example, say to myself when something disturbs me: I will worry about this when I am taking my walk. You remember that I told you that I run and walk wherever I am: sometimes for only fifteen minutes, sometimes for an hour or more. Exercise and time to think. What do you do for exercise?'

'Conducting is pretty good exercise, Maestro.'

He laughed and the grey eyes were warm again. 'For the brain and the upper half.'

'You have a point there.' They laughed at her joke and the invisible curtain, which had come down between them as they left Paris, lifted for a moment and she could see light, that exciting light one sees as the curtain lifts on an opera or ballet, revealing inch by inch just that little bit more of the joys to come.

'Perhaps,' he began, but the orchestra members were coming in, finding their seats, scraping their music stands over the floor so that they were in exactly the right position, and so she was left to wonder what he had been going to say. Perhaps we could go for a walk . . .

If that is what he had been about to say Juliet never did find out, for they began at once to work on the Brahms. Karel was a demanding taskmaster but he was also courteous; as instruments converse with one another during a piece so did Karel communicate with the instrumentalists. Almost to a man they found themselves trying harder for him. 'That was sublime,' he would say to an individual player, 'but somehow I always get an impression that you are holding something back, not going for gold, as it were. Don't you see yourself leading the orchestra one day and if not this great group, another perhaps, in Berlin, or Vienna maybe?' And the musician would concentrate more and think into his head the exquisite sound that the long-dead composer had intended.

'Bravo, bravo,' Karel would suddenly shout and then he would say nothing for five, ten or more minutes. But the orchestra knew that he was listening with every atom of his being and that when he did speak he would show that he had been aware of everything. He stopped the rehearsal immediately if an instrument or an ensemble was late or early, sharp or flat.

'God, kid,' one of the cellists said to Juliet as Karel went to take an urgent telephone call. 'What punishment-gluttons conductors are; hard enough to listen to one instrument without trying to listen to over a hundred of them.'

'But you don't merely listen to yourself or the other cellos. You would know if the trombones were late or early.'

'Yes, but it wouldn't be my problem.'

Mood was harder to influence than style or technique. No one played in this orchestra unless he or she was a consummate musician but they were all individuals with their own idea of how the piece should sound. Coming in on time was easy enough to get right but to understand the mood the conductor wanted to achieve, to accept and reproduce it, that was what made a good orchestral musician.

As each day flew past Juliet was finding herself more and more fascinated by the life she had chosen and could not imagine herself doing anything else and that included getting married and having children. Too difficult anyway with this type of career, working most days and also several nights a week, travelling all over the country and often across the globe. Mind you, there was the Australian, Simone Young, who had actually conducted the Metropolitan Opera when she was five months pregnant and the Vienna State Opera three months later. That must have raised some eyebrows, but being a guest conducting an opera even at these prestigious venues was not quite on a par with being offered the post of regular conductor with a major orchestra. On the other hand, Marin Alsop, who had a child and who still flew around the world five times a year, managing to check in at her home in Colorado every two weeks or so, was senior conductor with the Bournemouth Symphony Orchestra and rumoured to become the first woman to conduct the Amsterdam Concertgebouw in over a century. Was that perhaps because the conductor has to be seen to be a world-class musician, an expert in development, audience building and long-range strategy? 'How long,' Juliet wondered aloud, 'has it taken Ms Alsop to become a senior conductor?'

'Quite some time, Juliet, since I believe Maestro Alsop is almost fifty years old.' She had not seen Karel return. 'Why are you interested in her? She has conducted here, you know. The year 2000 was the Walton Centenary and she conducted his music here. Soon she will come and conduct Bernstein, one of her heroes. In fact she was his pupil. You hope to follow in her steps perhaps – not as a pupil, of course?'

'Not a bad course to follow, Maestro.' She could not tell him that she was wondering how the famous conductor managed to combine motherhood and a distinguished career. Around the world several times a year? It sounded daunting.

'I believe the American orchestras are more open to women than their European counterparts. We are perhaps too stick-in-the-mud, is that the term? But this is not preparing you for your next concert or for Paris. That should be very exciting and interesting, and then would you like to conduct your friend, Hermione, when she comes to audition for me?'

'Me? But surely you want to conduct her?'

'I will, with one piece. I have asked her to prepare two pieces and the orchestra will prepare also with the leader playing the solo part. It is important for me to watch her and to listen to her and it will be good practice for you, although you have conducted a violin soloist before, and you have conducted Hermione many times; so you will both be without nerves.'

Would it be totally facetious to say that Hermione was born without nerves? 'I doubt that, Maestro. What is she playing?'

She has chosen Chausson's *Poème* since she is playing it at this wedding in the Cotswolds and I will tell her in a day or two which concerto I want to hear. We will use one that is already in the orchestra's programme; I will let the leader select and then, perhaps, we can give her a week to prepare. Does she sight-read well?'

'I would say so.'

'Then warn her that I will probably also pull something for her to play that she has never heard.' He turned to the waiting orchestra. 'Ladies and gentlemen, shall we begin?'

Juliet rang Hermione as soon as she had dashed through the stinging sleet to her flat. They spoke about Hermione's audition for a while and then talked about Gregor and Heather. 'Gregor rang me about moles this morning.'

'I know; I told him moles are all part of living in the country and that the best thing to do was get in touch with Tom's gardener. He's there five days a week anyway and, by this time, has probably seen the hills for himself. They are a damn nuisance but Daddy's gardener always scoops up the hills for his seedlings, says the earth is beautifully soft and aerated.'

'That's positive, I suppose, but what do you think about Gregor and Tom? Are they? I mean . . .'

Hermione's voice was positive and even happy. 'Yes, and you have never seen such a change in a human being. I can't but be glad for him; he's just so much more confident.'

'So confident that he sounded frightened this morning?'

'Young love.'

'Are you all right with it?'

Hermione was silent for a moment; perhaps she was wondering whether or not to be, as she always was, completely truthful. 'No, but I want what's right for Gregor,' was what she decided to answer. 'Heather's getting bigger by the minute,' she went on and Juliet, seeing the quick change of subject, obligingly talked about her former flatmate's advancing pregnancy with something resembling interest.

When they had finished chatting Juliet hung up, went to the bathroom for a towel for her wet hair which had been dripping a cold rivulet of water down her neck during the phone call and then wandered into her tiny kitchen to find something to eat. This was when she missed Gregor most; he had been such a good cook and more importantly he had been interested in food, had liked preparing it, and had never, as far as she was aware, felt put upon by his three flatmates who were, each and every one, almost useless in the kitchen. I could take a cookery night class, thought Juliet as she tried to summon up enthusiasm over a rather dried-up-looking lamb chop, but I am supposed to spend my free time improving my French. She wrapped the chop in foil and put it in the waste bin, took some Serrano ham – only slightly curled at one edge – out of the refrigerator and garnished it with a tomato, quite firm, and a few olives. She found crackers nicely sealed in a tin and three tiny but only slightly soft satsumas. That, with a mug of instant coffee, decaffeinated, of course, made a respectable meal that she ate, her mother's voice echoing in her ears, at the small table in the kitchen.

She ignored her mother's strictures about reading at the table and read a day-old newspaper from cover to cover.

When she had cleaned up she looked out of the windows because the thought of a nice walk in the moonlight had appealed but there was no moon or at least she could not see one for the sleet-filled rain that was still driving against the windows. A good night to start reviewing her French vocabulary: there had to be some sites on the Internet, since she had certainly not brought any old textbooks to London.

She curled in a chair in the living room, laptop on her knees, accessing sites and making notes, a recording of Stephanie Blythe singing Handel arias playing softly in the background. The lamp on the table beside her chair was lit and she had left a single light on in the hall and the faint glow created a yellow path across the carpet. She was, she decided, content. She heard a crack and there was darkness, sudden frightening blackness, and silence.

'Damn, if that disc is ruined I will be furious.'

Juliet pushed the laptop aside, got up and, out of habit, tried the lamp beside her. Nothing. The blackness was complete; she could see nothing. She stood for a moment making quite sure that she knew exactly where she was and then cautiously she moved in the direction of the kitchen. In there she must have a torch and, if not, there were lots of candles.

It was the oddest feeling to be cocooned in darkness. No light at all shone through the curtain-less kitchen window. No stars shone in the spring sky and no pale moon slipped from behind a cloud. Juliet was marooned or mantled by blackness. No lights shone on the estate and the huge mass of the Defoe House apartment building which was on the other side of the spacious Thomas More Garden across the road guarded its privacy; not a chink or gleam of light showed. She opened the living-room curtains though, for, as her eyes adjusted she was aware that there was in fact more light outside than in and surely soon the street lights would go back on and her little home would be flooded by light.

Candles? Where were they? She had not lived in this apartment long enough to remember exactly where she had put everything; she had never before had to think about it, and it was definitely infinitely more difficult in the dark. Somehow, in broad daylight, one just seemed to know where candles were.

She pictured the Edinburgh flat. Third drawer down on the right of the sink. Bingo. Thankfully there were matches in the same drawer.

What a friendly light is a candle flame and how powerful is its beam. Juliet was surprised by just how deeply she could see into the corners of the room. There were two half-used candles in the candlesticks on the table – she had completely forgotten them – and she moved over to the table and lit them from the one in her hand. 'All I need now is a bottle of wine and a man.' She laughed somewhat ruefully and returned to the living room. On the floor near the sofa was a thick candle she had bought originally for decorative purposes; it would do now to help dispel the gloom. Once it was lit she moved it a little away from the wall; just possibly smoke from the flame would mark the wallpaper and when she had to move out she did not want to be handed a large bill for redecoration.

She sat back down in her chair and realised that her laptop was running on its battery. She sent up a silent prayer that power would be restored before morning; a coffee-less breakfast just did not bear thinking about. She decided to ring Hermione and moan about her circumstances but there was no answer from the flat and Hermione's mobile was switched off. Juliet began to feel really sorry for herself.

Dash it all: what can one do alone in the dark? A bath. Yes. She would indulge in a long, leisurely, hot, hot bath with lots and lots of beautiful-smelling bubbles. She began to feel quite cheerful as she carried some candles into the bijou bathroom. She almost dropped them when she heard a loud knocking at the door. It was not a sound she associated with London. There was a buzzer on the Podium door; she became familiar with it when Hermione and Gregor had visited but, because of her erratic working hours, she was very rarely at home and had not heard it since. The loud knocking came again and she realised that she had been standing candles in hand, staring towards the front door.

'Just a minute,' she called, putting down all but one of the candles. She went to the door and looked through the spy hole but could see nothing; it was even blacker out there. It had to be the car park attendant who could usually be found in the basement guarding the residents against all comers.

'Juliet? It's Karel.'

Karel. What on earth . . . 'Wait.' She closed the door so as to unhook the chain. 'What are you doing here?'

The shadowy figure lifted whatever he was carrying in his left hand and waved it in her general direction. 'I had gone to buy some food and, driving past, all the lights went out. I was in the street and wondered if you were all right.'

Vaguely she could smell curry. 'Come in,' she said, standing back so that he could pass her. 'You're very kind but, as you can see, I'm fine. How on earth did you get in here? The attendant never lets anyone in whom he doesn't know or that I don't tell him I'm expecting.'

'He knows me; he finds me a parking space every now and again, and, besides, this is an emergency. Other residents are driving the poor man crazy. It's not his fault the lights have gone out.' He looked around. 'You have made it very nice – with the candles.' They stood for a moment looking at each other. 'I will go now since you are well,' he said when the silence was becoming awkward.

She could not let him leave – how discourteous. 'That was kind of you, but would you like a drink or – your food must be getting cold.'

He laughed ruefully. 'Yes, I think perhaps; too long I waited in the car to see if the lights would come again. You have eaten? There is plenty; sometimes I can't make the decision and so I buy two and keep for the next evening.'

How sad and lonely that sounded. She wondered if any one of the thousands who had watched his conducting with great pleasure would ever have pictured him buying a takeaway meal or, to her even worse, heating up left-overs the next night. He seemed to sense her thoughts.

'It is not so awful as it sounds, Juliet. I am busy; I refuse the invitation and then I realise that I have forgotten to buy something to cook and so I go out. Sitting in a restaurant takes too much time; the takeaway is very convenient and I try different types, a cultural study.'

They were still standing near the door. Juliet held out her hand for the bag. 'Come in before it gets cold and eat it. I think there's a beer in the fridge.'

The semi-darkness made it easy to be relaxed. She could not see the expression on his face and realised that therefore he could not see her clearly either. The darkness also created an intimacy, a domesticity that she did not know how to destroy, not that she wanted to. This was tonight and they were two people caught in a blackout. Tomorrow would be different.

'There is only one beer, I think.'

'I'm not a beer drinker; I bought that for Gregor. There's a glass just above your head.' She reached into a drawer beside the cooker. 'And here's an opener.' She took a deep breath; having him so close in the dark was disturbing. 'I'll only be a minute in here. Why don't you take your beer into the living room? I'd say, put on some music, but . . .'

He took the metal bottle opener from her hand and his fingers brushed hers. A frisson of pleasure ran through her hand, up her arm, and down across her breast, and she turned away quickly praying that he had not noticed.

'You will share?' He gestured to the cartons.

'Does smell good.'

He laughed and returned to the living room and when she was alone she busied herself taking down plates and finding forks and water glasses.

'It is nice you keep beer for Gregor.' He was in the doorway again. 'He comes often?'

'He comes never. Your beer is probably stale.' Gregor. Thank God, a wonderful safe topic of conversation. 'Gregor is busily composing and, at this time, I think he's living in Sir Thomas Redpath's home near Edinburgh. Light a few more candles, please, and we'll eat here. This smells so delicious I'll have to have some.' She put the cartons on a tray and carried them to the table. 'Does this happen often in the Czech Republic?'

'This? Oh, the breaking of the lights. Sometimes, in the winter with the storms; we have much snow, more than here, I think.'

They talked about weather conditions and blackouts like two stereotypical Britons with nothing else to discuss because the air between them was, to Juliet at least, charged with its own electricity and she welcomed the innocuous subject; her nerve endings seemed to be on fire and she prayed for the impromptu meal to end and, at the same time, to go on for ever.

'Gregor is composing?'

She put a tiny spoonful of pilau rice on her plate very, very carefully. 'Yes. The last time I spoke to him he wasn't sure whether he was writing a symphony or a concerto but there is a violin solo for Hermione so perhaps it will be a concerto. He had great marks at college. "Total command of orchestral technique; keen sense of colour." That sort of thing. He had the mole problem, by the way.'

He put down his fork and reached into his pocket with an exclamation of annoyance. 'I asked about them.' He opened the piece of paper he had retrieved and read it. 'If he wishes to get rid of them humanely there is a little trap: the mole goes in as he digs and the door closes behind him. Then you pick it up and take him away to the country, I suppose.'

'Sir Thomas lives in the country. But that was kind of you to ask. He hasn't rung again so I presume everything is fine. Hermione reminded him that Redpath has a gardener; he'll know what to do.' She ate some of the rice, put a little sauce on the amount remaining and then put the fork down again. 'Is there something those of us who care about Gregor should know?'

He was silent but the light from the candles shone on his face and she could see doubt in his eyes.

'Gregor is twenty-five years old, Karel; he's had rather a difficult start in life and Hermione says he's really happy.'

'He is . . . how you say?'

'Your English gets worse when you're nervous. Is he gay? I think so. Yes, he is. He didn't know and it troubled him. Is Tom Redpath known for his particular proclivities?'

He laughed. 'My English was never good enough for such big words. Is he gay? Yes. None of the people with whom he associates complain; he is very generous but his liaisons do not seem to last very long. He is, perhaps, looking for something or someone special, like us all, no?'

She could not answer that. 'Gregor has little interest in money,' she said. 'Hermione is in love with him and her father is very wealthy. Gregor spurned her. The three of us love Gregor in different ways. He is my friend and I want him to be happy. I hope Tom Redpath has helped Gregor come to terms with his sexuality since that seemed to be a problem for him, but I don't want him hurt. I'm angry with myself that I never once thought there was a difficulty: some friend I turned out to be.'

'I think you are a wonderful friend to have. Hermione thinks so and, besides, Juliet, we cannot be mother to all of our friends. What of the third person in the flat?' He tore a piece of nan bread apart and mopped up some sauce. 'This is very good or I was very hungry.'

'Both. Heather is going to sing in Montpellier at Christmas.' She could not tell him about the pregnancy – it was not her secret to share. 'We are all so happy for her.'

His mouth was full but he nodded and Juliet toyed with her spoonful and watched his face as the candle flames flickered.

'It's very good,' she said.

'For a special meal I prefer French,' he said and looked directly into her eyes.

The lights came on as suddenly as they had gone out and shone into the kitchen. Glad but at the same time sorry that she need not say anything, Juliet got up and switched them on from the door.

'I liked without the lights, Juliet, but it is good that all is well again.' He stood up. 'It is very late and we have the early start. I can help you clean up.'

She could not bear such intimacy and said almost stridently, 'No. I mean thanks but you have to drive home and it will take only a minute. Thank you for coming in. Will I wrap this up?' She followed him into the living room where he lifted his waterproof jacket from the chair where he had left it. They stood again at the door looking at each other. Her feelings were in turmoil: what should she say, could she say? If she moved towards him, raised her hand . . . She did nothing, said nothing.

'I have had enough food,' he said at last. He leaned forward. 'Goodnight,' he said and kissed her cheek.

She stood there for some minutes after he had gone, her hand pressed against her face. What had it all been about? And his remark: 'For a special meal I prefer French.' Was he remembering their wonderful meal in Edinburgh? Was he thinking of that entire lovely episode which, so often, had seemed only a dream? For how could such an exquisite interlude have gone so dreadfully wrong?

'Lukewarm curry can be a rather special meal too,' she said to herself rather sadly and began to tidy her tiny kitchen.

24

Hermione closed the door and began to lock up for the night. Before fastening the dead bolt she remembered that Heather had been singing with her choir and so she slipped off her long leather coat, threw it over a chair that stood in the tiny hallway, and walked into the main room. No lights shone anywhere: Heather was either still out or asleep. She checked the time again and walked along the corridor to Heather's bedroom where she stood at the door quietly listening. Then she knocked and waited for a moment before turning the handle. The light from the street lamp just outside the apartment building showed that Heather had not yet come home and that the room that would welcome her was the untidy muddle it always was. Impending motherhood had not made the singer any tidier.

Hermione, who was fanatically and – to her friends – often annoyingly neat, shrugged her shoulders and closed the door. She was pragmatic in her dealings with others: *chacun à son goût*; if Heather chose to live in a tip that was her problem and, short of throwing her out, there was nothing Hermione could do to change things. Besides, she said to herself, in the great scheme of things being untidy is not such a very bad habit. She went into her own bedroom, kicked off her shoes, but immediately picked them up, took them to the wardrobe, found their shoe trees, inspected the shoes to see if any dirt had adhered to them and put them away.

That morning she had slept late and so she did not want to go to bed. She decided to wait in the living room for Heather. She curled up in an armchair near the window and lay back. She liked these moments of stillness when moonlight filled the room, often imbuing rather dull objects with an unearthly beauty. Had Gregor been in the flat all the curtains would have been closed.

'You're losing heat with all these big windows; that's wasteful and isn't good for the planet.'

But Gregor was still in the country and so she would indulge herself. The street outside sent up the usual sounds, a car screeching to a halt at a traffic light, the revving of a car or motorcycle engine, but the building itself seemed very quiet. Surely all residents were not asleep. Usually the low murmur of a television programme from one of the neighbouring apartments could be heard or Mrs McDermott's radio: Radio 4 or Classic FM. Even though she had so recently been ill and hospitalised, Mrs McD stayed up late and it was just after eleven. Hermione sat for a few minutes listening intently and then jumped up abruptly. She went to the fireplace, reached behind the French ormolu clock that sat in the middle and found a key and then, still shoeless, hurried out of her flat and along the corridor. She listened outside Mrs McDermott's door for any sound, the flushing of a toilet, the running of water, the whistling of a kettle, but there was nothing and after knocking moderately loudly she opened the door and went in.

The flat smelled musty and, as usual, felt cold. Hermione hesitated; she did not want to terrify the old woman who, after all, was still recovering from her enforced hospital stay but her instincts told her that something was wrong. The atmosphere in the hall where she stood was heavy and filled with foreboding. She went to the bedroom, knocked lightly, turned the handle, and opened the door. She could see nothing, for unlike Heather's bedroom where all the curtains were wide open these windows were shrouded by thick velvet curtains. There were tiny pinpricks of light in places where the material had worn but not enough to let her see.

'Mrs McDermott?' she said firmly.

Nothing.

She held her breath and switched on the light by the door. The room was empty and Hermione almost collapsed against the wall with relief. With a wildly beating heart she realised that she had been geared up to finding Mrs McDermott dead in her bed. But if she was not in her bedroom, where was she? Hermione walked along the corridor and into the sitting room switching on lights as she went. Mrs McDermott was sitting in a chair near what had once been a rather lovely marble and art nouveau tile fireplace, now blocked off.

'Hello, Mrs McD,' she said in a normal voice. 'Everything all right?' She advanced hesitatingly across the worn carpet.

Mrs McDermott did not stir. The book she had been reading was lying on the carpet beside her chair. Hermione bent to pick it up, noting automatically that it was in a language she did not recognise, and then she touched the paper-thin skin of the wrinkled old hands as she attempted to give the old lady her book. Hermione had never in her life seen a dead body before and she managed to stop herself from gasping at the initial shock. She stood looking down at her friend, the old lady who had lived next door, who had listened with apparent pleasure to rehearsals, even to scales, who had loved to share the simplest of meals – Gregor's scrambled eggs – or rather grander affairs. Hermione began to cry but even as the tears ran down her cheeks her mind was working furiously. What was the correct thing to do? She, even at the grand old age of twenty-five, wanted to ring her father: he would know what to do; he would do everything, take care of everything, but he was not here.

Hermione blew her nose and wiped her eyes with the frilly cuff of her little lacy cardigan, went to the telephone and dialled the emergency services just as Gregor had done a few weeks earlier. She waited patiently with Mrs McD until the ambulance arrived, kneeling on the carpet beside her, and holding her cold thin hand. Again she cried, for the old lady they had known for such a short time and for herself and her friends.

Our one and only uncritical listener. Did we do enough for you, dear Mrs McD?

She thought of times when they had tried to pretend that they were not in the apartment, times when they had shown exasperation at seeing the frail figure with gloves and handbag standing at the door. She remembered Mrs McDermott sitting on their sofa applauding one or other of them.

'Why you are not at Covent Garden, I do not understand.'

I'll try to remember you every time I play, Mrs McD. How cold death is.

But at last the reassuringly efficient ambulance men were there and all Hermione was asked to do was to give them the name of Mrs McDermott's next of kin.

'I don't know; I don't think there is anyone but I have her lawyer's name.'

She watched them until the ambulance drove away and then slowly climbed the stairs to the old lady's flat where she turned off all the lights before locking the door and, aware for the first time of her now very cold and dirty feet, walked back to her own apartment. Heather's pink duffle coat was lying on the chair in the hall, and, assuming correctly that she had returned on her own, Hermione locked the heavy main door and stood, her head against its solidity for a moment, feeling the warmth of the apartment surround her.

She had no idea of the time; it did not matter. She dialled her parents' number and her father answered almost immediately.

'Mrs McDermott's dead,' she said and began to cry again. Between sobs and nose blowing she told him the story. 'She was so cold, Daddy. How awful to die alone in a cold flat; it felt like a morgue in there. Poor old soul couldn't afford heating; she was always turning it off and coming in here.'

'This is the neighbour you called the ambulance services for before?'

She nodded, although she was alone in the living room. 'I just had a feeling; everything was so quiet, an unnatural quiet. I should have gone earlier, asked her to come in and have some tea, listen to music. She knew quite a bit about music, loved to hear us practise. Oh, Daddy, what if . . . what if . . .?'

'Hermione, stop at once. You were a wonderful neighbour. Mummy and I were saying just the other day that you – and the others, of course – were unbelievably patient with that old woman.

Look, darling, I'm going to drive down right now and stay with you for the rest of the night. Mummy's in New York but I'll try to contact her. Unfortunately I have to be in Berlin tomorrow; I can't change the arrangements; too many internationals involved but tonight I can be with my little girl for an hour or two anyway.'

Hermione made an effort to pull herself together. 'Daddy, I'm twenty-five years old. Heather's here and I'll ring Gregor because he'll want to know, and Juliet, of course. I'm fine; I'm over the shock now talking to you and I think I'll go to bed – after I ring Gregor.' She looked at her watch. 'He's unlikely to be in bed, and if he is, he would still expect me to tell him. Even if you leave now you won't get here until nearly morning and you would just have to leave again.'

He was adamant; he would leave for his business meetings from Edinburgh instead of Inverness. After promising to unlock the door Hermione hung up. Then she rang Gregor but there was no reply and so she telephoned Juliet who answered very sleepily and then was instantly wide awake when she heard Hermione's grief-filled voice.

'What's wrong, Hermione? Is it Heather?'

'Mrs McDermott's dead.' Hermione had not meant to be so blunt and so started to cry. 'I found her, Juliet, in her flat, sitting in a chair, cold as . . . cold as death.'

'Oh, darling Hermione, I'm so sorry. I'll come at once. Karel will understand. Who's with you? You mustn't be on your own.'

'Heather's here. She's asleep, doesn't know yet, and I've left a message for Gregor. Can you believe Daddy is driving down . . . Never mind that; it's too complicated. Oh, bloody hell, Juliet, she was a poor, lonely old woman and sometimes I pretended I wasn't in the flat when I heard her at the door and she never ever said anything caustic to any of us. Dash it all, Juliet, she was as forgiving as a dog.' She was quiet for a moment and then said again as if she could not quite believe it, 'She was so cold; I've never experienced such cold.'

'Look, I'll get the first flight from City Airport in the morning. I'll leave a note for Karel. He'll understand.'

'Can you really come? Daddy has to leave immediately for Berlin – why he is bothering to come, I do not know, but I don't want to be alone when I talk to the hospital or the lawyer.'

'You may have to talk to the police too.' Juliet was trying to remember what her father had said happened when someone was found dead at home. Was there an autopsy or was that only in suspicious circumstances?

'I don't expect police. The ambulance man said she'd had a heart attack, just slipped away quietly. She wasn't frightening to look at, just peaceful, and almost pretty. Her wrinkles seemed to have smoothed out and I could see what she would have looked like when she was young. I just didn't expect her to be so cold: she had been dead several hours. All the time I was out enjoying myself, she was sitting there . . . Poor old woman.'

'It sounds peaceful, Hermione. She probably had no idea and I'm positive that she would be delighted to know that you were the person to find her. Now, Dr Juliet talking, pour a little brandy and go to bed. There is nothing you can do now and you'll need your energy in the morning.'

Juliet tried to go back to sleep when she had hung up but her mind was too busy. After Karel had left she had abandoned the idea of a hot bath and had gone straight to bed, to lie and go over and over every word, every look, every gesture, and most of all to think of his coming to see that the major blackout had not affected her badly. She tossed and turned trying to find, not only a cool place but also an acceptable answer to the question, Why had Karel come to see her?

The 'he just happened to be passing when the power cut happened' was least satisfactory but probably true.

She tried to pacify her racing mind, now full of Hermione's shocked voice, together with pictures and memories of the old lady who had lived next door. Impossible to believe that she would never see her again, never open the door of the Edinburgh flat to find her on the doorstep, dressed, as always, for an afternoon visit. She would stay for the funeral, return to London immediately, and so she would miss only two or at most three days. She got out of bed and set her alarm clock and then she packed an overnight bag with the bare essentials: if she travelled in a black suit, which would do for the funeral, a pair of jeans and a few jumpers would take care of everything else. She zipped up the bag and stood looking at it for a moment. Yes, she was as ready as she would ever be. Would she have time in the morning to put a message on the office computer for Karel? Possibly, but she sat down and wrote him a note to leave in his office and she would telephone when she got to Edinburgh.

The offices were not yet open when she rushed over in the morning. Eventually, she found an assistant seated at a desk who promised to deliver her note.

'It's terribly important,' she said. 'You will get it to him?'

He looked at her somewhat belligerently. 'I'm not a delivery boy but I said I would, didn't I?'

Juliet tried to smooth down his ruffled and extremely unappealing feathers. 'I'm sure you will. Thank you. It's a death in the family, you see.'

He said nothing but put the sheet of paper in his breast pocket.

'Thank you.' Juliet said desperately and turned and almost ran from the building. She did not see him look after her, take the note from his pocket, read it, and then casually tear it into small pieces that he tossed into a waste basket.

'Bossy cow.'

It took longer to get from Edinburgh Airport to the flat than it had taken to fly from London to Edinburgh and Juliet was extremely frustrated when her taxi at last dropped her off. A white chauffeur-driven Rolls-Royce pulled up at the same time and Gregor got out and ran across the pavement to her and, for the first time ever, wrapped her in a bone-shattering hug.

'Juliet, I just knew you would come. Isn't this awful? Poor old soul. Hermione's sleeping. I talked to Sebastian and he was just leaving but said he'd finally got her to lie down for a while. She was waiting for me to phone but I never even looked at messages till this morning.'

Neither of them mentioned the expensive car that was now

purring quietly away. A few weeks before they would have laughed at this evidence of conspicuous consumption and Gregor would probably have said, 'If you have to have a Rolls, for God's sake have a black one.' Life and death had moved very quickly in the past few days though.

They walked past Mrs McDermott's door with bowed heads and Gregor reached in his pocket for his key to Hermione's flat. 'Can't believe she won't hear us and come in. "Can't understand why you're not at Covent Garden, Gregor." She had me in the Albert Hall for the Promenade concerts last time I played for her though. Hermione and I played her bits of my new piece.' He stood staring into space for a moment. 'I'm glad we did that.'

They were inside and the flat was warm and quiet but they heard water running in the kitchen and tiptoed along to the door. Heather, fully dressed, and now obviously pregnant, was filling a kettle. 'I heard you two,' she said and held out her arms for a group hug. 'Poor Mrs McD. I wish I'd been nicer to her.'

That comment embarrassed and annoyed Juliet but she supposed it was all part and parcel of dealing with death. She could not, however, bring herself to offer Heather any soothing platitudes but they were not needed since Gregor did it for her.

'You were fine, Heather. Mrs McD liked you a lot.'

'How are you? You're looking better than the last time I saw you.' Juliet took off her coat and hung it over the back of her chair. 'Here, sit down and let me make the coffee.'

They were sitting around the kitchen table, eating hot buttered toast and drinking coffee, when the telephone rang and all three jumped for it. Gregor, being closest, got there first. 'No, she's asleep. I'm afraid she's been up all night.'

Juliet and Heather stood and watched him waiting while the caller spoke. After a moment or two, Gregor spoke again. 'Is it absolutely necessary? I'm her flatmate, Gregor Morrison, and her other flatmates are here too. Yes, she is. Hold for a second. Juliet, it's Mrs McDermott's lawyer. He says he can talk to you rather than wake Hermione up just yet.'

Juliet took the receiver, said hello, and then listened for a few minutes. 'Yes, that will be fine; she should be rested by then. Thanks for calling. Yes, I am very sorry. We all are. She was quite a character, our dear Mrs McD.'

She hung up the telephone and stood puffing out her cheeks and then blowing. 'Mr Galbraith wants to come over to close the flat up but he wants Hermione there since she's been the one who has been so involved with Mrs McDermott.' She took a deep breath. 'The . . . body has been released for burial – no suspicious circumstances, and Mrs McD has left quite clear instructions which he will carry out. Poor sweet old lady; can you believe that, apart from a few relatives of her late husband who will be informed as a courtesy, there is no one, not one single person to be notified. She has no living relatives.'

'Sit down, Juliet, and I'll make fresh coffee. When is he coming?' Gregor took the coffee pot over to the sink. 'Heather, sit down before you fall down. Have you talked to your parents again?'

'No,' said Heather in a very small voice.

'Maybe you should give them another chance: the shock should have worn off by now. Don't you agree, Juliet?'

'Absolutely, but it's up to Heather. Is everything going well?'

'It was till this morning; it's not much fun to wake up with morning sickness and have Hermione's father tell me about Mrs McD. What a fright I got when I saw him.'

'He drove down through shitty weather to spend a few hours with his daughter. Gets my vote. Poor old Mrs McD.' He started to laugh. 'Remember how tipsy she got at Hogmanay.'

Neither of the girls said anything and he busied himself making coffee. 'I haven't spoken to my mother in years. Wonder if anyone would tell me if anything happened to her.' He reached into his pocket for his mobile, which was ringing, and Juliet was amazed at how his face changed when he answered it. 'I'm fine. Juliet's here and Heather, and poor old Hermione's having a sleep.' He covered the mouthpiece and turned to Juliet. 'Tom,' he said. He returned to his telephone conversation. 'Yes. You are so thoughtful. I'll stay here. Course. I'll give her your best wishes when she wakes up.'

Juliet looked at her watch. 'Maybe we should rouse Hermione.'

'I'm roused,' said a rather throaty voice from the door. Hermione looked at her friends and walked forward to put her arms round as many of them as she could reach. 'I'd say it was like old times but it can't ever be like old times again, can it?'

'Of course it can. Here, have some coffee. Tom's sending some food over from Sainsbury's, Hermione, to save any of us having to go out.'

Hermione took the mug and smiled. 'How thoughtful of him. That was sweet, wasn't it? The cupboard is bare, I suppose.'

'There's no apricot yoghurt for a start,' said Juliet, who was holding open the door of the fridge and staring at the illuminated interior. She closed the door and turned. 'Hermione, that nice Mr Galbraith is coming later this morning; he needs to close up Mrs McD's flat.'

'Does he want my key?'

'No idea. I would imagine he has keys but he did want you to be there.'

Hermione reached for a piece of toast, which she began to tear apart and crumble between her fingers. 'I don't think I want to go into the flat again. Will you come with me, Juliet? He can't object to you.'

'Stop murdering the toast and eat it. Of course I'll come. Maybe he'll speak to you here. Now I have to go and ring my parents; yet another trip north without visiting them.' She picked up her handbag and rummaged through it. Then angrily she put it on the table and went through the pockets of her coat. 'Damn, damn, and double damn,' she said and went out into the hall. A few fraught minutes later she returned. 'I cannot believe I am so stupid. Either I've left my phone in London or I left it in the taxi or I've dropped it. Thank heavens Karel knows where I am.' She took the telephone that Gregor was quietly holding out to her, said thank you, and went back out into the hall.

Patrick Galbraith of Galbraith, Wedderspoon and Galbraith arrived shortly after eleven. Hermione and Juliet met him at the door of Mrs McDermott's flat. He was not the same Mr Galbraith whom Hermione had met in the hospital when Mrs McDermott was taken ill earlier in the year. This Mr Galbraith was scarcely older than they were themselves and was far from being a dull, grey-suited archetypal solicitor; he was wearing a sports jacket and was in the act of fastening a tie around his neck.

'Sorry about the tie. I very rarely wear one in the office and my father handed me this as I was leaving.'

'It does nothing for that jacket,' said Hermione and was sorry to see his pleasant face flush with embarrassment. 'I'm sorry, it's a very nice tie. I should have kept quiet – nerves, probably.'

'Solicitors have that effect,' he said, 'especially at sad times like these. Shall we go in, ladies?'

'Is it necessary?' asked Juliet, since Hermione seemed to have become tongue-tied and was happily looking at Mr Galbraith who had lost his high colour and was almost gazing back at her. 'The flat is cold: ours is warm and there's fresh coffee.'

He turned to look at her. 'That would be lovely but, you see, you, Miss Crawford, and you, Miss Elliott-Chevenix, were named as executors by the late Mrs McDermott and it would be appreciated if you would see me remove certain items from the flat for safe keeping.' He picked up his briefcase which he had put down in order to put on the regimental tie.

Hermione and Juliet looked at each other in amazement as the solicitor opened the door of the flat and turned on the hall light. 'Executors?' they said together and followed him into the room.

'Yes. Highly irregular since you are each mentioned in the will, small bequests, but she was adamant.'

At that Hermione started to cry and he looked at her in either horror or terror, Juliet could not be sure which.

'It's all right, Hermione,' she said. 'Let's get this over.'

Hermione blew her nose on some rather dubious tissues that she unearthed from her pocket. 'It's just the thought: poor old Mrs McD. She didn't have anything to leave . . .'

'On the contrary, Miss Elliott-Chevenix, she had a great deal. Unfortunately there is no burglar alarm on the flat – we advised her several times – and so I have been authorised to remove several small but extremely valuable items from the residence. It is appalling but do you know that there are criminals who make a reasonable living by studying the Deaths column of their local papers and then breaking into the homes of the recently deceased? They love the day of the funeral. Shall we go into the bedroom?' he asked and blushed furiously again.

The solitary bulb in the light fixture did little to dispel the gloom in the room and he walked across to the windows and drew the curtains. 'Perhaps you ladies would be good enough to open and close the curtains as normal for the next few days? Best to look lived in.'

'Drawn was normal,' said Hermione quietly.

'She kept the sun's rays from her carpets, but she did open the front curtains and even the windows themselves; she was perfectly normal, you know, perhaps a tad eccentric but who wouldn't be?' He looked at them and saw that they had no idea what he was talking about. 'Mrs McDermott spent years in a concentration camp in Poland: she lost every member of her family there. After the war she married a minor diplomat in the British Embassy in Lisbon but he was killed in a climbing accident shortly after their marriage; there were no children. Mr McDermott's relatives were, shall we say, not so welcoming as he was.' Again he saw that they looked puzzled. 'Mrs McDermott was Jewish although she has not been in a synagogue for over fifty years.' He turned away. 'The first item is this small engraving.' He lifted down a small picture that was hanging on the wall near the boarded-up fireplace. 'Fragonard,' he said. 'Jean Honoré; 1732 to 1806. Extremely valuable.' He wrapped the engraving in a cloth retrieved from his briefcase.

Less than an hour later they left the flat. Juliet felt as if she had been holding her breath and she could see that Hermione was hanging on to control by the tips of her green fingernails. Neither of them had ever had to deal with death and it was a sobering experience.

'Coffee, Mr Galbraith?' Hermione had found her voice.

'Yes, please, and my name is Patrick.' His rather pale face had a slightly pink tinge and he was looking at Hermione much as a dog looks at a beloved human, just begging for even the tiniest acknowledgement.

'Patrick,' echoed Hermione who was also looking not quite her usual super-sophisticated self.

'Coffee,' repeated Juliet, who thought that left to themselves Hermione and Patrick might stand there on the landing perfectly happily for some time and she threw open the door of Hermione's apartment with more vigour than was perhaps necessary.

'The funeral will be at two tomorrow afternoon and will be conducted by the local Church of Scotland minister,' Patrick told them when all five of them were in the sitting room. 'It will be a small private ceremony just as Mrs McDermott wanted. Naturally we have informed her late husband's relatives. None of them is specifically mentioned in the will although certain items of family furniture will be returned to them. I will, of course, arrange to allow them into the apartment to see to the disposal or packing up of pieces. You four young people are each mentioned and so would it be possible for me to return here just after the funeral to read the will? Then Hermione . . .' He looked at Hermione and seemed to lose track.

'Hermione?' prompted Juliet.

'Yes, of course. Hermione and you, Juliet, as executors will be asked to sign documents stating that each legatee has received his or her legacy.'

When Patrick had left to return to his office, Juliet borrowed a telephone and rang her parents again.

'It looks as if Saturday will be fairly free, but I'm not sure. Can you and Dad come through here, Mum? There's just so much to do. Mrs McDermott named me as an executor.'

'How bizarre. And we can't go to Edinburgh because Daddy's playing golf – if it doesn't snow. Why don't you go to the funeral and come home for the weekend? Bring Hermione; a break will be good for her.'

'Mum, are you listening to me? Mrs McDermott is dead. She died alone in her apartment and I am going to her funeral. I really would appreciate some support from my parents. Sebastian drove down through the night to be with Hermione.' How utterly childish she felt as she heard herself say those words.

'He's not a doctor. Daddy can't just jump when you deign to call him, Juliet, and it's not as if you were close to this old lady. If you talked about her at all you were usually laughing.'

Impasse again. The inability of minds to meet or the unwillingness. Her mother was still talking. 'And where is Chloé, not rushing to Hermione's side?'

'She's in New York.'

'Obviously not dropping everything to return just because an old woman dies in her daughter's block of flats? Really, Juliet, you are so selfish sometimes.'

The words hit like a hammer blow. Selfish, was she selfish? 'I have to go back to London on Sunday.' She was pleased at how calm she sounded: not hurt, calm.

'On the Aberdeen to London train, Juliet, which happens to pull through Dundee.'

'Mother, please. I must ring Karel Haken because I took off without permission and I need to check in with him. I rang you first. Please come in and have lunch with us on Saturday. Now I have to go.'

When Hermione's mobile was finally free again it was too late, Juliet decided, to call Karel. Heather had gone to a choir practice and Gregor was meeting Tom for dinner; the girls had been invited but were tired and merely wanted to stay at home and rest and talk. Juliet was still upset by her conversation with her mother and was even beginning to wonder about her feelings for Mrs McDermott. Had she been genuinely fond of the old woman or was it merely that Mrs McDermott had given her and the others unconditional approval? She could see her sitting on the sofa, gloved hands in her lap, tolerating scales with a patient smile, glorying in their best efforts.

'I can't think why you're not at Covent Garden.' Dear Mrs McDermott.

Patrick Galbraith had rung Hermione once or twice ostensibly about requests from relatives of the late Mr McDermott that they might be granted access to the flat. Only one, a niece, had promised to attend the funeral and would represent the family at the reading of the will.

'Juliet, you look so sad. Are you upset over Mrs McD or is it Haken? Why don't you ring his mobile?'

Juliet tried to smile and shook her head. 'Not fair to disturb him outside office hours and besides, he'll be conducting now. I'd forgotten that; in fact I'm missing two performances.'

'You could leave a message, Juliet, tell him you'll be back bright and early on Monday morning.'

A note was impersonal and so too was a phone message. Much better actually to speak to him; she did not allow herself to think that after their interesting evening she was looking forward to hearing his voice. It would be even better to speak to him face to face so that she could try to read his expression but at least a personal call was more acceptable than leaving yet another message.

He in fact rang her.

They were changing for the funeral and Hermione had suddenly realised that green hair might be at variance with the tone of the proceedings.

'Mrs McD loved your green hair.'

'Oh, Juliet, she preferred purple. I have to cover it up but I can't find my black cap anywhere.'

Since the black cap in question made her look like the Artful Dodger – which had been the sole reason for the purchase in the first place – Juliet did not pursue that line. 'You look great and, do you know, Hermione, I think Mrs McD would prefer colour. Remember all her scarves and draperies, and are you going to answer that telephone?'

Hermione found her mobile phone under several abandoned outfits. 'It's for you,' she said, slight disappointment in her voice. 'It's Maestro Haken.'

Juliet's heart began to race and she prayed that her emotions were not written across her face. 'Karel, how nice of you to call.'

He said nothing.

'Karel? Hello.' Juliet was now feeling not only stupid but also nervous.

'How nice of you to call,' he repeated, and the fury in his voice was almost tangible. 'How dare you. Why on earth did you run away? Such immaturity, Juliet, and you think that I can possibly write that you are able to control an orchestra – you cannot control yourself. I expect you in the office at eight o'clock on Monday morning and we will discuss whether or not you have any future with the LSO.'

And then there was silence.

25

Early on Saturday morning Juliet telephoned her parents. Her mother answered.

'Hi, Mum, are you coming in today?'

Her mother's voice was very cold. 'How very kind of you to ring me. I did think you might answer at least one of my messages yesterday.'

'Yesterday? The funeral was yesterday and then there were so many other things to do.'

'And you were much too busy to ring your mother back. Our plans aren't important.'

'But I didn't get . . .' began Juliet. 'Mum, have you been leaving messages on my mobile phone?'

'Yes. Daddy phoned you on Thursday evening when he came home and I rang twice yesterday. It's very rude, Juliet, and distressing too.'

'My phone is in London. I'm sorry, Mum. I've either left it in my flat or lost it on the way to the train. I'm using Hermione's mobile,' she added quickly. 'It's just that I find I have to return to London and if you weren't planning to come in then I'd like to leave today.'

'What is more important in London than seeing your parents?'

Juliet, who had been in tears of one kind or another for nearly twenty-four hours, was ready to hang up in exasperation. 'My life is more important, Mother, my career, or what is left of it.'

It all came flooding back: Karel's angry voice and, more importantly, his implied threat. He was going to dismiss her from the course. What had she done? She had to speak to him, had to find out why he was so angry. Of course it would have been better had

315

she requested permission to leave but Mrs McDermott's sudden death had upset her more than she had understood at the time and now she saw that she had not been thinking clearly. She should have telephoned him or the Barbican offices when she heard the news – left a voice message, instead of leaving the note. But he had ignored the note, accused her of running away from him. How bizarre. Why on earth should she even contemplate that? Nothing had happened between them: they had shared a meal and a few hours of comradeship in a blackout. He had kissed her. No, that kiss meant nothing. It was European politeness, wasn't it? She looked down at the ring on the fourth finger of her right hand and, although she had been quite positive that there were absolutely no tears left inside, she began to weep.

'Juliet, you're crying. What's wrong, darling? I didn't mean to upset you. What's wrong?'

Juliet sniffed. She remembered her utter desolation when Karel had hung up on her; she remembered trying not to show Hermione that the foundations of her international life-long career seemed to be crumbling under her feet.

Patrick Galbraith had driven them all to the crematorium. A striking woman in her late forties, who introduced herself as Caroline de Lazlo, represented Mrs McDermott's husband's family. She was dressed in an extremely well-cut black suit over which she wore an unbuttoned black suede coat with a fake fur – Juliet hoped it was fake – lining. She had a no-nonsense face matched by a no-nonsense manner. 'Hello,' she said, holding out her hand. 'I am Andrew McDermott's niece; I'm afraid I had no idea of your friend's existence till a few days ago; bloody families. Pity about this legal stuff but it shouldn't take long and you'll forgive me if I dash after the will, etcetera.'

They gathered in Hermione's lovely sitting room. Gregor had filled every vase he could find with daffodils and the heat had already opened their cheery yellow trumpets. For some reason, possibly because he had once read everything Agatha Christie ever wrote, he had also assumed that wills were read to the sounds of mourners sipping sherry, and he had stopped at a local off licence and bought a bottle of what he was assured was good sherry.

Heather, very conscious of her baby, had forsworn alcohol for the duration of her pregnancy, Juliet and Hermione looked surprised by the offer and declined, Patrick said that he was driving, and so Gregor and the McDermott family representative duly sipped from crystal sherry glasses that Hermione was astonished to discover that she owned.

The will was very simple. The listed pieces of McDermott family furniture which included the Venetian bureau cabinet were to be returned to the family should anyone want them, Juliet and Hermione were each willed a ring, the Fragonard etching was to go to Gregor who, on hearing the news, looked totally astounded and then burst into tears – a phenomenon his flatmates had never seen before; the flat, with its remaining furniture, was left to Gregor and Heather to use or dispose of as they chose. Heather gasped and, getting up, attempted to run from the room but Juliet held her in a grip of iron, soothing her all the while. Mrs McDermott's small annual income had died with her and there was barely enough in her bank account to pay expenses.

'She was adamant that her estate should cover all costs,' said Patrick Galbraith quietly. 'She was a very proud and dignified lady and we will all miss her very much.'

'I suppose I should look at the furniture, Mr Galbraith. We can compare lists, if you like.' Caroline de Lazlo reached into her handbag and brought out a folded paper that she handed to Patrick. 'Frankly I can't imagine anyone wanting anything after all this time; it was hers to dispose of as she chose.'

'And she chose that her husband's family should have it back if they wanted it.'

She got up from her chair and Gregor and Patrick sprang to their feet. 'Let's get it over.'

'Would you like coffee, Mrs de Lazlo, or tea?' asked Hermione, suddenly conscious that this was her flat and that she was the hostess.

'No thanks.' She looked round and shook each of them by the

hand. 'I wish you all well and I'm sorry about your friend.' And with that she walked over to the door which was opened by Patrick who nodded to them.

'I have the rings, ladies. I'll bring them back.'

The four friends were left alone and for some time no one spoke.

'Who told her I was pregnant?' asked Heather at last but no one volunteered a confession.

'It has to be because of the baby. A flat. My God, I can't believe it; she's left me her flat but she didn't even like me.'

'She liked you very much, Heather. I think perhaps you didn't have much time for her.'

'Oh, bloody perfect Juliet. You were always so patient with her, weren't you? What is it, jealous are you?' She had a thought that was momentarily unpleasant. 'Gregor, we don't have to get married or anything stupid like that?' She put her hands on her stomach as if to reassure herself that she was indeed expecting a baby and then, almost theatrically, hit her forehead. 'I can't believe it. A flat. She's left me a flat, in this building. What will my bigoted, narrow-minded father say now?' She covered her head with her hands. 'I can't believe it,' she said again. 'This is totally unreal. I want to jump and scream and dance.'

'I'm a wee bit gob-smacked myself,' said Gregor. He got up at the sound of the doorbell and they all watched as he walked to the door to find Patrick Galbraith standing there.

'Hello, ladies,' said Patrick. 'I hope you don't mind that I waited until Mrs de Lazlo was gone to give you your rings. I also wanted to talk to you all a bit about Mrs McDermott's reasoning. First the rings.' He opened his briefcase again and handed a small green leather box to Juliet and a small black leather one to Hermione. 'Yours is an opal and diamond cluster ring, Hermione; it dates from the early twentieth century. Mrs McDermott thought you might like it. Yours, Juliet, is rather more valuable and was her engagement ring.' He waited until Juliet had opened the box, gasped and looked up at him with a stricken face. 'That's a three-carat Burma ruby and the diamonds are rather nice too. She admired you a great deal; in fact she would have left you two ladies more but decided that neither of you really needed help from her. Gregor, your etching is extremely valuable and I suggest you have it valued and insured immediately. The flat was left to you and Heather mainly because, Gregor, of your' – and he read from a paper in his hand – ' "unfailing patience, courtesy and kindness". She was very grateful to all four of you and agonised several times over the will; she wanted to be fair but to be sensible. Mrs de Lazlo has looked at the family furniture in the flat and I have the feeling that it will be left there, even the valuable pieces which are perfect, by the way, no woodworm. Her main home for the foreseeable future is in Singapore and so she neither needs nor wants it and she feels the very elderly family members will say the same. We'll wait for a formal letter of renunciation from the family solicitors. I think now I'll leave you all to think about today and perhaps' – he looked directly at Hermione – 'I could pop in again. You two' – he looked at the silent Heather and Gregor – 'might need some advice. We're always happy to help. The keys will be made available as soon as all the legal stuff is out of the way. Anything else I can help with before I go?'

Too much had happened for any one of them to think coherently; Juliet, in fact, was engrossed in the patterns the fading light from the tall windows was casting on the carpet. It seemed easier somehow than thinking about the beautiful ring she now held tightly clasped in her right hand, as if, somehow, through the generous and unexpected gift, she was in touch with her old friend.

Patrick stood up. 'Fine. I'll let myself out.'

At this, since Heather and Gregor seemed too dazed to react, Hermione got to her feet and walked to the door with him.

'I really can't take this in,' said Gregor. 'It never occurred to me that the old soul owned the flat. Always thought she was just a better-educated version of my mother – a spit away from being a bag lady. Shit, I wish I'd been nicer to her.'

' "Unfailing patience, courtesy and kindness",' quoted Juliet. 'Mrs McD knew worth when she saw it.'

'She never said anything about me.' Heather began to cry. 'I never had a minute for her. "Useless old bat," was one of the nicer things I said about her. God, I feel like shit.'

'You sang for her,' said Gregor. 'Remember. She was always saying that you should be at Covent Garden.'

Heather blew her nose loudly on the tissues that Juliet handed her. 'I sang for me, for practice. I feel I've aged ten years this afternoon. Is this what growing up is all about? Rotten taste in people, worse taste in boyfriends, and then something happens that makes you think.' She got up and began to stride back and forth across the room. 'What's taking Hermione so long? Show the ring, Juliet.'

Juliet opened her hand. The great red stone had dug deep into her palm but all three gazed at it in awe. Juliet moved her hand and the stones sparkled as the light from the table lamp hit them. 'It's the most beautiful ring I've ever seen.' She slipped it on her right hand; it could have been made for her.

'Oh, let's see it.' Hermione, a little pink, had come back from the door.

Juliet held out her hand. 'Another toad?'

'Absolutely not. It's perfectly lovely, Juliet. Won't that make the back stalls sit up as it flashes during performances? Look at mine.' She slipped the lovely old ring on and smiled with pleasure. 'Let's never take them off: we'll wear them in her memory.'

Juliet looked at the ruby ring again and shook her head to clear it of all the memories. 'Mummy, it's been quite a difficult weekend and Maestro Haken is furious that I left London . . . I think it's because I didn't actually speak to him. He didn't seem to know where I was. He must have phoned me several times and got my message service because I have no idea where my telephone is. Then, possibly because he was so angry he rang Hermione to see if she knew where I was.' But that could not possibly be the case because she had left a very clear message, had she not? Mrs McDermott had died and she had had to go to Edinburgh. Yes, that was clear. 'Anyway, he's threatened that he will terminate my contract: perhaps I agreed to stay and not to leave without express permission. I don't know; I was so happy and excited I signed everything without actually reading it thoroughly, without really taking it in.'

'Oh, darling, I am sorry. But he's being unreasonable. A death isn't really what one would term an everyday occurrence, is it? The one thing you don't seem to have thought about, darling, and don't bite my head off, but where did you leave the note? Perhaps he hasn't seen it, and when he finds it, on his desk or whatever, then he'll be sorry and he'll apologise.'

'Mum, you're wonderful. That's it, of course. I gave it to one of the front of house staff, I think they're called. If he just left it on Karel's desk, then God knows what pile of papers it's buried under. You have no idea the amount of paperwork that builds up every day. But I still want to go back today; his number is on my mobile and this is so terribly crucial and important that I need to ring him no matter what time. He's conducting and so he'll be around quite late. If I get in before ten I might even be able to see him.'

'Then that's what you must do. Daddy and I will come down to London next weekend, or if Daddy's too busy or on call or anything like that, then I'll steal away midweek by myself; I'd love to stay at your flat. Wouldn't that be fun?'

Juliet was feeling much better. How simple, how easy it was going to be to make everything all right. 'It will be fantastic and I'll show you my ring. It's glorious, Mum, the most enormous ruby and six, yes, I think, six diamonds. I'll never ever take it off.'

Who knows, her mind added, it might be the only ring you will ever have.

26

'My poor Karel; it's not your fault. The judges look only for musical ability. Working in such a close relationship with another is rather like marriage. If you have not lived together before you tie the knot, as they say, then each revealed facet of the other's character or personality can be either a painful realisation or a delight.' He looked directly at the younger man and then turned away, his splendid profile thrown into relief against the early evening light from the windows. Then he looked down at his well-shaped hands and sighed as if he knew he had to say something but was most reluctant to do so. 'To be honest, I have had my doubts about the Crawford girl from the start.'

Karel looked at him doubtfully. 'Really? You said nothing.'

Alexander frowned. 'What could I say, my dear boy? I was not the chairman of the panel of judges. Had I been, Miss Wells would have been the competition winner. She, no matter how delightful, is not really a threat to you and your place in conducting history.'

Karel stood up and walked to the window and then back again. He looked down at the older conductor, so calm, so controlled, and so urbane on the sofa. 'A threat? I haven't the slightest idea what you're talking about. Miss Crawford is not a threat. She is a superbly gifted young woman who is perhaps too emotional and . . . irresponsible. It's the lack of responsibility that worries me. I had spent some time with her the evening before.' He stopped talking. How could he say, I hoped we were where we had been in the summer. Damn it. He really believed that perhaps Juliet cared enough, a little: he had hoped that perhaps they could be friends. And to walk into his office next morning with a packed schedule that involved Juliet and find that, without a word to anyone, she had disappeared. He had been afraid that she had overslept but that would have been unusual and forgivable. Then when she had not turned up by noon and there had been no reply to several telephone calls he had begun to worry. He had gone to her flat, had eventually persuaded the manager to open the door, but the flat had been as neat and tidy as Juliet herself. At last when he was minutes away from contacting the police he had remembered Hermione. If anyone would know where Juliet was, it was she.

'She is frigid, perhaps, Karel. You know these tall thin Celts. I would have said no emotion instead of too much.'

This was too personal and he found such topics of green room conversation objectionable. Besides, he could not discuss Juliet, could not even think of her without shouting out that he had been a prize fool. 'I am interested only in her ability, her promise. She has worked hard, done everything I have asked of her. She was late once. On another occasion she had the wrong score – and I have serious worries about the hows and the whys of that incident; it merits further investigation. In everything I have given her the benefit of the doubt because the orchestra, to a man, admire her. She listens and they listen to her because, although she is so young, they respect her: she has earned the respect of one of the greatest orchestras in the world. I thought everything was going so well, and then—' He turned away as if afraid that his deepest feelings could be seen on his face. 'Just to go away without a word, without telephoning or leaving a message; I don't understand her.'

The calm voice of his mentor tried to reassure. 'Nothing to understand, dear boy. She folded under pressure. You must consult the board and have her removed.'

Karel turned back quickly. 'Too drastic a step, surely. Her whole future as a conductor is at stake here, and besides, Alexander, although Mrs Grey is not on the board, she thinks Juliet is wonderful and has even invited her to Acapulco; she will not be happy to have her replaced. What were her comments about the Shostakovich she heard? "Wonderful; I loved how she emphasises the warmth and colour of the music rather than dwelling on its austerity." I would be happy to have such an accolade about my conducting skills.'

Alexander Stoltze stood up. 'You receive such plaudits every time you stand on the podium, Karel; you are a genius and the day I found you was the happiest in many ways of my entire life. You should be gathering your forces together instead of worrying about a silly girl. She's not for you, Karel; you need a woman like Bryony who knows how to play the game. Miss Crawford is too intense: her music, her conversation . . . everything.'

Karel opened the door of his dressing room. 'I am realising that I too am rather intense, Alexander. Thank you for coming in. I shall wait until I have spoken face to face with Miss Crawford before I make any decisions.'

The two men stood in the doorway, not touching but almost locked together by some invisible force. Stoltze blinked first. 'Remember our plans, Karel, our dreams. A Czech conductor, you, acknowledged as the greatest in the world.'

Karel laughed. 'Alexander, I was nineteen years old, a mere boy, when I dreamed such grandiose dreams, fantasies even. I thought of you as the greatest; many others thought so too.' He did not add the word "then", but it seemed to lie there, unspoken, between them. 'And I will not brush aside any talented youngster who is working to get where I am. Indeed, I will hold out my hand and pull him up, as you did with me, Maestro. Music has been very good to both of us; we are in a happy place, my friend.'

'Don't lose sight of the dreams.' Stoltze gestured as if embracing the Barbican. 'This is good but one day you will conduct the Berlin, the Chicago, all the greats.'

'Your dream, Alexander, not mine. I am not lowering my sights, old friend, but I won't let ambition rule my life. Being asked to take over here was a tremendous honour; I want it to have been a fabulous success – for me, yes – but more importantly for this brilliant young woman. She is so much better than Miss Wells.'

'But not in bed.' Alexander Stoltze spat the words out and

strode away along the corridor totally ignoring two colleagues who stood bemused for a moment, looking after him.

Juliet arrived in plenty of time for the concert. She decided not to impose herself on Karel until the end of the evening but busied herself with the work that she normally did at such events. Several of the orchestral players spoke to her but others hurried away as if they feared perhaps to be in her environment.

'You really gave us a scare, Juliet,' confessed one of the cellists. 'The maestro was frantic, convinced something had happened to you in the blackout.'

'Nonsense,' she began but could say no more. If Karel had not admitted that they were together during the blackout, she could hardly disclose the information. 'I've been at a funeral.' And she had been at a funeral. She looked down at the glorious ring on her right hand. How strange that someone she had known for such a short time should have come to mean so much.

'He was beside himself. We all decided the two of you were dark horses with something going on behind those cool exteriors. The Wells was after him, you know; don't think I have ever seen a conductor move so fast, off the podium that is. Good luck to you.'

Had she not finished with that remark Juliet might have given her a broadside: not pleasant to be gossiped over. As it was she said thank you demurely and walked on. So Karel had been worried, but why? She had left a note. Ergo he had not received it. She stopped and stood still for a few minutes while she thought. It would be better to have the note or the messenger before she met with Karel. She made her way up to the front door and looked all over for the man to whom she had given the note but without success.

'We have a large staff, Miss Crawford, and if you can't even tell me the name . . .'

Juliet stood at the main desk and tried to think back to Thursday morning. 'He was tall, quite dark-skinned. Damn, I can't remember another thing. He was wearing a badge, a label with his name.' She could see it in her mind's eye but her brain absolutely refused to zero in on it. 'The rota,' she said at last. 'There must be a rota. Please, it's vitally important. Can you find out who was on the front door on Thursday morning – very early, before six?'

'That would be night duty, Miss Crawford. I'm afraid I don't know' – and as Juliet almost groaned – 'but I will be able to find out.'

They arranged that the name of the doorman would be left in Juliet's pigeon-hole as soon as possible.

'It may take some time, Miss Crawford, but of course records are kept and I will let you know.'

'It's terribly important. I just need to know where he left the note I gave him for Maestro Haken.'

'A note for a conductor. He would have left it in the maestro's pigeon-hole, no question.'

'That's what I thought but . . .' She could not discuss her predicament any more freely than she had already done. 'You've been wonderfully helpful' – she peered closer – 'Bernie. Thank you. I'll wait to hear from you.'

She was trembling and held on to the desk for a moment, her eyes closed. What a fool she felt.

'Are you all right, miss?' Bernie, solicitous, had hurried round his desk to hold her arm.

She managed to smile at him. 'Too much coffee today and not enough food. I'll grab a sandwich at the intermission.'

'Sit down for a minute, love.'

She sat down and wanted to close her eyes but poor Bernie was still hovering and so Juliet smiled brightly. 'I'm absolutely fine,' and watched him walk doubtfully away.

As soon as he was safely behind his desk she allowed her face, which seemed moulded into an artificial rictus, the grin of a gargoyle, to relax, and then sat quite quietly aware of nothing but the fact that this evening, this meeting, might possibly be the most important of her entire life. For weeks she had walked around this great house, everywhere, the auditorium, backstage, the gods, and had become more aware of the sound qualities of the hall in an afternoon than people who knew it well had learned in years of visiting. She had listened to performances from different parts of the house, sitting quietly, unseen, unnoticed, in the back row, perched in the highest, cheapest seat in the gods, ensconced like a duchess in the stalls, and all the time she had noted the reverberations, the ability of the strings to hold their own against the wind instruments – and vice versa. She had found herself asking, But he said fortissimo there. How loud is loud? How loud did he mean it to be? How slow is the adagio in that passage? Is that too slow or is it not slow enough? And more important than all, Can I do as well? Will I ever do it better? It can't be better because he is so gifted. Will the orchestra respond to me?

But now she asked only, Will *he*?

She decided to go backstage to listen to the concert from the wings, but not the side from which Karel would make his entrances and exits. Once there she found a folding chair, set it up and sat down, closing her eyes in an attempt to clear her mind of everything except the joy of the music. Her hands were in her lap and again she was conscious of her ring. One day, perhaps, it would be so familiar that she would notice it only by its occasional absence from her finger. Mrs McD. How much did you understand of all this, ambition, success, failure and love and loss? I can't bear to be thrown out of the programme: I can hardly stand it that Karel thinks badly of me. If I'm drummed out, what chance will I have of ever making a success as a conductor, and oh, dear God, which of the two is more important to me?

The audience began to clap; the leader would be walking across the stage. More enthusiastic applause: Karel. How quickly these Barbican audiences had warmed to him. She could see him, see his gestures, terse, controlled rather than self-indulgently voluptuous. She sat back and let the music wash around and over her, pounding her down as storm waves beat upon a rocky shore and then lifting her up and carrying her to a place of ultimate peace and safety. She forgot everything but the quality of the sound. At the intermission she stood up and stretched; the chair that she had found to sit on was distinctly uncomfortable.

Karel found her there.

'I thought I saw you as I made my entrance. What are you doing, skulking here?'

She jumped to her feet and hit out angrily. 'Skulking? How dare you. I'm not skulking. I wanted to hear the concert but I thought it better if we didn't meet beforehand. I had actually worked out that it would be easier for you if we didn't come face to face until after the concert. Then you could yell as much as you seem to want to.' She felt the tears in her eyes and turned away so that he could not see the sign of weakness.

He reached out and pulled her round. 'I don't want to yell.' His voice was quiet and sad, disappointed. 'Juliet, why didn't you tell me, why didn't you speak to me? I was almost out of my mind with worry.' She had bowed her head but he lifted her face gently with his hand. 'Oh, I've made you cry. Don't cry, Juliet, darling, darling Juliet.' He was looking into her eyes and he moved his hand to catch the tear that was just about to spill from her lashes and then he made a sound that was half groan, half moan and pulled her into his arms and began to kiss her, hard, demanding kisses.

At first, almost in shock, she stood in the circle of his arms and did nothing, neither fighting nor encouraging and then as his kiss became fiercer, she responded, raising her arms and pulling him towards her. At last they stopped, bemused, exhilarated, and he kept his arms around her as if he knew that without his support she would fall.

'I have to go; my poor assistant will think I have disappeared in air, like you did on Thursday morning. One more kiss. Oh, God, Juliet. I love you. You can't believe what it has been like all these weeks, seeing you every day, standing close enough to touch but afraid.' He laughed, looking at her bruised lips, her disarranged hair. 'Dare I hope you are not completely indifferent to me, Miss Crawford, the jewel in the orchestra's crown?'

This time she initiated the kiss from which they both withdrew, their professional sides loudly trumpeting that there was an orchestra ready to play a symphony, an auditorium full of people who wanted, expected, to hear wonderful music.

'Go to my dressing room; it's more comfortable there, and we will talk. Please.'

She nodded, unable to speak, and he kissed her quickly and almost ran from the wings. She became aware of a loud buzzing, like angry wasps whose nest has been disturbed, the audience wondering about the delay, and then there was clapping and eventually silence as the conductor raised his arms.

Juliet stayed exactly where he had left her while bubbles of joy coursed through her, leaving her weak as a newborn but at the same time exultant. She leaned against the door, unable to move for fear she would stumble over something and make a great clatter. They were going to talk; she knew that if she explained and asked about the note, then he would understand, and – would he, could he? – withdraw his threat of expulsion. She closed her eyes and listened to the symphony and thought she would never ever be as happy as at this moment; nowhere in the world would ever be more beautiful that this less used side of the stage with its wires and cables, its folding chairs stacked against the wall, because this was where Karel had first said he loved her.

When she heard the last notes of the music she opened the door behind her quietly and slipped out into the corridor and then she walked quickly towards the dressing rooms. Karel's assistant met her at the door of his room.

'Miss Crawford, you are not our favourite person today. Are you all right?'

'I'm fine, Joseph. A friend died; it was very sudden.'

'I don't know if this is a good time to wait to see him. Can I tell him you're back and okay?'

'He knows and he asked me to come here – to talk,' she added as he looked at her thoughtfully.

'Miss Crawford, was the maestro with you at the intermission?'

She nodded, trying to avoid his eyes.

'That explains a lot. But I still don't think it's the time or the place for a tête-à-tête. Maestro Stoltze is here and several other dignitaries; they're coming backstage.'

For less than ten seconds Juliet considered asking Joseph to tell Karel that she would return to her flat and wait to hear from him. 'He specifically asked me to meet him here.'

'Very well, very well, here they are, here they are.'

Alexander Stoltze led the way; with him were several other men and women including Margarita Rosa Grey who kissed Juliet on both cheeks. 'Miss Crawford. See.' She threw out her arms as if showing Juliet off at a sale. 'I knew it was all nonsense and here she is, safe and sound.'

She ushered them all into the principal conductor's dressing room. 'Alexander, what is all this, that Miss Crawford is leaving us? You are happy with the programme, Juliet?'

'Of course, madam, very happy.'

'Then why did you disappear on a day when you were supposed to conduct a children's string ensemble? Insupportable behaviour, unprofessional.' Alexander Stoltze looked at the other men and shrugged his shoulders inside his beautifully cut jacket. 'Hormones,' he said with a laugh, 'or a lover's tiff.'

'Alexander, how old-fashioned you are,' said Mrs Grey. 'We modern women are not governed by our hormones no matter how hard you antediluvian men try to insist that we are.' She patted his cheek and turned to Juliet. 'You missed a concert, Juliet?'

'Yes, madam. A sudden death . . . I had to rush home.'

'Miss Crawford has not had time to explain fully,' interposed Karel who had just arrived. 'She is here and will, no doubt, have acceptable explanations for what might, in some circumstances, be seen as unprofessional behaviour.'

Mrs Grey was now patting Juliet's knee, a look of deep sympathy on her face. 'Not a family member, I hope.'

'No, madam, an elderly friend.'

Margarita threw up her hands. 'A young woman who rushes to the deathbed of an elderly friend.' She got up after patting Juliet again. 'Next time, let us know. Come along, ladies and gentlemen, we will leave the senior conductor to deal with this and later, maybe they will elect to join us in my suite.' She looked at Juliet. 'But we will understand if you are too exhausted. Emotion is so debilitating. *Adios*.'

'Did she wink?' asked Karel when all the goodbyes had been said. 'You have a powerful friend there, Juliet. I'll close up, Joseph; I'll change later.'

'If you're sure, sir. Coffee's on. Goodnight, Miss Crawford.'

When the door had closed behind him Karel got up very quickly and walked over to the coffee pot that was plugged in near the mirror. 'I want to take you in my arms again but we must clear this up first.' He poured coffee and handed Juliet a cup. 'I drink two cups of coffee after I conduct; I have no coffee at all before.' He drank deeply from the cup and Juliet wondered how he could possibly drink such hot coffee so quickly. 'Why didn't you call me? Was it Mrs McDermott? I would have understood.'

'I know; it never occurred to me that you wouldn't. That's why I left so precipitately. But it was the middle of the night and I thought I'd leave a note and I did, Karel.'

'We have no luck with notes.'

'I meant to call from Edinburgh but a great deal happened and then I realised that I had lost my mobile; to be honest, dealing with the funeral and my parents was stressful and then it was so late again but I honestly believed that you would have got my note.'

'Where did you leave it?'

'I gave it to a doorman; he said he would leave it in your box and, no, before you ask, I don't know who he is but the one who is on duty tonight is going to find out for me. Probably he got really busy and forgot.' She looked straight at him. 'I did write a note, Karel; I wouldn't just take off.'

He bowed his head and then lifted it again and smiled at her. He put down his coffee cup and moved closer to her. He took her coffee cup from her hands and pulled her to her feet. 'I'm sorry, Juliet. I was angry until maybe ten o'clock, then I began to worry, then I got mad again and by the afternoon I was in despair. I went over to your flat and banged on the door like a crazy man and, I'm sorry, but eventually I persuaded the manager to let me in. He came too.'

'And my body wasn't lying cold on the living room carpet.'

He pulled her close. 'Don't make such jokes. I had persuaded myself that it was all over, that I had not fallen in love in Edinburgh. It was a – how you say – *Midsummer Night's Dream*, like the play by Mr Shakespeare. You were so cool, so calm, so completely dedicated to your studies. I thought – I too can be like Juliet. It was lovely but it is over and that's great, the best for the two. And then you did not come after our lovely evening in the candles and I knew that I had been – damn, I don't know how to translate it. The knowledge of my love hit me like the lightning strikes the tree in the park.'

'That's the way it was with me too. Oh, Karel, how much time we have wasted being unhappy.'

'You liked Erik.'

'Yes, I tried; I thought it might just work. What about Bryony?'

He was pulling her closer and closer. 'Bryony? I was never involved with Bryony and, after some remarks I have heard today, I am beginning to understand why she was . . . imposed on the project. But do we have to talk about Bryony and Erik and Alexander?'

For some time they did not talk, being otherwise, very pleasurably, engaged.

'We're going to be locked in here overnight and that couch is very narrow and not at all comfortable.'

'And you need your second cup of coffee?'

'Exactly.'

'There is coffee in my flat.'

He laughed and kissed her again, but very lightly, on her forehead. 'My darling, I love you, and I always will.'

She looked at him, at his eyes, which told her clearly what was going on in his head, and decided to tease him. 'Coffee then, unless, Maestro, you would prefer to go for your usual run.'

They went out and Karel locked the door behind him. There was only a handful of people in the main foyer. 'They do not want the evening to end,' said Karel. 'It is always like this; eventually they will have to leave. The curtain is down.'

'Why did you mention Maestro Stoltze?' Juliet asked as, unhurriedly, they strolled across the terraces, noting the planks that had been arranged so that non-flying ducks could waddle up out of the water.

'Because for the past ten years he has meant more to me than

332

anyone in the world except my father and, unlike my father, I am beginning to think he is not what I thought he was.'

She squeezed his fingers. 'Oh, poor Karel, he surprised me once too but since he meant nothing to me I wasn't hurt in any way.'

They stopped to look at the lake. 'Did you hear that two Canada geese have moved in and are eating all the ducklings?'

He had no thoughts to spare for the plight of the ducklings. 'He thinks highly of you, your conducting ability.'

'Didn't seem so tonight when I'm perfectly sure he was trying to get me fired. Why, I cannot imagine.'

'You should be flattered, my darling. He thinks you are a threat to me.'

Juliet stopped dead just before the gate leading to her building. 'A threat? I don't understand.'

'When he was my age, he had to struggle so hard to make his reputation. We lived in what was then Czechoslovakia, and perhaps he is right, but he thinks if he had not been a Czech, he would have become well-known earlier in his career. He always wanted to be the principal conductor of the Berlin Philharmonic; he has been their guest conductor many times as you know but always, always that shining jewel goes to someone else. We used to talk about how it would be the peak of my career.'

Realisation dawned on Juliet and she began to walk again towards her apartment building. 'And he would have it vicariously, and the prestige of having been your early tutor and constant mentor.'

'Yes, I think so.'

'You're not saying he fears I might one day be good enough to rival you for it? Well, well, well. That is a compliment and, of course, I fully intend to be their principal conductor one day, when I've finished with the Bournemouth, and the London Philharmonic and the Boston Symphony Orchestra . . .'

He stopped her mouth with a kiss.

'Is there food in your apartment?'

'Food? Gosh, no, I'm only just back from Scotland.'

He pulled her away from the door just as she was about to insert her key. 'Then we'll drive to mine.'

Fifteen minutes later, Juliet was standing with a glass of very good red wine at the picture window of his apartment. From the kitchen came the enticing smell of bacon being grilled.

'Smell good?' Karel had come up behind her and put his arms round her waist.

'Yes,' she said, turning in his arms.

'I turned it off because I find I cannot wait another minute to kiss you properly, dear Maestro Crawford, and I thought, since the bacon is just perfect, it will make a wonderful sandwich . . .' He kissed her eyes, her nose, her neck and then again her mouth and Juliet heard herself moan with anticipated pleasure. 'When we want it,' he finished.

27

Juliet woke up to the smell of hot buttered toast, bacon and coffee. She smiled and stretched in the unfamiliar bed. Her body felt wonderful, even more wonderful than it had felt all those months ago when she had first made love with Karel Haken.

'Good morning, sleepy head.'

Karel, showered and shaved, but wearing only a dark blue towelling bathrobe, appeared in the open doorway with a tray. 'Breakfast is served, madam.'

He put the tray on her lap, climbed into the bed beside her, and took it on to his. 'I have already had the cup of coffee that I missed last night. So, this is really the first for today, and a magnificent bacon sandwich, my favourite breakfast from today forward, because I am sharing it with you.'

Juliet bit into her sandwich and sipped some coffee. 'Fabulous,' she said when she could speak. 'I'm starving. Do you have this every morning?'

'If I say yes, will you come to live with me?'

'Absolutely.' She picked up the sandwich and put it down again. 'You're joking, aren't you? Karel, you don't mean it, that you want me to live with you?'

'I want to marry you, Juliet. I'm old-fashioned enough to hope that you want to marry me too.'

'Marry you? When?'

'That is a yes or a no?'

The butterflies that had lain down to rest in the pit of her stomach exploded into the air or perhaps her blood had been replaced by the most wonderful vintage champagne because something was whooshing through her so that she wanted to dance, to sing. Marry him? A dream; it was all a glorious, wonderful dream. 'Yes,' she said and then just as quickly, 'No. Karel, this is crazy. I'm still a student. There are three months of the programme still to go.'

'We'll wait until it's finished.'

She got out of the bed and looked for something to wear. Where on earth were her clothes? She looked around and blushed with embarrassment. Clothes were strewn all over the room and, naked, she felt vulnerable and at a disadvantage.

'Here.' He had gone into the bathroom, wrapped himself in a towel, and handed her his dressing gown.

'Thank you,' she mumbled but when she was completely covered she said, 'Karel, I love you, but I went to the concert last night afraid that I was going to lose my position and that has to be my focus, working with the LSO for the next three months. Please try to understand. I don't need complications. Damn. I don't even have a phone.'

'It's not in your flat?'

'No.'

'Take a shower, get dressed and we'll go and buy a new one and then you can call everyone.'

She looked at him. 'You don't mind?'

'I don't mind taking you to buy a new mobile phone.' He smiled at her. 'Relax, Juliet. I won't change my mind and when you are ready, if you are ever ready, just – I was going to say – call me.' He stopped talking for a moment and smiled ruefully. 'We had better go and buy you a new telephone. That way the odds are stacked in my favour.'

It was a beautiful spring day. Daffodils were in full bloom in the gardens, the trees in the park were showing off their dresses of pink blossom and the white magnolias were magnificent. Karel drove Juliet back to her apartment and waited in the car while she changed. 'You can come up,' she suggested. 'I won't be long.'

'I brought the Sunday paper. How many sections will I get through before you're ready? Off you go.'

In her bedroom Juliet examined herself very carefully in the mirror above the dressing table but she looked exactly as she had looked the day before, except perhaps a little less stressed. She took off her suit, hung it up neatly, changed her underwear and put on a favourite pair of jeans and an oversized man-style shirt. She wrapped a multicoloured belt that she had bought years before in a Spanish market around her waist, grabbed a leather jacket and she was ready. She locked up and almost ran to the outside door.

Karel seemed engrossed in the *Sunday Times* leader as she slid in beside him.

'You know, I look just as I looked yesterday, and so do you, Karel.'

'Good. I like how you looked yesterday. And I like very much how you look today.'

'Thank you, but I wasn't angling for a compliment and, by the way, how many sections did you get through?'

'I read the leader. I was thinking.'

'About music or about us? Don't you think it odd that something totally momentous happened to us yesterday and nothing shows?'

'No, but I'm pleased that something momentous happened.' He lifted her hand as if he had noticed her ruby for the first time. 'Something momentous happened in Scotland too. You have never worn that ring before; it's very beautiful.'

She told him all about Mrs McDermott and the will.

'So now Heather has a home of her own; how very generous.'

'Oh, it was. I believe that Mrs McDermott would have left everything to Gregor. They were great friends; he never ever got impatient and he really was the only one of us who never pretended not to be there when she came knocking.' She was twisting the ring round and round her finger. 'It seems so sad to me that she had this ring and yet she kept the heat off in her flat, and we don't know what she ate; the hospital says she was undernourished. Gregor used to share his scrambled eggs with her.' She struggled against them but tears began to flow. 'Every time she came, she wore her gloves; such old, worn leather gloves but it was obvious that she had been brought up to believe that ladies wear gloves. She loved listening to us, and she enjoyed everything, even scales. Once Heather warmed up for half an hour while that old woman sat there, so straight-backed, gloved hands so correctly in her lap, and listened with courtesy.' She turned her face away from him. 'Why is it that you don't see the worth of what you have until you've lost it, Karel?'

He reached across the controls and pulled her into his arms. 'Cry, sweetheart. You see you did value her because she valued you or you wouldn't have that glorious ring; she was saying thank you, and if you wear the ring every time you conduct, you will be remembering her and her love of music.' He wiped her eyes with the corner of his handkerchief. 'She was in a camp, you say. Perhaps once she studied, and you young people reminded her of golden days before the horrors of war. Think positively, Juliet.'

She started to laugh. 'Oh, Karel, you are physically so unalike but just now you reminded me of my agent. "Positive vibes, Juliet," is his mantra.'

He laughed, let go of her, and started the engine. 'Shall we go?'

'No, stop. Turn it off. I need some space. Do you understand that?'

'No.'

'Yesterday,' she began.

'I know all about yesterday and I'm glad for yesterday because it brought everything out. Now I don't understand because you say you love me, we have the most wonderful night, and you say you need space. You want not to be with me but I want you with me every second. I want to look at you, touch you, hear you, marvel at you and at us together. I want to buy you a damn phone and then bring you back and make love to you – and you want space, distance between?' He hit the steering wheel so hard with his hand that he winced. 'Stupid loss of control.'

Tentatively Juliet reached out her hand and laid it on his knee. 'It's too much too soon, my love. Oh, and you are my love, Karel; being with you, loving you is more than I have ever asked for. Please, please try to understand. Yesterday.'

'Dammit, Juliet, don't keep saying yesterday. Yesterday is gone.

Yesterday we found each other again. To me it is so simple. We love each other, yes? We are in love, yes? Are you afraid I can't be professional at work? Believe me, there you are just the brilliant and sometimes so annoying girl who is a "threat" to me.' He laughed half-heartedly. 'Poor Alexander. You are a threat to my peace of mind, not to my place in history as a conductor. If you become the principal conductor of . . . which orchestra? Let us go to the top, the Berlin Philharmonic, I will be so proud. I will write your name in the sky. Please trust me, Juliet.'

Juliet closed her eyes in the hope that that would make her thinking clearer. She knew that this conversation was one of the most important of her entire life. 'Do you aspire to a great position, Karel?'

'Of course. I want to be the best I can be.'

'We can't do it together. One post, one principal conductor. If you are in Germany I might well be in Outer Mongolia.'

'They say spring there is quite beautiful. We could meet on off-days. We will not be the only lovers in the world who live apart. Positive thought, please. You look always for the down side.'

'No, I don't, but I like to be prepared. Then I can plan strategy.'

'Strategy. You need a new phone. Let us go.'

She opened her car door, shaking her head as she did so. 'Tomorrow I will find the doorman who took my note.' She felt him tense and spoke quickly to defuse an explosion. 'I know you believe me as you believed me about the score. Now I don't think the doorman is in collusion with someone who wants to scupper my chances – he probably forgot and will be apologetic, but I need you to see the note. Did you ever hear that someone locked me in the green room during the competition? At first I thought it was my fault but after the score incident I knew that it was deliberate. Someone badly wants me to fail. I'm going to be the best winner of this competition they will ever have, Karel, and then in June, if you still want to, ask me again.'

And then she was out of the car and hurrying through the maze of the Barbican complex, past gardens, man-made lakes, and fountains that sparkled in the brilliant spring sun, to the sanctuary of her little flat.

From there she telephoned her parents.

'Everything is fine, Mum. I've spoken to Maestro Haken; problem was he never received my note and so he was' – she almost said worried but perhaps, for her mother, worried might be an emotive word. One worries about the people whom one cares about – 'concerned when I just didn't turn up. That's why he was so angry, thought I was unprofessional. But everything's hunky-dory and I'm looking forward very much to the next few months.'

'I rang you last night, dear, on the landline. I take it you haven't found your mobile because we tried that one too. No answer on either one. We went to bed at midnight.'

'I was at the Barbican.'

'Until midnight? My goodness, dear, you do work long hours.'

'There was a meeting after the concert, with Karel and Mrs Grey, Alexander Stoltze and several others. Being a musician isn't nine to five, Mum.' Meeting was possibly an exaggeration but the less her mother thought about where her daughter might be at midnight, the better.

'And where have you been this morning?'

'I had breakfast out. Mum, I don't need the third degree at my age.'

'We worry.'

'Please stop worrying. I'm fine and I'll see you and Daddy when I can.'

'Have you forgotten that I said I would come down this week? You have. Tuesday and Wednesday.'

Juliet groaned inwardly. 'Wonderful, Mum. I'm rehearsing an ensemble early on Wednesday evening but I'm sure it will be fine for you to be there, and then we'll have a late supper somewhere.'

They chatted on for a few minutes and finally, when Lesley was happier with her daughter, she allowed her to hang up. 'See you Tuesday.'

'I can hardly wait,' Juliet told the opposite wall which kept its own counsel. She got up from the sofa where she had been slumped and walked to the window and as she did she heard her stomach make protesting noises. Since she had eaten nothing at all the previous evening and only one bite of a bacon sandwich, she was extremely hungry and so, instead of ringing Hermione, which she had planned to do, she picked up her purse, her jacket and left the flat. She would go to the Waterside Café to have lunch, a large lunch.

She enjoyed her stroll: all her senses seemed heightened. She took time to admire the cloud formations in a pale sky, wisps like spider webs, plumper more solid ones, like cotton balls or the marshmallows her mother had very occasionally allowed on hot chocolate, isolated dark grey patches of gauze that hung there, unattached, as if they did not know whether to flee or to try to become part of the more substantial whole; she listened to the music made by jets of water as they fell back into the ponds, was aware of birds, small plump brown birds who balanced on the frailest of twigs and opened their tiny beaks in appreciation of a lovely spring day. There were flowers in many of the window boxes that hung from each floor of the tall towers, and crocuses sprouted in seemingly random plantings all over the grass, white ones, purple ones, and the golds that were so vibrant that they demanded that the viewer be cheerful. She hung over the Podium, admiring stretches of the Roman wall. Had Karel admired it; did he know what it was or was it, to him, just another old wall?

Is this love or is it the acceptance of love? But I feel powerful, wonderful. If I had a piano now I would play it as no one has ever played it before. Had I an orchestra I would conduct them so that they would be amazed at the beauty of the sound we produced. I am invincible. I am also very silly, she said with chagrin as she realised she must have said at least some of that nonsense aloud, if the looks directed at her were anything to go by. She bowed her head and hurried into the foyer.

And there, at the desk, was the man who had taken her note.

Am I not invincible? The gods are on my side.

'Hello.'

'Good afternoon, madam. May I help you?'

'It's me, Juliet Crawford. I gave you a note on Thursday morning just before six.'

He looked straight at her. 'Sorry, madam, you have me confused with someone else.'

The semi-insolent tone, the failure to meet her eyes, told Juliet more than anything that he was lying and deliberately. 'Were you on duty here on Thursday morning?'

He looked directly at her and smiled. 'Yes, madam; that was my shift. Here's my name, quite clear, on the duty roster. You would be the young lady as was asking.'

'I gave you a note and asked you to deliver it to Mr Haken.'

'Sorry, madam. This place is a graveyard at six in the morning. I'd remember you,' he added, looking at Juliet suggestively. 'Afraid you have me mixed up with someone else. Maybe you was upset or something, had a row with the old boyfriend?'

Juliet wanted to punch him right between his leering eyes. He was lying. He had been on duty and he had taken her note. She could remember his attitude when she had reiterated how important the note was. 'I'm not a delivery boy but I said I would,' was what he had said. And now he was denying all knowledge and it was her word against his. Damn it. Karel would take her word but positive proof would be better. She turned and walked away and heard him laughing quietly behind her.

She went to the Waterside Café. Her appetite was quite gone but she knew that if she did not eat she would feel dreadful later. She selected a small carafe of white wine and a plate of cheese and biscuits, hoping that the wine would calm her and that the cheese would prevent the wine from going straight to her head, a danger on an empty stomach.

'Hi, Juliet, how are you?'

Juliet looked up. It was Margaret Oakes, one of the wind players.

'Fine, Margaret, fine.' She was so aware of the half-empty carafe. Damn it, why? It held two glasses on a good day.

Margaret pointed to a table by the window. 'We're over there; my husband and my mother who lives with us and saves our marriage.' She laughed. 'Anyway, we saw you were alone and wondered if you'd like to join us.'

'How very kind,' said Juliet and meant it. 'I'd love to.' She was not unconscious of the fact that Margaret would be aware of her seeming defection from the orchestra and would be interested in the state of play. She picked up what was left of her cheese, left her wine and walked across to the window table. Margaret's husband stood up.

'Hi, I'm Bill. You forgot your glass. I'll just get it. We have a rather nice château extremely cheapo here.'

They were easy company and carefully avoided asking her about her absence and so Juliet felt obliged to tell them almost the whole story.

'So glad it worked out,' said Bill, a violinist with a radio orchestra. They then told her hair-raising stories of the difficulties inherent in a marriage where not only did both parents work several nights a week but also they were often different nights. Foreign tours were a nightmare too since Margaret and Bill were often abroad, but in different countries, at the same time. Margaret also had a good solo career.

'Mum's worth her weight in gold. I put my solo career on hold when I got married and while our two were little but now with Mum living with us permanently and Bill's sister occasionally, we manage.'

Mrs White, who had added little to the conversation now put down her cake fork and said, 'You'll be scaring Miss Crawford away from the idea of combining marriage and career. Good child care is important but it's love that counts.'

'What an old sop.' Margaret laughed and changed the subject. 'I wish whoever owns that phone would answer the damned thing.'

Several times while they had been eating they had heard a mobile phone ring and ring.

'Someone playing hard to get,' suggested Bill.

'Or it's been left behind,' said Juliet. 'You know I've misplaced my mobile but unfortunately I wasn't here on Wednesday evening.'

'Oh, the night of the big blackout. Wasn't that scary? Bill broadcast in the dark, didn't you, dear?'

Juliet was not really paying attention to the chatter because she was still thinking about the ringing mobile phone. 'My mobile must have been ringing all day Thursday. Karel rang me several times, and so did my mother.' She got up from the table. 'This has been lovely; I thoroughly enjoyed myself but I think I'll go off and try to find my phone.'

Had she had her telephone with her when she left the note for Karel? She must have had because she had brought it out of her flat. Or had she? She remembered looking everywhere for someone to take the note and then – yes, that dreadful man had been sitting at a desk reading a newspaper. She hurried to the entrance that she had used on Thursday morning. The desk there had been empty but, yes, she had put her things down there for a moment while she thought.

'Excuse me. Is it possible that I left my mobile phone here on Thursday morning? I think I dumped everything here.'

The man smiled. 'You know there was a phone driving everyone mad one day last week but what day or what they did with it, I've no idea. Maybe someone picked it up or could be it's in lost property.'

He had no idea how near he was to being kissed. Juliet thanked him and hurried away only to find that the office would not be manned until Monday morning. She went back to the flat and rang Hermione. 'I'm making progress. If the phone is there and was found on that desk then I can prove I came in on Thursday morning?'

'No, you can't. Who's to say you didn't leave it on Wednesday night?'

'Hermione, it's important to have concrete evidence that I'm not lying.'

'You are such a control freak, Juliet. The maestro says he believes you. Why do you want to push evidence in his face?'

'Because he says he wants to marry me.'

Hermione yelled so loudly that the telephone connection was

possibly immaterial. 'He what? Tell me all. I thought he was going to throw you out on your little pink.'

Juliet told her more or less what had happened. 'And if he asks again and I accept then I want there to be no shadows, even the palest ones, hanging around.'

'I'm coming down . . .' Hermione began.

'Oh, that would be lovely but Mummy's coming; leave it till later.'

'God, love really does do daft things to people. I can't. The wedding, remember, and my audition with the maestro is Thursday. Mother is coming with me and we're going to stay down until the wedding, have a few days' – she assumed a strong American accent – 'quality time together.' In her own voice she added that her father would meet them in time to go to their friends' daughter's wedding. 'We'll be at the Savoy. Bring Lesley for dinner Wednesday after that rehearsal you talked about. I bet there's nothing but apricot yoghurt in your flat. It would be nice if we could get rid of the mothers so that we can talk. I take it you're not telling Lesley.'

'God, no. Hermione, I don't think I've mentioned him ten times. She doesn't know about the summer.'

'I'm getting goose pimples all over just thinking of you finding each other again. You are sly, never so much as hinting.'

Juliet lay back against the cushions. How could she begin to explain the miracle that she did not fully understand herself? 'I tried so hard to cut him right out of my head, and my heart. It was the work: it's so intense and I knew so little. You have no idea how I've grown in the past few months. We're beginning to talk about the next phase. Already there have been one or two approaches from orchestras and I hope to leave here and step straight into an assistantship somewhere, preferably abroad.'

'Somewhere nice and warm and I'll be a regular visitor.'

'I won't be accepting a position on the basis of the climate.'

'That's extremely selfish of you. You should put the needs of your friends first. By the way, talking of friends, I think Heather and Gregor are going to keep the flat, for a while anyway. They

345

talked my head off yesterday. Should we sell and split the money? Should we rent and split the money? Gregor believes Mrs McD wanted him to live in it. I think she wanted him to have a nest egg and half an egg is better than none. Even in the state it's in, needing modernising, it will sell quickly and at top whack, but it's their decision and they're right not to rush. They can live here with me although Mummy knows about the baby and is rather edgy – sleepless nights, etcetera.'

'What happens if you start, when you start touring?'

'If was right, but I'll still keep the flat and can afford the rates which are, by the way, going to come as a big surprise to our young friends. I've mentioned them, as has Patrick.'

'Have you any idea what happened about the moles?'

'Oh, big-time trauma. The gardener gassed them but Tom has assured Gregor that it will never happen again. He wants Gregor back now, ostensibly so that he can work on his composition.'

'And?'

'Gregor has assured himself that Heather and I are fine and so he's leaving this evening.'

Juliet felt very sad and she could hear sadness in Hermione's voice. 'It's really the end then,' she said.

'No, Juliet, it's a beginning.'

28

Karel almost totally ignored Juliet on Monday morning and her heart, which had been fluttering with joy at the thought of seeing him, seemed to turn into a lump of ice. He spoke about the Saturday night concert, one or two things that he thought merited praise and one small item that he felt needed extra work.

'And you see that the missing Miss Crawford has returned. I'm sure we are all sorry about the sudden death of a close friend, which was the reason for Juliet's unexpected departure. She did leave a note, which was not given to me, but we have decided that, in matters of crisis, I can be reached by telephone at any time. Later in the week I am auditioning Hermione Elliott-Chevenix, and so I would like to work on the violin concerto that she will be playing. For now, I will play the violin solo and Miss Crawford will conduct.'

Juliet had not expected that but tried to remain calm. Listening to Karel play was so emotive that, at one point, she almost stopped conducting just to listen but recovered herself in time.

'The conductor can't stop in the middle, you know, Juliet.' It was a break time but he had asked her to stay to discuss her technique. 'Even if she is finding the soloist irresistible.' He pulled her into his arms and kissed her and once again her limbs seemed to melt and she found herself clinging to him, enjoying the feel of him in her arms, the faint smell of his aftershave.

'You were so mean to me this morning,' she said when she could speak.

'Not at all. I told you when we are working you are just another member of the orchestra. Now come, let's get some coffee.'

'I didn't know you played the violin,' she said as they entered the

347

cafeteria, which, at this time of the morning, was no peaceful haven.

'There is a lot you don't know about me. What do I know about you? That you never seem to have any food in your house and that I'm crazy about you. More than enough to build a lifetime on. Have dinner with me tonight.'

How she wanted to. After she had ended her conversation with Hermione the previous evening she had sat up for hours willing Karel to call her, trying to summon up courage to call him. But if she had called what would have happened? They would have spent the night in each other's arms and it would have been wonderful but it would not have helped her deal with her problem.

'I can't. My mother is coming tomorrow and I need to shop.'

'Do I get to meet your mother?'

'I don't know.'

They were waved over to a table where several members of the orchestra – many in casual and even bright clothing, so different from their usual black – were sitting.

The conversation was not about music but was general and wide-ranging and Juliet enjoyed being part of it, listening carefully to arguments and strongly expressed opinions. Here, Karel, the orchestra leader and the leaders of the various sections seemed to be just members of the orchestra; there was no hierarchy, and everyone felt able to participate.

This is perfect, thought Juliet, and I wish we could stay like this for ever. And she felt a little sad, for it would change. She looked at Karel, noting the animation in his face as he spoke, the brightness of his eyes, the laughter lines near his mouth, his beautiful mouth.

My love for him won't change, ever.

Karel did meet Lesley Crawford who took a taxi from the airport straight to the Barbican. She walked into the Waterside Café just as Juliet was leaving to return to the rehearsal room. 'I'm quite happy to sit here with some tea until the rehearsal is over,' she assured Karel when, after they had been introduced, he suggested that Juliet take her mother back to her flat.

'I'll give you the keys, Mother.'

'I will conduct the rehearsal, Juliet, and the leader will play the concerto while you go with your mother. We are rehearsing for Miss Elliott-Chevenix's audition, Mrs Crawford, and everyone will tell you that the leader of our orchestra is a much better violinist than I am – the orchestra is grateful to you for arriving so opportunely.'

Out of sight of nearby orchestra members, Juliet glared at him, but he smiled serenely. What price the cool aloof Czech now? And that is exactly what her mother said as Juliet walked with her across the terrace by the lake, stopping to admire the gardens, and on up to the Podium where each column of flats in Thomas More House had its own main door. Juliet, and every other resident, carried two keys, one to open any gate and the main door and then the one personal to his or her particular flat.

Lesley stopped again to take off her calf-length pale blue coat – London, she found, is often much warmer than Dundee. 'I thought you said he was very cold and restrained. I think he's lovely, very friendly, and the voice is charming, such a delightful accent.' She looked at her daughter who seemed very quiet. 'You're the one who's restrained, Juliet, but don't worry, I have no intention of disturbing you at work. Just let me in and get back; it will be lovely just to sit down and not have to do anything for a while.'

They had arrived at Juliet's flat. 'This is nice. So much better than when you moved in?'

'You're in the bedroom, Mum, if you want a nap. I'll sleep on the sofa. You're sure you don't mind if I run? There's tea and coffee, whatever you want.'

Lesley waved her away. 'Scoot; I'm absolutely delighted that you enjoy your work so much.'

'If you're sure you don't mind.'

Juliet hurried back to the rehearsal where they continued working on the concerto.

'Enough of that one for today,' said Karel when they had been playing for some time. 'I think we need to do the *Poème* which you will conduct, Miss Crawford.'

349

He interrupted her three times.

'Lift the tempo; it sounds like a dirge. Yes, it's morbid, but we can strike a balance, yes?'

Juliet tried not to flush at the criticism.

'No, no. Now it's too fast.'

Dear God, what did he want of her?

'Better, better. Support the soloist.'

How? She was doing that, wasn't she? Not even in her first days had he stopped her so often; even some younger members of the orchestra were sending each other questioning looks. The more seasoned had seen it all before. It was not personal. The conductor wanted perfection as he heard it in his head, as he hoped Juliet heard it.

When the orchestral players were putting away their instruments he spoke as if nothing had happened. 'Your mother? How long does she stay?'

She could be cool too. 'Till Thursday.'

'If she would enjoy it, invite her to a session. By the way, has Miss Eliott-Chevenix signed that contract?'

Mrs McDermott's death had put everything else out of Juliet's head. 'I have no idea. Would it make a difference?'

'To her audition? No, not at all. I was interested.' He opened his music case and began to put sheets of music methodically into the sections. 'Do you have a new mobile phone yet?'

'No, I think mine might be in Lost Property but I never seem to get there when it's manned.'

'Run now. Call me if it's there.'

It was. It had been found just under the desk and left on the desk in the hope that the owner might come back. After a whole day of hearing it ring the doorman had given up, switched it off and taken it to the Lost Property Office.

'Possibly it slipped out of my handbag when I put things down. I'm so glad to have it back.'

'From what Tom said, you'll probably have a million messages.'

She laughed, thanked him, and walked to her apartment, playing the messages back. There were three from Karel, one in the morning and two in the afternoon. By the third message his voice was showing his concern and, remembering how ghastly he had been about her conducting she hugged the thought of his worry to her. Her steps were buoyant as she hurried to meet her mother. Everything was going to be all right. They could work everything out.

Hermione was sitting cross-legged on her bed in her luxurious bedroom at the Savoy. Juliet was sitting in a chair facing her.

'Isn't this just fab, Juliet, what we dreamed about?'

'Aren't you nervous? I'm not auditioning for him and I feel sick.'

Hermione straightened her legs. 'Dash. Pins and needles; that'll teach me. You are an old worrywart, Juliet. I had better not tell you that I forgot my violin and Daddy had to send it to the airport in a taxi.' She laughed at her friend's expression. 'Of course I didn't; I even took it into the loo with me, and, yes, I'm nervous, but I think just the right amount. I really feel I'm auditioning for someone who will be aware of only my music, not me, not Sebastian Elliott-Chevenix's daughter. And don't tell me the other conductors were like that. I know that; but this time I feel it too. There's a terrific sense of freedom – and, with my best friend in the whole world conducting the orchestra . . . What could be better?'

'I want it to go so well for you but Karel has done nothing but find fault with me this week. Even with my mother sitting there, he said, "Please don't bludgeon the orchestra into submission." I could cheerfully have bludgeoned him.'

Hermione tried hard not to laugh. 'Sorry, darling, he seems to be showing you that you're just any old student, and possibly that he's absolutely furious that your mother is sleeping in your bed.' She looked at Juliet and saw not only unhappiness in her face but also fatigue. Poor Juliet; she really had so little experience with the vastly inferior sex.

'I have no intention of letting him sleep in my bed whether Mum's here or not. I think I made that perfectly clear.'

'Why? You love him and need him. He loves you and needs you. Believe me, Juliet, it is possible to have it all.' Hermione got off the bed and approached the chair. 'And you have to let him know that you do love him.'

'I told him I did.'

'Not, I hope, in the same conversation with "but you have to live like a monk until June"?'

'Girls, we're going to be too late.' Hermione's mother had knocked and then pushed the door open just enough to get her head in. Seeing her daughter in the beaded skirt and over-long cotton shirt in which she'd travelled, she pushed the door open further. 'Hermione, you're not even changed. Move.'

Hermione 'moved' and ten minutes later, wearing a very demure but quite stunning off-the-shoulder sea-green shift – 'I bought it to set off my ring and they have it in red which would be stunning on you' – she emerged into the sitting room of their suite.

'How lovely, Hermione. Juliet, isn't that a pretty dress?'

'Yes, Mum, and also available in red at a trendy boutique near you. I bought clothes at the Christmas sales that I haven't even worn yet.'

Chloé Elliott-Chevenix ushered her daughter and her guests out. 'Do you know, Juliet darling, you have just reminded me. Did you ever discover who sent you the marvellous gown? Someone with wonderful taste.'

Juliet was just about to say that she was no nearer to un-covering or discovering her saviour when it seemed as if a light went on in her head, bells started to ring and yet the corridor was quiet, and she would have sworn that she heard bird song. The happiest smile her mother had seen in some time lit up her face. 'I think I just did,' she said. The smile became enigmatic and she said no more.

Hermione stopped the words 'It had to be a man' as they attempted to escape from her mouth, and Juliet sent her a smile of thanks. Although Hermione's own mother would have found the remark amusing and her father would certainly have said, 'Well, thank God she's found someone solvent – and let's hope with his own teeth,' Lesley Crawford would probably have become quite upset at the thought of a man besides her own father buying expensive gifts for Juliet. Hermione tried to catch Juliet's eye in the lift but her friend refused to look at her.

The dinner was lovely and the conversation uncontroversial. Hermione steered it to thoughts about her forthcoming audition, suggestions for posts suitable or probable for Juliet when the programme was complete, and the clothes she and her mother were wearing for the wedding. 'In fact, let's have coffee upstairs, Mum, and Juliet can try on the hats. You must try Mummy's, Juliet; it is stunning.'

'We dark-haired women are easy, Lesley. It's difficult to buy a hat for someone who is green on Monday when you speak to the designer and purple on Thursday.'

They did not in fact return upstairs. Juliet suggested that Hermione should have what for her would be an early night to prepare for the audition and although Hermione said that she could not possibly be turned into Maxim Vengerov overnight and would therefore sound exactly as she did now, the older women agreed, Juliet's mother pleading a very early flight.

The Crawfords took a taxi back to Juliet's flat.

'What was Hermione trying to say to you as we left, Juliet?'

'No idea,' lied Juliet, who knew perfectly well that her friend had been attempting to semaphore, 'Call me as soon as you have talked to him.' She had no intention of sharing this phone call with anyone – if she could get it made in the first place. Lesley wanted to talk, about Hermione, about the Hon. Chloé, about the exquisite décor of the Savoy, and mainly about her own daughter's future.

Juliet decided to step right in with both feet. 'Mum, I've been doing a lot of thinking, especially after Mrs McDermott's wonderful generosity – of spirit as well as financially. She lost her entire family in a concentration camp and her young husband a few years after her wedding and yet she was always so positive. And her praise of our efforts was from knowledge; she never told us how much she knew and we were too self-absorbed to ask but she did know about music. She had heard many of the acknowledged greats and yet she happily listened to us doing scales and finger or voice exercises and I remember that Daddy very rarely did.'

'He's a man, Juliet, and not very musical. You know he isn't a great music lover; it's not important to him.'

'But I am?'

Lesley moved restlessly on the little couch and bent down to take off her high-heeled, rather narrow fashionable shoes. 'What has got into you? You are being odd tonight; too much wine and rich food. Of course you're important to your father.' She sighed loudly. 'And yes, I suppose he was disappointed that you didn't want to work with him; that's all he talked about when you were tiny and yes, he didn't attend all your recitals and concerts but he often had more important things to do.'

'Golf.'

Her mother stood up indignantly. 'How dare you. Oh, Juliet, he did his best.' She sat down again. 'Occasionally he played golf instead of listening to you perform but you have to understand that it was important for him to get away from the surgery, and he is making an effort to understand how important your work is. Mr Haken thinks the world of you.'

Juliet busied herself with the pot of decaffeinated coffee so that her mother could not see her face. 'I want Dad to think the world of me, Mum. I want him to be impressed by what I've done, by what I'm doing. I want him to see that in its way it's as important as medicine.'

Her mother put her arms round her shoulders. 'Silly girl. Nothing is as important as medicine.'

Juliet sighed like a deflating balloon and then straightened up. 'Bedtime, Mum. I have an early start.'

'Good girl; it was lovely to have this little chat.' Lesley picked up her shoes, kissed her daughter and, at last, went into the bedroom and closed the door.

Juliet looked at the door for some time. Then she smiled, somewhat grimly, busied herself tidying up, spending more time than she ever did in cleansing her face, pulling out the sofa bed and – mainly – watching the sliver of light under the bedroom door. Just when it seemed that her nerves were at breaking point the light went out. Juliet sat back against her pillows, her favourite, a small heart-shaped pillow of antique toile de jouy that was filled with lavender, held against her face while she counted to one hundred. That achieved, she added another fifty. Then she picked up her newly recovered mobile telephone and pressed a number.

It was answered immediately. 'Juliet?'

She whispered, 'Did you buy the gown?'

'Yes.'

Stupid, stupid Juliet. Who else, who else could possibly have cared enough? Who else would handle a difficult situation with such exquisite sensitivity? And I didn't know, didn't guess, didn't allow myself to dream, to hope, to pray. 'There has never been a more beautiful dress. Thank you, my darling Karel.' She breathed a small kiss into the receiver and disconnected.

Immediately the light went on in the bedroom. 'Did I hear Daddy, darling?'

Juliet smiled. 'No, Mummy, goodnight.'

Hermione's audition was arranged for two o'clock. Juliet had taken her mother to the airport, and had deliberately not caught any of the hints that Lesley had thrown out about a late night telephone call.

'I could have sworn I heard you speaking, darling.'

'These walls are paper-thin, Mum,' she said, which was not an answer and was, in fact, quite untrue.

'Do you say "Break a leg" to musicians? Whatever one says, say it for me. Will he give her a job if he likes her?'

'Mummy, I don't know what the maestro is planning. But he is with several orchestras, in Prague, in Paris, in Heidelberg, in Seattle. Orchestras plan years ahead. I'll ring you tonight and tell you how it went.'

'And you'll tell me anything else that's important, won't you, dear?'

Juliet hugged her mother. 'Yes, Mum, I'll tell you anything important when I know myself. Trust me.'

She hurried back to the Barbican, anxious to see Karel, wondering what, if anything, he would say when she arrived.

'Good morning, Juliet,' was all he said as he went on with his rehearsal of a small ensemble.

She sat down and tried not to think of him as anyone other than Maestro Haken, the conductor, but it was difficult to ignore her overwhelming attraction to him; she found that, instead of taking notes that he would discuss rigorously with her, she was playfully seeing him as a magnet and she no more than a small piece of iron filing adrift and lost until his force pulled her to him. Juliet looked up at him there on his podium and, once again, was filled with the joy of her knowledge of him. Is there a more glorious feeling than that of loving and being loved in return? She pictured herself in her beautiful gown, a gift from him. Is there anywhere a man more . . .? She did not allow herself to continue with flights of fantasy. Get a grip, Juliet, she castigated herself. You are in danger of losing the plot. Think of the cello. What is it saying? The viola? Is the timing off? Concentrate.

They did not break until lunch but still there was no opportunity for private conversation and Juliet found that she was pleased. It had taken all her mental strength to block everything but the music, and the effort had tired her. She did not know whether Karel was deliberately avoiding her or whether indeed there was just too much for him to do. She did not care particularly; today was Hermione's day and Juliet, the woman in love, was happy to be sublimated by Juliet, the conductor.

It was too new, too unexpected. She saw him and wanted to be alone with him, to hold him, to love him. Would the day ever come when she took this priceless gift for granted, when she would cease to be amazed by the wonder of it all, when she could walk into a room and see him and not want to tear off his clothes, and more, to have him tear off hers? Did she want that? Was that what marriage became? And surely it must because no one could possibly sustain this level of sexual intensity. Could they?

Ernest Chausson's *Poème*, Opus 25. Think of Hermione.

It was not so difficult as she had feared. In a cafeteria full of people she was alone with the sound in her head. It was sad yet exquisite. Bravo, Hermione.

'Well done, Miss Elliott-Chevenix, that was quite lovely.' The speaker was Karel. 'Well done, Miss Crawford. Now, would you like to take a short break, because I have some pieces I would like you to sight-read? Ladies, gentlemen, thank you. Some of you I will see tomorrow. That goes for you too, Juliet; a good day's work.'

'Have we time to go to your flat, Juliet?'

Hermione had thanked the maestro and, linking her arm in Juliet's, had walked from the room. 'I'm high as a kite and want to dance and I bet that would raise a few eyebrows here.'

'Hardly; it is a huge complex devoted to artistic expression,' Juliet said rather grandly.

'There's nothing artistic about my dancing. I don't want coffee; let's go outside and then you can tell me what the iceman really thinks.'

Juliet took them to what was essentially the main entrance on the Silk Street side. 'He told you what he thinks. He said, "Well done." Simple as that. What did he say about the movement from the concerto?'

' "Meltingly done"; that's praise I think.'

Juliet smiled. 'Absolutely: you're fabulous, Miss Elliott-Chevenix. You know that name is too long for record sleeves.'

'I've decided to use the two middle bits anyway, discussed it with Mummy, so I'm Chloé Elliott. Dad's happy with that too.'

'So you have signed a contract?'

'No. I thought a recording contract before Chloé Elliott has ever been heard was rather silly. Araminta is furious and can't make up her mind whether or not to let me go.' She stopped and turned to face Juliet. 'But something really important. Please. You and Karel?'

'He bought the dress, Hermione,' she said softly and did not know how her face took on a special softness. 'Can you imagine? We hadn't spoken for months; when we did meet I was fearfully rude and off-hand, and then he heard – I'm assuming he heard – the incident being discussed and he went out and bought the dress. You can't believe how awful I was to him the next day when he came to congratulate me; he brought a book and some lovely flowers in a vase because he said hotel rooms never have enough vases and I threw them away.' 'She remembered his face as he had dropped them in the waste-paper basket. 'I'd give anything to be able to go back to that day and to take them out of the bin.'

'Poor flowers.'

'They're not the only ones that have been chucked in the bin,' confessed Juliet, thinking of the rather splendid bouquet from Alexander Stoltze. 'But your sight-reading? How do you feel?'

'How do I look?' asked Hermione, standing with her arms outspread and her legs apart. Her pleated tartan kilt, like her last school uniform skirt, was barely decent, but her soft brown suede William Tell-type boots reached up well over her knees. Her hair was still a glossy green cap but her blunt-cut fingernails were a clear pink.

'You look fabulous, as you well know.'

'I was talking about my face – tense, fearful?'

'No.'

'Then it should. My stomach is churning. I bet he's found some obscure Czech composer for me to struggle through.'

The composer, Ivan Haken, was perhaps a little obscure outside his own land but his bagatelles were as delightful and melodic as any Hermione had encountered, yet with their own intricacies and difficulties. Karel allowed no one else in the rehearsal room and so Juliet had to wait until Hermione telephoned her.

'Why are you phoning? Can't you come?'

'I'm lost.'

Juliet laughed. 'Stay exactly where you are and I'll find you but tell me what he said.'

'That's your reward for finding me.'

Karel sat quite still, closed his eyes and listened. It was a magnificent instrument; he had indulged his senses, wallowing in its sound, in the colours the girl managed to produce during the Chausson and the Bach. The music was as well known to him as the skin on his hands; he had played it many times and had heard his father play it. The girl was remarkable, if slightly hesitant, and he found himself angry that she had refused two perfectly good opportunities to play with renowned orchestras. Spoiled brat: she needed discipline and playing with an orchestra would give her that, but there was a something, *das Fünkchen*, or maybe it was more than a tiny spark. She had it. He felt excitement tingling though his body and it was all he could do to remain still until she had come to the end of the pieces he had selected for her. She stood there looking at him, the priceless instrument held loosely in her left hand, her lovely eyes full of self-doubt.

Lovely Hermione, with your green hair, and your waif's body. What will you do to the international circuit?

He stood up. 'You are very talented, Hermione. Well done.'

'Is the composer a family member, Maestro?'

'My father.' In his life he prided himself that he never rushed things. He had rushed head over heels into love with Juliet and now he was about to ignore his principles again. 'A university orchestra in Omolouc is honouring him on his retirement in July. Will you play his concerto for him?'

She looked at the short extracts from various pieces that she had just attempted to play. 'His concerto?'

'Yes. The great Menuhin played it at its premier performance. Even if Maestro Menuhin were still alive I doubt very much that the university could afford him. Perhaps it can still afford Miss Elliott-Chevenix?'

'Miss Elliott,' she said. 'Plain Chloé Elliott would be honoured.' She began to put her violin away. 'My hair, Maestro?'

'Is your own business, and does not affect your playing and, besides, my father will love it.'

She smiled at him. 'Who knows what colour it will be by July?'

He held the door open for her. 'I am breathless with anticipation.'

'He is seriously attractive, Juliet, and has a great sense of humour.'

Juliet had found her friend wandering by the lake near the Guildhall School, an area certainly off-limits to casual visitors, and had walked with her through the Thomas More Gardens back to the apartment. She had listened while Hermione went over the entire audition in minute detail and she smiled with feeling when it became obvious that Hermione had thought of her only as the conductor and not as her friend. She had experienced exactly the same emotion. The violinist was merely the soloist whom she wanted to support as well as she possibly could. 'We both learned something today, Hermione. It is possible to divorce your professional self from your emotional one.'

'And that's important?'

'Oh, yes. Damn, I promised to let Mum know, and your mother will be chewing her fingernails.'

'I rang her as soon as Karel closed the door on me. Come and celebrate with us. We're going to eat at the RSA restaurant, fabulous food.'

'Very tempting, but some of us have to work, madame.'

Spontaneously Hermione threw her arms around Juliet. 'This is because of you. My agent's in a snit and probably isn't trying to get me anything but now I have actually auditioned for a prominent conductor.'

'He's only visiting: he has no real authority here. You do realise that, don't you?'

'Yes, but he's associated with several orchestras and the leader here was awfully friendly; can't hurt.' She went over to the table where she had left her violin. 'I'd better go, and I'll ring you on Sunday and tell you all about the wedding' – she paused for a moment and smiled provocatively – 'after I've talked to Patrick, that is.'

Juliet posed dramatically, arms outstretched, her back to the door. 'Patrick. Tell me all.'

'Goodness,' said Hermione with an attempt at insouciance. 'What is there to tell? Since my fellow executor took off to the big city, naturally all the discussions about Mrs McD's will and the furniture in her flat had to be discussed with the executor who took the office seriously. You would be surprised by how much work is involved in closing probate. He dropped in to discuss the signed permission to keep the furniture; naturally a thoughtful hostess had to offer him a cup of coffee. Then he was in Stockbridge and popped in to see if Heather and Gregor have decided to keep the furniture or sell it and, since it just happened to be lunchtime, he asked me to join him and so we had lunch.'

Juliet left the door and walked over to her friend. 'And?'

'And what? Does Gregor want to keep the family heirlooms or . . .' Hermione moved towards the door and Juliet grabbed the violin.

'You are the world's most annoying human being and, if you want this back, tell me why this lunch made such an impression.'

'Oh, it wasn't the lunch – which was excellent, he's into health food. It was the kiss, the first kiss. He walked me back to the flat and he kissed me and he apologised. Wasn't that wonderful, although any red-blooded male should have been able to read the signals I was sending out. He is absolutely adorable, Juliet, not at all toad-like. I talked to him earlier and he's thrilled at how well my audition went; I really must play for him sometime. We're having dinner on Monday. He begged for Sunday night – oh the temptation – but I told him a girl's got to wash her hair occasionally.'

Juliet hugged Hermione and handed her the violin. 'You wash your hair every morning.'

'But, darling, he doesn't know that – yet. If he plays his cards right he'll find out on Tuesday morning.'

Juliet felt tears come to her eyes and Hermione saw them and laughed. 'It's just right, Juliet, and Mummy will love him.'

Juliet walked her down to the road and saw her safely into a taxi and then returned to her flat. Hermione was in love and by the sounds of it Patrick was too. How absolutely wonderful. Patrick was not a toad. Juliet smiled and then she looked at her building and started to run. Karel was standing at the front entrance but was in the act of turning away.

'Hi.'

'Hi, Chloé Elliott has gone?'

She laughed. 'Yes. Thank you; she is really happy.'

'There is nothing to thank. To discover an exciting new talent is a great privilege. You are monitoring the Schools Orchestra this evening?'

'You know I am.'

'Is there food in your so-charming apartment yet?'

She smiled at him and he smiled back and visibly relaxed.

'My mum's been here and there is so much food that I might just need a friend to help me eat some of it.'

She turned and he turned with her as she opened the door. They walked slowly, side by side to Juliet's door and, once inside, Karel pulled her into his arms. 'Food,' she reminded him.

'Somehow, I'm not hungry any more. I could stand here all night just kissing you.'

What beautiful words. Juliet's heart sang. 'We can't. I work for the man with the worst mood swings in London.'

He looked aggrieved. 'I don't have mood swings: I am very calm. But how am I supposed to react when the woman I'm crazy about won't see me, won't talk to me, won't love me, won't marry me?'

She smiled at him. 'I can make a shrimp salad.'

They went into the kitchen and Karel stood, his back against the refrigerator, while Juliet assembled a salad. 'There's a half-full bottle of wine in the fridge behind you, Maestro.'

'Juliet, please don't ignore everything I say.'

She put down the red pepper that she had just washed. 'Karel, I'm not ignoring you. If life was perfect we'd be in bed together by now; that's what I want. I love you. I told you I loved you and I'm still so mystified by the rightness of it and the precious joy of it. But' – she looked at her watch and began to cut the pepper – 'in less than an hour we have to be back at work, or, at least, I do, and that has to be the priority.'

He turned and opening the refrigerator, reached in and took out the open wine in the door. With her knife she pointed to the glasses and he poured the wine.

'Can we stop being conductors for a moment and be Juliet and Karel who are in love?'

She put down her knife and took the glass and leaned towards him and he held her with one hand while they clinked the glasses together.

'We can make this work, Juliet,' he said and kissed her again. Her mouth tasted of the wine and he laughed. 'I am sharing your wine, let me share your life.' He released her and stepped back. 'The salad, Maestro; we don't have all night. See, I can be disciplined. Miss Crawford is not the only one who can put Art first.' His face became still again and he moved back towards her. 'Will you come back with me after the concert? We can love but we can talk too.'

Juliet began to tumble the salad on to two large white plates. She looked up at him and all the love and longing he could ever have wished for was in her eyes. 'We'll talk first, Maestro.'

29

'I took it for granted that you knew.'

Juliet, wearing nothing but a T-shirt that Karel had found for her, was sitting cross-legged on his bed drinking coffee. She was holding the mug just under her chin trying to stop her lips from trembling and a large tear fell into her drink.

Karel took the mug away and put his arms around her. 'I thought you knew.'

'I must have known – I don't remember. It was so exciting, winning, and then – I don't remember if I even read the letter. Hermione read it to me over the phone.' She could feel his lips soft against her forehead.

'Surely she gave it to you, but no matter; of course my assignment was just until Chris was well enough to stand for long periods and he feels after Easter is a good time.'

'But that's next week. Oh, Karel, we have just begun and it's over.'

He picked up the coffee and held it to her mouth as if she were a baby. 'Drink your coffee. Doesn't that taste good?'

Juliet sipped the coffee and he held her close and murmured softly against her hair as she tried to pull herself together. 'What are you saying, Karel?'

'I'll teach you Czech someday and you'll know, but it was only that I worship every inch of you, every hair, every fingernail, even this one that you have broken, darling, darling Juliet.'

'Oh, Karel, I can't bear it if you leave.'

'Think, my love. Perhaps it's good that I have to leave. Chris is more experienced, has many more contacts all over the world and, besides, you wanted some space.'

'I wanted you not breathing into my neck when I'm trying to make serious decisions. You in your flat, me in mine – that's a good distance. You in Prague and me here . . .' It was unfair; it was too soon, much too soon. She knew that deep down she must have known that Karel was merely filling in while the resident conductor was on sick leave; perhaps she had even been told the probable date of his return but it was still too soon. 'We don't even know each other yet.'

'We know everything that is important to know and, remember, my dearest, you want a career. We will never be together like ordinary married couples.'

'I know.'

'So dare I ask if that means that you have decided to marry me?'

At first she answered with a kiss that had all the promise, all the longing in it. Then, 'One day. When are you leaving?'

He climbed off the bed and stood looking down at her as if memorising the way her hair fell on her shoulders or how long her lashes were. Perhaps he was filing away the feel of her skin, soft against his or her scent, clean and fresh as a summer garden. 'I fly to Prague on Friday.' He held out his hand. 'Take my hand. Come with me,' he urged her. 'Share my life.'

She bowed her head and he walked into the bathroom and closed the door.

Juliet got off the bed and walked over to the kitchen. She rinsed the coffee cups and put them into the dishwasher. The jar of the jam he had spread on their toast was still there, open, on the table. She picked it up and sniffed the wonderful fruity flavours. She screwed the lid on and looked at the label. *Af Blabaer, Brom Baer, Jule Marmelade*. Now that wasn't Czech. Scandinavian, perhaps. Whatever it was he would not have finished it before Friday. She stood there holding the jar and weeping silently and he found her there and held her against his chest until she was quiet.

'They do say you shouldn't ask for something because you might just get it,' she said as she blew her nose on the tissues he brought her from the bathroom.

'Prague is a few hours away and we'll visit and I'll come when you are in Paris. We will make love all over the world. All right?'

She nodded, unable to speak.

'Then get dressed or we'll both be late and then what will the LSO say?'

They said goodbye on Thursday evening. On Friday afternoon he was flying from Gatwick and she from City Airport.

'Guess who called me this afternoon?' she asked and added, 'Erik Lyndholm,' before he could answer.

'That's nice. I sincerely hope he's still in New York.'

'Further away, Chicago, but he said something very interesting. He was in a café in the opera house and heard my name. Someone is bad-mouthing me, Karel.' She could see that he did not understand. 'Someone is spreading rumours; my fame has reached the Windy City. Seemingly I am given to tantrums where I don't bother to turn up and when I do arrive for work, I'm often late.'

He looked shocked. 'But this is untrue.'

'I know that and you know it but in Scotland we say, "Mud sticks." Who hates me, Karel, and why?'

He put his arms around her and held her close. 'No one does, sweetheart.' He held her against him while he thought, rubbing the back of her neck as he did so. No one could possibly hate her, but he knew that although talent wins many admirers it often breeds envy in the not so gifted. Theirs was an unbelievably competitive world and there were many gifted people doing their utmost to win the few glittering prizes that were available. How could he protect her from all of it? The simplest answer was the one that she was refusing to accept and although he could understand, he loved her and wanted to protect her. Dared he try again? 'I could make it so easy for you, Juliet.' He knew at once that he had said the wrong thing.

She pulled away from him, straightening her ruffled hair down with a shaking hand. 'So I seek refuge from my detractors in marriage to a world-respected conductor, the young lion. As his mate I would be accepted, would I? Well, let me tell you, Karel

366

Haken, that I have not worked for years just to give up the first time anyone says "Boo" to me. I will show managing directors that not only am I always punctual but hard-working, meticulous, unfailingly polite, and damned bloody good.'

He understood the body language. 'Juliet,' he began.

'No. I don't want us to fight, Karel, not tonight when we're not going to see each other for . . . for I don't know how long. I'm going back to the Barbican and you had better get on with your packing.'

He knew better than to ask her to stay. 'We'll talk every day, okay?'

'Okay. No, no more kisses. I can't even think when you're so close and I want to pretend that tomorrow is just another day at the office. Don't come with me. There are taxis right outside your building. I'll be fine and you have too much to do.' She pulled herself out of his arms, picked up her bag and her leather jacket and ran from the flat and along the corridor but she slowed down as she approached the lift and tried to compose herself; what would the neighbours say were they to see a distraught young woman running from a man's flat?

There was a celebratory lunch next day in one of the centre's many conference facilities and that meant that there was no time at all for Juliet to be alone with Karel. At times she posed beside him for photographs, so aware of his closeness but cognisant too that in a few hours they would be flying in different directions. Smile, Juliet. This is the way it is going to be. You can still change your mind. There is still time to take his hand and go with him.

Several members of the orchestra walked with him to the underground car park where he had left his rental car and so Juliet allowed him to kiss her cheek, press her hand, wish her well. She could not stay to watch him leave.

He telephoned from the airport. 'I feel as if a part of me has been torn off, Juliet.'

'Me too.'

'I'll meet you in Paris and you will come to Omolouc soon and meet my father.'

'Yes. I'll look forward to that.'

But her flight was called and they had to disconnect. She wanted to howl, but instead picked up her overnight bag and walked to the check-in desk. He's doing exactly the same. Get used to it.

Flying into Dundee was a pleasure. As the small plane approached the city Juliet could see not only the historical town with its mixture of ancient and ultra-modern buildings but the long silver ribbon of the River Tay stretching almost to its picturesque source, Loch Tay itself, far away up in the hills of Perthshire. Two magnificent bridges crossed the river between the Fife and Angus sides, the road bridge, and the rail bridge that replaced the original, which had been blown down in the terrible storm of December 1879. Stumps from the old bridge could still be seen at low tide, a chilling reminder of a terrible tragedy. But on a day like this when the sun caused the water to sparkle below them and long lines of daffodils tossed their golden trumpets all along the river road as if in welcome, Juliet allowed her heart to lift.

Her mother was at the airport in Dundee to meet her. 'Oh, I love the pink jacket.'

Juliet smiled. 'Christmas sales.'

They drove home in less than ten minutes and neither mentioned their talk in London; it was almost as if they had silently agreed never to bring it up again.

'What a difference from driving in London.'

'But you don't drive in London, darling, do you?'

'I don't, Mum, buses and the tube are great but friends drive and taxis, of course, sometimes take ages.'

The blossom on the trees outside her bedroom was not yet in bloom. 'I was looking forward to the spring flurry and now I'll miss it.'

Lesley opened the front door. 'It's been a funny old spring. Oh, it's lovely to have you all to ourselves for a few days. We have a few friends coming in for drinks on Saturday. Everyone wants to hear all. You don't mind, do you?'

'Of course not, Mum, but I was looking forward to relaxing.'

'It's only drinks, dear. Now pop your things in your room; I'll be in the kitchen if you want me. We could have a nice chat before Daddy gets home.'

Juliet went upstairs, seeing her home as if for the first time. So much had happened since Christmas but the house was exactly the same. The stained-glass window halfway up the stairs still caused shafts of coloured light to spill over the stair carpet. The flowers below them were different. Today there was a huge copper bowl full of daffodils; at Christmas the same bowl had held brilliant red poinsettias. Next Christmas it would be the same, but where would she be? Where was Karel? Somewhere in the air above Europe.

She sat down on her bed and turned on her mobile and then switched it off again. It was too early. She would go downstairs, be thrilled to be home, and she would help her mother with dinner, just as she used to do when she was home from boarding school or college.

The weekend was a success. Juliet played dutiful daughter, helped her mother, played golf, very badly, with her father, deflected all the inquisitive but well-meaning remarks from old family friends, and talked to Karel once or twice a day.

'Don't stay home alone in that tiny apartment, Juliet,' he said, his voice full of loving tenderness. 'If someone asks you to dinner or the theatre, dress up and go and have a good time. It's not good to spend every minute working on the next programme.'

'And you will be taking your own advice, Maestro? If someone asks you to dinner, you will dress up and go out and have a good time?'

'Maybe I won't dress up,' he said and she cherished the sound of his laughter. 'It's different for me, my darling.'

'Why?'

'Because it is impossible for me to be completely happy without you.'

What could she say in answer to that except that she felt exactly the same.

Late on the Sunday night Juliet rang Hermione for a long chat. Although she had spoken to her friend the night she had heard that

Karel was being replaced they had not spoken since and she had been unable to see her flatmates on this visit and wanted to catch up with them.

'How's Heather?'

'Blooming: she looks fantastic and her voice is even better. I think she worried pregnancy might change it – for the worse, I mean, but it hasn't and she's busy. I don't mean socially although the ghastly Peter keeps ringing; if she answers she hangs up and if I answer she tells me to hang up. I have a feeling that she's more of a catch now but it's obvious that she is no longer in love with him; I doubt that she even likes him. She is totally in love with her baby. Then she has her choir and the choral and she's doing some more radio stuff – flavour of the month is our Heather. Radio's fab because no one can see her. She looks gorgeous but you know what I mean.'

'I'm so pleased. And Gregor?'

'Besotted. Tom's not there much of the time which means that Gregor works and the piece – still not sure what form it has – is stunning. Tom is arranging a performance, invited audience including Kenneth MacMillan.'

'Fantastic. Do you remember at college when MacMillan walked past it was all we could do to keep Gregor from bowing? You're playing?'

'Yes, the violin solo. It is all happening for us, Juliet. On New Year's Eve we said this was going to be our year and were we ever right. Tell me about Karel.'

Juliet lay back on all the pillows piled on her bed and hesitated. What could she say about Karel? 'I don't even know if he likes liver,' popped out before she could think of something possibly more intelligent or at least relevant to say.

'Who cares?' That was Hermione Elliott-Chevenix. Cut to the chase.

'I suppose I mean I hardly know anything about him.'

'You know you love him.'

'But how can you love someone, I mean really love them enough to marry and stay married for fifty years, if you know nothing about them?'

'You know the important stuff, and whether or not he likes liver doesn't measure up. That you will find out the first time you make him breakfast.'

For a moment Juliet did not reply. She had seen the next few months as months of exploration, of discovery, as she found out, every day, more and more about this art of which she was a small but not insignificant part. Hand in hand with her growth as a conductor would be her evolving relationship with this special man; she would see him in various moods, see how he dealt with different situations. Yes, she had seen him almost every day for three months but everything was changed. She loved and was loved in return. She saw her world in a special light, for now it was a world that included Karel, not as her mentor but as her friend, her lover, but she had barely discovered her love and he had gone.

'There were so many things I wanted to ask, to tell him, things to find out. When is his birthday? Does he like Thai food? What does he think of New York? Does he ever watch television?'

'Juliet, are you crazy about Karel Haken? Do you go weak at the knees when he touches you? Does he ever make you laugh?'

'Yes.'

'Then, my dearest friend, you know all you will ever need to know.'

Before I met you I knew you. Corny twaddle, but was it possible? Was everything so right because they had waited for each other? Juliet returned to London and, although she missed seeing Karel, hearing his voice, seeing him smile that particular smile he seemed to reserve for her, she relished the opportunity to work with the resident conductor. A much older man, he had conducted several of the world's greatest orchestras and was prepared to share what he had learned with Juliet.

'What takes up most of your time, Juliet, as far as your work is concerned? Have you worked out how many hours you spend rehearsing, conducting, preparing? Have you spent hours sitting all over the house listening to how the orchestra sounds and planning to readjust your directions to the instrumentalists? Do you know the levels of reverberation in every nook and cranny? Is it twenty per cent of your time here, thirty per cent there – have you worked all this out?'

'Not really, Maestro. I'm afraid I'm still at the stage where most of my time, social or otherwise, is devoted to studying scores.'

He smiled. 'Welcome to the wonderful world of the professional conductor. You should have heard my wife every day these past few months. "You don't have to conduct anything for months. Why are you spending even more time studying scores? Find yourself a nice little murder story." But, of course, that is where the work is done, at home, alone in your study. You search for the spiritual meaning of the work. Think of the entire score, where is it going, where are the climaxes? It's an inexact science: my interpretation of pianissimo may not be the same as yours; but as long as we are convinced that – at this particular moment – we are right, then the orchestra will believe. Then there are the basics. This note – how long do I want it to be held? When should the flautists be able to breathe in this piece, the French horn – will we let him breathe at all?' He laughed at his own little joke but Juliet felt wonderful.

'It's exciting, though, to be alone with the music, to hear it in your head in an empty room, isn't it?'

'Yes, my dear, and the greatest joy of all is to do these hours of work that the public never sees, and then to discuss it with the musicians, to work at it together, and then to hear – if all the gods are with us – that the music filling the auditorium or the recording studio is indeed as beautiful as you heard it in your head. Now let's see what you learned with our brilliant young Czech.'

The next few months were challenging and exciting, and very different. She was not in love with the conductor and so an element was missing but she was glad of that. She had matured as a conductor with Karel but everything had been coloured by her sometimes mixed-up feelings for him. Now she was studying with someone whom she respected and admired but she was not troubled by her feelings and she scientifically set out to measure her progress. As always she confided in Hermione.

'I'm loving every minute, Hermione. Missing Karel is a given but my nerve endings aren't on fire, if you know what I mean; that can be quite exhausting.'

'When you have been married twenty years you won't even notice that he's in the auditorium.'

'Thanks for that. I'm off to Paris this week for three days and he may be able to join me for a day. Won't that be glorious? And you, what's happening?'

'Not one booking, my dear,' Hermione said sadly and then she yelled, 'Three. I have three bookings over the next year and two of them are thanks to Karel. So snatch him up before I do.'

'What about Patrick?'

Hermione laughed. 'Definitely not a toad. A frog, I think, who might just become a prince.'

Bryony returned to London in the company of a singer as well known for his *amours* as for his voice.

Juliet had popped out to the Piazza, a little café outside the Barbican tube station well known for its cappuccino and fabulous croissants. For once she did not have a score but was reading a novel, a murder mystery set in ancient Rome which had been highly recommended, and she was trying to turn a page and keep bits of croissant from fluttering all over the book when a voice hailed her.

'Juliet, my, how lovely to see you. May I join you? I adore the croissants here.'

Juliet tried to look pleased to see Bryony and tried to finish the croissant in her mouth and gesture to the chair at the other side of the table in what she hoped looked like a vaguely welcoming gesture. 'Hello, Bryony, back in London.' She could not bring herself to say, 'Lovely to see you.'

Bryony plopped her oversized handbag of very soft pink leather on the seat. 'Don't you just love Italian leather? Be right back.'

I am not going to discuss handbags, Juliet decided while Bryony was waiting for her order. 'It is rather splendid,' she said, cursing herself both for mentioning the bag and for sounding so very British. 'Useful size.'

'You can't imagine. Everything, but everything fits in.' She sipped quickly, said, 'Now tell me all,' and took a large healthy bite from her croissant.

'All? Work is going well. And you?'

'Darling, I know the work is going well – we inhabit a very small world.'

'I never hear a word about you, Bryony.' Damn, that sounded so bitchy but was in fact totally honest. 'I mean, I seem to work so hard: so much to learn, isn't there?'

'I hoped you'd tell me all about your love life – girls together against the world, as it were. What now that the gorgeous Czech has been, how can we put it delicately – replaced?'

'Maestro Haken hasn't been replaced. He took over from the LSO's senior conductor who was on sick leave; now he's well and back with his orchestra as Karel is back with his. No story there, I'm afraid.'

Bryony took another sip of her coffee. 'You know, that's not the way I heard it.'

Juliet would not give her the satisfaction of hearing her speak in defence of Karel who certainly needed no champion. 'What brings you to London, Bryony?' she asked mildly.

Bryony put her cup and the half-eaten croissant she had just picked up down. 'Darling, how sweet of you to ask. A coup.' She smiled enigmatically at Juliet – who did not react – and sipped her coffee again. 'Juliet, you know you're just dying to know so I'll tell you. Fabrizio Carluce.' She sat back and waited for Juliet.

'Good lord,' said Juliet before she could school her tongue, 'don't tell me he's still singing?'

Bryony scraped back her chair and stood up, grabbing her really lovely leather handbag. 'Why not? He is only sixty – all the acknowledged greats are older and they're still singing. Maestro Stoltze effected the introduction – he has been so sweet to me.' She paused reflectively and then went on. 'Fabrizio has demanded, not asked or suggested, but demanded that I conduct his recital at the Festival Hall. He was kind enough to say that my ability to conduct singers reminds him of the great Solti; that I bring not only deep

374

understanding and love of the music but also an understanding and love of the human voice.'

Juliet was sorely tempted. The words, "Especially your own", formed in her mouth but she swallowed them with the last of the cappuccino. 'Great. Solti was a master. I don't have much experience with voices but I'm off to Paris later this evening.'

Bryony seemed astonished. 'But I heard they cancelled that visit, Juliet: everyone was talking about it.'

Cancelled? Her attachment had been cancelled and 'everyone' was talking about it. A lump of solid ice formed in the pit of her stomach and, for a moment, she thought she might be sick. Get a grip, Juliet, don't let her needle you. Remember the email. You had an email from the director the previous evening. 'Don't believe everything you hear about me, Bryony, and I'll try to do you the same courtesy.'

Bryony glared at her for a moment, her mouth working as if she were desperately trying to spit something out and then she turned on her extremely high heel and stalked off. Juliet picked up her book and followed a few minutes later, reflecting that she and Bryony had only a love of music in common, and, therefore, to have alienated her completely was not a great loss.

I just know she's behind the rumours and I'm perfectly sure that she doctored my score; can't prove it, of course, since it has disappeared, but bad things happen to me when she's around.

And Stoltze, a little voice added.

Stoltze? Alexander Stoltze who knew that, although he was very good and much praised, he would never have the reputation of a Toscanini or a Furtwängler and who had settled for being the mentor of the young lion he was sure would one day be in that gilded circle. Would he lower himself to lock someone he saw as a potential threat in a green room? Surely not. But he and Bryony were the only constants. I should take it as praise: they're afraid of my ability and so they have tried to spike my chances.

For the rest of the day, a day devoted to discussions with the orchestra, her mind kept flying off to Paris. She was excited by the opportunity but uneasy. She had looked at the email from the opera house again. Yes, they were expecting her. She would not arrive in Paris to find herself unwanted. Damn Bryony. If she had wanted to unnerve Juliet she had succeeded admirably. Surely nothing could have happened between the time the email had been sent and the time she had met Bryony. Still, it might be wise to ring the director. 'Money well spent,' as Hermione would have said. She went outside on to a terrace by the lake and dialled the director's office. Monsieur le Directeur was unavailable but his secretary could take a message.

'You did not receive our message, Miss Crawford? We are very much looking forward to you joining us.' The voice held a shadow of doubt. 'All is well?'

'Oh, yes, madame. I wanted to ring to thank the director personally for his message. Please assure everyone that I am very much looking forward to the opportunity of working with such a magnificent company in one of the world's most beautiful cities.'

'The pleasure is ours, Miss Crawford. I look forward to meeting you.'

She tried not to remember that the last time she had gone to Paris Karel had accompanied her. Perhaps she would see him; if he could possibly get away he would fly to join her. She sat on the plane, the score of the opera, Strauss's *Ariadne auf Naxos* unopened on her lap, and gazed out of the window, seeing nothing, her belly tight with anticipation. Would she see him? Would the chemistry, or whatever it was, still be there? Would the opera company be surprised to see her, thinking that they had written asking her not to come?

That ghastly eventuality did not happen. Monsieur Duprez did not break his self-imposed rule and would not speak to her in English but they managed in German and, surprisingly well, in French.

'You have been studying, Miss Crawford,' he said. 'I hear a great improvement. That shows dedication, does it not, ladies and gentlemen?'

That remark proved to Juliet that there had indeed been

questions about her and her reliability and she vowed to make them see that their faith in her was well placed.

While she was in discussion with the resident conductor: 'You see, Mam'selle, it takes a very special skill to conduct the opera; the conductor must, how you say, juggle with the orchestra and the music in order to bring out the very best the singer can do.'

'*Par exemple*, Monsieur, would you consider transposing a piece if an otherwise wonderful performer had trouble with a few notes?'

'*Absolument*. You are aware, Mam'selle, that Mozart's keys were lower than modern ones: so it is only just, no?'

He was quite fascinating but Juliet was momentarily distracted by Monsieur Duprez, who was speaking so rapidly to a colleague that she did not have a hope in heaven of catching every word, but she was almost certain she heard the name Haken and then, in the same sentence, her own. Perhaps they were merely discussing the fact that Karel had been her mentor. She wished that she had spent more time studying French.

30

Karel was seated at the magnificent baroque organ of the Church of St Nicholas in the Malá Strana, or little quarter, of Prague. He was aware, as he ran his fingers over the keys, that Wolfgang Amadeus Mozart had played this superb instrument and that the patron saint of music, St Cecilia, looked down on him from the fresco above the organ, as she had once looked down on the great composer. For two hundred years leaky cladding had allowed rainwater and melting snow to seep insidiously in, causing – over time – extensive damage to this most magnificent of buildings but Karel had never seen the damaged church. Restoration in the fifties, long before he was born, had allowed the masterpiece to be restored and Karel never tired of sitting or wandering around inside. Juliet would love it, and Hermione, and he looked forward to showing it off to them.

He had not yet gone to Paris although he longed to see Juliet, to hold her in his arms, to hear her voice, see her smile; there had been too many rehearsals, too many meetings. At one of them he had arranged for Juliet to be invited to come to Prague in the summer when she had finished in London, to conduct a series of classical concerts. He looked up at St Cecilia who looked benignly down on him as if pleased with the sound he was producing.

'How will she react to what she will no doubt see as male interference?' he asked the painting but St Cecilia continued to gaze down in a most non-committal way. Karel smiled and closed the organ. If he hurried he would have time to pick up the antique gold earrings set with garnets that he had bought her. He would have liked to buy a three-stone Victorian diamond ring, each stone weighing over a carat, which the jeweller assured him would not stay with him long, so rare was it and so flawless the stones, but Karel knew his love. The time was not yet right. Besides, if she had discovered that he had interfered in Paris she might not even accept his earrings.

In the shop he waited while the earrings were wrapped and looked longingly at the ring, which would take every cent he had. No, he told himself sternly; she must never be taken for granted, this love of yours.

He arrived in Paris just as the first act ended. Tonight, it was not, he had been pleased to discover, *Ariadne auf Naxos*, an opera of which he was not particularly fond, but a much meatier work, Moussorgsky's *Khovanschina*. Juliet, wearing his gown, was in the box and he admired the straight line of her back and the gleam of her hair as the lights caught it. She was alone and so he bent over and kissed her exposed neck. 'Hello, my darling. Why aren't you outside drinking champagne instead of sitting here all by yourself?'

Juliet had got up and was now standing in his arms smiling up at him. 'Perhaps I was wallowing in all the Russian angst or maybe I was sure that you would arrive in time for the second act.'

They were in full view of the audience milling around in the auditorium and so he pulled her into the back of the box and kissed her thoroughly. 'I miss you.'

'I miss you too.'

'Tell me everything. I want to know who you have met, how many rehearsals you have audited, how many you have conducted, what your hotel is like, what you have eaten, how your facility with French has improved, everything.'

'We don't have time. Everything is wonderful; they have been so welcoming, supportive.' She put her arms around his neck and pulled his head down and Karel gave himself up to the pleasure of feeling her in his arms, the scent of her hair and the faint smell of the delicate rose cologne she always wore.

'Let's sit down,' he whispered into her ear, 'or I won't be responsible for my actions.'

She laughed and unclasped her hands. They moved back to the front of the box and looked down for a moment at the throng below. The noise of chattering and laughter and tuning instruments rose up to meet them and he held her hand and thought he had never been happier.

'I wish we had more time,' he said.

'We can walk around Paris in the moonlight, Karel, and have supper somewhere. We can pretend we're always together; we don't need to think, tonight, about saying goodbye.' She pressed his fingers and he returned the pressure. She was here; they were together. That was enough. He saw the lovely ring on her finger and thought again of the beautiful ring in the antique shop in Prague. At supper he would give her the earrings. He hoped she would like them.

She loved them.

They had left the opera house as soon as they had retrieved their coats. Juliet was not on duty and therefore had no need to speak to any of the management. They wandered down to the Seine and stood on a bridge, arms around each other, and looked at the wonder that was Paris at night.

'It rained all day,' said Juliet as they leaned over to see the city reflected in the still waters, 'and I so wanted it to be fine when you came.'

'And it is. But walking in the rain has its own charms. It depends on who you are with . . .'

'And how heavy the rain is,' said the more practical Juliet. 'Men don't have to worry about hair.'

He dismissed such trivialities. 'Come on. I'm hungry and I want some champagne.'

They wandered on across the bridge and along the bank. Several of the large boats moored on the riverside were restaurants and they walked until they found one that was not so noisy as the others. They stood near the gangplank for a few minutes assessing the restaurant.

'Someone in the kitchen certainly knows what he's doing,' said Karel as the warm odours of garlic, onions, tomatoes and fresh herbs assailed his nostrils.

There were no fine wines in the 'cellar' but the carafe of rough red wine was exactly right with the bouillabaisse that was served with great chunks of fresh bread.

'We will never find this boat again,' said Juliet. 'If we walked the banks of the Seine tomorrow it would not be here because it's too perfect to be real.'

'Then you will need something to remind you, my darling Juliet,' said Karel and handed her the small box. He was a little chagrined to see that she looked slightly relieved when the first box revealed a small square box and not a ring box.

She took them out and held them near the candle flame and the old garnets shone in the light. 'They are so perfect, Karel.' Juliet leaned across the table and kissed him and then she took her little gold clips off and put the earrings on.

'We have a lot of garnets in the Czech Republic,' he said as he watched her turn her head this way and that to make the drops swing. 'They go well with your gown. Thank you for wearing it. You know I never got to see you close-up.'

They laughed and talked a little about the dress and how Juliet had had no idea of who had given her the gift.

'I should have known, darling Karel, and I'm so sorry not to have thanked you. Maybe if I'd guessed I would have said and . . .'

He reached across and put his fingers on her lips. 'No "if only"s for us. Drink your wine – it matches your earrings – and tell me that everything is wonderful at the Garnier.'

'It is; they are so nice, so helpful and I love it. Conducting opera is so different but I might like to do more; it's such a challenge, the orchestra and all the singers. But I've just remembered something.' She dipped a piece of bread in her lovely soup and he waited, laughing with the pleasure of seeing her eat, while she finished it. 'Bryony is in London and she was surprised that I was going to Paris. According to her, gossip had it that I had lost the opportunity.' She looked at him. 'Karel, be honest with me. Did you know anything about it?'

He reached for her hand but she withdrew from his fingers and put her hands together on her lap. 'No. I can't think straight when you're touching me.'

He tried to make a joke. 'I can't think at all just being with you.'

'So you do know something. I heard Duprez mention you but couldn't quite catch what he was saying.'

'They had a letter from someone they respect.'

She interrupted. 'Alexander Stoltze.'

'They didn't tell me, just that they had had a letter. It said you were . . . unreliable.'

'So that's what I get for rejecting him. Has he contacted every orchestra in the world?'

He tried again to touch her but she held herself back against the chair and he gave up. 'No. He could not be so vindictive. The committee were concerned but I said that you had never been late while you were working with me, and that you had once had to leave town suddenly because of the death of a close friend but that you had informed me.'

'But you didn't get my note.'

He shrugged. 'As you didn't get mine, darling. There was no reason for them to know that, and obviously, from what you say, everything is going well.'

'I don't want you fighting my battles for me, Karel.'

'Had I been fighting your battles, my darling, I would have flown to Stuttgart, or wherever Alexander is, and punched his nose. I told the truth about a young conductor, a Miss Crawford, and that was my duty.'

He could see her thinking. He watched the emotions on her face and in her eyes and at last she smiled.

'Fair enough. I've had enough to eat, have you?'

He wanted nothing more than to take a taxi back to her hotel and to spend what was left of the night making love to her, but one day she would find out about the Prague Festival and, if she did not hear first from him, she would be furious. 'Maybe we should have some coffee.' He did not wait for her assent but ordered and then waited quietly until it came. 'In a few days, a week maybe, you will receive an offer of a contract from Prague. I have recommended you for a series of concerts in the beautiful church of St Nicholas and one in the main hall of Wallenstein Palace. It was offered to me and when I said that at the time I would be in Cincinnati, Ohio, United States of America, I recommended you, and yes, I did it because I love you, but I also did it because you are capable. Now don't yell before I finish, please,' he added as he saw her gather her forces. 'This happens all the time, conductors recommend soloists whom they have heard, as I have recommended Hermione, and they also suggest other people when they themselves can't accept a contract. Maybe before the offer comes in you will receive an offer from somewhere else and you will take that. This is when it starts, Juliet. Your record is excellent: you will be in demand. I would like you to accept Prague because I am selfish and I will return for my father's testimonial concert and oh, how it would please me to spend some time there with you but the decision is yours.'

She said nothing for a moment but sat, the coffee cooling on the table in front of her. A tear formed in the corner of her right eye and he watched, fascinated, as it hovered for a second on her dark eyelash and then ran down her cheek.

'Oh, beloved, I didn't mean to make you cry.'

She reached for a tissue with her left hand and flapped at the air with her right as if to chase his words away. When she was in control, she smiled mistily at him. 'Karel Haken, you are the nicest man. I will accept with pleasure the offer from Prague' – and then she smiled at him with devilment in her eyes – 'unless, of course, the Berlin Philharmonic calls before. Now I think it's time for that taxi.'

If anything their lovemaking was better even than their first time together. They had been with each other so few times but their bodies had learned what to do and what to feel. It was as if they had been together for always, emotionally and physically attuned to the likes and desires of the other.

The moon shining on the Seine shone through their windows as they undressed each other, stopping to kiss, to hold the other as if holding the most precious object. Rising desire set them fumbling with fastenings until at last they stood in the moonlight, each glorying in the body of the other. Unable to wait longer, they fell on the bed, caressing, murmuring, loving.

383

POSTSCRIPT

Three months later Juliet and Karel stood, hand in hand, at Ruzyně Airport, which is about fifteen kilometres north-west of Prague, and waited for Karel's flight to be called. Karel's father and Hermione, who had had a great success with the violin concerto and was staying on for a few days, had said their good-byes and were on their way back to the city. Juliet would wait until Karel's flight had left before returning by bus.

They said very little: everything had been said long ago. Karel would be in Cincinnati until September. In fact Juliet knew almost exactly where he would be for the next three years and he had several engagements in his diary for even later than that. Such was the life of an international star. She herself had only another week in Prague and from there she was going to Malta's capital city, Valletta, for a week of recitals in the lovely little Manoel Theatre.

After that she would fly home to Dundee to visit her parents. If it was at all possible she would have a day in Edinburgh visiting Heather and her brand-new son, Gregory McDermott Banner, who were living, with Gregor, in Hermione's flat.

'We won't make decisions before the New Year,' Heather had told her. 'Perhaps we'll sell the flat. If things don't work out for Gregor – and I hope for his sake that they do, we'll move in there together – mutual aid, as it were. But I want to get on my feet so that Gregor needs to think of nothing but of Tom and of his music. That's where I am really: baby first and then career. Everything will be clearer by Christmas.'

Juliet smiled at the thought of Christmas with Karel but before that, if he could find a window in his schedule, he would join her in

Dundee. If not, he would be with her, for at least a few days, in Melbourne where she would be until Christmas.

'This is to be the pattern of our lives, darling. Sometimes I feel as though I cannot bear it another moment. You know I will try to come to Dundee; it's time, is it not, for me to meet your parents. After all, you have met my father.'

'And fallen completely in love with him.'

'As he with you but, beware, he is fickle because he is also crazy for the purple-headed Hermione.' He kissed her then, oblivious of the travellers around him.

'We won't be sad, my darling. In no time at all it will be September and we will see each other and then, before we know it, it will be Christmas and we will have a whole week together.'

He held her close. 'A whole week and just the two of us. Where will we hide? New York is exciting at Christmas.'

The Tannoy disturbed them. 'Would passengers for Lufthansa's flight to New York, via Frankfurt . . .'

He pressed her even closer. 'Oh, God, I can't bear to say *Na shledanou.*'

'It's not goodbye. You see I am learning Czech – for the future. *Uvidime se brzy.*'

Once more he kissed her frantically, feverishly, covering her face with his kisses. 'Clever girl, see you soon too.'

He let her go so quickly that she staggered a little and then she stood watching until he reached the gate, turned and waved, and she waved back, the large antique diamonds on her left hand catching all the light in the hall and sending it spilling in all directions.

'*Uvidime se brzy.* See you soon, my darling.'

EILEEN RAMSAY

SOMEDAY, SOMEWHERE

She was painting the story of their lives . . .

In the attic of her beloved Aunt Tony's cottage Holly Noble finds a series of beautifully painted pictures depicting the world-famous opera singer Blaise Fougère – and her life changes forever.

Determined to trace what appears to be a secret love affair that spanned the decades, Holly meets arrogant Taylor Hartman, Blaise's nephew. Taylor refuses to believe that his uncle is the subject of the paintings: he sets out to prevent Holly from exhibiting to the world what he believes to be the deluded dreams of a frustrated artist.

But as each canvas is hung, and the story of 'Toinette' and the man Holly only knew as 'Uncle Fire' is told, the colour, the passion and the beauty of the paintings draw Taylor and Holly ever closer.

HODDER

EILEEN RAMSAY

A WAY OF FORGIVING

The past is never forgotten – but can it ever be forgiven?

When a terrible accusation ended her marriage five years ago Sophie Winter was determined she'd never be hurt again. With an exciting job at Scotland's new parliament and a fulfilling social life, she finally feels she has buried the bittersweet memories of her past.

But some things aren't easily forgotten . . .

A family wedding draws her back to Tuscany and Sophie encounters Raffaele de Nardis again. The world famous pianist is proud, passionate and devastantingly handsome. He is also her ex-husband.

Sophie realises that she can only face the future if she confronts the past.

HODDER

EILEEN RAMSAY

THE STUFF OF DREAMS

Fourteen years ago there was a fire. A famous actor died and his lover, a famous actress, was arrested . . .

Now Abbots House has been rebuilt, and a mysterious woman, who hides her face and talks almost to no one, has come to live there.

Kate Buchanan can't leave her tragic past behind – but nor can she remember what actually happened that night years before. In the peace of the Scottish seaside village, though, snatches of her memory start to come back – and an epic love story returns to haunt the woman who survived.

HODDER

GABRIELLE ZEVIN

MARGARETTOWN

This is a love story.

It could be about anyone – you, your parents, your best friends. But it's not. It's about a woman called Margaret Towne, and the man who falls in love with her . . .

The day he meets Maggie for the first time is the day he under-stands what it is to be in love. Deeply, wildly, terminally in love.

What he doesn't know is that loving Maggie means loving many women at once.

After a brief, intesne courtship the two young lovers set off to meet Maggie's family: Margaret, Maggie, Marge, Mia and May – five women of different ages, all living together in a house called Margaron, in a place called Margarettown. Nothing in Maggie's world is quite like anywhere else.

Part memoir, part fable, part journey through the many worlds of one woman, *Margarettown* is a novel about how love takes us over and changes our lives; how it makes lies out of truth and truth out of lies. It is the story of what it takes to love the same person for a lifetime – and about the impossibility of really knowing anything about who it is we have come to love.

HODDER

VALERIE-ANNE BAGLIETTO

THE MOON ON A STICK

'If a broken heart could be classified as a sickness, she'd been at death's door . . .'

In her early thirties, Amy Croft thinks she's settled for life. She has Nick Burnley's engagement ring, and their three adorable little boys. If Nick seems slow to set a date for the wedding, Amy's grudgingly willing to wait.

But then she finds out he's taken the plunge – with someone else.

Suddenly Amy needs three things she thought she already had. A home, financial security and a soulmate. And with the help of her widowed mother Elspeth and her irrepressible teenage sister Tilly, she finds everything she's always longed for, all over again, in some unexpected places . . .

HODDER

ELIZABETH ADLER

THE HOUSE IN AMALFI

Can you go home again?

Once Lamour Harrington was a carefree little girl, following her charming, hard-up, writer father to Italy: first Rome, then the lovely Amalfi coast. Lamour will never forget the tiny cottage where they spent the happiest years of her life.

Now, nursing a broken heart, she decides to leave Chicago and her career as a landscape architect to rediscover the Italy of her memories.

In Amalfi, the Castello Pirata with its Japanese garden still stands; their cottage still waits for her. It even seems as though love has come back into Lamour's life as the heir to the castello – glamorous Nico Pirata – sweeps her off her feet. But why does his father Lorenzo hate a woman he only ever knew as an innocent child? As Lorenzo plots to make Lamour leave Amalfi forever, long-hidden secrets come to dangerous life again.

HODDER